STAR OF ILL-OMEN

By

DENNIS WHEATLEY

THE BOOK CLUB
121 CHARING CROSS ROAD
LONDON, W.C.2

Printed and bound by Novello and Company Limited London W 1

CONTENTS

CHAPTER I

GENERAL PERON'S SECRET

KEM LINCOLN slid back the chamber of his automatic to make certain that it was working freely, snapped home a clip of bullets and repouched the weapon in his shoulder holster. He hoped that he would not have to use it. If Estévan Escobar was alone the pistol should prove redundant, but if he appeared driven by a chauffeur, strong measures might be necessary to get the better of the two of them.

It was mid-December, but nearly as hot as it would have been in June in central Morocco, for it was three o'clock in the afternoon and the latitude 33 degrees south. The spot on which Kem stood was about one hundred and sixty miles north of Buenos Aires. He had chosen it with care, as the highway there crossed the last low rise before merging into the great plain in which lay the basin of the River Plate. From it he could see a mile or more along the road to the little town of Basavilbaso, down which Escobar must come on his way to the capital; but there was no human habitation in sight and the landscape was entirely deserted. To the north the endless plain disappeared in a blue haze; to the west, coming right up to the road, stretched a belt of thorn-tree scrub; to the east the ground fell away to the distant mile-wide river in what a generation ago had been pampas but was now a part of the vast wheat-fields which were bringing the Argentine nearly as much wealth as her cattle.

Kem was dressed in a white linen jacket, an open shirt, twill riding-breeches and a broad-brimmed sombrero. In spite of the protection the hat had given him on his recent ride from Basavilbaso, and the fact that he had now taken refuge in the shade of the nearest tree, he was in a bath of perspiration; little rivulets of it trickled down his chubby brown face.

He was of medium height and twenty-eight years of age, inclined to plumpness but naturally so, and the strength of his back and shoulders made him a formidable opponent as a wrestler. Quite apart from the tan he had acquired during his three weeks in the Argentine, his skin was exceptionally dark for an Englishman. At first sight many people took him for a native of the south of France and in both physique and temperament he owed much to the fact that his maternal grandmother had been a Provençal. His hair was straight and black, his face round with full cheeks, his eyes dark brown and his lips thick. Men thought him an ugly fellow and could never understand what women saw in him; but women are rarely attracted by good looks alone. Kem's immense vitality, the laughter that was always twitching his full mouth and the quick humorous intelligence that danced in his dark eyes had proved better assets with the girls than a handsome profile.

As his keen eyes watched the empty, sun-scorched highway for the first little cloud of dust which would tell of the approach of his unsuspecting victim's car, he cursed the heat and thought idly of the strange chain of events that had brought him there, like a modern Claude Duval, lurking on the edge of the forest about to stage a hold-up.

At the opening of the Second World War he had been only fifteen, but by 1943 he had managed to get into the Commandos. A few months later he had had the bad luck to be knocked out and captured during a minor raid against the coast of France. The Germans had succeeded in holding him for less than a week and, once he had escaped, the ease with which he spoke fluent French had enabled him to make his way through France to the Pyrenees without difficulty; but soon after crossing the border into Spain misfortune had again overtaken him. Walking by night towards Burgos on his way south to Gibraltar he had been run down by a fast car and picked up many hours later still unconscious with head injuries and a fractured thigh. By that time his lucky stars had once more been in the ascendant, as it was a local doctor returning from a confinement at a lonely farm who had found his twisted body soon after dawn.

Like most Spanish professional men Doctor Manuel Duero accepted the Franco regime as infinitely preferable to Communism, but, all the same, cherished Liberal views which made him strongly anti-Nazi. As he lifted Kem into the back of his old Ford the young fugitive had become delirious and disclosed the fact that he was a British soldier; so instead of taking him to the local hospital, which would have resulted in his being interned for the duration, the good doctor had taken him to his own home. There, his two pretty daughters had nursed Kem back to health, but nine months had elapsed before his smashed thigh had mended sufficiently for him to regain full use of it.

Meanwhile the armies of the Allies had landed on the Continent, but the Germans were still putting up a desperate resistance and no one could yet say when the war would end, so Kem had felt compelled to take a reluctant leave of the Dueros and make his way to Gib. By mid-September '44 he was back in England and had rejoined his unit, but his disability was judged still too serious to permit of his resuming the more desperate forms of Commando operations; so when he was sent abroad again it was for attachment to the Special Intelligence branch of SHAEF.

There he had soon graduated from an office desk to outside employment and been let loose in Belgium in civilian clothes. His fluent

French, coupled with his round, innocent, cheerful countenance, had made him an excellent agent; so when the war ended, having been trained to no other profession, he had gladly accepted an offer to remain on as a permanent operative in the British Secret Service.

Although Kem had not realized it at the time, the shrewd chief who had made him that offer had then had innumerable resourceful young men to choose from, but comparatively few of them spoke good Spanish. It was that additional qualification, gained during his nine months' convalescence with the Dueros, which, as a long-term policy, had really been responsible for his selection. And now the shrewd chief's pigeon had come home to roost. At twenty-eight Kempton Lincoln was a fully experienced and very capable agent; he had carried out successful missions in various European countries, and when a really first-class man was needed to tackle a big job in the Argentine his chief had had no doubt in his mind whom to send.

Kem pushed his sombrero to the back of his head, mopped his forehead and grinned as he thought how far-reaching the effect of one unexpected moment in a man's life could be. Had he not been knocked down one night on the road to Burgos he would certainly not be where he was now, sweltering in the sun and waiting to hold up the man who was believed to hold the secret of a new, quick and inexpensive method of producing Atom bombs.

On first being told of his new mission he had not liked the idea of it at all, as his scientific knowledge was about as sketchy as that of the average fifth-form schoolboy. At the risk of getting a raspberry for telling his grandmother how to suck eggs, he had pointed out to the Director-General M.I.-X. that nine-tenths of success in spying lay in knowing what to look for, and that if he managed to get into a nuclear energy plant it would be as meaningless to him as the inside of a television set to an Australian aborigine; but the D.G. had brushed the objection aside, and said:

"My dear boy, in that only a handful of scientists are better situated than yourself, and obviously none of them can be employed on such unorthodox work as ours. Besides, no acquaintance with back-room wizardry is required to carry out the main object of this assignment. Early in 1951 the Dictator, Peron, announced that by approaching the problem from a new angle one of his scientists had discovered a cheap and easy method of producing atomic energy. If that is true its repercussions could be boundless. At present United Nations' production of these new weapons is strictly limited by the vast labour and expense their manufacture entails, and, thank God, we have no reason to suppose that their cost in effort to the Ruskies is any less. But if a way has been found to turn out these hideous things as easily as Ford cars, even a comparatively small country like the Argentine might quite well succeed in enforcing its will upon both hemispheres before she could be success-

7

ully destroyed or invaded. Fortunately General Peron is a declared enemy of Communism, but on the other hand he has never manifested any particular love for the democracies. Privately we may hope that he is a really great man, and that if he has such power he will use it to enforce a new era of universal peace; but officially it is our job to visualize ambition leading him to have a crack at becoming the Emperor of the World, and do what we can to tie his hands before he has the chance to get going."

"I see that," Kem had agreed, "but didn't he admit a few months later that his scientist was a fake, and the whole thing a mare's nest?"

The D.G. took a pull at his after-lunch cigar and stared thoughtfully at the plane trees outside his bow window before replying. "Yes. He confessed that he had been fooled, and took away a decoration that he had given the fellow for his supposed discovery. But what would you do, say you were a South African and had found alluvial diamonds on your farm? After the first excitement wouldn't you give out that you had been mistaken, or that they were so small as to be almost valueless, in order to discourage raiders until you could get the place properly protected? If Peron is out for world domination he would be crazy to start anything at half-cock, and even given mass production it would take him a year or more to form a stock-pile large enough to menace the east as well as the west. In the meantime he would naturally take any steps he could to divert attention from his preparations."

"If that's the case, sir, why should he have ever announced the discovery in the first place?"

"I don't know." The D.G. grinned broadly. "Perhaps through lack of forethought. Or perhaps the whole thing was a bluff from the beginning, and simply staged to increase the importance of the Argentine in the eyes of the world. But, if so, why should Peron lose face by retracting afterwards? Perhaps it is a double bluff and he never had it, but pretended he had, then denied it, hoping that people like myself would think on just the lines I am thinking—that he *has* got it but is playing for time and denied it only to discourage spying. As you know, the old Falkland question has reared its ugly head again recently. As long ago as 1770 the Spaniards claimed the islands, and as their heirs the Argentinos are still trying to kick us out. Should that boil up to a head, Britain might have to think twice about going to war with Argentine if we had grounds to suppose that Peron can turn out Atom bombs as easily as hand-grenades. Peron would certainly like us to believe that."

Again the D.G. pulled at his cigar, then went on, "Our own backroom boys seem positive that no short cut to production is feasible, so that lends a certain weight to the double-bluff theory; but there is always a tendency for scientists to stick in their own groove when they think they have found a good one, and pooh-pooh all others. Anyhow, it will be up to them to decipher the gibberish in any papers you may

8

be able to get hold of, and pronounce upon them. If you can manage to purloin or photograph anything that looks like a formula it would naturally be all to the good, but at this stage I'm not aiming as high as that. Your job is simply to find out if Peron is bluffing or not."

Kem had spent the rest of the afternoon memorizing the contents of a rather slender file. It contained General Peron's original announcement and his later disclaimer, a brief biography of the scientist who had claimed to have discovered the new process and a semi-technical appreciation of its implausibility by a committee of British atomic experts who had deliberated on the matter.

There was also a series of brief reports from two resident agents in the Argentine. These revealed little but the apparently sinister fact that, far from having closed down his atomic experimental station, Peron had in recent months increased it to a great plant that now employed several thousand people. It was situated in a fold in the great plain some ten miles north of Basavilbaso and the whole area had been cordoned off. None of the workers was allowed to go on leave or quit the hutment town that had swiftly grown up round the plant for any other reason. The highest degree of secrecy was maintained about what went on there and permanent camps had been built outside its perimeter to accommodate ample troops to guard the place with strong patrols by day and night. The whole undertaking was under the control of a Colonel Estévan Escobar.

Escobar had started life as an engineer officer and was an old friend of General Peron. Rumour had it that he had made a fortune from the illegal sale of military supplies. In any case he had left the Army at the age of forty to devote himself entirely to his hobby, which was astronomy. He had then spent some years at observatories in both the United States and Germany. The outbreak of the war had found him in Berlin, and he had entered the service of the Nazis as one of the scientific advisers to the Luftwaffe. For a time he had been at Peenemünde working on the long-range rocket projects. In February 1945, evidently having decided that the Nazi goose was cooked, he had abandoned his paymasters and returned to the Argentine. He was now fifty-seven.

While reading of the great plant and the extraordinary precautions taken to keep its secret, Kem had had his tongue in his cheek. Peron, he felt, would be shrewd enough to know that if he wished to scare other nations with smoke he must at least create some sort of fire. For a dictator who did not have to account to his people for the expenditure of national funds, and who could command labour and troops without any awkward questions being asked about their employment, it would require only orders to a few trusted men to establish a bogus plant of practically any size. So Escobar's costly activities really proved nothing either way, and Kem had sailed for the Argentine with an open mind.

From the beginning he had realized that he would stand little chance of obtaining any definite information, either by getting himself taken on as an unskilled worker at the plant, or ordinary snooping should he find it possible to penetrate the sealed-off area by night. Experience had taught him that the best dividends were obtained with the least risk by the exploitation of social charm as a means of sliding smoothly in at the top. In the present case he had been exceptionally lucky, and within ten days of landing at Buenos Aires had succeeded in getting himself invited out to stay with Colonel Escobar.

The scientist lived in a fine old estancia which he had modernized and equipped with every luxury. Both he and his beautiful young wife were fond of company and consoled themselves for being deprived of the gaieties of Buenos Aires by entertaining a constant succession of guests. Kem had been a member of one of their house-parties for the past week, but that had not got him very far in his mission, as the estancia, although within the cordoned-off area, lay up in the hills, more than two miles from the plant in the valley, and it was tacitly understood that no guest should ever go down there.

Nevertheless, he had learned one important fact. Escobar trusted nobody, and each evening when he returned from his office he brought with him a fat red brief-case containing his most important papers, which he promptly locked away in a wall-safe in his bedroom.

It was obvious that his several thousand workpeople must be employed on the manufacture of something, and Kem had no doubt at all that Escobar was using the knowledge he had gained at Peenemünde to make long-range rockets; but whether the war-heads of these were being filled with ordinary explosives or prepared to receive some nuclear compound remained the vital problem, and one to which it seemed certain that Escobar and a few of his senior staff were the only people who knew the answer. In consequence, after a few days at the estancia, Kem had decided that his best chance of finding out lay in getting hold of Escobar's papers.

Kem knew a lot about safes. It was part of his business to do so, and in 1947 his department had arranged for him to spend three months under the tuition of London's finest locksmith. He felt fairly confident that he would be able to crack Escobar's safe, but to tackle the job properly he required at least an hour secure from interruption in the Colonel's bedroom.

After some thought he had settled on a plan. A fine stable was kept on the estancia and on several occasions he had gone for rides with some of the other guests, but they always observed the siesta in the heat of the day, so rode only in the early morning or evening. He would say that he wished to make a long trip up into the mountains, borrow a horse and take a picnic lunch; but instead he would ride into Basavilbaso, and from there telephone Escobar's secretary, pretending that he was one of General Peron's aides-de-camp, with a message that the Dictator wished to see Escobar on a matter of urgency, and that he was to report in Buenos Aires at eight o'clock that evening.

If the trick worked Escobar would have to curtail his siesta and, leaving the estancia by half past two, arrive at the spot near which Kem stood about three o'clock, while the countryside was still sleeping. But he could not be allowed to go on to Buenos Aires; otherwise, as soon as he got there he would find out that he had been hoaxed and would telephone an alarm to the estancia. It would be necessary to put him safely out of the way until morning, with his people believing that he was in Buenos Aires, if Kem were to stand any chance of getting into his bedroom that night.

So far, all had gone according to plan. Kem had ridden out towards the north that morning, and had been courteously waved through the cordon of guards on showing the pass with which he had been provided; then, by a circuitous route, made his way south to Basavilbaso. When telephoning he had used the name of one of General Peron's junior aides-de-camp, and Escobar's secretary had shown no suspicion, either that he was not speaking to the man whose name he had been given, or that the call came from Basavilbaso instead of from Buenos Aires. There was, however, still the danger that Escobar might have smelt a rat on receiving the message and, having rung up to confirm it, discovered that it was a fake.

Anxiously, Kem watched the long swathe of road that wound down through the valley. At five past three a little cloud of dust appeared upon it. Rapidly it grew nearer until through the heat haze he could see the big Cadillac that was churning it up. His heart gave a bound: in a part of the country so sparsely populated such a car could belong only to Escobar. A moment later Kem saw that it was being driven by a military chauffeur. His mouth hardened and he slipped his hand under his jacket to make sure that his gun lay easy in its holster. Then he slipped out into the road and waved to the driver to stop.

CHAPTER II

THE FIGHT IN THE THORN WOOD

FEARING that Escobar's military driver might take him for a hiker cadging a lift, and ignore his signals to stop, Kem stepped right out into the middle of the road. It entailed some risk, but if he allowed the car to pass, his carefully thought-out plan for getting hold of the atomic expert's papers would be aborted at its outset, and he would get no second chance to put it into operation, for immediately Escobar arrived in Buenos Aires he would learn that the message which had brought him from his plant was a fake.

There came a horrid moment when Kem thought he would have to leap for his life, but he stood his ground just long enough. Good brakes brought the Cadillac to a halt within ten feet of where he was standing, and its glowering driver favoured him with a spate of Spanish curses. But Colonel Escobar had recognized him, and putting his semi-bald head out of one of the back windows cried:

"Why, Señor Lincoln, what are you doing stranded here? I thought you had taken a horse this morning to ride out towards Tala."

Putting on a crestfallen look, Kem stepped round the bonnet to confront his host. "I did, Excellencia; but decided at the last moment that the country to the south was prettier, so rode down this way instead. Then, I am greatly embarrassed to confess it, but an hour ago I met with an accident. The beautiful mare from your stable put a foot on a loose rock and fell with me into a twenty-foot gully. I was thrown into some bushes, so escaped with a few scratches, but she broke her neck."

Escobar shrugged his powerful shoulders. "That is sad, but please do not worry. I have a score of other horses just as good. The important thing is that you are not injured. Jump in and I will give you a lift into Parera. You will be able to hire a car there to take you back to the estancia."

The offer was exactly what Kem had expected. Getting in, he murmured his thanks, and added, "At such an hour, and particularly in a sparsely populated area like this, I was very lucky to meet a car at all and the last person I expected to pick me up was yourself."

The burly, middle-aged scientist threw out his strong square hands in a typically Latin gesture. "This morning I had no idea that I should be travelling this way myself. My annoyance at being roused in the middle of my siesta by an urgent call to Buenos Aires is now compensated for by my pleasure at having been able to rescue you from your predicament. I am only sorry that I should have to take you some ten miles in the wrong direction, but a summons from General Peron is a thing which one must put even before one's wish to place oneself completely at the disposal of a guest. However, I console myself with the thought that you should be home in good time for a shower and rest before *les cocktails*."

Kem was used to these flowery Spanish courtesies and replied appropriately. The car, meanwhile, had gathered speed and he was watching the road ahead intently. The back seat of the Cadillac was broad enough to hold three large people comfortably; and he inconspicuously edged up into his own corner in order to place as much space as possible between Escobar and himself. To the left of the road the seemingly endless wheat-fields dropped away towards the broad river, to the right the forest continued nearly as far as Parera. When they had covered the best

12

part of two miles he drew his pistol from its shoulder holster, pointed it at Escobar, and said in German:

"I greatly regret to upset your arrangements, *Excellenz*, but be good enough to tell your driver to slow down and take the turning to the right which lies about a half a mile ahead."

Escobar had not been looking at him. He turned with a start to find himself staring down the barrel of Kem's gun. His broad, florid face went scarlet. The fine, upcurled black moustache that he had retained on leaving the Army suddenly seemed to bristle, and his dark eyes went stony with rage. For a second it looked as if he meant to hurl himself forward and risk being shot; but his eyes swiftly narrowed, his lips drew back showing two rows of strong white teeth. Then he snapped:

"What the hell's the meaning of this?"

"That, you may learn presently," Kem snapped back. "Do as I said!"

"You must be mad. Your fall——"

"No, I'm perfectly sane. Quick! Give the order or we'll miss the turning!"

"I'll be damned if I do!"

"You'll be dead if you don't!" As Kem spoke he flicked up the safety-catch of his pistol. The significant little gesture was not lost on Escobar. He realized that even an unexpected bump in the road might now be sufficient to jerk the finger on the trigger and send him to Kingdom Come. "Guido!" he shouted at his driver. "Take the turning to the right."

The startled chauffeur stiffened in his seat. He knew the road to Buenos Aires well, and that the turning was no more than a cart-track leading to a few Indian villages in the belt of rough scrub and thorn woods that had not yet been brought into cultivation. A swift glance in the driving mirror showed him the faces of his two passengers. They were staring at one another. His master's bushy brows were drawn down in a ferocious scowl; the round, cheerful face of the young man they had picked up was now set with the jaw thrust determinedly forward. The pistol was held too low for Guido to see it, but it was clear to him that something was wrong. Slowing up, he jerked his head round, caught sight of the gun in Kem's hand and made a grab at the automatic he was wearing in his belt.

Kem had been watching him out of the corner of his eye. His voice came, now in Spanish, like the crack of a whip. "Both hands on the wheel, Guido, or I'll blow the back of your head in."

Guido obeyed the order with commendable promptness, and Kem went on, "That's better. Now round the corner. Drive on till I tell you to stop. Keep your eyes on the road. If you look at me in the mirror mine will be the last face you'll live to see."

As the car turned up the track and passed a clump of tall, blue-grey eucalyptus trees Kem heaved an inward sigh of relief. From the moment

13

he had seen that Escobar was being driven by an armed chauffeur he had feared that he might be compelled to shoot it out before he could get the car off the main road. That tricky part of his project had now been accomplished without bloodshed, but he still had to secure Guido's gun before he could consider himself fully master of the situation. He was wondering how best to set about it when Escobar burst out:

"You ought either to be in hospital or jail. If you injured your head when you fell I'm sorry for you; but if you didn't, by God I'll have you in prison for this."

Kem's full-lipped mouth broke into a broad grin. "Thanks, but my head is sound as a bell. In fact, I lied to you just now about having a fall. You don't seem to set much stock on your valuable mare, but it may console you a little to know that she's safe and sound too. I left her hobbled in the wood not far from here."

"Then you *are* a crook, and this is a hold-up. What are you after, eh?"

"Your money or your life," Kem replied, his eyes twinkling.

"Damn it, you *must* be crazy! I don't carry much more than the price of a good dinner on me. Who in their senses does? Anyone but a fool would have realized that. You must be an amateur at this game. It would have paid you far better to stay behind and make off with some of the valuables at the estancia."

"That's not a bad idea. Perhaps I'll go back there to-night and relieve you of the household silver and your collection of snuff-boxes."

Escobar gave a short, harsh laugh. "You'd better not. Our police will soon lay an amateur like you by the heels, and I'll use my influence to get you a maximum sentence."

"They'll have to catch me first, and all my arrangements are made for leaving the country to-morrow."

"We'll see about that. In the meantime I've had enough of this foolery. I've told you that I've had an urgent summons to report to General Peron. He's a good friend of mine, but all the same I can't afford to ignore his orders. If I'm not in Buenos Aires by eight o'clock I may find myself in serious trouble. In the circumstances I'm prepared to do a deal with you. Put away that gun and let me proceed on my way; in return I'll hand you over my wallet and give you my promise that I'll not report this idiotic hold-up to the police until to-morrow morning."

Kem appeared to consider the offer for a moment, then he replied, "Then you are prepared to risk the silver and the snuff-boxes?"

Escobar gave him a swift, shifty look and nodded; then his eyes suddenly narrowed and he exclaimed, "But wait a minute! If you lied about the mare having broken her neck in a gully you must have planned this hold-up in advance. How the hell did you know that I'd be on my way to Buenos Aires at this hour?"

The broad grin again appeared on Kem's round face, as he murmured, "Ah! Thereby hangs a tale."

By this time the Cadillac had penetrated a mile into the acacia dotted rough scrub and Kem was keeping a look-out for a suitable spot in which to tackle the most critical phase of his venture. As they rounded a bend the track sloped down and towards a more densely wooded stretch, although on the left the nearest trees stood some way back and were sufficiently far apart for the car to be driven in among them. In a sharp voice he ordered Guido to turn off the road and keep going through the trees until he could go no further.

After a second's hesitation the man obeyed, and the car bumped its way over the uneven ground until it finally lurched to a halt facing a rotten tree-stump.

"Now!" said Kem. "Put your hands above your head, Guido, and if you value your life keep them there." To Escobar he added, "You stay where you are, unless you want a bullet." Then he opened the door of the car and slipped out of it.

Walking round to Guido's door, he opened that, quickly relieved the chauffeur of his gun and heaved it twenty feet away into the thick undergrowth. Then he produced a length of whipcord, threw it at Guido, and said, "Now get out, and tie your master's ankles together tightly with that. Quick now!"

Guido was a tall, cadaverous man with lank black hair, sombre eyes and olive complexion that betrayed more than a dash of Indian blood. But for his smart uniform he would have looked the typical hardy, primitive-minded South American *peon*. With a scowl he caught the cord and wriggled from his seat, while Escobar cried in alarm:

"*Nom de Dios!* You cannot mean to tie us up and leave us here. This wild country is almost uninhabited. It may be days before we are found. In the meantime we may die of thirst."

Having secured Guido's pistol, Kem was feeling much easier in his mind. Up to that point, too he had been extremely careful not to give away any part of his real intentions; but he bore Escobar no malice, and now felt that he could afford to disclose enough to reassure him. With a smile, he said:

"You need have no apprehension about that. I am going back to the estancia, and I'll leave a note there for your people, telling them where to look for you in the morning. You need not worry about General Peron either. He is not expecting you. It was I who telephoned your secretary in order to get you out here."

"I guessed as much when you said you'd lied about having an accident," growled Escobar. "You're not such a fool as I thought, but a real crook. Damn you, I'll——"

Kem cut him short by a threatening flourish of his pistol; then he pointed it at Guido and snapped, "Go on! Get busy! Tie up his legs as I told you. And tight, or it will be the worse for you."

With the cord dangling from his left hand, Guido stepped forward.

To reach Escobar he had to turn his back to Kem and come between them. At the car door he stooped, apparently to pass the cord under his master's knees. Suddenly he swung round. The sunlight glinted on a knife that he had whipped out from beneath his tunic.

He was within four feet of Kem and with a panther-like spring was upon him. Only Kem's Commando training saved him from that first surprise assault. He could have shot Guido dead, but the force of the Argentinian's spring would have driven the knife home before he dropped. In a flash Kem saw that his only chance of escaping a dangerous wound lay in deflecting the wicked blade. Mentally cursing himself for his lack of forethought in not having taken into account the fact that every *gaucho* in the Argentine carried a stiletto, he swerved aside and brought the fist that held his gun down with all his force on Guido's wrist.

Their two clenched hands met with a terrific impact. Kem's gun exploded but was dashed from his grasp. Guido's knife fell with a tinkle on the ground. The bullet caught him in the calf of his right leg. With a howl of pain he lurched forward, flinging his long arms round Kem's neck. Kem lost his balance and they crashed to the ground locked in a wild embrace

With a shout of encouragement to Guido, Escobar jumped from the car and frantically cast about for a weapon with which to aid him. Kem's gun was now underneath him, but Guido's knife lay a few feet from the writhing pair. Escobar's eyes lit on it, and running forward, he stooped to snatch it up. With a violent effort Kem freed himself from Guido's clutch and rolled over. Jerking out his right foot he landed a kick on the side of Escobar's head. It caught the scientist off his balance and he toppled sideways a second before he could grasp the knife.

All three of them were now sprawling on the ground. Kem's brain was racing. He was not given to panic, but he knew that he was up against it. There was no escape now from a fight to a finish, and in a hand-to-hand tussle he feared that the two of them might prove too much for him. If they did that would put a grim end to his mission. The best he could hope for was a long spell in an Argentine prison; but, judging from the murderous glare he had seen in Guido's eyes, it seemed more likely that they would kill him and leave his body to rot there in the bush. Guido's wound had not prevented him from pressing his fierce assault, and Escobar, although over fifty, was both vigorous and powerful. Kem's only advantage lay in his superior agility and the combat training which had taught him a score of ugly tricks that could be used in an emergency.

He was first on his feet, but up only for a moment. He had barely kicked the knife well out of his reach when Guido seized him by the ankle and brought him crashing down again. Escobar had got to his knees and now hurled himself on the prostrate Englishman. Kem drew back his first and landed a blow on his attacker's left kidney. The big man gave a screech, relaxed his hold and squirmed with agony. Following up his advantage, Kem jabbed him with his left beneath the jaw and wriggled out from under him. But, in the meantime, Guido had found Kem's gun. As he rolled over he saw the Argentinian raise it and point it at him.

For a desperate second Kem thought his end had come, but he kicked out wildly. The toe of his boot caught the end of the barrel at the instant Guido fired and the bullet whizzed harmlessly overhead. Before Guido could level the weapon and fire again Kem had turned a somersault and leapt at him, a whirling mass of arms and legs that sent him spinning. Next second Kem had seized his wrist, twisted it violently and forced him to drop the gun. But with his left hand, brown, wiry and strong as a talon, Guido had him by the throat. Its sharp nails dug into his neck until little rivulets of blood ran from them, and all his efforts to wrench his head away failed to loosen that agonizing grip.

Guido was underneath but had pulled Kem down on top of him and was holding him too close for him to use his fists effectively. In vain Kem pummelled at his ribs and the sides of his head; the tough *gaucho* seemed immune to any punishment. Kem seized his ear and gave it a savage twist, but still he hung on. Hunching his body, Kem exerted all his strength and brought his right knee up, jabbing it into the Argentinian's crutch. At last the awful pressure on his windpipe relaxed and he was able to tear his throat away.

As he did so he heard a twig snap behind him. Jerking his head round he glimpsed Escobar. Sweat was running in rivulets down the burly scientist's red and furious face, but he had recovered sufficiently from the two savage blows Kem had dealt him to enter the fight again. In his hand he grasped a heavy length of broken branch that he had picked up to use as a club. He was just about to bring it crashing down on the back of Kem's head.

Still struggling with Guido, Kem forced himself to keep his head steady while he counted three, then he jerked it aside. The great lump of wood missed it by barely an inch, to come smashing down in Guido's upturned face. As Guido glimpsed the coming blow he gave an awful cry, then suddenly shuddered and lay still. Before Escobar could strike again Kem had heaved himself to his feet and jumped clear of Guido's body. Still gasping from Guido's stranglehold, he paused for a moment to get back a little breath; then he sailed in. His left fist landed squarely on the point of Escobar's jaw and a smashing right followed it to his solar plexus. With a moan the scientist slumped to the ground and lay writhing there.

Panting and dishevelled, Kem surveyed his handiwork, more with relief than any sense of triumph. Guido was out cold, his nose smashed and his face a mess of blood; Escobar would give no further trouble, provided a watchful eye was kept upon him. But it had been a near thing, and Kem was highly conscious that half a dozen times in the past few hectic moments it was he who had been within an ace of becoming as helpless as the bodies at his feet.

Recovering his gun he tucked it back in its holster; then, picking up the length of whipcord, he turned the squirming Escobar over on his face and tied his hands behind his back. Next he examined Guido's wounds. The *gaucho's* face was a horrid sight, but the blow had not fractured his forehead; so he was in no serious danger. The bullet had torn the muscle of his calf, which was bleeding, although not badly. As he had met with his injuries only through doing his duty, Kem was relieved to think that after a week or two in hospital he would emerge, perhaps with a permanent limp, and certainly more villainous-looking than ever, but otherwise none the worse for his adventure.

Kem bound up his wounds as best he could, carried him to the car and propped him up on its back seat. Not wishing to cause him many hours' additional pain by trussing him like a chicken, Kem put another length of the thin cord round his neck, knotted it, and tied its two ends to the outside handles of the car doors, so that when he came-to his hands would be free to keep the flies from his face, but he would not be able to reach and release his master.

Escobar had got back his wind but was still dizzy when Kem returned to him and made him get to his feet. With a muttered curse he allowed himself to be pushed towards the car and into the driver's seat. A threat to reduce his face to the same state as Guido's was sufficient to prevent his offering any resistance while Kem firmly lashed his ankles with a third length of cord, then rifled his pockets. The few papers they contained were of no interest, so Kem stuffed them back; but to keep up his character of highwayman he took the money from the wallet. Then he went round to the back of the car, opened the boot and swiftly ran through Escobar's suitcase: it contained only his things for a night away from home. When he had satisfied himself there was no other place in the car where Escobar might have put any secret papers, he removed the sparking plugs from the engine and disconnected the lights and the horn to prevent any possibility of Escobar signalling with them, then turned to him and said:

"I'm sorry about your man, and that you will have to spend some uncomfortable hours here; but I could think of no other way to get rid of you for the night."

The atomic expert gave him a suspicious scowl, and muttered, "I don't believe you would have gone to these lengths only to make it easier to get away with the silver at the estancia. What's your real game, eh?"

Kem's full-lipped grin spread over his round face. "If you want the truth, it's not your silver or snuff-boxes I'm after, but your wife's emeralds."

Almost imperceptibly Escobar relaxed. "Ah, well!" he shrugged. "They are heavily insured. If the police get you, though, I'll charge you with attempted murder, and we'll see to it that you never have a chance to stage another hold-up."

Slamming the car door, Kem turned away with a wave of his hand, to walk the three miles to the place where he had left his mare hobbled. As he set off he was thinking that had he been due for a really lucky break Escobar would have had his cherished brief-case with him. But perhaps that had been too much to hope for. Evidently he had left it in the safe in his bedroom. Even in his absence it was not going to be any too easy to get hold of.

"Still," thought Kem, with another grin, "if I play my cards properly I can persuade the beautiful Carmen to help me there."

CHAPTER III

THE FLYING SAUCER

FOUR hours later, immaculate in a suit of cream tussore, his dark hair neatly parted at the side and brushed smoothly back, Kem Lincoln sat on the wide loggia of the estancia. The building was a large one in the Spanish colonial style and had been erected by a wealthy grandee early in the nineteenth century. Its rooms, built round a central arcaded court-yard, in which a cool fountain splashed, were airy and spacious, and Estévan Escobar had spared no expense in furnishing them suitably when he had taken the place over as his private residence.

The inner side of the loggia was formed by part of the colonnade, the arches of which gave on to the courtyard; the outer by a low stone balustrade, beyond which a garden of shallow terraces sloped away towards the depression where, two miles off, lay the atomic plant and town of hutments that housed its several thousand workers.

It was the cocktail hour, and with Kem in the loggia were now assembled the Escobars' house-party, which consisted of five other guests. They were a Colonel Gonzales, who was on General Peron's staff, and his middle-aged wife; a painter named Jorge Avila, engaged on some murals in the house; Pedro Belasco, a young astronomer whom Escobar regarded as his most promising pupil, and Yolanda Milleflores, a pretty but rather shallow young woman who had been educated at the same convent as Carmen, Escobar's wife. Carmen herself and her elderly aunt, Doña Julia Partaga y Calderon, who lived with them completed the party.

Carmen was twenty-four and, Kem thought, one of the loveliest women he had ever set eyes on. A Partaga y Calderon by birth, she was descended from a long line of Spanish hidalgos, and the strong yet delicate bone formation of her thin face had the indelible stamp of the aristocrat. Her hair was black, her skin had the matt whiteness of magnolia petals, her cheekbones were high, her dark eyebrows tapering and below them her fine eyes were almond-shaped, vaguely suggesting that from somewhere far back she must have inherited a dash of Chinese blood.

She had been married only three years and was heiress to a great fortune; so why she should have married a man like Escobar, who was more than twice her age and of little social standing, remained something of a mystery. She had had no children, but appeared to be on good terms with her husband and content to live with him in social exile at the estancia for the greater part of the year; although, apparently, her money gave her more independence than that enjoyed by the wives of most South Americans, as she made two trips to Paris every year to buy clothes, accompanied only by her aunt.

It was her most recent trip which had given Kem an exceptionally lucky break at the outset of his mission. After receiving his instructions from the D.G. he had gone to the Foreign Office for briefing by an expert on South American affairs. Naturally he had made further enquiries about Escobar and it had transpired that, just by chance, the man he was interviewing had learned in casual conversation a few nights before that Escobar's wife was then in Paris. A high priority signal to the British Embassy had elicited the information that Carmen had left Paris for Lisbon and was reported to be sailing home the following day in the *General Peron*, one of the Dictator's new motor-powered liners. Within an hour Kem had collected his passport and crammed the essentials for a voyage into three suitcases. A special service aircraft had taken him to Lisbon overnight and he had sailed in the same ship.

The liners of General Peron's new fleet were most luxuriously appointed, but quite small and built to accommodate a limited number of first-class passengers only; so it had been easy for Kem to draw the attention of Carmen to himself on the second night out. From his boyhood he had been interested in conjuring and in time had become an accomplished amateur of that art. After dinner, in the charming little lounge, he had started to amuse the people at his table with some sleight-of-hand tricks, and amazed them by the facility with which he picked their pockets. Soon most of the forty or fifty passengers present, attracted by his entertaining patter, had left their tables to gather around, Carmen and her aunt among them. Without particularly singling them out, he had included them among his victims; so when they appeared on the promenade deck the following morning it had been quite natural for him to greet them as acquaintances.

As the wily Kem was a past-master at getting himself into the good graces of elderly ladies, the Doña Julia Partaga y Calderon took a great liking to him, and their acquaintance swiftly ripened into one of those shipboard friendships in which his almost constant attendance on her and her niece had been readily accepted. But, for all that, South American convention demanded that she should continue to play the dragon; so the occasions on which Kem was able to enjoy Carmen's company on his own had been short and infrequent.

At first that had not worried him particularly, as his object was simply to achieve a degree of intimacy which would ensure an invitation to meet her husband when she got home. In fact he had rather doubted the wisdom of attempting to have an *affaire* with her at all, as that might bring about complications contrary to the interests of his mission. But Carmen obviously loved admiration and found him an amusing companion; so during the long lazy days running down through blue seas towards the equator he decided that it would appear abnormal if he did not enter into a flirtation with her.

A ship being a world apart with no distracting influences, and almost every hour of every day offering chances for subtle innuendo or stolen glances, such approaches, once begun, are apt to advance with surprising rapidity; thus, having launched himself upon this slippery slope, Kem had soon found himself committed to the role of Carmen's would-be lover.

Being constantly in her presence had half intoxicated him already; so, putting behind him the fear that if they became too intimate on the voyage she might refuse to see him afterwards, he had deliberately settled down to woo her; while she, from a natural reaction against the restraint imposed upon her by the chaperonage of her aunt, went halfway to meet him. By the time they crossed the equator they were daily resorting to little subterfuges which enabled her to be alone with him for short periods, and so the fascinating game went on until she agreed to come up from her cabin at night and meet him secretly on the boat deck.

In the veins of both Carmen and Kem ran hot southern blood; so they came to their meeting with no illusions as to its probable outcome. After ten days spent in talking neither expected the other to waste precious time admiring the Southern Cross or discussing the ethics of their relationship. With only a few murmured words they went straight into one another's arms.

On the next night they met again. At two o'clock in the morning Kem saw her down to her cabin. In a whisper he asked her to let him come in and say good-night to her there. Flushed, and trembling a little, she had consented. Once inside their passion mounted to fever heat. The good-night was never said, and Kem stole away at dawn. For the three nights that followed she did not come on deck; but as soon as all was quiet he went down to her. During hours that sped all too swiftly they

21

gave free rein to the lovely madness that had seized upon them both and, oblivious of past or future, revelled in the highest delights that youth can give.

Then had come the last night of the voyage, and when the ship's bell tolled the sad tidings that it was time for them to part, Carmen said with a sigh:

"These stolen nights have been wonderful, and I have loved every moment of them. But as I told you in the beginning, there can never be anything permanent between us, and I have made myself think of them as though they were dreams that have never really happened. You know how rigid the social code is in the Argentine, and it would be much too dangerous for us to attempt to carry on our *affaire* once we have landed; so now, Kem darling, we must say good-bye for good."

Her attitude was just what he had feared it might be, but he had already taken precautions against that, so was able to reply, "My angel, I would never forgive myself if I brought trouble on you, but it is too much to ask that I should forgo my chance of ever seeing you again. Only yesterday Doña Julia insisted that when I had concluded my business in Buenos Aires I must come on a visit to your estancia for at least a week, and unless you positively forbid me to do so I mean to accept the invitation."

At first Carmen had protested at the risk involved of their not being able to conceal their passion for one another from her husband; but Kem had argued that since they had succeeded in doing so from her aunt, who had had nothing to do and had been constantly in their company, it was unlikely that a man like Colonel Escobar, who must have many important affairs to occupy him, would prove more perspicacious; and he had then solemnly sworn to observe the utmost discretion during his visit.

Through lack of opportunity, but not of inclination, it was the first time that Carmen had surrendered herself to a young man of near her own age, and, being still in the throes of awakening to the supreme heights of physical passion, she had yielded to the temptation to prolong her clandestine *amour*. She did so with considerable misgiving for, as she told Kem, even if he stayed at the estancia for a month there might not occur a single opportunity on which they could safely make love again. Nevertheless, when the ship was about to dock twelve hours later, as mistress of the estancia she had formally endorsed her aunt's invitation.

That her misgivings had been well founded Kem had to admit after his first forty-eight hours as a member of the Escobar house-party. Carmen dared not break away from the customary routine by which, morning and evening, the party all rode, swam in the pool or sat about together; and Escobar invariably returned to the house both for the siesta hours and at cocktail time every evening. So far, only three times during Kem's stay had a chance arisen for Carmen and himself to snatch a few whispered words and kisses. But to-night the coast would be clear.

He had no intention of allowing anything to interfere with the accomplishment of his mission, and had put behind him any scruples about having planned to use Carmen unconsciously to aid him in it; yet he would have been less than human had he not also planned to seize the final opportunity of revelling again in the wild delights they had known together.

At the moment, however, a quite unforeseen happening that afternoon had drawn the whole company into an excited discussion, which temporarily debarred him from any chance of getting a whispered word with her of his intention of coming that night to her room. A Flying Saucer had appeared over the valley.

Unfortunately it had made its appearance during the siesta hours; so, of the house-party, only the painter Jorge Avila, who preferred to doze in the loggia rather than in his room, had seen it. Pedro Belasco, the young astronomer, was frankly sceptical and at first twitted Avila with having dreamt it; but a telephone enquiry to the offices of the atomic plant produced corroboration, as a dozen, or more workers lounging in the shade had also seen and excitedly reported the strange visitant.

Pressed to give details, Avila described it as a huge, round, gleaming disc, whitish in colour and not less than a hundred feet across. He said that it appeared to be spinning like a great top and flying at about three thousand feet, but showed no evidence of propulsion and was completely silent. He had opened his eyes from a doze at about a quarter to three to see it hovering right over the plant. It had remained stationary there for some four minutes, then suddenly and noiselessly streaked away in a westerly direction at a terrific speed, so that it was lost to sight in a matter of seconds.

That tallied with the bulk of the reports which had been published about the sighting of such objects in the United States and elsewhere, but Belasco refused to be convinced.

"I grant that you saw something," he conceded, with a shrug of his narrow shoulders, "but not what you suppose. It must have been a thing called a sea-hook, which is a form of balloon used to gather meteorological information."

"Nonsense!" retorted Avila sharply. "Such wind as there is comes from the north-west, so how could a balloon travel against it? And at such a speed! I give you my word this thing made off faster than any jet: it was doing at least a thousand miles an hour. It could only have been a space ship."

Again Belasco shrugged. "You admit you were half asleep. It was a sea-hook that you saw, then you dozed off again and only dreamt its swift disappearance."

His was the type of argument which had been adopted the world over by natural sceptics of the normally inexplicable after the official board of enquiry known as "Project Saucer" had been closed down by the United States Government, and the statement giving sea-hooks as the explanation of these strange appearances had been issued; but Kem thought it very far from being fully convincing.

As a secret agent, whose special business it was to keep abreast with the development of all new types of weapons, he had followed the Flying Saucers controversy with considerable interest. It had started in June 1947 with a level-headed American business man named Arnold, when flying his own aircraft in Washington State, sighting nine discs in close formation weaving in and out among the peaks of the Rocky Mountains. Within a month scores of people in Portland, Oregon, and Seattle reported seeing similar discs, including such trained observers as the captain and crew of a United States air liner, all of whom vouched for having watched a flight of them manœuvre for ten minutes.

At about the same time had occurred the strange case of Maury Island. An official of the Port of Tacoma, named Dahl, had been near the island in a patrol boat with a crew of two men and his son, when they had all suddenly sighted six great discs flying silently about 2,000 feet above them. Five of the discs were circling round the sixth, which seemed to be in trouble, as, although it was moving too, it was swiftly losing height. After a few minutes it was down to within 500 feet of the sea. There it hovered: there came a dull boom and it let fall what appeared to be some metal objects that must have been intensely hot, as they raised a cloud of steam on plunging into the water. The disc then rose again, and with its five companions streaked away across the Pacific.

In the following January had come the high-spot of the saga. At three o'clock on the afternoon of the 7th, State Police at Fort Knox, where the greater part of the available gold in the world was now buried, had alerted the military authorities that they were receiving telephone calls from scores of people about a Flying Saucer which was overhead and making in the direction of Godman Air Base. Colonel Hix, the Commandant at the Base, had immediately ordered up three fighter aircraft and gone with his staff to the control tower. Within a few minutes Colonel Hix and his companions all picked up the Flying Saucer through their binoculars. It was far bigger than any previously reported and estimated to be a good 500 feet in diameter. Also unlike its predecessors, this colossal airship—the floor space of which must have exceeded that of St. Peter's in Rome—was belching blasts of red flame as it proceeded at quite a moderate pace through a sky only partially obscured by thin cloud. The three fighter pilots also saw it, reported by radio to their base and gave chase. Soon, apparently taking alarm, it began to climb at 400 miles an hour. Two of the pilots lost sight of it almost at once, but their senior, Captain Mantell, kept it in view. His last words, spoken to Base, were that he thought he could stand an altitude of 20,000 feet and meant to go to that in the hope of getting a closer view of his quarry. How close he got no one will ever know, or the exact cause of his death, but later the wreckage of his aircraft was picked up scattered over a wide area.

To reject the unprejudiced testimony of such highly qualified observers as Colonel Hix and his staff seemed arbitrary in the extreme, and fifteen months after the tragedy at Godman Air Base it had been supported by evidence of an unquestionably scientific nature.

At White Sands, New Mexico, the United States Government had established an experimental station for the development of long-range rockets. On the firing of each rocket the expert in charge, Commander R. B. McLaughlin, was responsible for recording its speed, direction and performance, this being made possible by a number of teams stationed several miles apart registering the flight of the rocket by means of theodolites. In April 1948 one such team was checking the flight of a weather balloon when into the field of view of the theodolite sailed a Flying Saucer. The instrument showed it to be sixty miles up and moving at the fantastic speed of 18,000 miles an hour. McLaughlin had not been present with the team, but a month later he and two officers with him saw the same or a similar disc, and a month after that another of his teams reported two very small discs that chased, circled and passed a rocket which was hurtling at enormous speed up into the stratosphere.

Both before and since these outstanding episodes, the sighting of Flying Saucers had been reported, mostly in the United States, but also in several other countries, and the number of separate cases now totalled nearly eight hundred. Owing to the sensational publicity given to the early sightings, on December 30th, 1947, the U.S. Government had decided to set up "Project Saucer"—a committee composed of astrophysicists, specialists in electronics, meteorologists and other experts—to investigate all the available evidence. At first their reports had admitted that much of the phenomena described was incapable of explanation on any accepted scientific grounds, but later a U.S. Army Air Force spokesman declared that all cases submitted had been disposed of as having natural causes, and in September 1949 "Project Saucer" was closed down.

Like many other people, Kem had regarded the vague official attempts to explain away specific cases and the culminating bald announcement as at least suspicious. It seemed next to incredible that men like Colonel Hix and Commander McLaughlin, who had had a lifelong training in identifying aerial objects, could have mistaken weather balloons for giant space ships of hitherto unknown design and performance, or, as it was suggested, that the unfortunate Captain Mantell had been deluded into chasing the planet Venus at three o'clock in the afternoon. It was, too, a little too much to insist that thousands of sane respectable citizens had suddenly become the victims of mass hysteria, and that groups of them at hundreds of different times and places had all been led to tell a tissue of lies as a result of hallucinations.

With the superior air of a young don who has been somewhat spoilt by early academic successes, Belasco had been delivering a lecture to

Avila upon the astro-physiological barriers which would make it next to impossible for any space ship, except in the form of a rocket, to accomplish the voyage from one world to another. Then Colonel Gonzales cut in to remark:

"Because no satisfactory explanation has yet been offered to account for the appearance of these things, it does not follow that they are space ships. They may be a new secret weapon. That is the opinion of many well-informed people. When I was on a mission to Spain last year I was shown a photograph of one over the Balearic Isles that had been taken at night by a newsreel camera-man named Enrique Muller. It looked like a plate of fire, with five great jets of flame swirling from its circumference as it revolved. The man who showed me the photograph at the Spanish War Office was convinced that it was a diabolical invention of the Russians."

Kem shook his head. "I find it hard to believe that the Russians are so far ahead of everyone else in aero-dynamics, Colonel."

"That none of us knows," the Colonel retorted, "and colour is lent to the theory that they are Russian by the fact that by far the greatest number of sightings so far have occurred over American air bases, and experimental stations. If the Russians have such an aircraft, it follows that they would use it to spy out as many of the military secrets as possible of their potential enemies."

"Perhaps. But how, then, do you account for the sightings down in the Antarctic? Commander Orrego, who is in charge of the Chilean naval base there, has reported the appearance of quite a number of Flying Saucers and, it is said, secured good photographs of them. What possible interest could the Russians have in the South Pole?"

"The Chilean Government refuses to release the photographs," Carmen remarked, "and what I cannot understand is why they, and the American Government, should make such a mystery of the matter."

"That is easily explained, my dear," smiled the Colonel. "It is the duty of all governments to do their utmost to maintain the tranquillity of their people. The odds are that no one, apart from those responsible for their appearance, yet knows definitely what these things are or whence they come. But say they did, and an authoritative statement were issued, either that they are a new Soviet weapon, or possibly the forerunners of an invasion from another world: think of its effect. Either might cause widespread panic and in any case would have disastrous effects upon the world's stock markets. Naturally the authorities will strive to prevent anything of that kind, as long as keeping secret what they do know will enable them to."

For another hour these intriguing speculations about the Flying Saucers went on, and it was not until they were about to separate to change for dinner that Kem succeeded in getting a few words alone with Carmen.

As the party broke up he had caught her eye and she had moved over to the far end of the loggia, ostensibly to admire the sunset with him. But Doña Julia was still collecting her work-things within twenty feet of them, and Belasco was helping her hunt for a missing needle.

"To-night," murmured Kem under his breath, "I'll come to your room."

"No, Kem, no!" she whispered back. "It would be too dangerous."

"On the contrary. With Estévan in Buenos Aires we have nothing to fear."

"No, no! I dare not let you."

"Please! Please, Carmen," he urged her. "This is a God-given opportunity, and our last chance of a few hours together. This morning I received a letter that I cannot possibly ignore, and I have to leave to-morrow."

She drew in a sharp little breath and he saw the knuckles of her hand go white as she clenched the balustrade. After a moment she whispered, "Must you . . . must you really go?"

"Yes; and my company has ordered me to the United States. I shall always love you, but it will be months, perhaps years, before I can get back here. Surely you won't deny me the memory of this last night together when the gods have been so kind in making things easy for us?"

Biting her scarlet lip, she hesitated, torn by conflicting emotions; then her low voice came again, "Darling, I want you so much. It crucifies me to say no, but the risk is so appalling. Estévan would kill me if he found out, and I'm sure that his creature, Belasco, already suspects us. I knew it from the look he gave me after he came upon us in the garden the day before yesterday. He's watching us covertly now. He's bound to realize that with Estévan away we shall attempt to seize on this chance to deceive him. I feel sure he'll stay up and spy on us. He'll lie in wait somewhere between your room and mine. I dare not risk it. I simply dare not."

Kem gave her a steady, confident smile, as he whispered in reply, "I've thought of that. I saw the suspicious look he gave you, too, but I've thought of a way to fool him. At dinner I mean to pretend to be ill —a touch of the sun after my long ride today. That will be excuse enough for me to go to bed two or three hours before the rest of you. It will be one o'clock or so, as usual, before the party breaks up. At midnight I shall leave my room, lock the door and go to yours; so if he does wait up he'll have his wait for nothing, because I'll already be in your suite. Then when dawn comes I'll leave by your window. Carmen, you must let me do that. You must! I can't bear to go away without holding you in my arms again."

Again she hesitated, then she gave a little gulp and breathed, "All right. It . . . it shall be as you wish. May the Holy Mother forgive and protect us."

Kem was a born actor. At dinner, instead of being his usual amusing self, he appeared distrait and poor company; then towards the end of the meal he gave an admirable rendering of a near faint and complained of a splitting headache. Everyone present showed much concern and he was packed off to bed with varying advice as to the best treatment for slight heat-stroke.

On his way upstairs he grinned to himself at the thought that he had pulled off the second step towards his great coup. Estévan Escobar was safely out of the way for the night and while overcoming Carmen's scruples he had, in accordance with his carefully-thought-out plan, deftly secured for himself an uninterrupted hour in their private suite. The thought of her saddened him a little. She was so lovely and so lovable, and to use her in this unscrupulous way was hateful to his natural instincts. Yet he could not allow such a consideration to interfere with the accomplishment of his mission.

There remained the worrying uncertainty about whether his skill as a locksmith would prove equal to cracking Escobar's safe; and while he had seen no other way to get at it than by involving Carmen, he was aware that he might yet have to pay a price for that, for the most dangerous complications would arise should he not have completed his nefarious task by the time she arrived in her room.

As he closed the door of his own room behind him he wondered a little grimly how the night would end.

CHAPTER IV

A THIEF IN THE NIGHT

IN the Argentine the upper classes followed the Spanish custom o dining late, and even in the country rarely sat down to dinner before nine; so it was past ten before Kem reached his room. There, he at once undressed and got into bed, as a precaution against anyone coming up to enquire after his feigned indisposition, and he soon had cause to be thankful for his wariness. Within five minutes of his getting between the sheets there came a soft knock on the door and Doña Julia, an imposing figure in black lace and stiff satin, rustled in.

With her the old lady brought well-proved remedies for heat-stroke, and proceeded to swathe his head in bandages soaked with some sweet-scented solution of herbs. She also produced a fearsome-looking draught of thick, blackish liquid; but having gracefully submitted to her other ministrations Kem, fearing that it contained a soporific sufficient to dull his wits dangerously, perhaps at some critical moment during the coming night, persuaded her to leave it for him to take only should he find difficulty in getting off to sleep.

Once she had gone he felt that he had no need to fear a second visit, as after dinner every night the house-party at the estancia always settled down to a game of baccarat, and Doña Julia apparently found no difficulty in reconciling her passion for gambling with a most exemplary piety.

He had already done most of his packing before dinner, but he now got up and completed it. Then, with his head still bandaged and wearing his dressing-gown, he carried his two suitcases down the back stairs and out to the garage. As he had foreseen might be the case, some stable hands and chauffeurs were lounging in the yard, enjoying the cool of the evening. To one of the latter he explained that he had a touch of the sun, but in spite of that must start for Buenos Aires first thing in the morning. Then he tipped the man lavishly to stow his baggage in a car that he had hired before leaving the capital, and to service it with air, water, oil and petrol. Having waited to see that the job was done properly, he returned to his room, and wrote a brief note describing the state and place in which he had left Escobar, then propped it up on the dressing-table, where it was certain to be found in the morning.

When packing he had left out with his day-things a dark lounge suit, and he now dressed himself in it for three good reasons. Should he hear anyone approaching when he made his way stealthily to Carmen's room he would, against a dark background, stand a better chance of remaining unseen than he would have had in a gaily-coloured dressing-gown; if he were unlucky enough to run slap into anyone his being fully dressed would be much less likely to suggest that he was on his way to an amorous rendezvous with the beautiful mistress of the house; and, lastly, he was far too old a hand to risk having to make a quick getaway without his trousers, should some unforeseen event cause matters to go seriously wrong.

By the time he had dressed and removed the bandage from his head it was a quarter past eleven; but anxious as he was to get to work he felt that he dared not do so yet. At the estancia the servants, like their masters, kept late hours; so it was possible that Carmen's maid might not yet have come up to prepare her mistress's room for the night. He felt confident she would have done so within the next half-hour, but it was better to sacrifice that than risk disaster by walking in on her.

Controlling his impatience as best he could, he took up a book, but after a few moments found that he could not concentrate on it. For a little he thought with joyful anticipation of the hours he planned to spend with Carmen, then his mind drifted back to Flying Saucers.

Even allowing for numerous hoaxes, unscrupulous publicity-seekers and mass hysteria, there seemed far too much testimony by trained

29

observers of known integrity to accept the official denial that any such things existed. It was Kem's opinion that they did. He had also reached the conclusion that they could not be a secret weapon manufactured anywhere on this planet.

The construction of such huge machines would require a vast plant with thousands of employees. If the United States, Britain, the Dominions or any of the free nations of Europe had such a plant its purpose would be bound to have leaked out ere this. Besides, both America and Europe were now so criss-crossed daily by airlines and private flyers that someone would certainly have seen from the air Saucers on the ground at any factory or base where they were prepared for flight.

Asia outside the Iron Curtain could be ruled out, because none of its peoples was sufficiently advanced to produce such a scientific wonder, except perhaps the Japanese, and they were still under American supervision.

Russia, too, could be ruled out. For her to have sent scores of Saucers over the United States would have been to risk that at any time one of them might be compelled to make a forced landing, with the result that American scientists would gain possession of its vital secrets; and if the Russians had achieved such a stupendous advantage for waging a future war against the United Nations, they would never be such fools as to throw it away before they were ready to use it with maximum effect.

Finally, Kem was convinced that, indifferent in some respects as United Nations Intelligence might be, it was very far from being so behind on vital matters for no single one of its agents to have ferreted out the base from which the Saucers came, if such a base existed anywhere on earth; and that had they done so he would, in his job, have been informed of it.

The unlikelihood of any human agency being responsible for these mysterious visitors was further strengthened by the fact that several entirely different types had been reported; and while British, American or Russian scientists might conceivably have designed one revolutionary type of aircraft, the odds were much greater against their having perfected several simultaneously.

Of the discs so far sighted the great majority appeared to be of a standard type, about 100 feet in diameter with a central hub, like a short mast, projecting from its upper surface. But the giant that had appeared over Fort Knox was said to have been 500 feet across, and the same, or perhaps an even larger one, which had been sighted later, was estimated to have a span of from 700 to 1,000 feet, whereas the discs that had chased and passed Commander McLaughlin's rocket had been registered by the theodolite as spanning two feet only.

Size apart, these could be considered as of one type; but the thing that Captain Chiles of Eastern Airlines had seen at 2.45 in the morning of the 23rd of July 1948 bore no resemblance whatever to them. While flying his plane from Houston, Texas, to Atlanta a long cigar-shaped monster had come hurtling out of the night towards him. It had no fins; its fore-cabin was brilliantly lighted; a purplish band of light glowed from nose to stern down its side, and there spouted from its rear end a 50-feet-long orange flame. Apparently as a result of seeing the airliner, the monster suddenly turned on its full power, the tail flame doubled in length, and like a bullet from a gun the mystery ship shot up towards the stratosphere.

Chiles could not have imagined the occurrence, as his First Officer had seen it, too, and corroborated every detail: in addition, the only passenger who happened to be awake vouched for the streaking past of something which had momentarily lit up the interior of the plane with a baleful, unearthly glare, the like of which he had never seen.

And this was by no means the only case in which these great aerial torpedoes, with flame gushing from their sterns, had been reported. While piloting a big DC-6 at night near Mount Vernon, Captain William Sperry had met what he described as "a submarine with lights." He was flying at 300 miles per hour, yet so terrific was the speed and manoeuvrability of this terrifying night-rider that it circled twice round his aircraft before disappearing.

Then there were the things that the scientist, Mr. Gerald Heard, had so aptly termed "Thinking Lights" in his admirably lucid and unbiased book on Flying Saucers. The most spectacular case in which these had appeared was at Fargo, North Dakota. National Air Guard Lieutenant Gorman was about to land his aircraft there after participating in an exercise that ended after dark. Although he had been given the "all clear" he saw a light flying across the airfield below him. Yet it was not the light of another plane; it was not attached to anything and had nothing whatever to support it. Greatly mystified, he dived down to get a closer view. It dodged him. He turned and chased it. Then for a full twenty minutes the light played tag with him, ducking, swerving, swooping and jumping while he fruitlessly pursued it. Finally, apparently having had its fun, and taken him up to 17,000 feet, it put on a burst of speed and disappeared upward into the night sky. Again, there could be no question of Gorman suffering from hallucinations, as the officials in the control tower witnessed the whole extraordinary performance.

So these newcomers to earth's skies varied both in type and in bulk; or rather, as a small flame has no body, from lack of it to a mighty disc which had been sighted simultaneously in towns 150 miles apart; thus, by simple triangulation, proving it to have been flying at an immense height, and to have been of enormous size for it to have been seen at that height at all.

But were they newcomers to earth's skies? Research among old scientific journals had unearthed letters reporting the inexplicable appearance of hovering lights and great airships being seen among the clouds on numerous occasions during the last century. That these appearances had been few and far between in the past, yet had increased to almost monotonous frequency since the opening of the Atomic Age on earth, might in itself be a factor of extraordinary significance.

If, as seemed the only possible explanation, they came from some other world, they must be manned by beings scientifically far in advance of ourselves. Life on that world might have started a million years before life started here. If so, and life there had followed a similar pattern to life here, its inhabitants might have reached the Atomic Age while earth was still populated by prehistoric man.

Perhaps they had watched the development of life on earth for several millennia and been content to inspect it only at long intervals, until one day they had been suddenly given cause for grave alarm by seeing us explode what could only be an Atom bomb. They would have good cause for their alarm, as they would know that if we mishandled this terrible power we might blow up the earth, and in so doing throw the whole solar system out of gear, which would play havoc with their own seasons, oceans and climate. Such an anxiety could well account for their sudden increase in visitations, particularly as the greater part of them had taken place over United States air bases and secret weapon experimental stations.

For Kem the final proof that these aerial objects did come from another world lay in their extraordinary performance. No human pilot could conceivably have stood up to their terrific accelerations and violent swervings without blacking out. It was even a possibility that they were manned by beings totally unlike ourselves, for no intelligence that we can visualize could exist in a flying flame, and nothing resembling a human in a flat disc measuring only two feet in diameter. But perhaps the solitary lights and smaller discs were pilotless. Possibly they contained only some form of camera and scientific instruments; and were controlled by radar from the giant disc sighted at Fort Knox, which normally floated far out of sight above the earth and acted as a mother ship to the standard discs. In support of such a theory evidence had come in from numerous airfields that radar signals had been picked up which could not possibly have emanated from any aircraft in the vicinity, or been the result of natural causes such as thunderstorms.

Who makes these signals, if not our mysterious visitors from outer space? Whence do they come? Are they in any way like us, or soulless, abhuman intelligences? That they are not infallible was shown by the disc that got into difficulties over Maury Island and that on two occasions discs were compelled to make forced landings. But on both they left no trace, other than a great patch of burnt grass, which suggested that they were made of some very strong but easily combustible material, such as tough cellophane. It suggested, too, that their crews may have deliberately committed suicide rather than disclose their secrets and intent.

What form of power can the discs use which enables them to spin, roll and dart at enormous speeds in utter silence, with neither flame nor smoke coming from them, yet, as has been witnessed more than once, when flying low cause great forest trees to bend in their wake as though swept by a typhoon? And why, with the invisible power at their disposal, should they use another type for their cigar-shaped ships, causing them to spurt great tongues of flame like erupting volcanoes?

What are the intentions of these beings so far in advance of ourselves? Will they be content merely to explore our earth? Will they one day land, take charge of us, and with benign wisdom smooth out the incredible muddle to which our fears, greed and folly have now brought us, so that a new era of peace and prosperity dawns on earth? Or do they, when they have gathered all the intelligence they require, mean to invade it; perhaps bringing with them a destruction even more terrible than any we may fear from the Hydrogen bomb—which is said to be as much more powerful than its atomic forerunner as that was to any explosive previously devised by man?

While Kem was speculating on these fearsome problems which in our own lives may foreshadow either the coming of a Golden Age or the obliteration of the whole human race in a Flaming Hell, he glanced from time to time at his wrist-watch. At sixteen minutes to twelve he banished such thoughts from his mind as completely as one can wipe clean a slate with a stroke of a wet sponge, stood up, and cautiously opened the door of his room.

The long corridor of the bachelors' wing was lit only by the reflected glow of the lights on the main staircase. It was empty, but he remained there listening intently for a moment. No sound disturbed the silence of the house; so he closed the door behind him, locked it, pocketed the key, and, with no suggestion of furtiveness in his movements, walked quietly down the corridor.

At the main landing he paused and peeped over its elaborately scrolled iron-gilt balustrade. A big Moorish lantern, hanging at his own level, threw its light on the colourful Persian rugs and brocaded settees in the hall below. A faint breeze gently billowed the curtains, but otherwise all was utterly still and silent. Kem moved on, the rubber-soled shoes he was wearing carrying him as silently as a ghost across the tiled pavement that floored the upper arcade surrounding the central courtyard of the house.

The Escobars' suite was self-contained, and situated in the cool southeast corner of the estancia. On reaching its outer door Kem knelt down to see if any light showed beneath it. There was none; so gripping the door-handle firmly he turned it right back, pushed gently, then stepped through into the dark hallway of the suite. Closing the door behind him, he switched on a small electric torch.

Two doors now confronted him and two others lay to his right and left. Opening each in turn he flashed his torch round the room into which it led. The first was Carmen's boudoir, a charming room in Wedgwood blue, with white fluted pillars flanking arched alcoves containing shelves of books and a collection of biscuit china. The second was her bedroom, a setting that any film star might have envied done in rose and gold. The third was a spacious bathroom typical of Latin-American exotic taste. It was mainly black marble, with a freize of cupids picked out in white, and had its entire ceiling covered with mirrors. The fourth was Escobar's dressing-room, but apparently he usually slept there, as the bed in it was made up and the pillows were slightly creased.

After his swift examination Kem decided that this last was the most likely room in which to find the safe. Closing the door behind him, he locked it, then switched on the light and looked slowly round. His glance came to rest on a medium-sized flower painting hanging at shoulder level above a tulip-wood chest of drawers. With unerring instinct he walked over and took down the picture. There behind it was the circular door of a wall-safe; and the sight of it produced on Kem's chubby face a happy grin, as it was of a pre-war pattern, not equipped with the electric timing devices which would have proved his worst headache.

Adjusting a stethoscope that he had brought with him for the purpose, for the next twenty-five minutes he concentrated entirely on it, working methodically and swiftly as he strained his ears to catch the fall of the lock's tiny tumblers. At last he got the combination and the thick steel door swung open. It contained two shelves, and on the lower reposed Escobar's precious red brief-case.

Having taken it out, he wondered for a moment what to do with it. Before leaving, it might be difficult to find an excuse to return to Escobar's room to collect it, and in no circumstances must he let Carmen see that he had it, as it was certain that she would recognize it as her husband's. Turning, he walked through the bathroom to her bedroom and hid it on the floor behind the draperies that framed a pair of french windows giving on to a balcony. Carmen would not see it there, and as he meant to leave that way in a few hours' time it seemed the easiest place from which to retrieve it without her noticing him do so.

Had he been able to foresee the manner in which he would actually leave Carmen's room, brave man as he was, Kem Lincoln would have gone white and palsied with terror; but his future was mercifully veiled from him.

Instead of dread, he was conscious of an almost breathtaking elation as the beam of his torch swept across the filmy night-dress that Carmen's maid had laid out on the wide low bed for her. That afternoon he had taken a desperate gamble, but not in vain; for now by far the most important mission that had ever been entrusted to him was as good as safely accomplished. During it, despite himself, he had become involved in a delightful love-affair; and to crown his success the stage was set for him to carry away with him a glowing last memory of a lovely woman of whom duty had compelled him to make use, but whom he would always remember with tenderness.

In that moment he felt that he had good reason to count himself one of the spoilt children of the gods. He forgot that the gods so often make playthings of their children.

CHAPTER V

A BEDROOM SCENE

FOR a minute or two Kem continued to shine his torch round the luxuriously appointed bedroom. Although Carmen was only twenty-four, like most South American girls she had reached full womanhood early, and the room betrayed no evidence of lingering girlish tastes; its counterparts could only have been found in those of highly sophisticated leaders of fashion in the world's great capitals. Yet in herself she was still unspoiled and, passionate though she was by nature, had had little experience in the arts of love. Kem noted the array of costly toilet preparations on her dressing-table, but noted also, standing in an alcove, a *prie-dieu* beneath a simple statuette of the Madonna, and he knew that she still practised her religion.

Again he blessed the good fortune that had sent him such a perfect mistress, then he was suddenly overcome with a wave of depression at the thought that in a few hours he must part with her for good. He wondered miserably what she would think of him when she learned the truth, as she must as soon as Escobar was released and returned to find that his safe had been burgled. Knowing the depth of the feeling he had aroused in her, he hoped that it would not make her too bitter. But perhaps the revelation of deceit would be all to the good, as it should cause her to banish quicker any craving for him from her mind. In any case, she had been resigned to the ending of their *affaire* when they landed at Buenos Aires, and only the necessities of his mission had impelled him to insist on prolonging it. Both of them had known then that they could only hope for a few more brief meetings before final separation.

With a sigh he switched out his torch, went through to Escobar's room and began systematically to go through the remaining contents of the safe. As he had left his room at a quarter to twelve it was as yet only a little after half past. The nightly game of baccarat at the estancia never broke up before one and sometimes went on until two. Feeling confident that he could count on a clear half-hour, at the very least, before there

35

was any likelihood of Carmen being able to come upstairs, he did not hurry himself, but examined everything carefully.

He had seen at once that Escobar's brief-case contained too many papers for him to photograph them all in the time at his disposal, so that he could leave the originals, apparently untouched, as he would have liked to do; but he thought there might be other papers in the safe which it would be worth while recording with his micro-camera.

At first it looked as if he was going to be disappointed, as the greater part of the safe was occupied by stacks of bonds and share certificates, and a score or more of Carmen's jewel-cases. But right at the back of the top shelf he came upon a japanned black box about twelve inches long and four deep. On forcing its locks he found in it a pile of letters, and a quick look through them showed that some bore dates as far back as the nineteen-thirties. Thinking it probable that they contained some of the secrets of Escobar's private life which it might be useful to have on the files, Kem took them over to the bed and began to examine them more carefully.

Many were love-letters, and he was only three-quarters of the way through sorting these out from the official and business correspondence when, to his consternation, he heard the outer door of the hall open.

It was barely a quarter to one. It was possible that Carmen had managed to get away unexpectedly early. On the other hand it might be her maid, who had forgotten something when preparing her mistress's room for the night, and returned to rectify her oversight rather than risk a scolding. In either case discovery now lurked round the corner.

Holding his breath, Kem listened while footsteps crossed the hall and there came the sound of another door opening. Then, without the loss of a second, he swept up the letters, crammed them and their box back in the safe, and closed its door. There was no time to reset the combination and lock it, as he had meant to do, but he quickly rehung the picture over it. Switching out the light, he tiptoed into the bathroom and stood there in the dark, listening intently.

There was no light in the bedroom; so whoever it was must have gone into the boudoir. He had been there only a moment when the bedroom lights were switched on and Carmen's voice called softly:

"Kem! Where are you?"

Greatly relieved, he let go his breath and stepped through the doorway. She gave a little cry of delight and came running to him.

Next moment he had her tightly in his arms.

After a few breathless kisses, he said, "Darling, you gave me such a fright. However did you manage to get away so early?"

"They say lucky at cards unlucky in love, but I get it both ways to-night," she laughed at him. "Knowing you were waiting for me here, every moment I had to remain down there was torture. From midnight on I bancoed every hand, in the hope that if I lost enough it would give

36

me a good excuse to stop playing. But I had a fantastic run of luck; so it was the others who declared I had won quite enough for one night and asked me to pack up the game."

"My sweet, how clever of you to think of a way of gaining us an extra half-hour. And every moment is precious, as I must leave well before dawn, otherwise one of the servants might spot me climbing down from your balcony." As Kem spoke he picked her up and began to carry her towards the bed.

"No, Kem, no!" she protested in a swift whisper. "Please put me down. Don't spoil everything by being too impatient. This is the only chance we've ever had to make love properly."

With a smile, he set her on her feet, and said, "What a vandal you must think me. I'd deserve to be shot if I failed to make the utmost of being with you without fear of interruption in this perfect setting. I meant only to kiss you some more before undressing. Let me act as your maid and help you take your things off."

Taking a step away from him she shook her head, and he saw a sudden blush spread over her magnolia-petal cheeks. "No, please!" she protested. "You may think it silly of me, but I'm really terribly shy. I'd rather not undress in front of you. Please, darling, go into my boudoir and take your things off there while I get ready for bed. I promise you I won't be long."

He knew that she had never taken a lover before she had been carried away by himself on those last three moon-mad nights in the liner, and he thought once more how doubly attractive the combination of sophisticated elegance and inward modesty made her. Had he not wanted to delight his eyes with her graceful figure unadorned, in all its natural loveliness, he would have been less than human; but he restrained his impulse to press her, and, hoping that she might prove willing to indulge him later, said at once:

"Just as you wish, my sweet." Then he added with the naughty-boy grin that made his plump face so attractive. "I'll give you five minutes' start, then race you into bed. So you'd best be quick if you don't want me to catch you in your nothings."

"Oh, darling!" she laughed. "How I adore you!"

They embraced again, then he went into her boudoir, pulling the door to, but not quite closing it behind him.

After he had glanced at his watch, it suddenly occurred to him that he might have suggested undressing in Escobar's room, as he could then have seized the opportunity to relock the safe. But the thought had come too late. It would not be fair to re-enter Carmen's bedroom now that she had started to undress, and anyway he could think of no plausible excuse for making the change. For a moment he contemplated tiptoeing across the hall; but if he did she might hear him, and that would necessitate awkward explanations. Then second thoughts told him that whether

37

Escobar found the safe locked or unlocked when he got back next day made not the least difference; so he dismissed the matter from his mind and filled in the lead he had promised Carmen by looking through her books.

When the five minutes were up he took off his coat and trousers and laid them on a chair. He had just unstrapped the shoulder holster that contained his gun, and pushed it under them, when he heard Carmen calling him. Her voice was low, but urgent with alarm:

"Kem! Kem! Quickly! Come here!"

On stepping through the door into her room he saw that she had switched out most of the lights. It was now lit only by a rosy glow that came from among the silk draperies of a small canopy over the head of the bed. She had on only a pair of lace scanties and long silk stockings, but was in the act of wriggling into a dressing-gown. As she hurriedly tied its broad sash round her waist she exclaimed:

"Oh, Kem! This is the most ghastly luck! The safe's been burgled."

"Are you certain?" His voice held swift concern that sounded natural to her, but was inspired by very different reasons from her own.

"Yes. I've just found it unlocked."

"Perhaps Estévan forgot to lock it," he suggested, in the forlorn hope that she might accept such an explanation. But she shook her head.

"No. When I went to put away the jewels I was wearing I found everything upside down It's been thoroughly ransacked."

Her jewels! So that was what had given the game away. Mentally he cursed himself for not having foreseen that it was probably her custom to lock away those she had worn, before going to bed. To gain a moment's time he asked, "Are any of your others missing?"

"I don't think so. I only looked to see if my emeralds were there, and they are still in their cases."

"That's a bit of luck, anyhow."

"Luck!" she cried bitterly. "But don't you see, Kem, that this makes it impossible for you to remain here. Oh, just to think that of all nights it should have happened on this—the one night we had a chance to spend together!"

"Why shouldn't we do so still? It was probably my coming in here that disturbed the burglar. If he had to make a hurried exit without taking anything you can easily straighten up the contents of the safe. Then if you say nothing about having found it unlocked, no one will be the wiser."

"But he did take something. Estévan's brief-case is gone."

"He may have taken it with him to Buenos Aires."

"No, he always leaves it in the safe. When he has papers he wants to take he uses another—a green one."

"What do you intend to do then?"

"Telephone the police. Oh, Kem!" Her voice was near to tears.

"Our night together is ruined; but what alternative have I? You must leave me and get back to your room as quickly as possible, so that I can rouse the servants."

"There is nothing they can do."

"They can search the grounds. The thief may still be lurking somewhere about."

"No. I've been in your suite for a good bit over an hour; so the job must have been done before a quarter to twelve. It's a certainty that he will have got clean away by now."

"He may not have got through the military cordon, though; and when I telephone the special police at the plant they will turn out the whole garrison."

"Even then," Kem argued tenaciously, "in the bush, on a dark night like this, he'll stand a good chance of eluding the patrols. He may have done the job while we were at dinner. If so he would have had ample time to have slipped through them already."

"We can't be certain of that; and if I telephone at once there may still be a chance that they'll catch him."

"If you do the police will come up here to investigate. On their motor-cycles they'll be here within ten minutes. That means we won't even have time to say good-bye to one another properly."

"I know. Oh, it's tragic! But what else can I do?"

Suddenly he took a pace forward and grasped her hands. "Carmen, my love! Why should we let this misfortune deprive us of our last hours together? Let's forget it till the morning. No one will ever know at what hour you found that the safe had been robbed, and you might not have discovered it till then."

"I daren't, Kem. Estévan knows that I always lock my jewels away at night. Besides, his brief-case contains the most vital secrets, and it is of the utmost importance to him that everything possible should be done to recover it."

"Listen!" he said firmly. "It is also of the utmost importance to me that you should not call in the police to-night. As you know, I meant to leave to-morrow morning, anyway. Now I shall set off much earlier than I intended, leaving a note for you that you can show to the others, excusing my hurried departure on the grounds that I have enjoyed myself so much here that I forgot the date, and should have left to-day to keep an appointment in Buenos Aires at mid-day to-morrow. You don't usually get up until nine o'clock, and if you put off telephoning the police till then, by that time I shall be well outside the cordon."

She gave him a puzzled look. "But why all this mystification, Kem? And what have you to fear from the police?"

"Surely, my sweet, you must realize that, as the only foreigner here, suspicion is bound to fall on me. If you call in the police to-night, it's a certainty that they won't let me go to-morrow. You know how

39

arbitrary the police are here. Unless they catch the man who did the job I'll be lucky if my Embassy is able to get me out of their clutches in under a month."

Suddenly he saw suspicion dawn in her eyes. Her face went deathly white and her mouth opened a little. Then she whispered, "You . . . you pretended to be ill at dinner, and . . . and you were upstairs on your own for nearly three hours. Oh, Kem! I believe . . . Yes, it *must* have been you who forced that safe."

Since her discovery that the safe had been rifled, he felt that he had played a poor hand as skilfully as possible; but he knew now that he had not a single lie left that would take a trick. If he denied her accusation she would never believe him. The circumstantial evidence in itself was pretty damning, and he had further blackened his case by admitting his anxiety to evade questioning by the police.

Only two courses were open to him—swiftly to overcome her, gag her and leave her tied up there, and one other. He chose the latter.

Walking over to the french windows, he pulled out the brief-case from behind the draperies and threw it on the bed. As it slipped off on to the floor, he said:

"Well! There you are. What are you going to do about it?"

For a moment she stared at him, then her voice came a trifle hoarsely. "Kem, why did you do this? Was it for money?"

He shrugged and replied with a cynical smile, "Partly, since I earn my living by doing jobs like this. But not altogether. Have you ever heard the phrase 'Making the world safe for democracy'? It was coined by Lloyd George, though he didn't manage to do much about it, as since his day we've had a second World War, and at any time may find ourselves up to our necks in a third. Anyway, the honest achievement of that old election-winning catch-phrase is still the faint hope of the United Nations, and I am an agent employed by one of them. The job of people like myself is to find out, and if possible counter, any ugly surprises that the dictator countries may have up their sleeves for us; so that if it does come to a showdown there may still be a reasonable chance of freedom not perishing from the world. There isn't much real freedom anywhere to-day; but what there is I, personally, would go to any lengths to preserve. And I can honestly tell you that if I had a private income I would go on doing the work I am doing without any pay, simply for its own sake."

Carmen's dark eyes looked intolerably sad as she said, "You need not have told me that you would go to any lengths—seeing the uses you have made of me."

"Oh, Carmen!" he said softly. "I admit that I used you; but owing to the set-up here I saw no possible alternative. It does not in the least alter the fact that I love you."

"How can I possibly believe that?"

"I swear it!" he exclaimed, and as he spoke he knew that, now it seemed that he had lost her, he really did love her, and more than he had ever loved any woman before.

For a moment they stared at one another in silence, but her expression gave no indication whatever that she had been touched by his avowal. Seeing no spark of response in her sad eyes, he said abruptly:

"Since you won't believe me, I'll—go now. I have no alternative left. And I dare not take the risk of your setting the police on to me. There is too much at stake. I've never had to do anything that I hated more, but I've got to tie you up and gag you, so that you can't alarm the house. I beg you not to make things more difficult for me than they need be."

As he spoke he took a step towards her. She sprang away and tried to dodge him; but he was on her in a flash. Seizing her round the waist with one hand he clapped the other over her mouth and forced her back against the bed. She went over on it backwards and he flung himself on top of her. Carmen was lithe and strong: she struggled violently, but made no attempt to shout when he took his hand from her mouth for a moment to get a better grip on her. As they wrestled on the bed both of them were breathing hard. Suddenly they caught their breath and went rigid. They had heard the outer door of the hall open.

Releasing his hold, Kem jumped back off the bed on to his feet; but Carmen remained panting where she lay. In the struggle her dressing-gown had come undone, revealing her half-naked limbs. Kem was still standing over her as the bedroom door was flung open and Escobar came bursting in.

CHAPTER VI

AWKWARD EXPLANATIONS

HAVING flung the door wide, Escobar halted in his tracks. For a moment all three of them remained utterly still, as though posed in a *tableau vivant*. Escobar, big, burly, his scant hair ruffled and his clothes disordered, just as Kem had left him ten hours earlier; his heavy face suffused with rage as he stared at his wife. Carmen still lay stretched out on the bed, facing away from him, her breasts now naked, her lower limbs scarcely veiled by lace-edged *crêpe de chine*, and her long silk-stockinged legs dangling over its edge. Kem, in his shirt-sleeves and pants, his feet still touching hers, stood right over her. Had a photograph of the scene been produced in court no jury could have failed to give Escobar a verdict on his having caught his wife *in flagrante delicto*.

Suddenly they all came to life. Carmen grabbed the folds of her dressing-gown and pulled it over her; Kem took a pace backwards; from the far side of the bed Escobar roared at him:

"So this was the reason you held me up and planned to force me to spend the night in the bush! You swine! By God, I'll kill you for this—and her too!"

Long training in facing difficult situations had given Kem a capacity for remaining calm at moments of major crisis. His brain was working with incredible swiftness. He knew that his only course now was to fight his way out and head for the frontier as though all the devils in hell were after him. He had left his gun in the next room; but Escobar was not carrying a weapon either, otherwise he would have produced it. Apparently, too, he had not expected to find his now unwelcome guest still there, or he would have roused the house on his arrival and brought the servants to help capture him. He must have let himself in and, with the thought of finding out whether Carmen's emeralds had been stolen uppermost in his mind, come straight up to his own suite.

It was for her that Kem was now principally concerned. He was also troubled by the guilty knowledge that, once having got possession of the brief-case, he ought not to have prejudiced the successful conclusion of his mission by staying on, even for an hour, to make love to her. When he had planned his coup the temptation to do so had been so great that he had easily persuaded himself that a few hours either way could make little difference, provided he left her before dawn; now he was terribly conscious that by lingering there after he could have got away he had jeopardized everything, including his own life. But that was no fault of hers. In fact, although unconscious of his major motive, she had endeavoured to dissuade him from taking the risk of coming to her room at all. That she was guilty in having already become his mistress, and had been incredibly careless in failing to lock the door of the suite, made no difference. Those nights on the liner were now hidden in oblivion; her marriage would have remained safe if he had kept his mind on his job, and refrained from taking advantage of a situation that had exposed her to discovery.

Somehow, he decided swiftly, he must save her from becoming the victim of his folly; and within thirty seconds of Escobar's shouted threat he replied firmly:

"You have plenty of cause to abuse me, Colonel; but none whatever to imply a gross insult to your wife. I assure you that you are entirely mistaken in supposing——"

"Mistaken!" Escobar snarled. "D'you take me for a child, or think to deceive me against the evidence of my own eyes? There's only one reason that I know of for a woman to undress in her bedroom with a man who is not her husband. If I hadn't been a trusting fool I'd have guessed as much from the way the two of you have been looking at one another during the past week. How long have you been her lover?"

"I am *not* her lover," Kem insisted. "If you'd give me a chance I could explain."

"You're lying! All that hold-up stuff this afternoon was just a clever bluff to get me out of the way. You're no professional thief, although you took my money. That was just part of the act you put on, so that you could sleep with her to-night without my suspecting her afterwards. But I'll make you pay for this, and I'll flay the hide off her back with a whip before I kick her out of the house."

Kem saw that as long as Escobar's furious anger lasted there could be little hope of persuading him of Carmen's innocence. But his attitude was already just a trifle less like that of an enraged bull; so, to give him further time in which to calm down, he put the question:

"How did you manage to get back here?"

Escobar gave a harsh laugh. "There was one thing you left out of your calculations. To-day was market day in Parera. A party of drunken Indians who had been in to sell their mangy cattle noticed the car this evening when returning to their village. If you hadn't made off with the sparking plugs I'd have been back hours ago. As it was I had to tramp to Parera before I could get another car; then as Guido was in such poor shape I felt bound to go out of my way to collect him and have him patched up at the hospital in Basavilbaso. *Nom de Dios!* That gives me an idea. Instead of turning you over to the police right away, I'll put you in the cellar for the night, then give you to Guido for him to bash your face in, before I have you hauled off to prison."

"Thanks, but it's best first to catch your goose before thinking of refinements in ways of cooking it."

"You're caught all right. I've only to shout for the servants. And don't you think you can get away by climbing over the balcony. A call by me to the plant will bring two hundred police and three thousand troops out. They'll catch you before you've gone a mile."

Kem knew the odds he would be up against—provided Escobar were ever allowed to give the alarm. But he hoped to prevent him. At the first moment of his appearance he had contemplated diving at him and knocking him out. He had refrained only on account of Carmen; for if he left without giving any explanation Escobar was bound to continue to believe that she was his mistress, and even, perhaps, that she had helped him to steal the brief-case. Now, it seemed, was the time to attempt to clear her. With a shrug he said:

"Anyhow, you're completely wrong about your wife."

As Kem spoke he had intended to add, "I returned neither to make love to her nor to steal her emeralds; but for this!" then to retrieve the brief-case from the floor and hold it up, hoping by the suddenness of such a dramatic disclosure instantly to convince Escobar that he was telling the entire truth. But Carmen forestalled him.

The instant she had finished retying her sash she had slid off the bed, and for the last few moments had been standing a few feet away from Kem, staring with dark, anxious eyes alternately at him and her husband. Now, before he could speak again or had made any move towards the brief-case, she snatched it up, flung it on the bed, and cried:

"There! That's the proof of what he says. That's what he came here to get. He's not my lover, but a thief and a spy."

Escobar's eyebrows shot up; then he sprang forward and seized the precious brief-case.

Kem made no attempt to stop him, but smiled at Carmen a little wryly. "I admit it; but at least you might have left it to me to show the proof of your innocence."

"I require no parody of chivalry by anyone like you to help me clear myself," she flared. Then she turned to her husband and hurried on: "He pretended to be ill at dinner, and went early to bed. None of us suspected anything, and I came up just before one. When I had undressed I went, as I always do, to put my jewels away. As I entered your room I saw by the light from the bathroom that the door of the safe was open. An instant later he sprang upon me and overpowered me. Then he carried me in here. When you found us he was trying to tie me up and gag me."

Kem did not blame her for the line she had taken. It was the only one by which she could save herself. Had they not been lovers things might have happened more or less that way. It was not very different from the story he had himself meant to tell Escobar, except that hers had certain holes in it. Intently he watched the Colonel's face for a sign as to whether or not he would believe her.

At first his expression showed relief; but suddenly his eyes narrowed, and he asked, "Why did you not call for help when he attacked you? A woman's scream is very piercing; so someone would have heard you."

"I couldn't," she replied quickly. "He had his hand over my mouth."

"Why didn't you bite it? He's not all that bigger than yourself, and it is quite a way for him to have carried you. Surely you could have freed your face for long enough to give a scream. Besides, how did the brief-case get here?"

"I—I don't know," she faltered. "He must have brought it in with him."

"What, while carrying a struggling woman in his arms and preventing her from crying out? As he has not three hands, that would not be possible."

She gulped. "It's the truth! At least as near the truth as makes no difference. I was struggling, but I didn't cry out because I feared that if he were found here it would create a scandal."

Escobar's face had darkened again to a scowl as he snapped, "Next I expect you'll ask me to believe that when burglars crack a safe they always start by taking their trousers off. You're lying! He is your lover!

44

Yes; and I believe he seduced you into becoming his confederate. Combination safes aren't easy to crack, and you knew the combination. That's it! You opened it for him: then, believing me to be safely out of the way, you two beauties meant to have a last fling together."

Kem saw that the time had come to intervene. "No, it was not like that," he said quietly. "Since you must be told the truth I'll tell it you. I've already admitted that I am a secret agent. It is part of my job to know a lot about safes. I faked illness to get to bed early, came along here, and cracked yours about midnight. But the thing that Carmen hasn't liked to tell you is that she knew I was in love with her."

"He is not!" interjected Carmen, in sudden fear that he now meant to give everything away. "He only endeavoured to make use of me. He is lying! Don't believe one word he says!"

Swift as a hawk Escobar seized upon the point. "Since you admit that he tried to make use of you, why did you not inform me of it? If there hadn't been something going on between the two of you, your natural course would have been to ask me to tell him to leave the house."

Again Kem intervened. "She refers only to the fact that I took advantage of our shipboard acquaintance to get myself invited here." Then he turned and looked Carmen straight in the eyes.

"It is true that I love you. The fact of earning a living the way I do doesn't make a man any the less liable to fall in love. If you hadn't appeared to be reasonably happily married and so damnably rich I would have asked you to go away with me to-night."

Carmen quivered as though she had been struck, and suddenly an entirely new expression came into her eyes. Momentarily forgetting her husband's presence, she stammered, "Do you—do you really mean that?"

It was true that during the past week Kem had toyed with the idea, but only as the sort of daydream in which one lets oneself build "Castles in Spain". He had no wish to tie himself up by marriage yet, and, in any case, he could not possibly support a woman like Carmen happily on his slender income, even had she been willing to run away with him. But in the stress of the moment he had voiced the idea because he knew he would not be able to prevent Carmen from calling for help when he made his bid to overcome Escobar unless he could get her on his side, or at least render her temporarily neutral.

"Yes," he said. "I would have begged you to go with me if I'd thought there was a decent chance of my being able to make you happy."

For the past twenty seconds Escobar had been glowering at them in silence. Now he snarled at Carmen, "Your attitude makes it clear beyond dispute that you have been carrying on an *affaire* with this man behind my back."

Kem swung round upon him. "You can hardly call it that; for it was entirely one-sided. I've shown that I was in love with her, of course; but that is a compliment any pretty woman may accept. I've done

45

nothing that would give her cause to complain of me to you—until to-night. And now you'd better hear what remains to be told about that. Passion can make any man unscrupulous if he feels it strongly enough, and I planned to take both your papers and your wife. When I had burgled the safe I brought the brief-case in here and hid it, as I meant to take it with me when I left by the window of this room. Next I went into Carmen's boudoir, took off my coat and trousers and waited there. Half an hour later, suspecting nothing, she came up to bed. I gave her time to undress, then came in here."

"And then?" Escobar muttered thickly.

Kem gave a little shrug and went on:

"I was gambling on two fairly good cards. One, that the liking for me she had shown might prove to be a little more than friendship when it was put to the proof, and that if she did not care for you very deeply she might take pity on me. Two, that even if she refused, seeing that I was already half undressed, she would be too frightened of a scandal to call the servants and let them find me with her in that state.

"At the moment she saw me she had no reason to assume anything but that I was her socially respectable guest, and guilty only of having fallen so desperately in love with her that I had seized on the chance of your being away to attempt to seduce her. Naturally she didn't want a scandal if it could possibly be avoided, so she didn't scream, but she wouldn't let me even start to make love to her, and begged me to go away. I refused. After a few minutes she began to lose her temper, and threatened to ring for the servants. By that time I was terribly wrought up. The sight of her with hardly any clothes on made me lose my head, and I was prepared to stoop to any means rather than not have my way with her.

"Suddenly it occurred to me that since she wouldn't even let me kiss her she must be very much in love with you, and that I might be able to use her love for you as a lever. I produced the brief-case, told her the truth about myself, and offered to strike a bargain. I reckoned she would know how much those papers meant to you, and I offered to leave them behind if she would give way to me. But she wouldn't, and tried to reach the bell. I seized her and threw her on the bed. That's how things stood when you came in."

It was a good story, as it accounted for everything, and Kem knew that a hot-blooded South American like Escobar would regard it as quite plausible that a young man might go to any lengths when fully roused by passion. That Escobar accepted this last explanation was immediately apparent from his expression. Tapping the brief-case, he said:

"So you could have got away with this if you hadn't had your wits bemused by thinking about my wife."

Kem did not dare glance at Carmen. He was still unable to guess whether, when the showdown came, she would help or hinder him.

Since his prospects of escape hung almost entirely on that, he could have embraced Escobar for his remark, as it enabled him to reply:

"Yes. If I had left as soon as I had done my job I should be outside the military cordon by now. But there are times when love makes fools of us all."

The Colonel grunted and remarked sourly. "By the time you have done your five years in a fortress for espionage you may have learned that it doesn't pay to mix women and business." Then he suddenly sidestepped and reached out for the gilded bell-rope that dangled beside the bed.

With extraordinary swiftness Kem was on him. Just as he had been taught during the war, at that school "somewhere in southern England", he threw himself forward with all his force, turned a somersault on the bed and shot off it, to cannon into Escobar and send him flying. But he could not prevent the loud cry that the Colonel let out as he went over backwards.

For a moment or two they were a whirling mass of arms and legs, as each strove to get an advantageous grip on the other; then, for the second time within ten hours, they became locked in a desperate embrace.

Kem's foremost anxiety was to stop the Colonel's shouts for help, as if they were heard they must prove his ruin. Escobar had already emitted three or four before his young antagonist succeeded in checking them by a sharp jab in the midriff. In the comparative silence that followed one heartening fact impinged on Kem's brain—Carmen had not added her cries to those of her husband. While he had the chance he grabbed Escobar by the throat, and silently prayed that the yells he had already given had not reached the ears of anyone beyond the hall door of the suite.

Of the two Escobar was far the stronger. With a violent jerk of his head he broke the grip on his bull-like neck; but he had no breath left for further shouting. Instead, he tensed his powerful muscles and threw Kem from him. Rolling over, Kem came at him again, like a hound at a wild boar. Again they clinched and, panting with their exertions, strove for mastery. It was at that moment that Kem heard a loud knocking on the outer door.

CHAPTER VII

A DESPERATE SITUATION

At the sound of the knocking Kem was instantly conscious of a nasty feeling in the pit of his stomach. He knew that, short of a fluke, it would require his utmost exertions for several minutes yet before he could

47

finally overcome Escobar. The door was not locked, so even if Carmen remained neutral and, to cover herself from not letting in whoever was there, pretended to faint, it would not save him. Should he receive no reply, the person who had heard Escobar's shouts for help would try the door, find it open and, in less than a minute, come dashing in.

If he were then still struggling with the Colonel he would be completely at the mercy of the newcomer and must expect to be promptly knocked on the head. On the other hand, if he abandoned the struggle before rendering Escobar unconscious, snatched up the brief-case and made off out of the window, he would not stand a dog's chance of getting clean away. In either case a hue and cry must start almost immediately, but with Escobar howling-mad on the end of the telephone it was certain to be redoubled in intensity.

At the moment he was on top of the Colonel, grasping his throat with one hand and using the other clenched to jab him in the ribs and so keep him half-winded. Escobar, too, had one hand on Kem's throat. With the other he seized Kem's ear and wrenched at it. The pain was excruciating. Instinctively Kem shut his eyes. Only by clenching his teeth could he prevent himself from yelling.

Distantly, through a brain clouded by agony, he heard the sort of sharp thud that metal makes on bone. After that, almost instantly, Escobar's grip relaxed, his hand fell from Kem's ear and he suddenly went limp as a jelly.

Opening his eyes Kem saw that the skin of his adversary's forehead was now broken, and that little globules of blood were already oozing from the abrasion. As he lifted his eyes they fell on Carmen's legs, then on her long fingers grasping the silver-gilt hand-mirror that she had snatched up from her dressing-table. With it she had struck her husband unconscious.

As Kem struggled to his knees she held the mirror out to him and said, as if in a daze, "Look! I've broken it. That's an omen of terribly bad luck, isn't it?"

"It was lucky for me you did," he gasped. "Quick! See who is at the door and try to get rid of them."

His swift words seemed to act like a cold douche, and instantly brought her back to her full senses. Turning away, she ran out into the hall. The knocking sounded for the third time, but whoever was making it could not have been there for much more than a minute.

Kem heard her voice, sharp with annoyance:

"Who is it? What do you want?"

There came the sound of muttering, then her voice again: "Oh, it's you! No, the shouts you heard are nothing to worry about. Estévan returned unexpectedly ten minutes ago, and he's in a filthy temper. We were having a private row, that's all. He's just gone into the bathroom, and when he's got the dust from his journey off himself he'll feel better. I'm sorry you were disturbed. Please go back to bed."

A moment later she returned to the bedroom, closing the door behind her. She was deathly pale and her dark eyes were distended with mingled fear and excitement as she whispered:

"That was Pedro. I told you I thought he would stay up to spy on us. Thank God he didn't see you come to my room. I expect he saw Estévan pass, though, and knowing that you would not be aware of his return was waiting to see if you would run your head into a hornets' nest. Estévan's shouts were not very loud, and I don't think he could possibly have heard them through both doors unless he had been hanging about outside."

Kem had got to his feet, but was still panting from his exertions. He gave her a faint smile. "Well, that's a relief, anyhow. It means there's very little chance of anyone else having heard them."

They listened anxiously for a few moments, but could hear nothing. After the violent altercation and the struggle that had just taken place, the house now seemed as silent as the grave.

Carmen's glance fell to her husband's blood-stained head and unconscious body. With a swift intake of her breath she stammered, "I haven't . . . He's not dead, is he?"

"Good Lord, no!" Kem quickly reassured her. Then kneeling down, he turned up one of Escobar's eyelids and added, "He will be out for some time though; and I can never thank you enough for having come to my assistance so splendidly. I wouldn't have stood a dog's chance of getting away if you hadn't."

She gave a nervous little shrug. "I had to do something. If I had allowed Pedro to come in while you were still struggling it would have been all up with us."

Suddenly a look of consternation leapt into Kem's eyes, and he exclaimed, "Oh God, what a fool I've been! I should never have told you to send Pedro away, but simply to lock the door and remain silent."

"If I'd done that he would have fetched the servants and broken it down."

"Of course; but it would have taken him ten minutes or a quarter of an hour. Long enough, anyhow, for me to have laid Estévan out and got away with a flying start. Don't you see that I've allowed you to compromise yourself completely?"

"I had burnt my boats already, by hitting Estévan over the head."

"No. You could have said that you meant to hit me and hit him by mistake. That very thing happened this afternoon when he tried to smash my head in with a log. I moved just in time and the blow landed on Guido's face instead. But you would never be believed after having sent Pedro away and told him yourself that everything was all right."

"What does it matter? . . . unless . . ." Her mouth drooped and she stared at him in sudden doubt. "Oh, Kem, you did really mean what you said about wanting me to run away with you, didn't you?"

Had his mind not been so fully occupied during the past few moments, he would have realized already that she would never have attacked her husband had she not made up her mind to leave him. And now that she was so hopelessly compromised no other course was open to her. His decision, that he must take her with him, was almost instantaneous, and he replied:

"Of course I did. I refrained from saying anything about it before only because I thought you were content to remain with Estévan, and because I can't possibly afford to give you the sort of life you have been used to."

She looked down at her husband's body. "He's been quite kind to me, so I don't hate him. But I was forced into marrying him against my will. My father is one of the old Liberal aristocracy. He sacrificed me to secure Estévan's influence and save himself from being imprisoned for having been involved in a plot against the regime. Our marriage was no more unsatisfactory than many others, I suppose, although he must have found me very cold. Anyhow, I don't feel that I owe him anything. The first real happiness I've ever known was with you, and after that I don't think I could have stood his making love to me any more. As for money, don't worry about that. I have plenty of my own."

Kem stepped over Estévan's unconscious form, took her in his arms and murmured, "My sweet, I swear I'll do my damnedest to make you happy."

When they had kissed, she smiled at him fondly, then gently pushed him from her. "We'll have plenty of time for love-making later on, darling. There are other things we must think of now. What did you intend to do on leaving here?"

"My luggage is already packed and in my car, and I have my pass for getting through the cordon. I meant to drive into Basavilbaso, then head east for the frontier at Concepcion. I've written a note describing the place in the bush where I left Estévan, but I counted on that not being found till well after eight o'clock—when the servant who calls me had failed to get a reply, so became alarmed and fetched someone to force the door of my room. By then, as it is only about forty-five miles from here to Concepcion and I had planned to start at a little before dawn, I should have been across the river and safe in Uruguay."

Carmen nodded. "That sounds a good plan; so let's stick to it. As Basavilbaso is on the road to Buenos Aires they are certain to think that we've made for the capital and are trying to get away on a ship. How long can you give me to pack some things?"

"As matters are now, the sooner we leave the better. But I hadn't intended to start for another four or five hours, and since you prevented Pedro from rousing the house we need be in no desperate hurry."

"Then I've time to do something about Estévan's head. Poor man, it isn't his fault that we've brought all this trouble upon him; and I'd hate to leave him like this."

"Yes; he's certainly had a raw deal," Kem agreed, "and I can hardly blame him for the horrible things he threatened me with while in a raging temper." Between them they hoisted the Colonel's limp body up on to the bed. Then Carmen fetched hot water and lint from the bathroom, bathed the wound and bandaged up her husband's head.

When she had done, Kem said, "I'm afraid I must tie him up, otherwise he may come to and manage to reach the bell-pull or the telephone before we are safely across the river."

Carmen made no demur and produced some string, with which he secured Escobar's wrists and ankles; and to muffle his cries, should he attempt to shout for help, they knotted a towel loosely over the lower part of his face.

They then went out to the hallway and took out from the baggage cupboard there Carmen's dressing-case and two suitcases, as there was plenty of room in the back of Kem's car, and she naturally wanted to take with her as many of her personal possessions as she could. While Carmen packed Kem collected things for her, as she directed, from cupboards and drawers. They spoke only in low voices and, in spite of what Kem had said about there being no need for them to hurry unduly, both instinctively worked as though everything depended on their speed.

When Carmen went to get her jewels from the safe, Kem took the opportunity to stuff the brief-case into one of the suitcases under some of her clothes. She had made no mention of that side of the business, so he was still uncertain how she felt about it. As her family had been Liberals he now had a good hope that his little lecture on "Making the World Safe for Democracy" had fallen on fertile soil and excused his theft in her eyes. But it was possible that she might have patriotic scruples about letting him make off with one of her country's most closely-guarded secrets; so he thought it as well to avoid drawing her attention to the brief-case again, and all its theft implied, while he had the chance.

Within twenty minutes of having rendered Escobar *hors de combat* the packing was finished. It remained only for them to dress and get away. Kem told Carmen that as soon as he had got his clothes on he meant to climb down out of the window. She could then lower the suitcases to him on two knotted lengths of curtain, which he was making ready as he spoke. He would carry the cases round to the car, then return for her. By that time she should have finished dressing and be ready for him to help her down to the ground.

On her agreeing, he left her and went into the boudoir. As he did so it suddenly struck him how greatly the prospects of his whole life had changed since he had come from it, less than an hour before. Then, he had been looking forward only to a few joyous hours with Carmen, before facing the sadness of having to put her out of his life for good. Now, she was coming with him, and with luck there would be many happy times in store for them.

He wondered about her marriage. As Escobar was a Roman Catholic there could be no question of his divorcing her, but he might secure an annulment. Such matters could usually be arranged in Catholic countries, and the fact that she had had no children should make it easier. If they did get an annulment it was certain that she would expect him to marry her, and that would mean good-bye to his carefree bachelor state. But after all, that was not much to give up for a wife like Carmen. And he was twenty-eight, which was quite a good age to stop indulging in casual affairs and settle down. Besides, there was no longer cause to fear that discontent and bitterness might come between them on account of lack of money. Carmen had said that she had plenty of her own, and Kem, being a practical man, was not such a fool as to harbour any silly notions about its being unmanly to permit a rich wife to provide the luxuries of a joint household. Really, it looked as if those "Castles in Spain", that he had only amused himself by dreaming about, were actually fine solid buildings and soon to become his. Now, he felt that there could no longer be any doubt about it. Overnight he had indeed become one of the darlings of the gods.

He had just pulled on his trousers and done them up, when he heard a loud rending noise in the next room. Next second Carmen's voice came in a low cry fraught with utter fear.

Grabbing up his coat, he dashed into the bedroom. A few feet inside its doorway he halted, rooted to the spot. He could hardly believe his eyes, and his scalp prickled with terror, as he stared at the monstrous thing that had thrust its way through the window.

CHAPTER VIII

REAL CAUSE FOR TERROR

CARMEN's bedroom was a fine apartment nearly thirty feet in length and twenty wide. It was situated at the corner of the house. Three windows on its longer side, the central one of which consisted of double doors opening on to the balcony, faced south; in its east wall, near which Kem was standing, there was a fourth. At the moment his distended eyes were riveted on the exit to the balcony.

The French window had been smashed open and through it protruded a thing, the like of which he had seen only in the make-believe pictures of nursery-story books. Had it portended any normal danger he would have hurled himself at it in Carmen's defence; but momentarily petrified by fear of the unknown he stood staring at it, feeling certain that he **must** be dreaming a hideous nightmare and would shortly wake, safe and sound, even if in a bath of perspiration.

The thing, the sight of which had turned his blood to water and paralysed his brain, was a gigantic hand and arm. Kem had seen giants in circuses, but this mighty limb was far larger than any ever recorded as belonging to a human being. It was naked to the shoulder, as thick round the bicep as the haunch of a horse and eight feet in length. A tangle of coarse red hairs partially covered its forearm and the whole of the skin was pasty white, marked here and there with unhealthy-looking bluish pimples. The nails on the huge hand, as big as five-shilling pieces, were horny, cracked and broken. Its fingers, a foot long, were thick and clumsy; but, like the tentacles of an octopus, they, and a thumb the size of a rolling-pin, clasped Carmen firmly round the body.

Mercifully, she had fainted. She was slumped forward, with her head dangling down over the giant paw, her dark hair mingling with the red bristles that sprouted from its back. Under Kem's horrified gaze the hand lifted her off her feet as easily as if she had been a puppet; then, quite slowly, the arm began to withdraw, carrying her towards the window.

The sight of the movement gave Kem back the use of his limbs but failed to restore his wits. Instead of dashing back to the boudoir for his gun, he sprang forward and began to caw wildly at the great fist in a frantic attempt to stop it taking Carmen from the room.

As he did so he caught a glimpse of the face of the monster to whom the arm belonged. It protruded above the edge of the balcony, and was thrust forward over it, just outside the shattered window. The head was completely bald. What could be seen of its nose was flattish and its chin receded. It was wearing some form of breathing apparatus clamped over its nostrils and mouth. The eyes, too, were protected, but by a separate shield that looked like an elongated, transparent celluloid blister. Through it, as through thick lenses, the eyes were magnified, in this case to the size of saucers. They were a pale watery blue and their complete lack of expression gave them a malevolent, soulless quality.

Kem might as well have attempted to check an elephant that was pulling away by hanging on to its trunk, as to halt the steady withdrawal of the huge arm. No sooner had he got a good grip on it than he found himself being hauled forward, too. Suddenly he realized the futility of continuing such an uneven tug-of-war. His brain began to function properly again. The monster was not armoured. If he could get his gun a single shot through the eye should kill it.

Releasing his grip, he turned and dashed towards the boudoir. After two paces his flying feet faltered to a halt as a result of what he saw. While his back had been turned, the wire mosquito blind of the east window had been burst in as though it were made only of paper. Another huge hand was reaching through it and seemed to be searching

53

blindly across the floor. The door of the boudoir was open, but the hand was within a few feet of it and partially blocked the way. Kem's throat contracted. He gave a gulp, as he realized that to get through he must jump the hideous thing that sprawled across a square yard of carpet.

As he hesitated, at the awful thought that it might grab him, he noticed that it was another right hand. That meant that at least two of the great brutes were attacking the house. He wondered if some of them were at that moment dragging other members of the house-party from their bedrooms. But he had heard no screams or shouts for help. Perhaps they were all too terrified to cry out. He could not recall having shouted in the hope of bringing aid himself, desperately as he needed it. This terrible occurrence had come upon them so totally unexpected, and developed with such swiftness, that he doubted if any utterances he had made during the past few seconds had been more than spontaneous noises engendered by animal fear. In any case, no amount of shouting could now bring help in time to save Carmen. He, with a gun in his hand, stood the only possible chance of doing that.

Cursing himself for a coward, he subdued his fears, ran in and jumped. As he leapt the hand lifted. The toe of his left shoe caught the knuckle of the middle finger. Deflected from his course, he plunged forward head first and came crashing down inside the doorway. The breath was driven from his body and his head hit the wall, knocking him half unconscious.

The hand, having felt the impact of his foot, began to grab about in search of him. Suddenly he felt its finger-tips fall heavy on his legs. More by instinct than through any conscious effort he jerked them away and rolled over towards the bed.

For a few minutes he lay there, panting and still dazed, his head aching intolerably and his body incapable of making any further effort. Vaguely, he heard things being dragged about and sensed rather than saw the huge hands fumbling slowly here and there. Exerting all his will-power, he forced himself to open his eyes and sit up. Sick, bruised and shaken, he stared dully round the room.

In those few minutes it had become a shambles. Carmen had disappeared, her dressing-table had been overturned and the bed dragged from its place to near the french window. Escobar had gone from it and the first monster, now leaning right in, was using both his hands to pile everything within his reach on to the tumbled counterpane.

Again, making a great effort, Kem staggered to his feet, but his head was swimming and he still could not focus his sight properly. He wanted to run, but his feet refused to obey him. Mute and helpless, he could only stand there, swaying drunkenly.

Suddenly he realized that the monster must have seen him get up from the floor, for its goggle eyes were now gazing steadily in his direction.

As it reached out a hand to grasp him, he turned and lurched away. But the other one, over whose finger he had tripped, was now halfway through the east window and stretching out to seize him.

Before he could move another yard the huge hand of the first fell like a sack of potatoes on his shoulder. It swung him round and flung him face down on the bed. His nose came sharply in contact with one of Carmen's suitcases and from the pain of the impact he became thoroughly bemused again.

His ideas about what happened next were extremely vague. Dimly, he guessed that the giant, using the bedding as a big sack, had gathered its corners together with both hands and dragged it out of the window. He felt a nasty bump as the great bundle was hauled over the parapet of the balcony, and another as it reached the ground.

There, the coverings in which he was enveloped fell back, and for a moment he glimpsed the stars overhead. But only for a moment. The silk of a frock that Carmen had slipped on while he was getting into his trousers brushed his cheek as she was thrown in beside him; then Escobar's heavy body descended with a soft thud across his chest and face, blotting out the stars. Feebly he heaved at it, trying to push it off him, but before he could do so the corners of the bedding had been pulled together, pressing it down on him more firmly than ever.

The journey that followed proved to be a new phase in the nightmare. How long it lasted Kem had no idea. His head was still aching too painfully from the knock it had received for him to think coherently, his mind was further confused by terror, and such efforts as he could muster were given almost entirely to a fight for air.

Within a few moments the close, hot darkness became positively stifling and every breath he drew only a prelude to renewed agony. By dragging his arms up and crossing them over his face he managed to form a little cavity in which to gasp more freely, but on every side either the belongings or the limbs of his unconscious fellow captives were wedged tightly against him.

Only a few physical facts penetrated to his brain. There was fur under the nape of his neck, and it must be that of a mink coat that he had got out of a cupboard for Carmen to wear. He could smell the scent of her hair; so her head must be somewhere near his. Two hard objects were digging into his stomach, and the feel of them told him that they must be the toes of Escobar's shoes, held together by the string that still tied his ankles. He was, too, quite definitely aware that the great bundle was moving all the time; the constant jolting and bumping to which he was subjected left no doubt that it was being dragged slowly and, apparently, laboriously along the ground.

After a time the pains in his head, in his stomach and in his lungs seemed to merge into a single torture that racked him from top to toe. In semi-delirium, as his degree of suffocation increased, he imagined himself to have been buried alive. Then his suffering was blotted out by oblivion.

When he came to he could again see the stars twinkling brightly in a cloudless sky. A moment later he realized that he was lying on his back on coarse grass, and began to wonder vaguely how he had got there. As he moved his head a little the pain shot through it again, bringing back memory of his recent ordeal in all its fantastic details.

In spite of his aching head, his lips twitched in a smile at the very idea that he should have been the victim of such extraordinary hallucinations. It seemed to him that they could have only one explanation—he must have met with an accident and been operated on; his imagination had run riot while he had been under the anaesthetic. He began to wonder how seriously he was injured; then why he was not in a hospital bed, but lying out in the open.

At that moment there floated into his area of vision a small, bright, bluish flame. It was about twenty feet above his head and burned without even the suggestion of a flicker. He watched it dispassionately for a few seconds as it made a graceful swoop and circled twice above him, thinking how pretty it was. Then something clicked in his brain.

That light, moving so purposefully above him, yet apparently attached to nothing and having no apparent means of support—he had never seen such a thing before, but he had read descriptions of it. It was—could only be—one of the Thinking Lights. And they were one type of the inexplicable phenomena which suggested that a people from another world might be about to invade the earth.

People from another world! Those monstrous beings that resembled humans only in form! Surely they could have been only creatures of a nightmare? But no! He was now awake and there above him floated the mysterious light. He had had no accident, but had really been brought there, like a ferret in a bag. In a second, all sense of the grace and beauty of the light was swept from his mind. It suddenly became for him a thing of evil fraught with the most potent menace.

Lifting his head a little, he saw that some two hundred yards away the night sky was blacked out by a curving screen of tree-tops, which told him that he must be in a clearing of the bush. With a sharp intake of his breath he lifted his head a few inches higher, now dreading, yet knowing already, the thing that he would next see. And there it was. In the centre of the clearing, only forty feet away from him, reposed a Flying Saucer.

From where he lay it had the appearance of a flattened dome about a hundred feet across and twenty-five feet high, with a thing like a small lighthouse rising a further six feet from its centre. It was made of some white, semi-transparent material, through which there showed a dark band occupying about three-quarters of its width and the middle two-thirds of its height. Above this, except where it joined the central mast, the flattish segment formed by its roof appeared to be empty, as did also the V-shaped segments ending at its rim. A pair of double doors were open in its upper surface and through these two giants were loading the things brought from the estancia.

It was the first time that Kem had seen more than the head and arms of any of these terrifying people. Both of them were standing on the ground, and the tops of their heads came up to within a few feet of the roof of the Saucer. They were twenty feet high, broad in proportion and, from what he could make out in the starlight, appeared to be naked. His head was now hurting frightfully again, and as he stared at them through a mist of pain he saw one of them pick up Carmen.

She must have regained consciousness; for, as the monster pushed her through the doorway of the Saucer, she let out a piercing cry. Had Kem just arrived on the scene in full possession of his senses and as fit as he had been that morning, he could still have had no possible hope of saving her; but her cry, like a warning bell, roused him anew to the acuteness of his own danger.

As he struggled to his feet he saw the other giant turn towards him. Lurching round, he staggered a few yards, then fell. In five great strides the monster was upon him. He felt the huge hands seize him round the middle and lift him into the air. Kicking and squirming, he let out a shout with all the remaining power of his lungs. He had no chance to give another. The great hands shook him as a terrier shakes a rat, reducing him to breathless silence. Half stooping, as though burdened with something much heavier than Kem, and dragging its feet as if terribly weary, the monster carried him to the Saucer and thrust him into its dimly-lit interior.

Again his consciousness ebbed and for some minutes he had only the vaguest ideas about what was going on around him. It was not till his head cleared a little that he could even take in his immediate surroundings. Then he found that he was lying sideways on a surface like opaque glass, looking at Escobar's bandaged head. Turning over on his back, he saw that the ceiling of the Saucer was made of the same substance. With a groan he hoisted himself into a sitting position and gazed about him.

He was in a chamber that, had he been a caterpillar, would have had the proportions of a shallow, inverted soup-plate; except that it had a central pillar some eight feet high and seven feet in diameter. The pillar was also made of the opaque material and appeared to be hollow, as the only light came from there and he could see shadows moving about inside it. The double doors of the Saucer were now closed and the two giants were lying side by side on their backs about thirty feet away from him. They were both absolutely still, and looked as if they were sound asleep. Escobar, still unconscious, lay huddled on his right, and beyond him Carmen was lying with her eyes shut, faintly moaning. Nearby the things brought from the bedroom were heaped in an untidy jumble.

Round the central pillar was ranged a circle of three-feet-high square tanks. No machinery was visible, and the great low chamber contained nothing else at all.

Almost imperceptibly the Saucer lifted and began to rock a little. Also it began to spin, although Kem did not realize it at the time, because the floor on which they were lying was gyroscopically controlled, and the ceiling, having no pattern or anything attached to it, did not appear to be moving. There was no drumming of any engine, no hiss or roar of escaping power. The Saucer was utterly silent; the only sound in it was Carmen's low moaning.

The speed of the ascent increased, until Kem was reminded of being carried up in the express lift of a skyscraper. Panic seized him at the realization that he had left the earth—perhaps for ever. He tried to stand up, but the pressure increased every second. His limbs seemed to have become as heavy as lead; an invisible weight pressed down on his aching skull. With a groan he surrendered to the force of gravity, and slumped back at full length on the floor. That brought him no relief. He felt as though some unseen contraption held every part of his body in a vice, and the turning of a thousand tiny screws were inexorably drawing it tighter. The air was forced from his lungs; his nose began to bleed; his eyes were bulging. He now lay sprawled out on the floor and crushed against it, incapable of lifting even a finger. Under the awful pressure the very life was being squeezed from him.

Fear had left him; but all his life Kem had been intrigued by mysteries, and the urge to learn secrets still lingered in his overwrought brain. He was conscious of one last thought. It was a pity to die when fate had given him this unique chance to solve the riddle of where the Flying Saucers came from. Imperceptibly the pressure lessened, as the Saucer was now passing out of the field of the earth's gravity. But Kem did not know that. He had fainted.

CHAPTER IX

KIDNAPPED

WHEN Kem came round again his body was still racked with pain, but he was also conscious of an entirely new sensation. Instead of being crushed against the deck of the Saucer, he was barely touching it. His body seemed to have no weight at all. As he moved slightly it floated sideways several feet, as though it were a log in a still pool that had been given a little push, before coming to rest again. After a while it impinged on his overwrought brain that the Saucer must have passed out of the field of the earth's gravity and that only the almost imperceptible pull of its base kept him from drifting up to its ceiling. He was too exhausted and bewildered by his recent ordeal to think further coherently, and mercifully fell into a dreamless sleep.

On waking his mind was clearer; but on realizing his situation he was seized with panic, and with a gulp of overmastering fear jerked himself up into a sitting position. The result was terrifying. The impulse from his hands on the floor shot him straight up to the ceiling. It was spinning at great speed; so the second his head touched it he was thrown from it at a tangent, as violently as if he had been grazed by an express train. For some moments he was whirled round and round the chamber, but at gradually decreasing speed, until he managed to clutch its central pillar and get his feet back on the floor. Even then his unaccustomed lightness made his balance uncertain, and his least movement had the most unpredictable results.

Clinging to what he supposed to be the control tower, he stared about him. The two giants were lying side by side still asleep. He saw that he had been right about their nakedness. Neither of them had a stitch on, except for the masks that covered a large part of their faces. These were divided into two parts: above the nose a single, transparent, protective cover for both eyes; below it another transparent cover for the nose and mouth, to which was attached a breathing apparatus like a box respirator. The lower cover bulged out over the nostrils, chin and cheeks, but in its centre there was an oval dimple which brought its surface close to the mouth. Below the oval, over the centre of the chin, there was a small knob, which suggested that the oval could be slid up like a visor, thus enabling food to be popped into the mouth without removing the breathing apparatus. Through the lower part of the masks he could see that neither of the giants had beards or moustaches; instead they had great tufts of stiff hair fanning out from their nostrils and ears. Apart from that and their size they differed in no obvious way from human beings. Both were males, the hair on both their bodies was red, and both of them were completely bald.

His glance shifted to Carmen. She was lying motionless on the far side of the deck from the giants, either dead or asleep. Near her lay Escobar, his wrists and ankles still tied, but moving his head slowly from side to side, which suggested that he had regained consciousness.

Striving to keep his feet firmly on the deck, Kem headed for Carmen, but overshot the mark, and succeeded in pulling himself up only by grabbing her dress, which drew her some distance with him. Her face was deadly pale and dried blood was caked about her ears and nostrils, but he could see from the steady rise and fall of her chest that she was still alive and, apparently, in a sound sleep. His involuntary tug on her sleeve had been quite gentle, and had not roused her; so he thought it kindest to leave her in happy oblivion until she woke of her own accord. Meanwhile Escobar had caught sight of him and, invoking his patron saint, cried out:

"For San Estévan's sake, come here and untie me!"

Reorienting himself cautiously, Kem glided over and, with the grace of a ballerina in the finale of *Le Lac des Cygnes*, sank down beside his late antagonist. Escobar's struggles to free himself had tightened the knots of his bonds, so it was some time before Kem succeeded in un-picking them, and while he was busy at it they exchanged a crossfire of abrupt questions and answers. The scientist had been conscious for three hours and during them had believed that he must either be mad or dreaming. He remembered nothing since Carmen had hit him on the head, so had escaped the shock, terror and exhaustion suffered by his fellow captives; but he had no clue whatever to the extraordinary situation in which he found himself on coming round. Kem's explana-tions were the reverse of reassuring, but at least they convinced Escobar that he was sane, since he could not ignore the evidence of his own eyes, and everything about him confirmed Kem's story.

The injury to his head was evidently not serious, as he said that the pain in it was already easing, but his limbs were stiff from having been bound for so long and hurt him acutely as soon as he tried to move them. After a bout of pins and needles his circulation returned to normal, and he sat up, with the immediate result that he slid forward and began to rise, like an aircraft that has just taken off. Kem seized and pulled him back, upon which, to their mutual surprise, they found themselves locked in a tight embrace and grinning into one another's faces.

As Kem released his hold, he said, "It seems a bit futile now to apolo-gize for all I did to you; but our present situation is no fault of mine, and we're both in it up to the neck; so I hope you'll do your best to forget what happened yesterday."

It was the bright sunlight now flooding the compartment with a golden glow which made Kem suppose that he had slept through the balance of the night. In fact he had, but they were not to experience night again for a long time to come, as the Saucer was already so far from Earth that it could no longer be dimmed by Earth's shadow.

Escobar nodded. "It would be senseless on my part to bear malice. Nothing that happened in the past can possibly have any bearing on our future. For our mutual protection we must stand together. But what, in the name of Jesu and all His Saints, can the future hold for us?"

"God alone knows!" Kem sighed. "One can only suppose that these people are carrying us off to another world."

"As specimens, eh? Just as a naturalist might collect some creatures from a pond in a glass jar."

"That's about it."

Escobar flung out his hands in a gesture of helplessness, and promptly

60

went over backwards. When he had recovered himself, he said, "That we have been kidnapped is obvious. But these great ugly beings, who you say carried us off, have the appearance of *homo sapiens*, only of the most primitive type. And they lie sleeping there; so evidently they have nothing to do with navigating the Saucer. There must be others—of a different race perhaps—whose high degree of intelligence will be apparent from their expressions and the development of their crania. Where are they?"

"I've seen no one except these two," replied Kem. "It was they who carried us from the estancia and pushed us in here. I've seen no sign of any others, either. It was dark when we took off and the deck was lit by a steady glow from the central column over there. Above it there is a sort of squat lighthouse projecting about six feet from the roof. The column is hollow, as I noticed some faint shadows moving about inside it, and took them to be parts of the machinery that had been set in motion. It seems obvious that the hub of the thing, formed by the column and the lighthouse above it, contains its control room; but as far as I can see there is no way by which one of these huge creatures could get into it."

"I agree, and their brutish appearance convinces me that they can be only servants or slaves of other infinitely more advanced types, who must be about somewhere. Evidently their quarters are in the roomier part of the Saucer, below this deck. Come! We must find them and plead with them to take us back to Earth."

The only possible approach to the underside of the deck lay at its edge. This did not touch the outer shell of the Saucer, as the circular deck was some ninety feet across, leaving a uniform gap of about three feet all round between its rim and the spinning roof which sloped down towards it. Awkwardly, they propelled themselves to the edge and, gripping it with their hands to keep themselves steady, lay there on their stomachs peering over.

Beneath them they could see a slightly convex wall formed by what looked like thousands of strands of wire. It was about twelve feet in depth and there was no gap at either its top or bottom, where it met the upper and a lower deck. Pulling themselves along by their hands they made the full circuit of the deck on which they lay, hoping to see some break in the wire or doorway in the wall it made; but there was none. The huge coil appeared to be solid and cut them off completely from any chamber which might lie inside it between the two decks.

After a moment, Escobar said, "Under the lower deck there must be a compartment similar to this. Perhaps the giants with the master-minds who control this thing have their quarters down there."

"How could they?" Kem protested. "It would be upside down, and they could not possibly sit on a curved floor that is gyrating at God knows what speed."

"They would not have to. Gravity being virtually non-existent in space, they could sit quite comfortably on the ceiling, and are probably accustomed to doing so. One can only assume that they are somewhere below us and do not wish to be bothered with us during the voyage; so have left us up here with these loutish lower-race people to look after us."

Kem found it hard to visualize people of any kind going about their normal tasks while upside down; but on kicking his feet into the air he turned upside down himself and found that he could remain so without the slightest inconvenience, as the lack of gravity prevented the blood from running to his head. Pulling himself down beside Escobar again, he remarked unhappily:

"Anyway, wherever the supermen are, there seems no way in which we can get to them; so unless they come to us we won't be much wiser about them till the end of the voyage. I wonder where they come from."

Escobar shrugged. "Your guess is as good as mine. The universe is so vast. Much of it is probably still unknown to us, but from what we already know it is estimated to contain 300,000 million stars."

"Three hundred thousand million!" Kem gasped. "Surely not; otherwise the whole sky would be like the Milky Way!"

"Not necessarily: like our solar system, on an infinitely larger scale, the whole universe is flattish in form; so that if it were solid it would have the appearance of a disc, inside which our own minute system is revolving. But apart from that, on a clear night the human eye can pick out about 3,000 of the nearest or brightest stars. To form some conception of the immensity of the universe you must imagine each of those representing another sky in which you can see as many again. That would give you nine million, the number it is possible to see with a five-inch telescope. Then you must stretch your imagination once again, to visualize each of those representing another sky having yet again as many. And that gives you only 27,000 million—less than a tenth of the total. There are at least 200 stars for every man, woman and child living on Earth."

Kem's chubby face suddenly broke into a grin. "Everyone knows that the universe is a pretty big affair, but I had no idea that it was quite as colossal as that. All the stars are other suns, though, aren't they: so there couldn't be any life on them?"

"Certainly not life as we understand it. But many of the near stars are known to have their own systems of planets; so it is reasonable to suppose that the number of planets we cannot see is far greater than the number of stars that we can."

"Then our possible destinations are as numerous as the places in Baedaker?"

"Yes. The spectroscope has shown us that all known heavenly bodies are composed of similar materials, although in different proportions. It is, therefore, a fair assumption that a high percentage of them have passed, are passing, or will pass, through the same processes as Earth. The great majority of the sidereal planets are either still molten or have cooled to a point where their surfaces consist only of barren rock like our Moon. But each presumably passes through a phase, perhaps the equivalent of no longer than a single hour in the life of a man, during which conditions would make it possible for it to support life. Therefore, although the overwhelming majority of these distant worlds can have no life upon them, their total being so enormous, everything points to there being some form of life on a small proportion of them; and in this case even a small proportion might run to several hundred thousand."

It was a staggering conception, but Kem had no doubt that Escobar knew what he was talking about; and, after a moment, he said, "I know very little about astronomy, but, of course, I knew that many of the stars had solar systems of their own; so it seemed a fair bet that some of them had life of some sort on them; but don't you find it a bit surprising that, apart from size, these Saucer people are so like human beings?"

Escobar shrugged. "As yet I am not fully convinced that I have not suddenly gone insane, or am imagining all this in a delirium. But if I am in my right senses they are much the sort of beings I would expect to see. All life is governed by natural selection and the survival of the fittest. The development of the man-animal to his present form has enabled him to overcome all others on our earth. His head, in relation to his body, is much larger than that of any other species, so enables him to accommodate a bigger brain. Apart from the apes, he is unique in having converted his forelegs to their present use. The upright position gives him an immense advantage over any other animal his own size, as it enables him to see further. Above all, the turning of the fore-paws into hands and separation of the thumb from the fingers must have proved decisive. It enabled him to grip things, to use first a club, then a stone axe, as a weapon; to build himself a shelter and later, by rubbing two pieces of wood together, to make fire."

"You think, then, that on every planet where there is life it must have followed the same course of development as it did on earth?"

"Given the same chemical constituents, in more or less the same proportions, it would be unreasonable to suppose it to have done otherwise. As the planet cooled, the beginnings of life would emerge in the warm seas; as the seas receded vegetation would creep up on to the beaches; for eons of time on land there would be only the great swamp forests of giant ferns and spongy growths that are now our coal seams. But sooner or later, according to local solar conditions, animals would emerge to inhabit the jungles, and sooner or later man, or something very like him, would become the lord of that particular creation."

63

"It's queer, though, that these people should be giants. That gives the whole business a farcical resemblance to Jack and the Beanstalk. All the fairy stories for grown-ups always describe imaginary beings from another world as little people—like super-intelligent pigmies."

"They might be. That would depend entirely on the gravity of the heavenly body from which they came. If it were far larger than our Earth, yet similar to it in other ways, its gravity would be much greater. Its people would not require such weighty bodies to keep them down and enable them to go about their business with maximum efficiency; so they would be the sort of dwarfs that sensational novelists have often portrayed. But if their world were much smaller than ours the reverse applies. That, at least, is one thing of which we can be reasonably certain. As these people are about three times our size the odds are that they come from a relatively small planet; possibly one considerably smaller than Earth, and anyway one that has only about one-third of Earth's gravitational pull at its surface."

Kem was still pondering this, and thinking how remarkable it was that man had already acquired sufficient knowledge to make deductions about huge spheres so distant that they appeared only as specks of light, when he saw that Carmen had opened her eyes.

Hardly touching the deck, she lay on her side looking at him, but her look showed no trace of recognition. Both the men moved over to her. At first they feared that she had lost her reason, as she continued to stare blankly at them without uttering a word; but suddenly she closed her eyes again and began to pray out loud, crying:

"*Mea culpa! Mea culpa!* O Holy Mother, I know that I have sinned and deserve to be cast down into Hell; but I beg you to intercede for me at the Throne of Grace. Have mercy on me, I implore! I beseech you to mitigate the just anger of your Divine Son, so that He will send His Angels to save me from the power of the Evil One."

In that vein she continued for several minutes; and, although she repeated herself frequently, she prayed with an earnestness that bore no resemblance to the ravings of a mad woman. When at length she ceased, Escobar whispered:

"I don't think she has gone off her head, but her mind still refuses to accept our situation as reality."

"In any case she is suffering from severe shock," Kem replied. "Just feel how cold her hands are. We had better wrap her up."

The long mink coat that had been lying across the foot of her bed when the giants appeared at the estancia was floating near the ceiling. They caught it, pulled it down and wrapped it round her. As they did so she opened her eyes again and began to moan:

"Water! Water! Oh, I know that I have deserved Hell! I know that thirst is an ordained torture! Satan mocks the damned by pouring the precious drops on to the red-hot stones. But dear Lord, have pity upon me! Don't let me be consumed by these internal fires. My throat is parched—burning. Have mercy and assuage my awful thirst, even if my punishment must last longer."

Escobar and Kem both looked helplessly round the large, low-roofed chamber. They, the sleeping giants, the row of tanks ranged round the base of the control tower, and the scattered oddments from the estancia, were the only things in it. There were no basins, pipes or taps which would have implied that water was laid on; no big jars, bottles or drinking vessels.

For the first time it occurred to them that probably many hours had elapsed since they had been carried off; and they suddenly realized that they were both hungry and thirsty, which made Carmen's craving for water a much more normal matter than it had at first appeared.

With a sideways kick of his feet Kem propelled himself over to the one suitcase that had been brought with them, turned it the right way up, and opened it. The case contained only some of Carmen's clothes and the now ludicrously useless red brief-case. Following his example, Escobar drew her dressing-case from beneath a large embroidered Spanish shawl, which had formerly graced her bed, and began to run through it. Round its sides there were rows of gilt-topped glass jars, each in a separate fitting, and among the morocco-leather cases containing her jewels were packed a number of little pots and bottles. There were powders, lotions, ointments and perfumes in considerable variety, but nothing fit to drink. The only things he could find which might prove useful in the present emergency were bromides and aspirins.

He held them up for Kem to see, but Kem shook his head, and muttered, "It's no good giving her those for the moment. We've got to find her something to drink." Then he glided over to the nearest tank.

It was made of the same opaque material as the Saucer, and its flat top appeared to be a lid, as there was a hair-line break all round about an inch below it. But apart from that it formed a three-feet-high cube with a dead-smooth surface, and he could discover no means of opening it. As he moved over to the next, Escobar came to his assistance, and between them they began to examine all the tanks. After trying another unsuccessfully Kem came upon one the lid of which opened at a touch; but it was empty and its purpose obvious. It contained a large-mouthed fixed funnel leading down to a pipe about a foot wide, at the bottom of which daylight could be seen. It was clearly a lavatory on the same principle as those installed in railway trains, but lacking any form of trap, or, as far as could be seen, any sluicing apparatus. Nevertheless it was spotlessly clean and had no odour, but was too large and high for a human being to sit upon without discomfort. Hoping to find a wash-basin in one of the other tanks. Kem and Escobar swiftly tried the lids of the remainder, but all were firmly shut and defied every effort to open them.

Carmen was still moaning pitifully for water all this time, and her appeals to God, the Virgin and numerous saints, filled them with acute distress at being unable to ease the torture that she was obviously suffering.

With sudden exasperation, Escobar exclaimed, "There must be water somewhere in this accursed flying-machine." Then he turned towards the giants, and added, "Wherever those great brutes have come from, I'm certain of one thing—they couldn't live without it."

Kem followed his glance and went a little pale, as he muttered, "I suppose you're right. That leaves us no alternative. We've got to wake one of them and find out where they keep it."

The blood drained from Escobar's ruddy face, and after a moment he said thickly, "I'd rather confront a charging bull without a matador's cloak than rouse one of those giant ape-men and chance his waking in a temper."

"Water!" moaned Carmen. "Oh, Holy Virgin, take pity on me! Water! Water!"

"It . . . it's got to be done," faltered Kem miserably, and he took a hesitant step towards the nearest monster.

CHAPTER X

SPACE AND SPEED

NERVING himself against the probable anger of the sleeping giant Kem laid a hand on his shoulder. On touching the coarse skin he found it much tougher than he had expected. It was almost as rough and hard as the hide of an elephant, and it flashed through his mind that this was probably the reason why the monsters could do without clothes. As the Saucer was subjected to the full and constant power of the sun, its interior should normally have been as hot as a furnace; but evidently its temperature was controlled in some way, for it was far from hot and so near chilly that any naked human being would have found it difficult to sleep from shivering. That the giants were able to do so without apparent discomfort suggested that they were used to low temperatures and that nature had toughened their skins to make them cold-resistant.

After a few shakes the giant opened his eyes, shook his bald head and sat up. He was still wearing his two-part mask and through the upper section of it his great expressionless pale blue eyes stared at Kem. Fighting down an impulse to turn and run, Kem made the motions of drinking and pointed with his finger to his mouth.

The monster was much too tall to stand upright in the chamber, but he rolled over on his side, slid across the deck to the control tower and rapped upon it with his knuckles. After a moment a small trap-door, about six inches square, high up in it, flicked open. The giant pushed up the little transparent visor over his mouth and made some strange clucking noises in his throat. The trap promptly shut again but almost instantly, as if by magic, two of the tanks sprang open.

With his twelve-inch-long finger the giant gave Kem a gentle prod in the back, which sent him floating towards them. He saw that one tank was half full of a green vegetable that looked like beans, the other contained only a coiled length of rubbery-looking pipe attached to a short standard with a press-button top.

Escobar had propelled himself over to Kem's side and said at once, "The water must be sucked from that pipe. No other way of drinking is possible up here. If one tried to pour out any liquid it would float away in globules."

Between them they pushed, rather than carried, Carmen through the air to the tank, put the pipe-end in her mouth, pressed the button, and watched her avidly suck in the water. When she took her mouth from it some of the water spilled out and, as Escobar had said it would, danced through the air in a number of round, shiny balls.

Instantly the giant struck Kem's hand from the button, flicked up his visor and, sticking out a tongue the size of an ox's, greedily lapped the water balls into his cavern-like mouth. The episode gave them two pieces of information. Water was evidently precious, and the giant had no teeth. When he had succeeded in catching all the balls, he allowed Kem and Escobar to drink, but only sparingly; then he gave them five beans apiece from the other tank. Some unseen lever closed both the tanks down, the giant turned his back on them, yawned, rolled over and went back to sleep.

Carmen, her craving satisfied, had closed her eyes and lay white and still, but breathing gently. The two men remained standing, dubiously eyeing their beans. Simultaneously both decided to try one. They were moderately soft and had a sweetish, not unpleasant flavour.

"They're not bad," Kem pronounced. "But surely this isn't the only food we're to be given?"

"It may be," replied Escobar glumly. "The master-minds who run the place we are going to may have perfected some vegetable containing all the vitamins necessary to support life. That would be possible by selected breeding over a period of centuries. This ration they have given us may prove sufficient to stave off hunger for several hours."

Kem groaned. "Oh, God, this is too awful! Just think of having to live on a diet of beans indefinitely, added to everything else!"

"Perhaps the beans are a form of concentrate used only on these space journeys, when keeping the cargo light may be an important consideration. Among a highly developed people it is virtually certain that we shall find other forms of food when we get there."

"Have you any idea when that will be?"

"How the hell should I know?" Escobar snapped irritably. "Such a journey might be accomplished in a few months; but it is equally likely that it will take twenty years."

"Twenty years!" Kem exclaimed, aghast.

"Yes; if we are being taken to a planet outside our own solar system. The nearest planet that the astronomers consider might be habitable revolves round a star named Wolf 359. It is eight light years away from Earth, or, in lay parlance, 47 million million miles; and that is a mere nothing as astronomical distances go. The nearest globular cluster, ω Centauri, is 22,000 light years distant from Earth, and the farthest extra-galactic nebulae some 140 million light years away."

"We can't conceivably be making such a journey. It's not possible!"

"There I agree," Escobar conceded more reasonably. "Even travelling at the speed of light, it would take us about three times as long to reach the nearest globular cluster as any known form of civilization has existed on Earth; so we should be dead before we had completed all but a tiny fraction of the journey. It seems hardly likely that enquiring minds would get much satisfaction out of human remains many thousand years old, after having had ample opportunity to observe living people from the skies."

Kem nodded. "If the top boys of this other world had been content to receive our mummies the logical thing would have been for them to give orders that we were to be knocked on the head and embalmed as soon as we had been got away in the Saucer. Anyhow, the giants would not have been allowed to spare us any of their precious water, if they did not mean to keep us alive."

"Yes. That cuts the length of our journey down to within definite limits. But it would have been obvious to them that you and Carmen are still young people, and they may have thought that I looked good for another quarter of a century; so it's on the cards that we have to face imprisonment in this thing for quite a number of years."

"From what you say, even if we were flying at the speed of light, it would take us eight years to reach the Wolf 359 system. But light travels at 186,000 miles per second, and the fastest the Flying Saucers have ever been actually checked as travelling is only 18,000 per hour. If that is all they can do, we would still be dead centuries before there was any chance of our reaching the nearest habitable planet."

Escobar shrugged his broad shoulders. "No one knows how fast the Saucers can travel. They may achieve speeds too high for the human eye to register. In any case they would be able to go far faster in the stratosphere, where they are not subject to the resistance of the atmosphere, which is wrapped like an invisible blanket round the Earth. I do not consider it outside the bounds of possibility that they should travel as fast as light."

"Surely our bodies could not stand up to 186,000 miles a second?"

"Why not? You are confusing the issue with sensitivity to sudden acceleration. It is not the speed at which a pilot is moving that causes him to black out, but the strain on the human system of forcing it to withstand any pressure greater than that equal to four gravities for more than a few minutes. That is one of the worst headaches plaguing the scientists who are already exploring possible ways of sending a manned rocket to the Moon. Obviously the faster the rocket-ship reaches a high velocity, and can get clear of Earth's atmosphere, the less fuel it will need; so the nearer it will come to being a practical proposition as far as what is termed its mass-ratio is concerned. But the trouble is that the motors will have to be kept running for at least eight minutes; for if the rocket were driven clear of the atmosphere in less than that its acceleration would have to be so great that the crew would black out."

"I get the point," Kem nodded. "To run it for eight minutes would use up so great a weight of fuel that the rocket would not have enough left to complete its journey and stand any chance of getting back."

"In broad terms that is what it amounts to. One way of getting over that would be to first send up an aerial raft. When I was working for the Germans during the last war they were planning to do that; but not of course with any idea of using it as a stepping-stone to the Moon. Their object was to operate from it certain secret weapons. Anyhow, it is a perfectly practical proposition to send a form of static airship up by means of several rockets, which together would carry it to the strato-sphere. There, with very little engine power, it could be kept at a suit-able altitude, and it would behave like a very small moon, circling round and round the earth. Further manned rockets would be sent up, and on reaching it each would contribute to its tanks a quota of fuel. Then the Moon rocket could be despatched, refuel at the raft, and go on its way with enough fuel on board to get to the Moon, and return. Once the Moon rocket was well away on its big lap, its crew would no longer feel the least inconvenience on account of its speed. In fact, they would be able to swim about in the air of their cabin if they liked, just as we could here. And that brings me back to a very elementary example of speed and its effect, of which I was about to remind you. Everyone on earth is hurtling through space at 72,000 miles an hour, because that is the pace that Earth must maintain to accomplish its annual journey round the sun; yet nobody even feels it."

Kem put his hand over his eyes as he thought about this astounding but transparently obvious truth. He was quick to pick up the inference that if man could travel at 72,000 miles an hour without knowing he was doing so, there seemed no reason why he should not continue to function normally while moving at far greater speeds; but, all the same, his mind baulked at the idea of doing 186,000 miles per second, and he said:

"I admit that I am completely out of my depth, but do you really think it possible that any machine could go as fast as light? Even given atomic power, or something like it, that seems improbable."

"They may be using a form of power that with us is as yet only believed to exist theoretically," Escobar said thoughtfully. "I do not pretend to be a top-ranking scientist myself; but I understand enough about Einstein's Unified Field Theory to give you some conception of it. He postulated that all forms of nature, stars, planets, light, electricity —everything with the possible exception of the minute particles of which the atom is composed—obey the same universal laws. Further, that all matter is frozen energy, and that matter differs from energy only temporarily. He also proved that gravity is really electro-magnetism. Of course, there is a great deal more to it than that, but there is no point in going into his Space-time concept at the moment, as it is his views on magnetism with which we are concerned.

"It is now agreed that everything from a postage stamp to a battleship has its magnetic frequencies, and that any force which can break those frequencies would disintegrate the object operated on. Such disintegration, if controlled, would provide virtually limitless power. It has been proved by the means of the tenescope that there are 1,257 magnetic lines of force in every square centimetre of matter. If a way could be found to cross two or more of those lines the power so generated could be used to propel matter in any desired direction at speeds hitherto regarded as outside the bounds of possibility; and Einstein contends that by these means matter could be made to travel at the speed of light.

"That is as far as he does go, but several of the greatest living authorities on magnetism now go even further. They argue that Einstein's Unified Field Theory leaves out of account the behaviour of the particles of the atom, and that to fit this into the picture it is necessary to concede that certain frequencies, or invisible rays if you prefer, travel very much faster than light. If they are right, given the secret of how to harness magnetic waves, an object could be carried through Earth's atmosphere by them at the rate of 280,000 miles per second, and beyond it there would be nothing to stop that object from travelling at a million miles a second."

Slowly, Kem shook his head. "I understand what you say, and I'm sure you know what you're talking about; but I'm afraid that the idea of moving through space at a million miles a second is too much for my mind to grasp."

"I shouldn't worry about that. It could not grasp the idea of moving through space at a hundred miles a second, either. That is one of the natural limitations of the human brain. And, after all, the speed at which we are travelling has very little bearing on our situation."

"But it has! It makes an enormous difference in the time required to complete our journey. If we are travelling at some fantastic speed we may get there quite quickly."

"Not necessarily. That depends on our destination. Supposing that we *are* moving at a million miles a second, it would still take us approximately eighteen months to reach Wolf 359. But they may be carrying us off to some much more distant system."

Kem groaned again, and lowered himself to the deck; but suddenly his eyes brightened and he exclaimed, "By Jove! I believe you're right about this magnetic business, though. That wall we saw when we looked over the edge of the deck was made of thousands of strands of wire. I believe the middle section of this thing is one huge magnet."

"So you have tumbled to that at last," Escobar smiled. "I realized it at once, but I have been leading you up to it by easy stages. It explains much that we have heard about Flying Saucers. They were reported to have been seen whizzing round and round one another. When doing so they must have been temporarily recharging themselves. Then on a number of occasions they were seen in the Antarctic. No one could offer an explanation to account for their going there, but evidently their goal was the South Magnetic Pole. By hovering over it they would be able to pick up a full load of power before starting on their long journey home."

"That's about it," Kem agreed. "Anyhow, it makes your million miles an hour stuff a bit easier to believe. Unfortunately, though, you've also made it damnably clear that we're condemned to remain cooped up in this thing for, at the very least, eighteen months. Oh, God, what a thought!"

Escobar eased himself down beside Kem and laid a hand on his shoulder. "I fear we must make up our minds to that as our most probable fate, but there is one possible alternative. I have hesitated to mention it before because it sounds so trite and theatrical. There is just a chance that we may be going to Mars. If so, even at a speed far less than that of light, we might arrive within the next few days—or hours."

Kem seized upon this proffered straw of comfort, and for a moment was immensely cheered by the thought that perhaps, after all, they were not to be torn from the old solar system, and their last link with things that, though immensely distant, had always been familiar. Then a new wave of depression surged over him, and he exclaimed :

"Oh, what the hell's it matter where we're going, when there's not the faintest hope of our ever getting back!"

CHAPTER XI

THE OLD ADAM

FOR a time Kem and Escobar sat side by side in dejected silence; then Carmen began to pray again. When they turned to her she still did not recognize either of them; so they forced her to swallow two of the bromide tablets, then bathed her face with eau-de-Cologne, brushed her hair and made her as comfortable as possible. Kem feared that she had gone completely out of her mind, but Escobar did not agree. He maintained that her general state confirmed their original belief that she was suffering from shock, and thought that, if they could keep her under bromide, provided she were not called on to face any fresh crisis in the near future, there was a good hope that she would soon recover her wits.

When they had done the best they could for her, they set about making a more careful examination of the things that had been brought with them from the estancia. Besides the brief-case, Carmen's suitcase contained only clothes. Her dressing-case held her jewels, toilet things and a number of oddments that might come in useful: a work-bag with scissors, pins, needles and thread; a mirror, a writing-case with paper, pencils and a fountain-pen; a tube of seccotine, a perpetual calendar, a small torch, a rosary, a cigarette lighter, a bottle of lighter fuel, and a box containing the best part of a hundred Turkish cigarettes.

At the sight of the last Kem felt a sudden desire to smoke. So far his mind had been too fully occupied with other matters to give it more than a casual thought and realize, to his annoyance, that he had lost his cigarette case with his coat in Carmen's bedroom. But normally he was quite a heavy smoker and the urge came upon him with sudden strength. With a slightly guilty glance at Escobar, he asked:

"Do you think Carmen would mind if we took a couple?"

Escobar shook his head. "That is not the question. I lost my case during our fight in the wood; so I have none either. The same idea occurred to me; but dare we light up? There is good reason to suppose that these Saucers are highly inflammable. There must, too, be certain currents in them which maintain the temperature at a fixed level and supply us with enough oxygen. It is possible there are others, the purpose of which we do not understand, but which would act as conductors of fire. We don't want to blow the whole thing to pieces."

"That's true," Kem agreed slowly, "and anyhow there are only enough here to last us for a few days. If we are in for a long journey the sooner we get used to doing without the better." Then, with sudden resolution, he carried the box over to the lavatory and emptied its contents down the chute, adding, "There, that's put temptation out of our way for good."

As the cigarettes floated slowly downwards he noticed a curious thing. Not one of them hit the mouth of the funnel or touched the side of the long foot-wide pipe. When he mentioned it to Escobar, the scientist said:

"That is interesting. Normally, a proportion of such objects would be certain to brush the sides of the pipe in an eighteen-feet drop. It must mean that the sides of the thing are magnetized to repel any matter going down it. That would explain how it is kept so spotlessly clean without the use of water. There must be, too, some ray making an invisible trap at its exit; some force that matter can penetrate owing to its weight, but is sufficient to seal it off so that the atmosphere in here cannot escape that way."

"No doubt you're right; but unfortunately it doesn't get over the fact that it is about as public as an advertisement hoarding and we'll have to share it with the giants. That's not going to be very pleasant for poor Carmen when she comes to her senses."

Escobar shrugged, and muttered callously, "Oh, she will soon get used to it."

Kem looked round the bleak chamber, then his glance fell on the jumbled bedding. "Anyhow," he said, "help me to arrange these things somehow so that they will give her a little privacy."

Together, they sorted out the other items. There were the beautifully embroidered Spanish shawl that had been used as a bedspread, two sheets, a pillow and two blankets. Among them they found another bottle of sleeping tablets, a cut-glass decanter and broken drinking glass, an onyx ash-tray, a Roman Catholic missal and a novel in French by Paul Morand, all of which had been swept from Carmen's bedside-table.

Floating the bedding across to the far side of the control tower from the lavatory, they held the sheets out over two of the tanks, then let them settle, so that they covered the tanks and the gap between them, which then formed a cave three feet high, about four deep and at its widest nearly five feet long. From outside, the erection had the appearance of a flat-topped tent and, although owing to the very low degree of gravity it was a most diaphanous affair, as there were no draughts in the chamber to lift its edges, it showed no tendency to float away as long as it was handled carefully. Having placed the dressing-case on top of one tank and the suitcase on the other, so that what little weight they had would help to keep the sheets in position, they drew Carmen across the deck and settled her in her new quarters.

Both the men were now feeling very tired. It was not that either of them had been active for long, but both had returned to consciousness with head injuries that still pained them. Moreover, the full realization that they had been riven from Earth, were prisoners compelled to submit to a journey of unknown duration, and were condemned to an entirely unforeseeable future, had proved a great strain on their minds. Only nervous excitement caused by finding themselves in such a fantastic situation, and acute anxiety about what fate might have in store for them, had enabled them to speculate for an hour on the Saucer's possible speed and destination.

As Kem was still in his shirt-sleeves, his tiredness now made him also feel a little chilly; so he caught hold of the Spanish shawl, folded it cornerwise and, having wrapped it about his shoulders, tied its ends round his waist. Then, with hardly a word said, they used the blankets to cover the gaps between the tanks on either side of Carmen, so as to give their eyes some protection from the full light, eased themselves into these flimsy shelters and soon fell asleep.

How long they slept neither of them had any idea, but they were woken by the blankets being flicked from above their heads and a piercing scream. Coming to his feet, Kem saw that one of the giants had chosen this method of rousing them: he was kneeling opposite their triple-bayed tent, which had now ceased to exist, with the blankets and sheets clasped between his mighty hands.

Escobar had also risen, but Carmen still lay on the deck, staring with terrified eyes at the monster. Her husband and her lover cried almost simultaneously:

"It's all right! Don't be frightened! He won't hurt you."

Carmen gasped, but her expression of terror relaxed, and she whispered, "It—it's really true, then?"

"I'm afraid so," Kem said quietly; and Escobar added, "I, too, thought I had gone mad when I first came round. But it is neither an hallucination nor a nightmare. All three of us are awake and sane."

As she swayed into a sitting position, her long dark hair floated out behind her head and remained there like a streamer. "What . . . what does it mean?" she stammered. "Where are they taking us?"

The giant's intervention prevented them from telling her of their speculations as, at that moment, he gave Kem a prod with his forefinger, which sent him swimming through the air to the far side of the control tower, then pushed Carmen and Escobar after him. The monster's intention was quite clear, as round there the tank containing the water and the other that was partly filled with beans both stood open. The second monster was squatting in front of the open tanks, and motioned them to drink. Evidently on the first occasion the tanks had been opened for them as a special favour, but normally they were opened only at fixed hours for an issue of rations.

After each in turn had had a fair suck at the pipe, the squatting monster took it from them, so that they should not waste the water by drinking

74

more than they actually needed. Then he handed them five beans apiece and, as the tanks closed down of their own accord, slithered away to join his companion on the far side of the deck.

Carmen's expression of dismay, as she looked at the five beans she had been given, was so comical that Kem had difficulty in suppressing a smile. "Pretty poor fare, isn't it?" he remarked. "But I'm afraid it's all we're going to get; and not even a choice of having them *à la Portugaise*, or fried in butter, for a change. Still, they don't taste bad and they do satisfy hunger. Estévan and I were given some several hours ago and I've not got any appetite back yet."

It was the only possible consolation he could offer her in the circumstances; but he was by no means surprised when she took it with an ill grace, then went on to exclaim and lament at there apparently being no bathroom or even a wash-place.

Escobar had been regarding her with a curious expression. Suddenly he snapped at her impatiently, "Oh, shut up! You've got only what you deserve, and you would be little better off had we not been kidnapped by these people."

Round-eyed, she stared at him. "What on earth do you mean?"

"Well, you did your best to murder me, so that your lover could get away, didn't you?"

"Oh, come!" Kem protested. "I thought we'd agreed to forget all that."

The aggrieved husband swung round towards him. "As far as you and I are concerned, yes. When I was a younger man I might have acted as you did; both in trying to get hold of those papers for my country and in seducing any pretty woman who gave me the least encouragement; so I bear you no malice. But her case is very different."

"You are being unjust to her. She meant to hit me on the head and hit you by mistake."

"I do not believe that. Neither would anyone else. Had I been found next morning by the police she would have been charged with attempted murder and given a long prison sentence. That is what I meant when I inferred that within a few days, anyway, she would have been deprived of all her comforts and put on a diet little better than water and beans."

Kem was about to say, "Oh, no, she wouldn't; because we should have been over the frontier into Uruguay, and passing under different names, before the Argentine police even knew anything about the matter." But he was forestalled by Carmen.

With sudden humility she hung her head, then burst out, "It is true! I deserve all this! I should not complain of my punishment, for I have sinned grievously. I did not mean to kill you; but I broke my marriage vows on the ship. Then, led on by my guilty passion, I used violence towards you with the intention of abandoning myself to a permanent life of sin. It is a terrible thing to have done. O Holy Mother, witness

75

my repentance and let this confession weigh a little against my wickedness!"

Greatly embarrassed, Kem could think of nothing to say; but Escobar remarked with sharp malice, "No amount of repentance is going to get you your marble bath back; so you had better make up your mind to that."

"Listen!" urged Kem. "All of us are in about as bad a spot as any three human beings ever found themselves. Being either morbid or quarrelsome can only make our situation more miserable than it is already. For what occurred in the past I am entirely to blame, as I took advantage of Carmen's weakness when she had been away from home for a long time and was in the sort of surroundings where such things are particularly liable to happen. You, Estévan, say very generously that you bear no malice; and since I am prepared to shoulder the sins of both Carmen and myself I can see no reason why she should either. There remain the two of you. For God's sake enable us to face whatever we have to face united, by refraining from making any further references to what happened in a life that is now as distant as if we had lived it in ancient Rome."

"No one can take another's sins upon his shoulders," said Carmen unhappily.

Escobar spread out his hands. "For my part I will make her no further reproaches; but you cannot expect me to pretend that I would not put her from me on account of what she has done, were we still down on Earth."

It was a far from satisfactory compromise, and Kem would have given a great deal to be able to bestow Anglo-Saxon mentalities on his two companions. Carmen might then have been just as deeply religious, but not so hag-ridden by the teachings of her Church, and so the better able to bear any guilt she felt she had betrayed an unloved husband without making such a parade of it. Escobar obviously did not love her any more, and owing to her coldness to him Kem would have given long odds that since early on in their marriage he had been consoling himself with a series of mistresses whenever he visited Buenos Aires. He was suffering only from injured pride, and had he not been a Latin of little breeding he would not have been so callously realistic. In such a situation as the present he would, in the first place, have refrained from all mention of his wife's *affaire*, and had the subject been raised in spite of that, would have at least pretended to forgive her.

For a few moments they chewed their beans in awkward silence, then Carmen regained her *savoir faire* and remarked in the calm, conversational voice that she might have used in her own drawing-room, "Well, do either of you know where we are being taken? I suppose it is certain to be Mars."

"Estévan thinks that most improbable," Kem replied. "He favours a planet in one of the star systems, and as all of them are a great way off I'm afraid we've got to make up our minds to a long journey."

76

"No, no!" Estévan corrected him quickly. "I did not say that Mars was altogether unlikely. My view is that it is only one of a great number of possibilities, and that, therefore, the odds are against it."

Carmen wrinkled her smooth forehead. "But, surely, Mars being the nearest place where there is thought to be life makes it the most probable?"

"Not necessarily. As I was explaining to Kem a few hours ago, if the Saucer is travelling on a magnetic wave it could cover vast distances in a comparatively short time. That alone reduces the chance of Mars being our destination to equality with a score of other possibilities. It is further reduced by the fact that, while it is now agreed that there is a form of life on Mars, it is believed to be only of a very low type."

"One could hardly have lower types than these people," replied Carmen with a sidelong glance at the two giants.

"These two are not running the Saucer," Kem put in. "They are obviously quite incapable of either building or navigating an amazing scientific instrument like this. We haven't seen any others yet, but they must have their quarters on the lower deck, and be as different as an Oxford Don is from a Hottentot. These chaps evidently belong to a slave race. From what I remember of our being kidnapped, all their movements were very slow and laborious; so in spite of their size it probably needed all their strength to do the job at all. The odds are that they were brought only for that purpose and because they are much stronger than their masters. Anyhow, you can be certain they are not the brains behind this business."

Estévan nodded. "You can be certain, too, that the people who do have the brains are very advanced types indeed. But when I spoke of low types just now I did not mean anything resembling a human being at all. As far as we know, vegetation is the only type of life that exists on Mars."

"What about the other planets?" Kem enquired.

"With the possible exception of Venus, it is most unlikely that any of them could support any form of life, as we understand it. Little Mercury had always been difficult to observe owing to her nearness to the Sun; but we know that she revolves very slowly indeed—in fact only once in her year, which is equivalent to 88 Earth days—and her day being as long as her year results in her having the same hemisphere perpetually exposed to the Sun. In consequence the centre of that sunny side can be nothing but baked glaring rock, and when her orbit brings her to her minimum distance from the Sun the temperature there is 770 degrees Fahrenheit. At that both tin and lead become molten, so nothing could conceivably live there. Her dark side would, of course, be equally uninhabitable owing to unchanging intense cold."

"What about her twilight belt, though? That might be inhabited."

"No. Quite apart from the necessity for a livable temperature, life cannot exist where there is no atmosphere. A planet's life-blood is its water, which gradually lessens as it ages, both by absorption into its surface and conversion by the Sun's rays into atmosphere. But atmospheres also lessen by gradual dissipation into the stratosphere, and the rate of their lessening is governed by the gravity of the planet concerned. Mercury's gravity is only .27 of that of Earth; so her atmosphere would have been dissipated much faster."

"Can you be certain that she has none left?"

"Yes. We can see atmospheres and measure their density. Of course, on the dark side of Mercury there must be a huge pack of ice. In the unlikely event of some celestial calamity—such as a great comet colliding with the planet—that might alter the whole situation. If she were thrown on to a different axis, or given a speedier rotation, the Sun's rays would turn the ice to water and she would then be provided with a new atmosphere. But, as things are, if there is any atmosphere at all on Mercury it must be too rarefied for anything to live in it."

"What about Venus, then?"

"Venus is the nearest to Earth, yet remains the greatest mystery of them all; and that is because she has too much atmosphere, or something very like it. The whole of her surface is almost always covered by dense layers of cloud several miles in depth. That is why we know practically nothing about her, except for the facts that she is very nearly as large as Earth and has a year of 224 days. The only chance we get to observe any markings on her is when there are occasional breaks in the clouds, which are believed to be caused by terrific volcanic eruptions. We do not even know the length of her day or the tilt of her axis in relation to her orbit. Some authorities are of the opinion that, like Mercury, she may have perpetual heat in one hemisphere and perpetual cold in the other; but that seems unlikely owing to her cloud formations. So far the spectroscope has failed to find the oxygen on Venus that plant life would certainly produce, or water; so a theory has been advanced that her cloud formations do not consist of water vapour, but a perpetual sandstorm caused by the tearing of high winds at a dry, reddish soil about as hot as the boiling point of water. One thing the spectroscope has revealed is that her atmosphere contains a far higher degree of carbon dioxide than the atmosphere of Earth. That would have the result of making conditions at her surface like those in a greenhouse. Should the solution to the puzzle be that there is water on her surface, but for some reason its vapour cannot get high enough for the spectroscope to detect it, we might expect to find there the type of vegetation that she has been depicted as having by sensational novelists. There would be thousands of square miles of steaming swamps, with giant ferns and other vegetation growing in them, similar to that of the age of the dinosaurs on Earth."

"Then there may be life there," Carmen interjected. "Anyhow, animals like the brontosaurus and strange birds like the pterodactyl. If so, why not men?"

Escobar shook his head. "The age of those giant beasts and that of man is millions of years apart in the progress of evolution. Even if there is any animal life at all on Venus it cannot be intelligent life. The range of vision on her surface is too limited. The combination of heat and water would create an almost impenetrable mist, through which, owing to the thick cloud layers, the Sun would never penetrate. Only certain primitive types of fish and reptiles could exist in that dank, hot semi-darkness. Light and sun are essential to the development of even an intelligent species of mammal, let alone man. As the lives of planets go, Mercury is an old, burnt-out world; Venus millions of years too young to be a possibility."

"What's next on the list?" Kem asked.

"One that has already gone the way that Earth may go if our scientists are not very careful," Escobar replied with a faint smile. "In order of distance from the Sun the planets run: Mercury, Venus, Earth, Mars; and it is a curious fact that they do not seem to have taken up their positions arbitrarily, as each revolves in an approximately increasing ratio from the centre of the system. Between Mars and Jupiter there comes a wide gap; but between them, and just where we should expect it to be if we adhered to the ratio, there is strong evidence that there was once another planet. Now we see what must be its remains in the form of thousands of asteroids which continue to circle the Sun on what must have been its old orbit. Most of them are quite tiny; the largest, called Ceres, is only 480 miles in diameter. They are all that is left of a world that may once have been very like ours."

"Do you think its scientists blew it up, then?"

"Possibly. It may have exploded owing to internal causes. Earth is quite liable to do so at any time; although the people we have left behind us have not much cause to worry about that in view of the millions of years it has survived already. Again, it is possible that the world now only represented by the asteroids may have met its end owing to a collision with a big comet. But it is not at all outside the bounds of possibility that life developed there very much as it has on Earth, until one day somebody discovered how to split the atom. At any time after that a chain of reactions might have been released, which clever people like myself found it impossible to stop, and the whole planet was blown to pieces."

"God, what an age to be born into!" Kem groaned. "Just to think that everyone is now living under the constant threat that some fool monkeying with a Hydrogen bomb may put an end to everything without a moment's warning."

"Not quite everyone," Carmen corrected him. "Naturally I should be sorry for my friends if they were all blown sky-high; but at least we no longer have to fear that sort of fate for ourselves."

Kem's broad grin suddenly lit up his face. "You're right. If the back-room boys do slip up, from the place where we're going we may even see the big bang. Then we'd be the last survivors of the human race. Perhaps this is a sort of Noah's Ark without the animals, and it will be up to . . ." He had been about to say ". . . to us to carry on the old firm by begetting a new generation of mankind." Instead, he ended rather lamely, "to . . . er, pass on as much knowledge of our own civilization as we are able to between us."

Both the others guessed what he had really had in mind, and on account of all that it implied a rather awkward silence ensued. He broke it as soon as he could by asking Escobar, "Well; what comes next?"

"Jupiter; the big boy of the Solar family," the scientist replied. "His mass is 317 times that of Earth and it would take you over ten times as long to make a journey round his equator. He is ice all over, and ice miles deep at that, with a surface temperature of minus 210 degrees Fahrenheit. No life could exist in such intense cold, and, that apart, life would be made impossible by the fact that his clouds are formed from ammonia crystals and his icy atmosphere mainly of methane gas. The only children Jupiter has ever had are his eleven moons, and all of them are, if possible, even deader than ours.

"Saturn, the second largest of the family, comes next; with his nine moons and his beautiful rings formed by thousands of tiny asteroids. They are probably the fragments of two more moons he once had that collided. Anyhow, in this instance it is quite certain that no living being caused them to blow up, as his composition is similar to that of Jupiter and no form of life could possibly have arisen in seas of frozen methane.

"Uranus, Neptune and Pluto complete the family. The two first are small by comparison with Jupiter and Saturn, but still big brothers compared with Earth. To them Pluto is relatively a midget, about halfway in size between Earth and Mercury. There is no possibility of life on any of them. Their atmospheres, too, are mainly composed of poisonous gases, and owing to their great distance from the Sun they are unbelievably cold and dark. If one were standing on Pluto and could see the sky through the clouds at all, it would be difficult to detect the rising of the Sun unless one knew where to look for it. The little planet is nearly forty times as far away from it as Earth, and at that distance the Sun would appear no larger than many of the other stars."

So ended the last discussion upon their possible destination that they were to have for some time. All the possibilities at all feasible in the light of man's present knowledge had been reviewed and, unless there were other possibilities still entirely outside his range of speculation, it boiled down to one of two things. Either they were journeying towards one of the less distant stars, to land on a planet about which nothing whatever was known, but would be one of the comparatively few which it was logical to suppose had reached a period in its evolution during which beings of advanced intelligence could exist upon it; or they were being taken to Mars, about which a great deal was known, but which it was believed was capable of supporting only the lower forms of life.

As they could see outside the Saucer only by peering down the lavatory chute, they had no means of finding out in what direction it was going. Neither could they form any estimate of the speed at which they were travelling; and even had they been able to it would have told them little, except that had they known it to be of the order of a million miles a second, or even the speed of light, that would have ruled out Mars, as the orbit followed by the red planet would have been long since left behind.

Inside the Saucer there was no dawn, no evening and no night. As it whirled soundlessly through space its interior remained one unending day of never varying sunlight, dimmed only to the extent that, having had to filter through the Saucer's roof, all glare had been eliminated from it. Kem's wrist-watch had had its face smashed in at some point in his struggles that he could not recall. Escobar's thin gold timepiece had come through unharmed in the breast pocket of his jacket, but had stopped before it occurred to him to look at it; so by the time he rewound it they had only the vaguest idea how many hours had passed since they left Earth. But when rewound it enabled them to keep a count of days, and this led to the discovery that Saucerian time coincided nearly, but not exactly, with Earth time.

At intervals the lids of the tanks containing the water-pipe and the beans sprang open, apparently of their own accord, and the two giants supervised the issue of rations from them. After this had happened a few times the captives jumped to the conclusion that the issue took place every twelve hours; so began to look forward expectantly to this small excitement and feel annoyance that it always seemed to lag a little behind schedule. But on actual timing it was found that the issue took place with irreproachable punctuality after each lapse of twelve hours and nineteen minutes.

As far as thirst was concerned they wished that the intervals had been shorter; although they never suffered any acute inconvenience, because the temperature in the chamber was always kept at a degree only a little above chilly. Hunger never troubled them at all, as the beans, although deadly dull, seemed to fill this need and leave them with only just enough appetite to eat again when the next issue was handed out. Escobar was proved right in his prediction that the beans were a concentrate containing all the vitamins necessary to human nutrition, as after a few days of this grim diet, and having had time to recover from the shock and injuries they had sustained, the captives found themselves only a little thinner and once more in excellent health.

Apart from supervising the issue of rations, the two giants did nothing whatever. For a great deal of the time they slept flat on their backs;

during the remainder they squatted cross-legged side by side, staring goggle-eyed at the captives. Very occasionally they exchanged a few brief sentences in their throaty, uncouth tongue. They had nothing to occupy them and did not appear to desire it; but they were always awake when meal-times came round, and ate the larger ration of beans that they took for themselves with eager relish.

The idea that they were little more than animals was reinforced by their likeness to each other. Their features were flat and had no distinguishing marks, the eyes and nostril hair of both were the same colour; and, except that one was a few inches taller than his companion, it would have been as difficult to say which was which had they been two sheep. Kem christened them Gog and Magog, and in one of his brighter moments said what a marvellous box-office draw they would make if only he could turn the tables and bring them back to Earth as prisoners.

No other members of the crew appeared, and they gave only one brief sign of their presence. On what the captives counted as their second day out, while the giants were sleeping, Kem tried to open the little trap in the control tower, through which they had communicated with their masters on his rousing one of them to ask for water. Although the trap would have passed as invisible at a casual glance, he found it without difficulty; but its edges fitted so neatly into the pillar that they showed only as hair-lines, and it was shut fast. After examining it carefully, he came to the reluctant conclusion that it would be impossible to prise it open, even with the aid of the most suitable small implement he could find among Carmen's things. In consequence, he decided to try the procedure the giant had used, and rapped sharply on the pillar with his knuckles.

Almost at once the trap sprang open, but it was too high up in the column for him to see into it. Swiftly he kicked the deck from under him, but overshot the mark and hit the ceiling. The second his head touched its whirling surface he was hurled away from it and spun round and round the chamber in mid-air, just as he had been soon after first regaining consciousness in it. While he was still floundering about and endeavouring to get a foothold on the deck, whoever was inside the control tower had evidently used some means to communicate with the giants, as they both woke. Magog seized him round the middle and shook him till his teeth rattled; meanwhile the trap snapped shut. As he jumped he had caught only a glimpse of what lay beyond it, and on recovering his breath could tell his companions no more than that the inside of the tower appeared to be filled with a complicated structure of girders.

Boredom soon became the worst enemy of the captives. They slept as much as they could, but out of every twenty-four hours there were long stretches during which they lay in the gaps between the tanks, under their light screens of bedding, wooing sleep in vain. All of them read

Carmen's French novel through twice, then when she was not using her missal the men borrowed that in turn until they could find no more interest in it. They played guessing games and spelling games until they were sick of them, and talked of this and that until it seemed that they had exhausted every subject of conversation.

Escobar made matters no easier by his attitude to Carmen. He kept his word about reproaching her no further, but his resentment against her had evidently gone very deep, as he never smiled at her, and spoke to her only with the distant politeness he would have used towards a stranger. She did not appear to resent his unspoken condemnation, and made no effort to win back his goodwill.

After their first talk she had suffered a temporary relapse, and for long periods lay completely silent; but she showed no further signs of going out of her mind and after a few days gradually became more active, until she seemed quite normal, although she remained very subdued and spent much of her time at her devotions.

In such cheerless company, even Kem's natural exuberance wilted. Owing to the extremely low degree of gravity most forms of exercise were near impossible, but he kept himself as fit as he could by flexing his muscles and swimming round and round the chamber in its buoyant air. For his own amusement and that of the others he also practised his conjuring tricks, but again lack of gravity made sleight of hand unusually difficult.

Inevitably their occupations palled and as the days passed he found himself looking covertly at Carmen more and more frequently. At first all of them had longed desperately for a bath, or at least the means to wash themselves. That desire had gradually worn off, and as the Saucer contained not a speck of dust none of them appeared to become any dirtier. Owing to lack of water with which to shave both the men had grown beards, which, still being in an early stage, were far from improving their appearance; but Carmen, having all her toilet requisites with her, continued to look as beautiful and desirable as ever.

Her attitude to Kem was not encouraging, as although pleasant it was entirely impersonal. In vain he watched her for a clue which might help him to guess how she now regarded him. His feelings towards her had been only temporarily submerged during the fright, excitement and strangeness of their kidnapping; and, once they settled down, had returned with renewed persistence. Quite reasonably he argued that, since she had been so desperately in love with him, it was unlikely that her feelings had suffered any permanent change either. But what about Escobar?

For some days Kem wrestled silently with his problem. Escobar had behaved generously to him about the past and now treated him as a friend; so was it fair again to attempt to seduce his wife? On the other hand he had made it perfectly clear that he no longer felt even affection for Carmen, and his treatment of her implied that had he still been on Earth he would by now have thrown her out of his house, even if his own pride had made him stop short of bringing a charge against her that would have resulted in her being imprisoned. Now there was no possibility of anyone learning of her infidelity and laughing at him about it behind his back, it seemed probable that he would not really care much what she did. But as long as the three of them were confined together in the Saucer it would be impossible for her to carry on an *affaire* without his knowing of it; and he might strongly resent being placed in such a position. Moreover, if he did cut up rough, that would put an end to the unity which Kem considered it so important for them to preserve in view of their uncertain future. Yet, did that really matter so very much, after all? It did not if their journey was going to last for years, as by the time they reached their destination Escobar would have become accustomed to the new situation and condoned it. He would have to unless he were prepared to be sent to Coventry, perhaps for the rest of his life. And if it was their wretched fate to have to endure their present lot for a stretch of years, Kem felt that that was all the more reason why, if Carmen was willing, he and she should not continue indefinitely to deny themselves all the joy they could take of one another.

While Kem turned these thoughts over again and again in his mind he became more and more highly conscious of Carmen's allure. Her pale face and big lustrous eyes perpetually haunted him between waking and sleeping. The grace of her lithe body as she moved about made him ache to hold it. One day he was seized with an overwhelming desire to place his hand on her shapely instep; on another he could barely restrain himself from running his fingers through her dark hair, as she turned her head suddenly and it floated up in a gentle wave from the nape of her neck. The sight of her red mouth was a constantly tormenting temptation.

At last, when they had been on their way for just over a fortnight, he could bear it no longer. The Old Adam in him triumphed over all scruples and counsels of prudence. When their next sleep time came round, and they had settled down in the covered gaps between the tanks, he waited for a while to give Escobar time to drop off. Then, emerging from under his blanket, he gently raised the sheet that formed Carmen's tent and slid inside.

CHAPTER XII

WORLD FAR FROM OURS

As he laid his hand on Carmen's shoulder, she woke with a start.

"Hush!" he whispered. "It's only me—Kem. Don't make a noise."

"What do you want?" she murmured drowsily.

"I want to talk to you."

"What about?"

He noted the swift, nervous tension that had entered her voice now she was fully awake; so, as he eased himself down beside her in the narrow space, he replied as laconically as he could, "Oh, about ourselves."

"No, Kem!" She caught her breath, then added quite firmly, "There is nothing to be said between us that cannot be said in front of Estévan."

"There is! Carmen, I love you."

"I know you do; but I don't want you to tell me so. Please go away."

"Not till you've told me why you don't want me to tell you that I love you. It's not so long ago since you used to beg me to tell you so over and over again. Don't you care for me any more?"

"Yes. I still love you, Kem. Just as much as ever. But everything is different now."

At her admission he tried to put his arm round her shoulders, but she pushed it away and murmured unhappily, "No! Please, Kem! Don't make it harder for me."

"You're being hard on me, too," he protested. "Damnably and unnecessarily hard, if you still love me. And even if our circumstances have changed, we haven't. We are still the same people."

"I know. But things are different. I can't let you make love to me any more."

"Why? On account of Estévan?"

"Not altogether; although I don't want to hurt him more than I have already."

"You needn't worry about that. He doesn't care a rap for you. I don't think he ever did—or anyhow not since he found you disappointing to sleep with. It's quite on the cards that he made you marry him in the first place only on account of your family connections and wealth. No doubt he wanted a wife who would do him credit. Anyhow, it is pretty clear that for a long time past he has regarded you only as a valuable possession. Lots of people must have envied him his lovely, rich, aristocratic wife; and he must have got a big kick out of their believing you to be his loving and faithful spouse. When he found that you had kicked over the traces with me, that threatened the pretty picture he had built up; so naturally he was furious about it. But it was only his pride that was hurt, and there is no one here to make spiteful innuendoes about his having lost you. So why should you be so absurdly considerate for him?"

"If it were only that, I might feel differently," she sighed. "But it is really something fundamental. As you are an heretic I can hardly expect you to understand. But after what happened on the boat, I couldn't go to Confession. Not with the knowledge that you were coming out to stay at the estancia and that it might happen again. So, you see, I am still in a state of mortal sin."

Although Kem did not regard himself as an heretic, he let that pass; but as he had no reason to believe that Catholic women usually had better morals than Protestant ones, he said:

"Whatever religion a woman follows it is a sin for her to break the Sixth Commandment; but I've known quite a number of Catholic ones who did, and they didn't seem to think there was anything very terrible about having done so. Most of them got it off their chests by going to Confession afterwards, and I can't see why you shouldn't have done that, too."

Carmen sighed again. "I wish I had been capable of fooling myself into believing I could have received absolution like that; but I was not. The priest's words count for nothing unless one feels real repentance and has honestly made up one's mind to resist the same sort of temptation in future. And now it is too late. I shall never receive absolution at all."

"I'm sorry you feel so badly about it. When we became lovers on the boat, you showed no scruples about deceiving your husband."

"That has nothing to do with it."

"But your attitude was so different then. I took you for a woman of the world."

"I meant you to. I had been acting the part since soon after I married. I thought of myself as one, too. I had just come from having a gay time in Paris, and most of the women I knew there had their lovers. I wanted to take one myself. Sometimes at night I felt the urge to let myself go simply terribly, and I might have if I hadn't been so heavily chaperoned by Aunt Julia. By the time I met you I was on my way back to another six months with Estévan at the estancia, and I was obsessed with the thought that I was letting the best years of my life slip by without knowing what real passion could be."

"Well, when you did find out, with me, you enjoyed it, didn't you?"

"Of course I did; but although I didn't let you know it, I was haunted all the time by the thought that I was committing a sin."

"Darling, I cannot for the life of me understand why you should make such a bogey of that. Other women don't believe in these days that

86

because they follow the dictates of their hearts they will be damned for all eternity."

. "Perhaps. I wish I were like them, then. But all my family are deeply religious, and it's something I feel right inside me."

In the half-light that penetrated through the sheets Kem could see her strained face quite clearly. Leaning over her, he took both her hands in his and, in spite of her movement to pull them away, held them tightly, as he said, "Listen, Carmen. If you had received absolution I could understand your not wanting to fall into a state of sin again. But as you haven't, what difference can it make if we go on living together?"

She shook her head. "No, Kem. I can't. Please don't ask me to."

"How can you expect me to do otherwise? We may be cooped up in this damned thing together for years."

"I know. But all the same, I can't do it. Now that I feel repentance, to give way again would be an even greater sin."

"You mean you won't!" he muttered angrily. "Because you're just being thoroughly selfish. You'd rather see me driven half insane with longing for you than face being worried for an hour or two afterwards by a guilty conscience."

"No. It's not that. I'm not really being selfish. At least, I don't think I am. I want you just as much as you want me."

"Then for goodness' sake make an effort to put all these ideas about hell-fire out of your mind, and let me make love to you."

"No, Kem. I really mean what I said."

She had on the long fur coat that she wore both waking and sleeping, on account of the slight chill in the atmosphere, but it had fallen open when she had struggled to release her hands from his clasp. Now his thigh was pressed close against hers; he could feel its warmth through the material of his trouser leg, and her thin silk skirt. Her nearness drove him almost to a frenzy, and he began to plead with her in frantic, urgent whispers:

"Please, Carmen, please! I can't go on like this! I need you terribly! I didn't mean what I said just now about your being selfish. Seeing that you feel as you do, it would really be unselfish of you if you took pity on me. It is I who am the selfish one, to press you. But I can't help it. I've held myself in for days; but I can't any longer. I want you so desperately."

Suddenly, exerting all her strength, she thrust him from her and sat up. Then she said firmly, "Now it's your turn to listen, Kem. I know just how you are feeling, because I feel the same myself; but I'm not going to let myself weaken. You may not agree with me, but I believe that our having been carried off like this is God's choice of a way to chastise us for our sin. Perhaps that sounds far-fetched, but if I hadn't come up early to bed, intending to commit adultery with you in my bedroom, we might not be here now. In any case, what we are suffering

87

on this journey will be counted against the punishment that we wantonly invited. But that is not enough. As God is merciful we still have it in our power to gain His forgiveness, and He alone can protect us from the unknown horrors that we may have to face in the future. If I were in a state of grace I feel sure that the Holy Virgin and the Saints would intercede with Him successfully for us. As I am not, all I can do is to show my repentance by denying my body its desires, and to pray for help with faith that my prayers will not remain unanswered. Estévan often swears by the Saints from habit; but he is really an agnostic, and you do not take your religion so seriously as I do mine. You must let me be; so that with a clean heart I can continue to implore mercy for us all."

In the face of such a declaration Kem felt that it would be almost sacrilegious to press her further. The wave of passion that had shaken him so terribly had passed, and he looked at her now with new eyes, as though she were a woman dedicated and holy.

"I understand," he said slowly. "And I won't make a nuisance of myself again. I shall pray that your prayers may be answered." Then he left her as quietly as he had come.

There followed many days of deadly monotony, unbroken by any major incident. Only one occurred during the third week out. The last beans in the tank were used up, and when the next issue was due another full tank sprang open. This led to some excited speculation by the captives. Obviously the length of the journey must be governed by the supply of beans on board. They counted the tanks and in various ways endeavoured to assess how many beans each would contain, then worked out the number of days the beans would last, allowing ten per person for themselves and thirty per head for the giants, every twenty-four hours. Unfortunately, however, there were too many imponderables in the problem for them to arrive at a solution which stood a chance of being anywhere near the mark. In the first place, the giants must have consumed a considerable number on their way to Earth, and there was no means of discovering how many to deduct from the total on that account. Then the total itself might be hopelessly wrong; as one of the tanks consisted of the lavatory and another held the water-pipe, so others might contain other items such as spare parts, or be empty and filled with beans only on occasions when the Saucer was about to start on a journey to another world yet more distant from its place of origin than Earth. The only thing of which their calculations made them feel reasonably certain was that its present voyage was unlikely to last more than nine months.

That cheered them a little, but only temporarily; for, owing to the monotony of their routine, it seemed to them that instead of eighteen days they had already been imprisoned in the Saucer for as many weeks; so to have to endure a further eight months under such conditions sounded like a life sentence.

While they were discussing it Kem remarked, "I remember reading somewhere an article on sending a rocket to the Moon. It said that at a certain point where the gravitational attractions of the Earth and the Moon balance each other the rocket would have to turn round; so that as it came down it would descend base first, and by turning on its jets again be able to check the speed of its fall. When the Saucer turns upside down we shall know we have reached that point, and that may tell us something."

Escobar shook his head. "You are right about the theory of the thing; but even if it happened it would not tell us the proportion of our journey that we had covered, because we do not know the gravitational pull of the planet to which we are going as compared with that of Earth. However, the fact is that when the Saucer does turn over we shall not even know it. For all practical purposes we passed out of the field of gravity of Earth within a few minutes of taking off, and the only gravitational pull we have been subject to since is that of the giant magnet on which we are sitting. To whatever angle the Saucer may tilt, and even if it turns upside down, we shall continue to feel as though that remains beneath us. The Saucers have frequently been reported as flying sideways, on their edge, and while in an atmosphere that is the way in which they would meet with a minimum resistance. It is quite possible that we are flying sideways to our trajectory now."

Having become reluctantly resigned to the probability that they would have to remain for many weeks in their prison, they gradually adopted a routine of regular occupations.

Carmen made herself a little oratory by sticking a small crucifix to one of the tanks with seccotine, then decorating the deck below it with a mat of crimson silk, cut from one of her dresses, on which she laid out all her jewels. On her knees before the crucifix she spent many hours in prayer, and for a quarter of an hour before each issue of rations was due she read prayers aloud, in which Kem joined her, but Escobar curtly refused to participate in what he considered to be futile mummery.

Kem occupied himself for quite a while by converting the Spanish shawl into a coat. Carmen offered to do it for him, but he refrained from accepting, because it was one of the few ways in which he could kill time, although he gladly availed himself of her help in the matter of directions.

Escobar amused himself by making scientific calculations, doing his sums in minute figures in the margins of Carmen's French novel, as they wished to save her notepaper; but to make the book last as long as possible he allowed himself only one page a day for this purpose. He also spent a lot of time peering down the chute of the lavatory in the hope that he might see some heavenly body that he would recognize, and so be able to make a guess at the direction in which they were going. That would have been easy for him had it been perpetual night outside, but as it was always full daylight his chances of seeing anything were extremely slender. They would have been non-existent had not the Saucer been moving away from the Sun, but that it was doing so he soon detected through the very fact of seeing a star at all. It was so faint that at first he could not be sure that he had really seen it, but his impression was confirmed a few days later by seeing another. That they were visible in daylight, even against the deep blue colour that space assumed up in the stratosphere, proved that they must be very large and luminous bodies, but without a telescope it was impossible to identify them; so his observations got him no further.

Every day now they exercised themselves regularly as well as they could, played question-and-answer games for a set period, and took turns in selecting a subject for discussion. But, even so, the hours between ration issues seemed to drag interminably. And when ration-time came there were only the mentally unsatisfying few mouthfuls of water and five beans apiece to chew. They had soon come to loathe the very sight of the beans and their minds became obsessed with a craving for good food. They talked for hours of the delicious dishes they had eaten in the past, until it was decided that to do so was an additional torture; so for the future food should be taboo as a subject of conversation.

Under the strain one or other of them occasionally gave way to fits of anger, brought on by some trifling cause that normally would not have seemed of the least importance, or for a few hours sank into a state of sullen apathy; but, "while there is life there is hope" being one of the truer sayings, in the main, the certainty that their journey must end some time, somewhere, kept them buoyed up with a nervous expectancy.

It was on the forty-ninth day after they had left Earth that Escobar, who had just lifted the lid of the lavatory tank, looked down its pipe and gave a sudden shout:

"*Nom de Dios!* Quick! Come here!"

Kem and Carmen hastened to his side and leaned over the edge of the tank. The foot-wide round of daylight at the bottom of the pipe was no longer empty. Near its centre shone a brightly-coloured circle, which appeared to them to be about the size of a tennis ball. Their first impression was of its likeness to some fabulous jewel, for it might have been fashioned from a big, many-hued stone. Its predominant tint was rose-ochre, but in parts it was robin's-egg blue, and both were set off by a nearly complete, much smaller, circle of dazzling white, a segment of which was severed by the rim of the larger.

"It's Mars!" exclaimed Escobar excitedly.

"Are you sure? Do you know for certain?" Kem cried with equal excitement.

"Yes; by its markings. The reddish parts are deserts, the white spot is one of the polar caps, and the blue areas are its so-called seas. All of them are well known to astronomers and have long been named. Look!

90

Those two dark patches near its centre, but some way apart: they are easily recognizable, when seen in relation to the ice-cap and other features, as Mare Cimmerium and Mare Sirenum."

Fascinated, they stared down the chute for several minutes without speaking. As the planet remained in the centre of the pipe's orifice it was clear beyond doubt that they were heading for it, although in that short time it did not appear to grow appreciably larger. At length, Kem said to Escobar:

"Do tell us about it. Tell us all you know."

The scientist stroked the pointed beard he had grown which, in conjunction with the upturned moustache that he had always had, now gave him something of the look of a French financier. "Well," he said rather thoughtfully, "although I have devoted a lot of my time to astronomy, I have never specialized in Mars; so I can give you only the main facts that I remember. You had better have the figures first. The mean distance of Mars from the Sun is about 142 million miles. The nearest it ever gets to Earth is about 35 million. In many respects it is more like Earth than any other planet of our system, as it spins on an axis less than two degrees greater and has a day only thirty-seven minutes longer."

"That makes it more certain that this is a Martian aircraft, then," Carmen put in, "as rations are issued in it every twelve hours and nineteen minutes."

He gave her an unsmiling nod. "Yes; I ought to have considered that as a possible indication of our destination, but it never occurred to me."

"As Mars is spinning on much the same axis as Earth, I take it that the seasonal changes are similar, too?" Kem suggested.

"Yes; but they last nearly double the length of ours, because Mars takes much longer to complete a journey round the Sun. Her year has 687 days, or reckoned by her own slightly longer revolutions, 668. Her seasons also vary in relative length from Earth's, owing to her path round the Sun being more elliptical in shape. In her northern hemisphere summer lasts about a month longer than winter, and in her southern hemisphere the reverse applies. But to whichever hemisphere they take us, for most of the year I'm afraid we shall find it a good bit colder than the Argentine."

Carmen shivered. "If the temperature in this thing is their idea of comfortable central heating, we certainly shall."

"It may not be too bad in the day-time, but the nights in winter will be bitter. Mars is half as far again as Earth from the Sun, and it has been worked out that she gets only four-ninths of the warmth Earth gets. That means that, were the two planets the same in all other respects, Mars would be so cold that in the open we should be certain to freeze to death there. But, fortunately for us, they are not. On average, 50 per cent of Earth's surface is always sheltered from the Sun's rays by cloud, which makes it much cooler than it would otherwise be. Mars, on the other hand, has practically no cloud at all, except a narrow fringe of water vapour round the edge of the ice-caps when they melt in their respective springs. In consequence, practically the whole of her surface gets the full benefit of the Sun's heat; in fact 99 per cent of the possible maximum. That goes a long way towards evening things up; and calculations have shown that the mean temperature on her surface is 48 degrees Fahrenheit compared with Earth's mean surface temperature of 60 degrees."

"In what other ways does Mars resemble Earth?" Kem asked.

"As far as I know, in very few. Everywhere except in the desert areas her landscapes will present an appearance having little similarity to those of our World. She has no seas, no rivers, no mountains, and I find it difficult to believe that she has any forests in the sense that we use the word. But if you like desert scenery . . ." Escobar paused and pointed downward.

"Look how large a proportion of her shows a reddish tint. Look at that deep belt of red along her equator and for hundreds of miles to the north of it. That runs unbroken right round her and, as you can see, in places great triangles of it run up nearly to her poles. The whole of that is desert. Five-eighths of her total surface is an arid waste. The deserts of Arizona and the Sahara are tiny by comparison; but, of course, unlike them the deserts on Mars do not shimmer with heat. The probability is that, although their altitude is negligible, they are very like the cold, windswept uplands of Tibet. That they are swept by terrific winds we know, as we can see through our more powerful telescopes the dust-storms that these tornadoes churn up. We can measure them, too, and know that they are often several miles high; so they must be infinitely more terrible than any we experience on Earth."

"You are giving us a pretty grim picture," said Kem glumly. "Can't you suggest some more cheerful possibilities?"

Escobar shrugged. "To do so would be only guessing; but if we are lucky we may find a civilization there far in advance of anything we can as yet even conceive."

"If this Saucer is a fair example of it, I'd rather be taken to a place where primitive man is still running wild in the woods."

"The Saucer may represent only the degree of scientific and technical advancement they have achieved. The development of culture and the arts often runs parallel with more material triumphs. If it has done so on Mars we can look forward to many wonderful experiences. In fact we may be privileged to see a state of life which, unless the Martians bring it to Earth, our World cannot hope to reach for many thousands of years to come."

Escobar paused for a moment, then went on, "Until comparatively recently Percival Lowell, for many years the Director of Flagstaff

Observatory, Arizona, was regarded as the greatest authority on Mars. He made the study of the planet his life work, and even to-day most of what is known about it we owe to him. He used to say that Mars is the prophet of Earth, as everything that has taken place on one must inevitably take place in due course on the other. He was not, of course, referring to the evolution of man, although he always maintained that there was every reason to suppose that some form of intelligent life existed on Mars. But as far as the physical life of the two planets is concerned he was undoubtedly right.

"I think I mentioned once before that water is the life-blood of all planets. At one time Earth's oceans were much more extensive than they are to-day and nearly the whole of such land as existed was covered with vast forests. As the oceans have gradually shrunk through evaporation, the forest areas have also lessened until many of them now are deserts uninhabitable by man. Mars, being a much smaller planet than Earth, and having a lesser gravity, has less power than Earth to hang on to her water; so the process of absorption is much further advanced with her than it is with us. Through lack of water the whole of what were once her continents have become deserts, and even her ocean beds are now dry land. They are the last refuge of life on Mars, and when they too dry out completely all life on the planet must cease to exist.

"However, that inevitable annihilation will not take place for a long time yet; because Mars still has a final, but dwindling, reserve in her ice-caps. They are no longer permanent, like Earth's, and are not believed to consist of much more than a few feet of snow. In the course of each Martian year both of them melt completely, then re-form during the winters of the two hemispheres. Their melting enables the lowlands of Mars to be irrigated twice annually, and it is by that means only that vegetation can continue to flourish in them. But the subtle, silent enemy, evaporation, never ceases to take his annual toll of water; so year by year the ice-caps are gradually becoming smaller. When there is no longer enough water to form them Mars must die. And that is the way in which Earth will die, too."

"No wonder Gog and Magog are so stingy with the water," Carmen remarked.

"And as Mars is so much smaller than Earth that would account for their being giants," Kem added.

"Yes," Escobar agreed. "The gravity of Mars is only .38 that of Earth; so one would expect any species resembling a human being there to be about three times our size. But I was about to add that as Mars has aged physically much more rapidly than Earth, there is a good hope that its inhabitants will be much older mentally than we are; so wise, tolerant and benign."

Kem made a comical grimace. "I only hope you are right; but we've no evidence of that as yet. In fact all the evidence we have to date points the other way; except as far as their scientific achievements are concerned. Incidentally, now we have some data to go on, it would be interesting to know at what speed this thing is flying. We know roughly how long the journey has taken, and you said just now that Mars is 35 million miles from Earth, so it should be possible to work it out."

"Ah, but the figure I gave you is the distance between the two planets at their closest opposition. That occurs only once every seventeen years; at the other end of the scale there is a gap of 65 million miles between them when they pass. Besides, they come into opposition only at intervals of two years and two months. For all the rest of the time they are hurtling away from each other at tremendous speeds. As it is a long time since I have given any thought to Mars, I can't remember what her position in relation to the Earth is now; so it is impossible for me to even attempt the calculation you suggest."

After a moment the scientist added, "In any case, as the Saucers have visited Earth frequently during the past few years, they obviously do not have to wait for oppositions, but are capable of covering the big distances that separate the two planets while they swing round the greater part of their orbits."

Later, Kem worked out the sum for himself, taking the minimum distance as a base, and found that had Mars and Earth been at their closest opposition the Saucer would have been travelling at about eleven miles a second. But in view of what Escobar had said it seemed certain that it was doing several times that speed.

In the meantime, although it seemed unlikely that their landing would take place for many hours yet, they could hardly bear to drag themselves away from the viewpoint of their destination. The sphere of Mars did not appear to increase much in size, although its rotation from west to east was easily detectable from the gradual movement of the dark patches on its surface. When they had temporarily gazed their fill at it, they attempted to settle to their ordinary occupations, but every few moments they could not resist the urge to break off what they were doing to have another look. At last, tired out from staying awake much longer than usual to watch developments, they settled down under their bedding screens; but even then they were still so excited that it was quite a time before sleep would come to them.

When, several hours later, they woke, their first thought was to make certain that they were still heading for Mars. One glance down the pipe was enough. There was the brilliant-hued planet, and the circle it made had increased in size so considerably that only a narrow rim of daylight now seemed to separate it from the pipe's sides. The markings on it were much clearer and Escobar named several of them, which led Kem to suggest that the scientist should draw them a map of the planet, so that they could get a better idea of the principal features on both sides of it.

He agreed to do the best he could from memory, and the other two

94

followed him with immense interest as he sketched on one of their precious pieces of paper the great deserts and dead seas. The names he wrote in across them—Elysium, Ophir, Atlantis, Propontis, Lemuria, Ausonia, Fons Juventae, Utopia, and others with similar associations— suggested white palaces set among hanging gardens and palm-fringed lakes, rather than barren uplands, so tended to lessen their forebodings and made them more eager to arrive. Yet, in spite of the fact that by the time Escobar had finished the orb of Mars appeared to block the outlet of the pipe entirely, so it seemed that they must now be approaching it very fast, he said that the planet was still relatively far away and they would have to control their impatience to learn its secrets.

As the hours passed the major markings became still clearer and new ones were constantly appearing in the gaps between them. When they first woke, lines joining many of the seas and oases had been just perceptible; these became darker and as sharp as if they had been drawn with a ruler, while a whole network of fainter lines showed criss-crossing both the dead oceans and the deserts.

Like the majority of people Kem and Carmen had both heard that some astronomers believed there were canals on Mars, but neither had seriously considered the implications of such a possibility. Now they were looking down on them, while Escobar explained the theory that had been advanced regarding their origin and purpose.

"Lowell suggested," he said, "that long before the last seas of Mars dried up the Martians must have realized that drought would eventually bring all life on their planet to an end; so they took such steps as they could to conserve the water that remained. When the polar ice melted each spring, instead of letting most of the water it made run to waste in the bottoms of the old sea-beds, they canalized some of it and brought it to their most fertile areas. Now, the odds are that every single gallon of it is controlled and automatically directed into smaller channels that irrigate their fields. The colour changes that have been observed to occur seasonally in the bluish regions goes far to prove that. They wax and wane from a greenish hue in summer to a yellowish tinge in winter. It is that which has caused it to be now generally accepted that they are vegetation. But without the canals to feed them they too would become arid deserts."

"I find it amazing," Kem remarked, "that anything so narrow as a canal should ever have been seen from Earth, even through the most powerful telescope."

"That is partly due to the fact that dead-straight lines are always easier for the eye to detect than irregular ones, as you must have noticed in the case of roads when flying in an aircraft. But, of course, it is not the canals themselves we see; they are indicated only by the parallel belts of verdure that grow on their banks; and they are estimated to average ten miles in width. Between four and five hundred of them have been detected to date and some of the main ones are two or three thousand miles in length. As you see, many of the most prominent are doubles. So far no satisfactory theory has been advanced to account for that; but there is another thing about them that you will not notice at first sight, for which there is an interesting explanation. In the northern hemisphere the majority of them show a westward trend towards the equator, and in the southern hemisphere an eastward trend; so the people who planned them must have made due allowance for the fact that a planet rotates more swiftly at its equator than it does near its poles, and oriented them in such a way as to ensure the minimum resistance to the water they were designed to carry during its transit and, in consequence, a minimum cost in unavoidable loss."

"To create such a system," Kem said, a little awed, "must have been a gigantic undertaking, when one thinks of the labour entailed in cutting through little bits of land like those at Suez or Panama."

"Yes. It would have taken us thousands of years to do such a job, and it probably took the Martians many generations to complete it. But they had one thing in their favour: the fact that the lower gravity on Mars must make any physical work very much easier. A sack of these beastly beans that would weigh a 100 pounds on Earth weighs only 38 pounds on Mars, so there you could lift it without effort. In view of their size that must make an enormous difference in their capacity for labour."

At intervals the captives tried to make the hours of waiting until they could hope for liberty, or at least a change of prison, pass swiftly by endeavouring to think of other things. But their efforts were in vain; they could not keep their minds for more than a few moments from speculation on what sort of reception they would meet with on the unknown world they were approaching.

As they rushed towards it their field of vision down the pipe gradually decreased, until they could see only a circular area that included a great blue-green promontory shaped somewhat like India, which was called Syrtis Major, and a number of canals radiating from it. Then, with startling suddenness, the map below them disappeared, to be replaced by blank dark blue space.

Apprehensively they looked at one another. It was Kem who was first to realize the significance of the change, and reassure the others. "It's all right," he said. "The odds would naturally be against the Saucer's base being situated on the part of Mars that happens to be under it at the moment. It must have turned on its edge to partially circumnavigate the planet until it gets over its landing-ground."

His companions agreed, but they all continued to stare down the pipe a little anxiously. Half an hour later he was proved correct; as with a suddenness nearly as swift as the first change the daylight faded, then the aperture grew dark. Simultaneously the glow through the Saucer's roof dimmed, lights appeared inside the control tower and, within a few moments, the chamber was lit only by the soft radiance emanating from its central pillar. It was clear that the Saucer had traversed more than a quarter of the planet's circumference, and that it had now entered the cone of shadow that every twenty-four hours and thirty-seven minutes brought night to the inhabitants of Mars.

Still they looked down the chute, but nothing now broke the blackness of the circle below them. They had thought that the oases might contain cities with great populations, and that linking them together there might be flood-lit autobahns along the canals; but not a glimmer of light was to be seen.

Almost imperceptibly at first, then with increasing strength, they began to feel the pull of gravity. Recalling accounts of what his companions had suffered from the same cause when leaving Earth, Escobar called out:

"Don't be alarmed! The pressure won't be anything like as great as that you had to endure before."

But they were given little time to think about it. Their feet had hardly registered an unaccustomed firmness on the deck when two of the tanks sprang open; and Gog and Magog, who for the past seven weeks had either slept or squatted for hours on end almost unmoving, suddenly displayed an unwonted activity.

From the tanks they took a number of packages which, when unfolded, proved to be big sacks made of some transparent material like thick cellophane. They were about eight feet long and each had a bulky apparatus attached to it. Into two of them the monsters stuffed the bedding and all the other things that they had brought from the estancia; then, by the use of some self-sealing device, they closed the mouth of each sack so that it became air-tight and had the appearance of a sausage-like balloon, through the skin of which the contents could be clearly seen.

By the time they had done, the three captives, although in no actual pain, were breathing heavily, half fainting and incapable of any effort, owing to the increasing pull of gravity. As they watched, Gog slowly took up another sack and opened its mouth wide. Then Magog reached out and grasped Carmen in his huge hands.

Her mouth opened to scream, but she had no breath to do so. As Kem saw the terror on her face he made a feeble effort to reach her, but he and Escobar had already been forced to their knees by the increasing pressure. Horrified they watched while she was pushed into the sack and its mouth was sealed above her head.

Escobar was crouching nearer to the giants, so they seized upon him next; then Kem's turn came. Neither was capable of offering any resistance.

Once Kem had been sealed inside the sack he suddenly found that he could breathe more easily. It occurred to him then that part of the apparatus attached to it was probably an oxygen flask. Through the material of which the sack was made he could still see the chamber in which he had been so long confined. Gog and Magog were evidently now also seriously affected by the pressure, for their movements had become exceptionally laborious. As Kem peered at them he saw them go over to the lavatory tank and remove the funnel-shaped pan it contained; then they pulled up from it several long sections of the pipe.

He now lay nearer to them than either Carmen or Escobar. Slowly they reached out and grasped him, drew him along the deck and lifted him until the mouth of the sack, the apparatus attached to it, and his head were over the rim of the tank. He saw that the removal of the pan had left the tank empty and that where the pipe had been there was now only a wide, well-like shaft, at the bottom of which lay impenetrable darkness.

Gog and Magog gave a heave. Kem kicked out wildly; but that did not prevent his being tipped over the edge of the tank upside down. Head first he shot down the shaft, and ten seconds later he was hurtling from the Saucer into the black night below.

CHAPTER XIII

CHAMBER OF HORROR

DURING those moments while Gog and Magog had sealed Kem in the sack, then dragged him to the chute and thrown him down it, reason had told him that the Martians would not go to such trouble to kidnap them and bring them all that way only to dash them to pieces on arrival; but as he dropped like a stone head foremost from the Saucer's vent the thought did nothing to lessen his terror.

For what could only have been seconds, but seemed to him an eternity, he plunged downwards with ever-increasing speed. Only one thing penetrated his panic-stricken mind. It was much lighter outside the Saucer than in its shaft, yet the light was diffused and did not come from below him; the Martian earth was still hidden in a pall of darkness.

Suddenly, he was subjected to a sideways tug. At the same moment the speed at which he was falling lessened. The sack turned right over, bringing him head uppermost. His descent was further checked until he was floating down no faster than a piece of paper thrown out of a window, and he began to sway like a pendulum. The oxygen was still working and he took a deep breath, then he looked upward, guessing now what he would see. The apparatus attached to the sack had contained a large parachute; it billowed out above him like a huge umbrella.

It hid the Saucer, but the sky below its edge revealed the source of the light by which he could now see clearly. From horizon to horizon it was sprinkled with a multitude of stars; never, on the clearest summer night, had he seen from Earth one tenth of their number.

After a moment he realized that some of the brighter ones could not be stars. They moved too swiftly and were following him down. It dawned upon him then that they must be some of the Thinking Lights. He tried to count them, but became confused and gave up, after assessing their number to be somewhere between twelve and fifteen. Next, against the canopy of stars, he spotted a dark object a little above him to his left; then another and another, and knew that they must be the parachutes carrying down his companions and Carmen's belongings.

He had hardly sighed with thankfulness at the thought that their parachutes had also functioned properly when, turning his head, he caught sight of the Saucer. Its 100-foot diameter showed only as a big black patch against the stars. As he watched, a little cluster of the Thinking Lights appeared over its edge and came floating earthwards. Suddenly a bright spot showed in the centre of the Saucer. It glowed red and rapidly increased in size; then a tongue of flame licked from it halfway across the Saucer's lower surface. It was on fire. Next moment it was ablaze all over. For a few seconds it burnt with the brightness of a huge magnesium flare, blotting out the starry background all round it. Then it was gone, as utterly consumed as if it had never existed.

Kem was still staring upwards at the place where it had been when his feet struck the ground sharply, sending his knees up to his chest and driving the breath from his body. There followed a confused impression of bouncing, being dragged, turned head over heels and dragged again.

When he came to rest he was still winded; but as soon as he had recovered a little he scrambled up into a kneeling position and peered about him. The starlight now showed the landscape plainly—if it could be called a landscape. No tree or shrub broke the smooth contours which cut off the sky low down on either side; and the ground about him did not even boast tufts of coarse grass. He had come down in a shallow pan of sandy earth that was entirely featureless.

Instinctively he grasped two folds of the balloon-like sack that enveloped him and exerted his strength in an attempt to tear it open; but although as clear as glass it was as tough as silk and defied his efforts to break through it. As he released his hold second thoughts told him that perhaps that was just as well; for the sack was serving him as an oxygen tent and, had he succeeded in getting out of it, he might have found himself in grave danger owing to the atmosphere on Mars having different qualities from that of Earth.

The thought brought in its train a wave of depression. If that were so it might mean that he would be condemned to spend the rest of his life inside a captive balloon, or tank. He had hoped to regain a degree of liberty sufficient to see something of this strange new world; instead he might have to suffer the indignity of playing the part of an animal in a zoo for the interest and amusement of its inhabitants.

Presently he noticed that two of the Thinking Lights had come down and were circling round and round one another about twenty feet above his head. It consoled him a little to think that anyway his position had been picked up; so, presumably, someone would soon arrive to collect him. Almost immediately afterwards, with mingled feelings of relief and apprehension, he suddenly became aware that newcomers had already appeared upon the scene.

The sack in which he was crouching was sound-proof and they came upon him from behind, so he neither heard nor saw their approach. It was a slight turn of the head that caused him to catch sight of a big machine which had come silently up to within a few feet of him. From his position on the ground he could see only the under-part of it, but that was enough to convey that it was a form of truck. Its large, flat, open deck was reminiscent of an aircraft float, but there the resemblance ended, as it had no tender or driver's cabin and instead of wheels was supported by two rows of big balls that appeared to play the part of caterpillar tracks. As Kem swung round, a giant slipped down from its six-foot-high side, caught hold of him, and tossed him up on its deck with as little effort as if he weighed no more than a sucking pig.

Kem held his breath, expecting to hit the deck with a most painful thump, but to his surprise he landed on it quite gently. He remembered then that the gravity of Mars was, near enough, only one-third that of Earth, which meant that he would now turn the scales at not much above three and a half stone, and to the giant was the equivalent of a mere sixteen-pound bundle. It was his greatly diminished weight now being distributed over the same size body that had caused him to come down like a bolster instead of a sack of potatoes.

As he rolled over he saw that two of the other sacks were already aboard; the nearer contained some of the bedding and the further Carmen. She was lying propped up on one elbow, so evidently had sustained no serious injury in landing, and at the sight of him her face lit up with swift relief; but he glimpsed it only for a moment. Beside both sacks were heaped the parachutes that had brought them down, and after a single glance his view of her was cut off by his own parachute being thrown up to descend so that a number of its folds settled gently across his body. Only by craning his neck could he now see any part of the machine except its front. Another of the giants was squatting there cross-legged. Presumably he was its driver; as, a moment later, it began to roll in the direction he was facing, across the depression and up a slight slope.

But for the low gravity the movement would have been most uncomfortable, as the flat deck had no springs beneath it, and half bumped, half bounded, forward across the uneven ground. After a few minutes it rocked to a halt and another sack was loaded on to it, but Kem could not see if the sack contained the rest of Carmen's things or Escobar. There followed another short, wild ride and the fifth sack was put aboard. As the parachute attached to it sank on the deck in a rumpled heap Kem saw the driver stand up, leave his place and pick his way through the jumble of sacks and parachutes towards the back of the trolley. Next moment it had started off again, but now what had been its rear was in front; so evidently it could be driven from either end.

The next lap was considerably longer. For the best part of a quarter of an hour the trolley zigzagged over ground that had few gradients but could hardly have been a road, as the surface was too rough. Nevertheless its bumping was not sufficiently serious for there to be any fear of its passengers being thrown from it; and Kem, now lying on his back, was able without difficulty to keep his eyes fixed on a little bevy of Thinking Lights that danced above them as they careered along.

Beyond the Thinking Lights the star-spangled vault of heaven remained unbroken in every direction. No dark silhouette of trees, crag, tower or radio mast reared up to cut it as they passed; but Kem did notice one thing that warmed his anxious heart a little. Among the myriad of stars he could pick out that old familiar constellation, the Plough—or Dipper. It struck him as extraordinary that, although he had been transported many million miles through space, it should look no different from when he had last seen it, except that its stars were far brighter than when seen from Earth. It was, he felt, a practical demonstration of what Escobar had told him, of the whole Solar system being no larger than a grain of sand in the Sahara compared with the unfathomable vastness of the Universe; yet the sight of those seven great distant suns that he had known from childhood was strangely reassuring.

He wished that he could tell Carmen about it, but although he was free to move about inside his sack, he could not crawl while it encased him; and, even as he contemplated attempting to roll across the rumpled parachutes, he remembered that should he succeed in reaching her the sack would prevent her from hearing anything he said.

Next moment he was given something else to think about. It seemed as though a sharp-edged curtain of velvet blackness was being pulled up on invisible wires in front of the trolley. The curtain rose so swiftly that in a few seconds it loomed overhead blotting out half the starry sky; then the trolley plunged right into it, and was swallowed up in stygian darkness.

The way was smoother now, and raising himself a little Kem looked back. He could see the end of a twenty-five-foot-high tunnel, and following them down it were several of the Thinking Lights. A few hundred yards further on the trolley slowed down, then halted. The Lights came up with it and zoomed round and round overhead, faintly illuminating as they did so the shadowy roof of a vaulted chamber hewn out of solid rock, which was the same height as the tunnel but very much broader.

For the first time Kem saw the Thinking Lights against a solid background, and he could now see that they were not, as he had previously thought, pure flame. Seen closer they had the appearance of incandescent mantles tightly enclosed in wire mesh globes, similar to those which are still sometimes used to protect the naked flame of gas-jets, but much smaller. They had, too, what appeared to be several short wires trailing from them and at one side a round knob that cast a black shadow when seen against the light. The wires and the knob confirmed him in his first impression that they must be some form of aerial instrument that was controlled by wireless, but he could not even guess at their purpose.

He was not given long to speculate about it. The two giants who had brought the trolley there were detaching the parachutes from the sacks. As soon as they had done so, one of them climbed through a large circular hole high up in the wall; the other then passed the sacks through it to him. When Kem's turn came he saw that the inner chamber was smaller, somewhat lower and had a flat roof. It was illuminated only by two of the Thinking Lights that hovered in one corner near the ceiling. The place was uncarpeted and completely empty; it was a bare, round, stone cistern about thirty-five feet across. When the second monster had passed in the last of the five sacks, he wriggled through the hole after it.

Kem had had no previous opportunity to get a good look at the giants who had picked them up, but as far as he could see they were twin brothers to Gog and Magog and differed from them in appearance only in that, although they wore protective eye covers, they were not using the mouth-mask breathing apparatus. Both were about twenty feet in height, naked, bald, whitish-grey skinned, with red hair on their bodies and fanning out from their nostrils. For all he knew they might be the same two stupid, repulsive-looking brutes whom he had studied so often; but, somehow, he did not think they were. Then, as one of them stooped to undo the mouth of the sack in which Escobar was sealed up, he became certain of it, for the monster had a big birthmark behind his left shoulder.

As Kem watched, Escobar was pulled out of the sack. He stumbled to his feet, apparently none the worse for his experiences during the past hour; but next moment he was given cause for fresh alarm. One of the giants held him round the waist while the other pulled his coat off. Despite his struggles they then proceeded to deprive him of his trousers, shirt and underwear, until he stood stark naked mouthing useless curses at them.

Next the two monsters took Carmen from her sack. She must have seen how they had treated her husband; for, the moment she was free of it, like a Roman galley sailing between the legs of the colossal statue that once straddled the entrance to Rhodes harbour, she dived between the legs of the nearest giant and dashed for the hole in the wall.

As it was more than twice her height from the floor, it did not look as if she could possibly reach it, but the low gravity of Mars converted her flying steps into great leaps. She was across the room before the monsters even had time to turn, and, bounding up, grasped the lower edge of the opening. Desperately she strove to pull herself up and wriggle through it; but one of them took a ten-foot stride, stretched out a great hand, grasped her by the calf of the leg and pulled her, screaming, back into the middle of the room. She scratched and bit, but her strength soon seemed to fail her and in another few minutes the monsters had stripped her too of her clothing.

Turning over, she lay face down on the floor, her arms round her head, her dark hair falling across them and along her back. Kem saw one of the giants reach out for him; but, even in that moment, the uppermost thought in his mind was of Carmen's beauty and distress.

As he was pulled from his sack he saw that Escobar had sunk to his knees and was breathing heavily. A moment later he knew why. Now that he had been deprived of the additional oxygen he found it difficult to get his breath. The air in the chamber was very thin and after a few breaths his heart began to pound uncomfortably.

Having seen what had happened to his companions, he realized the futility of resistance, and offered none. He even helped the two monsters to get him out of his clothes. Then he sat down on the floor, panting slightly.

The giants next took up the two sacks that held Carmen's belongings, opened them, shook out their contents and scattered them about. Kem was sitting with his back towards the hole in the wall, but the sound of hissing behind him caused him to turn his head. The end of a hose had been thrust through it, and from its nozzle a whitish vapour was spurting to form a small cloud overhead.

The cloud grew in size very quickly. The monsters squatted down on the floor, so evidently the vapour was harmless to them; but the panic fear flashed into Kem's mind that it might not be harmless to humans. He got to his feet, but had taken only a step forward when he found himself faint from lack of air.

As he stood swaying there, he got a whiff of the gas. It was pungent and, like ammonia, made him gasp. Being short of breath already, the pain stabbed into his lungs like a knife. The whole chamber was now misty with the stuff. Vaguely he noticed that Escobar had fallen forward on his face. He could no longer see the Thinking Lights clearly, but only as two bright blurs high up near the hole in the wall. Suddenly they disappeared and the last glow from them was cut off by a cover being closed over the hole. The chamber was plunged in darkness. He choked, gasped, choked again, then fell with one of his arms across Carmen's back. It seemed as if his lungs were being torn in pieces. He gave a final gasp and shudder; then lay still.

CHAPTER XIV

TRIAL AND TRIBULATION

KEM was recalled to his senses by Escobar shaking him. He found that he was still naked but lying under several layers of coarse fibre matting. There was enough light to see by and it came from an oblong window high up in the wall. As there had been no window in the chamber in which they had been overcome by the white vapour, he knew that they must have been moved while unconscious; then, as he glanced around, he saw that they were in a lofty oblong cell large enough to accommodate a score of people, but as bleak and bare as a barrack yard.

He no longer felt any pain in his lungs, but was cold and utterly miserable. Sitting up, slowly, profanely and with intense feeling, he began to curse Mars and all its inhabitants. Escobar, who was standing over him, still without a stitch of clothing on, gave his shoulder another shake, and said:

"Pull yourself together, man! Swearing will not do you any good."

"You're right," growled Kem. "All the same, I wish I had the means to blow this bloody planet to hell. While we were on our way here there was at least hope that we'd meet with a decent reception. But this is worse than the Saucer. And the way they treated us! What in God's name did those brutes think they were up to?"

Escobar shivered, sat down and drew over himself some of the rough coverings under which he had been lying before he roused Kem. "I think that has quite a simple explanation and is unlikely to occur again. They were decontaminating us and all the things we brought with us, so that we should not give them any of the diseases we have brought from Earth."

"If that was the idea, I could have saved them the trouble by vouching for a clean bill of health."

"Oh no, you couldn't. Any number of bacteria must have developed on Earth which do not exist here. We have become immunized to them by breathing in small quantities all our lives, but we probably carried enough to start a series of plagues that would have wiped out the entire population on Mars. Whole tribes of North American Indians perished from measles when white settlers first brought it among them, and even the common cold can spell death to a race of savages that has never experienced it."

"If I had known that, and had the chance," said Kem viciously, "I would have brought a few bottles containing bubonic, syphilis and T.B. in my luggage."

"We would be no better off if you had. In fact worse, for when the diseases became rampant we should certainly have caught them ourselves."

"I suppose so. Anyhow, what you say explains quite a lot. It is evidently why we were not allowed to land at an airport, but delivered in sealed bags. That, too, must be why the Saucer took fire a few minutes after we were thrown out. It would have been full of our germs, so they preferred to destroy it rather than risk infection. I wonder what happened to Gog and Magog."

"They must have been burnt with it. I saw it burning as I dropped, but no sign of them. Their masks gave them 95 per cent protection from infection while they were with us, but they would have carried it on their bodies, so spread it among their people if they had landed; and they were much too big to come down that chute as we did, in some form of self-sealing sack."

"But what about the others? I mean the navigator and his pals; the intelligent ones whom we never saw, but who must have had their quarters on the deck below the magnet?"

"They must have been burnt up, too. Any bacteria in the air of the Saucer would have travelled from the upper deck to the lower. They would have known that, and probably considered themselves contaminated."

"In that case, why didn't they land and have themselves decontaminated in the same way as they decontaminated us?"

"Probably because there was no aperture large enough for them to get through and make a parachute descent. The Saucers that have made forced landings on Earth are reported to have burnt themselves out; so it is reasonable to suppose that their crews are quite prepared to commit *hara-kiri* if they feel circumstances require it of them."

"I couldn't care less," muttered Kem bitterly. Then he looked over to a pile of the matting under which Carmen lay, and added, "How has Carmen come through our last little jollification? Have you looked at her yet?"

"Yes. She is breathing quite normally and seems none the worse. I think she must have passed from unconsciousness into a sleep of exhaustion without coming round."

"That's a mercy anyway. But I wish I had a Sten gun to use on some of these brutes. They could hardly have treated us worse if they had been trained by the old Gestapo. When we left the Saucer we seem to have jumped out of the frying-pan into the fire. What the hell are we to do?"

"There is nothing that we can do," replied Escobar dully, "except await events."

Their short talk had taken a lot out of them, as they no longer had the oxygen flasks that had been attached to the sacks, and in the rarefied atmosphere they found it difficult to breathe. Every word meant an effort, and their hearts were labouring heavily. Too tired to discuss their miserable plight further, they settled down under their rough coverings, and tried to get to sleep. But they were so uncomfortable on the hard floor, and so cold, they could not get off, and lay there in the depths of depression, wishing they were dead.

Dawn came with unexpected suddenness. One minute only starlight lit the big bare chamber with a chill radiance; two minutes later every crevice in its rock walls could be seen and a slanting shaft of sunlight crossed it from the high window. It roused them to face another day of fearsome possibilities, but as Escobar sat up he said with an attempt at cheerfulness:

"Sunrise and sunset must always be like this on Mars. The refractive medium of the much thicker air on Earth brings some light to us earlier and causes it to linger later. But there are never any clouds to intercept the sunlight here, so at least we can always be certain of fine weather."

Carmen opened her eyes at that moment and said, "That is little comfort if it is always as cold as this."

Kem looked across at her and, with an effort, raised a smile. "So you're awake. How are you feeling?"

"Not too bad, considering what we've been through," she replied, with a sigh. "I've been awake some time, and endeavouring to compose my mind, so that I will be able to meet with some sort of dignity any fresh humiliations they may inflict on us. I'm sorry that I made such an exhibition of myself last night."

"There's no need to apologize. I thought it jolly brave of you to kick and bite that brute the way you did. Anyhow, it wouldn't have been natural in any girl to stand still while she was being stripped."

"A Christian martyr would have done," replied Carmen quietly. "I should at least have tried to show indifference and fortitude, and in future I mean to do my utmost to follow the example set us by the blessed Saints."

"If your religion will enable you to do that," cut in Escobar, "I think that, after all, there must be a lot to be said for it. In any case your determination not to give way to hysteria, in a situation that would terrify most women out of their wits, does you great credit."

It was the first kind remark that he had made to his wife since they had left Earth, and evidently he was conscious of it, as he added, "I suppose you must always have hated me in secret, for the way I blackmailed your father into making you marry me. I thought it possible at the time that you might revenge yourself on me by taking a lover; but I greatly underestimated your strength of character. I had no idea that you were of the stuff of which martyrs are made—or that, if you once got the bit between your teeth, you would not stick at attempting to murder me."

"I've never loved you, Estévan," Carmen said gently, "but on the other hand, I have never hated you either; and I swear to you that I had no wish to harm you. I would do what I did again, if I had to; but I would have done it to anyone who had it in his power, as you had, to stop Kem getting away."

He nodded. "All right. I accept that. Perhaps I should have put the whole thing behind me sooner. Anyhow, we are so utterly cut off from our past now that nothing that happened in it should be allowed to have any bearing on the future. Had this proved a land of milk and honey, and you and Kem were about to take a honeymoon in it, I might still feel resentment—although perhaps illogically. But as things are, it would be selfish of me to play dog in the manger and pretend to any rights over you. I'm afraid we have a hard time ahead of us; so we had better regard ourselves as people who had never met before we were carried off; and if the two of you can comfort one another, that, at least, will be something to the good."

"Thanks," said Kem, a little awkwardly. "That's damn' decent of you."

Carmen, however, shook her head, and replied in a solemn voice, "I am grateful for your forgiveness, Estévan, but, wherever one may go, a sacrament of the Church continues to be binding; so I shall continue to regard myself as your wife."

It was a strange conversation to be held soon after dawn by three people whose nakedness was covered only by some coarse fibre mats, but their circumstances were without parallel in human experience.

For a while, partly owing to their laboured breathing, they fell silent; but not for long. The great door of the chamber, which was made of several thicknesses of wattle-like material, was thrust open, and the two giants who had stripped them the previous night came in. Slung in a sheet between them they carried with ease all the captives' belongings; and as they spread the sheet out on the ground Kem was quick to notice that among them were a few other items.

Ignoring the clothes and Carmen's cases, one of the monsters picked out a flat object, which appeared to consist of a number of tubes of different lengths that had been graduated and welded together, so that they resembled a large "Pipes of Pan". He gave it to Escobar, who examined it a little suspiciously, then shook it. The faint noise resulting gave him the clue: the pipes contained water, and the quantity held varied in accordance with the size of each. Evidently it was a type of flask that had been designed to ensure that its user should practise maxi-mum economy, by opening for each drink only the pipe containing the quantity nearest to his requirements, while those still sealed continued to be protected from evaporation.

When the three captives had drunk from it, the other giant knelt down, opened a great fist, and held out to them a palm full of beans.

Estévan swore, and Kem's round face went red with rage. Having eaten nothing else for seven weeks, the very sight of the beans made him choke with fury. To have had to put up with them, and nothing else, as an emergency ration during the voyage, had been bad enough; but the thought that they might be the Martians' normal and only food, which meant that he would get nothing but beans to eat for the rest of his life, seemed beyond endurance.

It was Carmen who showed good sense by stretching out her hand, taking one and saying, "Come on. I know they are horrid, and we are all sick to death of them; but we must eat to keep up our strength."

A little shamefacedly the two men took their shares of the beans and chewed them glumly. Then the giants pointed to the pile of clothes and indicated that they should get dressed.

Again Carmen set the example. With a glance at the two men she said, "I'm sure you won't mind looking the other way for a minute or two. I don't mind their seeing me. After all, they are only animals. Then she pushed aside the fibre mats in which she had wrapped herself and stood up in all her splendid nudity, like another Aphrodite rising from the waves of Homer's wine-dark sea.

When she had dressed the others followed suit, and as Escobar pulled his clothes on he commented, "You may regard these people as animals, and I think you are right; but they must receive their orders from a far superior type of being. Do you realize that every single thing we brought with us has been most carefully examined during the night?"

It was only then Kem noticed that, although everything appeared to have been returned to them intact, that was not actually the case. The scents and ointments in some of Carmen's bottles were slightly less than when he last remembered seeing them; so evidently samples had been taken of them all. A button was missing from his trousers, one of the metal tags from his shoe-laces had gone, and every single piece of material had had a snippet cut from its edge, presumably for analysis.

"I suppose," he said, "that's why they collected all the gear they could reach through the windows of Carmen's room. Not with any idea of providing us with a few comforts on the voyage, but because they wanted to find out all they could about the things we use."

"Anyhow, thank goodness they've let me have my fur coat back," Carmen put in. "Without it I'd freeze to death."

"It is still early yet," Escobar sought to console her; "but it will warm up soon. Before mid-day you will probably be more comfortable without a coat. I have no idea what part of Mars we are on, or what the season is here now; but owing to the lack of cloud, and thinness of the atmosphere, parts of the planet must have a day-time temperature not far off that of the South of France in summer."

The effort to dress had been considerable and they were breathing heavily again; so they all saved their breath and forbore to comment when the giants fixed transparent protectors made of a mica-like substance over their eyes. The protectors were similar to, but smaller than, the ones the monsters wore themselves, and, as they had supposed, adhered to the forehead and cheeks by suction. They had hoped to be given oxygen flasks again, but now that they had been landed safely and could manage without them it seemed that to expend further oxygen simply to ease their breathing was considered to be an unnecessary extravagance.

Now that they had been watered, fed and equipped, one of the giants pulled open the great door and beckoned them to follow him through it. They had, during the past few hours, been subject to so many fears that they felt fear no longer, but only an intense curiosity, as they supposed that they were at last to be taken before those great intelligences who ordered life on Mars, and so learn some of its secrets.

The two men made way for Carmen and she stepped briskly forward; but her next step faltered, she gave a low cry of alarm, pointed, and stepped back.

Following her pointing finger, they saw at once the thing that had scared her. In the corner near the door, unnoticed by them before, there was either a small animal or a huge insect. It was about four inches long and seemed to be a cross between a bee and a beetle. It had the horns of the latter reaching out from its head, but its body was covered with fur like that of a bumble bee. It made no move to attack them and stood there quite motionless; so, after a moment, Carmen plucked up her courage, and walked past it out into the tunnel.

It was lit only by a dim daylight coming from the partly open doors of a row of rooms, all of which were on the same side of it as the one they had just left. As they followed the giant they took a quick look into several of them while passing, and saw that they differed in no way from that which they had occupied. The walls opposite the doors were broken only by single windows, and all of them were empty except for piles of rough matting littering the bare floors.

A short distance down the tunnel they came to the broader chamber to which the trolley had brought them the previous night. Along its sides a number of similar trolleys were ranged and, taking hold of the front of one, the giant pulled it out from the wall. As he did so they halted, expecting to be lifted on to it; but the second monster, who had been following them, now moved ahead and beckoned them over to an archway on the far side of the chamber from the sleeping rooms. The light there was so faint that they could at first see nothing beyond it;

but as their sight became accustomed to the semi-darkness they made out the features of a broad, lofty passage. On both sides, what at first appeared to be a four-foot-high step ran along the walls, but at intervals there were large holes in its flat top: they were long rows of giant earth closets.

Inconvenient as they were to scramble up and perch upon, the captives were glad to take advantage of them, while the monster who had led them there waited in the archway. When they had done they returned to the big chamber, to find that the trolley now stood in its centre ready to move off. The giant who had pulled it from the walls was squatting on its deck grasping one of the control levers that stuck up from each of its ends. The other lifted them on to it and scrambled up behind them. The driver pushed his lever away from him. Instantly the balls beneath the deck began to revolve and the trolley ran forward.

Through the semi-darkness of the tunnel, far away in the distance, they could see a square of light that could only be its entrance. As they rumbled towards it, Carmen said, "I didn't like the look of that creature at all. I hope we are not going to meet more nasties like that."

"It was probably quite harmless," Kem shrugged. "In an underground place like this it is quite natural that there should be beetles, or something like them; and we must try to get accustomed to the fact that all insects or animals here will be three times the size of anything resembling them on Earth."

Escobar grunted. "You are right there. I only hope that they keep their dogs, if they have such pets, well under control."

The thought of coming face to face with an Alsatian as big as a donkey was certainly frightening, and Kem laughed a little nervously. "I'd rather take a chance on being able to make friends with an outsize dog than find myself cornered by a cat the size of a small panther. Anyhow, we had better keep clear of the deserts if we can. I have never particularly fancied myself unarmed against a lion, and to come round a rock on one as big as an elephant would give me a heart attack."

"I am going to have a heart attack anyway soon, unless I can get some oxygen," Escobar panted. "For anyone not used to it, the strain of living in a place several thousand feet above sea level is bad enough; but it is nothing compared with this."

As the trolley rolled out of the tunnel into bright sunlight they got their first proper sight of a Martian landscape, and it did nothing to lighten their depression; for as far as they could see there stretched an endless plain broken only here and there by a low ridge of reddish rock. On looking back they saw that the place from which they had come was also a flat-topped ridge, and differed from those in the distance only in having a uniform row of windows cut in its one perpendicular side. It was a mile or more in length, so its row of windows seemed to stretch away interminably, and were far too many to count. Apart from them and the tunnel entrance, which pierced a mound at right angles to them, the place had no other features that would have indicated it to be an habitation, and Kem remarked:

"If that is a fair specimen of their architecture, I don't think much of it."

"Be patient," Carmen said. "That warren houses only these brute types. The place to which we are being taken may be very different."

They could see now why the trolley had zigzagged so erratically when bringing them to the giants' warren the previous night. At intervals of every few hundred yards the parched, red-brown earth was severed by great cracks, and some of these dangerous crevasses were a hundred feet long by ten feet wide. Evidently they had been brought across country, for the track on which they were running now was as smooth as a billiard table and, except in places where drifts of sand had blown across it, showed an actual polish which could only have been acquired through constant and prolonged use.

The sky made an inverted bowl of fleckless pale blue, broken only about twelve degrees above one horizon by a sun so glaring that it was difficult to look at, and, nearly overhead, by a single Saucer. They had no means of estimating the Saucer's size or altitude. Owing to the extraordinary clarity of the atmosphere it appeared to be quite low down, but nevertheless, they had a feeling that it was many miles up; and if that were so it must be of the same type as the great 500-foot-wide space-ship that had created such excitement over Fort Knox.

After the trolley had carried them about a mile, Kem asked Escobar, "Have you any idea how this trolley works?"

"By magnetism, I suppose," replied the scientist briefly. "I know of no other force which could keep the balls on which it runs from careering away in all directions instead of remaining in contact with the grooves in its under-surface."

On topping a low ridge a new flat vista opened out, but in the distance a belt of greenery broke the monotony of the arid waste. As they approached they saw that it stretched from horizon to horizon and that here and there groups of figures protruded waist-high above it. The figures were soon distinguishable as giants and the vegetation as row upon row of some plant that was uniform in height, colour and appearance. The track entered the plantation and continued in a dead straight line across it.

"Beans!" exclaimed Kem disgustedly as he got a nearer view of the plants. "Look, there must be thousands of tons here and those awful brutes are harvesting them."

As the trolley passed, the groups of giants paused in their work to stare at its passengers. Many of the monsters were children and females, but the latter were distinguishable from the males only through being somewhat shorter and having breasts the size of pumpkins. Both sexes were naked, bald, wore eye protectors, and had reddish hair flaring out from their nostrils. The children and young ones ranged from six to eighteen feet in height. They could easily be picked out by their skinny, undeveloped figures; but they neither laughed nor frolicked as human youngsters would have done while helping their parents in the fields. Until the trolley approached them, old and young alike seemed to be completely absorbed in their toil.

They were picking the beans into big floppy baskets of the same colour and texture as the mats under which the captives had spent the night, which, as could now be seen, was woven bean fibre. Here and there trolleys, on which the monsters presumably came to work, were parked and some of them were loaded with baskets of beans, but there was no other evidence of mechanization.

At a speed of about forty-five miles an hour the trolley rolled smoothly on through the bean-fields, until its passengers sighted what they took to be a solid barrier some twelve feet in height across the road ahead. As they neared the object at reduced speed they saw that it was a covered way, crossing the road at right angles and extending to either side of it as far as the eye could see. In form it resembled a huge drain-pipe, the lower half of which was buried in the earth, and its convex upper surface shining brightly in the sun. But it did not prove to be a barrier, as it was spanned by a parapetless bridge, the ramps of which were made of the same material, and so not perceptible until the trolley was within a hundred yards of it. As they shot up the short slope and ran down the other side, Escobar murmured:

"That must be one of their canals."

"Or a huge drain," suggested Kem.

"No; they don't seem to have any sewers. That was a canal all right. You may be sure they would have built covers for them all to protect them from the sun, and so reduce to a minimum the loss of water by evaporation."

"I simply can't understand it," Carmen said. "How could anyone even resembling these primitive brutes possibly know about such things, or achieve great feats of engineering like that miles-long pipe, and the Saucers?"

"Why not?" replied her husband. "If you were shown the skeleton of a man like Einstein and another of a cave-dweller I doubt if you would be able to tell which was which. Anyhow, it seems probable that these two are about to deliver us to whoever gave orders that samples of humans should be brought from Earth; so, with luck, we shall soon learn the answer to the riddle."

On the far side of the great conduit there were more bean-fields to a depth of several miles, with more groups of giants labouring tirelessly in them. Carmen waved to some of them, but they made no response and looked up only for a few moments to stare at the trolley as it passed.

Seven or eight minutes later it emerged from the bean-fields and entered another area of desert. Here again there were only harsh brown rock and parched reddish sand, split in places by long, jagged crevasses. There was no form of life to be seen anywhere, and they commented on it; as, even in the bean-fields, they had not seen anything resembling cattle, poultry, a dog or a rabbit, but only a few small birds hovering, on the look-out for dropped beans, over the groups of pickers.

"I wouldn't be surprised if they have exterminated all the other species in order to save the water they would consume," Kem suggested.

"You're probably right," Escobar agreed. "Water is the key to every form of luxury; and as these people are vegetarians, keeping either wild or tame animals alive would certainly be one of them. To manufacture nearly everything also requires the use of water, and there can be no doubt that its scarcity accounts for the exceptionally hard conditions which we have so far had to share with the slave race of Mars."

He had hardly finished speaking before they were confronted with another phenomenon, which was to make life on Mars for them still harder.

CHAPTER XV

THE GREAT REVELATION

ONE moment the desert had been still and empty. The next what looked like a small eddy of sand appeared on the horizon. With incredible swiftness it gained in bulk and height, until it became a huge whirling dust-devil. Towering to the sky, it came swooping down on them with the speed of a race-horse. Before they had time to grasp its full significance the whole desert was in a ferment. Winds of extraordinary force screamed through the wilderness, tearing the loose sand from the ground as they passed and hurling dense clouds of it in all directions. The blue sky turned to yellow; a reddish fog seemed to rise from the earth; the light faded; the sun showed for a few moments as a hard-rimmed orange ball, then was blotted out. Black night descended and, in it, every perception was banished except that of howling wind and stinging, blinding, choking, driven sand.

Escobar shouted a belated warning, then threw himself flat with his arms wrapped round his head. Kem pulled Carmen down beside him, so that her face was pressed to his chest and his own buried in the fur of her coat. The trolley slackened speed but did not stop. Through the raging, pitiless sandstorm it continued on its way.

Kem wondered how its driver could possibly continue to control it;

then he remembered the eye protectors that the giants always wore, and with which they had also provided their captives that morning. Evidently the dust-storms on Mars must be so frequent, and arise with such suddenness, that it had long been customary for everyone to go about in them.

He was now most thankful that he had made no attempt to prevent one being affixed to his own face; as the driven sand penetrated everywhere, and his eyes alone were kept free from it by the transparent mask. The sand stung his hands and forehead, rustled sharply through his windblown hair, was borne on swift gusts up the openings of his trouser legs and down the back of his neck. Firmly as he kept his face pressed to Carmen's coat, it somehow forced a way through the fur into his mouth and nostrils every time he took a breath.

It was as he attempted to spit out the sand that was forming a film upon his teeth, and to clear his nose by snorting down it, that he recalled the fans of hair that sprouted from the giants' nostrils. The reason for them was now obvious. Through the course of many generations Nature must have caused them to develop and become a normal feature of the species, for use as an air filter and protection against suffocation during sandstorms.

When, some ten minutes later, the trolley halted, its passengers were half-choked and half-stupefied. The violence of the storm had lessened slightly, but it was still blowing gustily, and the air continued to be so thick with particles that it was impossible to see more than a few feet in any direction. In consequence, they could form no idea of the outer appearance of the place to which they had been brought.

They knew only that, gasping for breath, they were lifted off the trolley, carried a short distance, and pushed into what seemed to be a hole in another cliff-face. A tunnel lay before them that was lighted at its far end, but it was less than a third of the height and breadth of the tunnel into the giants' warren. They could stand upright in it comfortably, but the two giants, who followed them in, had to crawl down it on their hands and knees.

At the end of the tunnel the air was comparatively clear. Breathing more easily, they looked about them and saw that, unlike the chamber in which they had passed the night, its walls were smooth and highly polished. Urged on by the giant behind them, they turned left along another tunnel that ran at right angles to the one down which they had come. It was from the second tunnel that the light had penetrated, and they now saw that it came from three Thinking Lights that floated some way along it near its ceiling. At intervals on both sides were doorless archways, varying in height from three to five feet, but none of the rooms beyond them was lit; so nothing could be seen of them except a small area of highly polished stone floor just inside each arch.

As they advanced, the Lights flitted through an archway about thirty feet ahead of them, and somewhat larger than any they had yet seen. Proceeding through semi-darkness again, they reached the now glowing arch; then the giant who was crawling along in their rear pushed them through it. Beyond was a long, rather narrow room, about ten feet in height. Its walls and floor were of smooth stone and spotlessly clean. It was lit only by the three Thinking Lights, which now hovered at its far end, and was empty but for one thing; yet that one thing had a curious effect upon them. At the sight of it their hearts beat a little faster from the momentary feeling that they were back on Earth again. Very nearly the whole of the wall at the end of the chamber where the Lights hovered was occupied by what might have been a cinema screen.

They had hardly taken in their surroundings when the three Lights dived down behind the screen, plunging the room in shadow except for a bright band of light which, coming from behind the screen, illuminated the strip of ceiling above it. The screen itself, however, remained unlit. In the meantime, on hands and knees, the two giants had followed their captives through the arch. As the room was nowhere near lofty enough for them to stand upright in it, they squatted down with their backs against the wall and their heads nearly touching the ceiling.

Curiosity having overcome every other feeling, Kem and his companions looked eagerly about them, wondering what was going to happen next. The room in which they were, and the corridors of this underground habitation, being so much nearer to human proportions than those of the giants' warren, they were hoping that some being approaching their own size and mentality would soon appear through the archway; but for several minutes nothing happened at all. Then the screen lit up and, without any preliminaries, a moving picture appeared on it.

The picture was very sharp, in black and white, and had obviously been taken from an aircraft that was circling above the scene portrayed; but it conveyed nothing of any special significance to its audience. Neither, at first, did others which followed it at short intervals. Each of them lasted for only a few minutes, and they were all variations of two themes. Some were of ancient, mud-walled cities; the others of great terrestrial upheavals, such as earthquakes and volcanic eruptions. That they were shots of Earth seemed certain, but there was nothing about them to indicate any recognizable part of it. A few were momentarily exciting, as they combined the two themes: showing densely populated metropolises dissolving into ruin through fire and flood, or small ships being whirled about, then engulfed by great tidal waves; but none of them lasted long enough to tell a story.

This strange, disjointed travelogue had been proceeding for over half an hour when a shot was shown of a flat-topped pyramid with a broad ramp running round it from its base to its summit. Pointing at it Kem said, "I've seen pictures like that of the star-gazing towers built by the Chaldeans."

Escobar nodded. "And that's probably what it is. It seems fantastic, but I believe all these shots were taken of actual happenings on earth that occurred thousands of years ago."

After a scene of a tropical island fringed with palm trees suddenly being submerged in a boiling, steaming sea, his belief was confirmed. The shot that followed was unquestionably of the Great Pyramid, for the Sphinx could be seen nearby.

From that point their interest quickened, as they guessed then that they were being shown a potted history of the development of civilization on Earth, interspersed with visible records of the great calamities that had befallen its peoples. They recognized Alexandria as it must have been in its heyday by the Pharaohs and Lake Meotis, and Athens crowned by her Acropolis. Shots that they thought were probably of Carthage and Syracuse followed, then one that Escobar identified by the Forum, the Capitol and the splendid buildings on the Palatine Hill as the Rome of the Caesars. Next came Vesuvius in eruption, with the lava pouring down its sides to engulf the terror-stricken people of Herculaneum, who could be seen as tiny dots fleeing from it. Pompeii was also shown, but showers of floating ashes obscured the final phase of its destruction.

From time to time the series moved to Central America or the Far East, to show the great temples of the Incas, the pyramids of the Aztecs, the Boro Budur in Java and the triumphs of architecture achieved during the long-dead civilization that had produced the Angkor Vat in Cambodia.

They were brought back to mediæval Paris, renaissance Venice, and London being consumed by the Great Fire. There were more shots of tidal waves and eruptions, apparently in Asia, Africa and America, then one that Escobar thought must be of the terrible earthquake that destroyed half Lisbon in 1755.

So fascinated were they by watching this extraordinary review that they gave no thought to time, but it had been going on for the best part of three hours when pictures taken in comparatively modern times began to be shown. The ascent of a balloon—they thought from Paris about the time of the Revolution—marked the beginning of a new era. There were others, including one from Hyde Park in which the Crystal Palace erected there for the great exhibition of 1851 could be seen. A shot of New York, showing its first skyscrapers, was followed by a close-up of an early dirigible. After the San Francisco earthquake came various types of airships and the first aeroplanes.

From then on progress in aeronautics became the main theme. Zeppelins had been recorded flying over their great base on Lake Geneva, and the smoke of a battle in the first World War with aeroplanes fighting above it. The types of airliner used in the nineteen-twenties and -thirties

116

followed, then the bombing of Rotterdam by the Germans in 1940. Unknown to its personnel, the armada that had sailed from Britain to North Africa had been photographed more clearly than was yet possible with lenses made on earth; and, as though moving with them, the little audience saw the flying bombs falling on London.

None of them had spoken for a long time when Escobar exclaimed, "*Nom de Dios!* That's Peenemünde, where I worked for the Germans during the War," and from a group of carefully camouflaged buildings they saw an experimental long-range rocket go hurtling up into the stratosphere.

The next shot was of the devastation caused at Hiroshima by the first Atom bomb. Apparently no Martians had been about when it was dropped, but their cameras had caught the second one, at Nagasaki, and registered from various angles the huge mushroom of dirt and debris it had thrown up. They had also been present at Bikini, and had since secured photographs of the principal rocket-testing grounds, although there was nothing to show which were in the United States and which in Russia, or elsewhere.

For another ten minutes the audience was shown the latest types of aircraft, both civil and military, and a number of the latter fighting over Korea. Then, for them, the film came nearer home. A distant view of Escobar's plant dissolved into a close-up. Next moment all three of them gasped. By some scientific wizardry a photograph had been taken through the roof of one of the buildings. They were looking down into Escobar's private laboratory; and there he was in it, fingering one point of his upturned moustache as he studied a graph pinned to the wall.

On that the show ended, although it was not to be the last of their surprises for that day.

Kem was the first to speak, and he grinned at the others. "Well! Even if it was a documentary, I've never seen a better five bobs' worth."

"I think the way these people have been spying on us is disgusting," Carmen declared emphatically.

"You mean the close-up. I don't see anything so terrible about that." Kem's grin broadened. "Of course, it could have been a bit embarrassing if Estévan had been playing tag with a neat little number in blonde secretaries. Anyhow, the lens they used must be a wonderful piece of magic to have taken that interior shot from somewhere up in the sky."

"Such an invention would have been easy to perfect by people so far advanced in science as these," Escobar told him. "It is many years since our own scientists first discovered how to photograph objects through solids. Ordinary X-rays of the human body pioneered the way, and now we can take photographs through sheet steel. Of course, we cannot yet get plates that would convey anything to anybody except experts; but the achievement of perfect clarity can only be a matter of experiment and time. As my laboratory is on the top storey of the building there would have been no complications, and it would have been simple for them to film me at work through the roof."

"But the only afternoon a Flying Saucer came over your plant you weren't there. I had left you tied up, miles away in the bush."

"Oh, the film must have been taken at some other time; perhaps weeks before we were kidnapped. It doesn't follow that the Saucer would have had to come down low enough for us to see it when the photographs were taken. I have no doubt that they possess telescopic lenses of tremendous power."

"I see!" Kem grinned mischievously again. "I only wish I had had a camera like that when I was at my old job. I would have got some sporting R.A.F. type to fly me over the Kremlin."

"I thought the early pictures—I mean the ones they showed us after the first half-hour—tremendously interesting," Carmen remarked.

"Yes," her husband agreed. "I would like to have seen a lot more of early Egypt, Greece and Rome, and Europe during the Middle Ages."

"But what was the object of the operation?" Kem asked. "That's what I want to know."

"Presumably to inform us that they have been watching our world for thousands of years, and know more about the development of civilization on Earth than we do ourselves."

"I don't think they are interested in our civilization so much as in the great upheavals to which Earth is subject, and the development of modern weapons."

"Given very powerful telescopes their attention would naturally be caught by any great disturbances, either natural or artificial; so it follows that most of their films would be records of eruptions or wars—particularly our more recent wars in which great quantities of high explosives have been used."

"Yes, but what is giving us this show leading up to?"

Neither Escobar nor Carmen could suggest an answer to that; but Kem was not to wait very long before receiving one.

After they had been standing there for a few more minutes, one of the giants crawled out into the passage and beckoned them to follow. Twenty yards further along it he wriggled through another arch. The place beyond was in only semi-darkness and as they peered ahead over his massive shoulders they caught a glimpse of one of the Thinking Lights slowly circling about eight feet up from the floor. With a downward swoop it passed out of sight behind the giant's body; then the steady glow it had given was suddenly replaced by a much brighter light, but one that constantly flickered as though it came from a powerful electric bulb that had a faulty connection.

Entering the room they saw that its floor and walls were of plain polished stone, but that, unlike the little cinema, it was furnished with a great variety of familiar objects. There was an armchair and three upright ones, two side-tables, a desk, a filing cabinet and, along one wall, a bench with scales, phials, retorts and other scientific impedimenta set out on it; and the brilliant flickering light came from bulbs on the desk and near the ceiling.

Throwing up his hands, Escobar gasped, "But this is my room at the plant! All the things in it, except that machine over there, are replicas of the things in my laboratory."

The others saw at once that, although the furniture appeared to be made of plastic instead of wood and leather and many of the items were unusual in texture and colour, in size and shape they were exact duplicates of those they had seen on the screen ten minutes earlier.

The one exception was a squat, square machine made of some transparent substance through which an incredibly complex array of wires, levers, pipes and pistons could be seen. It stood near to the desk. As they were looking at it two creatures similar to the four-inch long bee-like beetle they had seen when leaving their cell that morning flew out from behind the armchair and alighted on its top.

Next moment the machine began to make a whirring noise and many of the parts inside it became blurred through intense activity. But they were not looking at the whirring machinery. They could hardly believe their eyes; yet they knew that they had not imagined what they had seen. One of the big insects had lifted its right horn, clipped with the claw at the end of it a tiny lever and, by depressing the lever, set the machine in motion.

The implications of the movement were tremendous. In a flash it revealed to all three of them that no race resembling the giants, but of greater intelligence, had designed the Saucers and were responsible for the film of progress on Earth. The brains behind those great achievements were those of the insects, who in darkness became the Thinking Lights. Incredible as it at first appeared, the fact was inescapable. These bee-beetles must be the masters of all life on Mars.

CHAPTER XVI

THE MASTERS OF A WORLD

FOR a few moments their thoughts were chaotic. All through their uneasy, monotonous, seven-week journey in the Saucer; all through the trials, tribulations and anxieties of the past twelve hours, they had hoped to find on Mars beings with whom they could communicate. Somehow, it had seemed impossible to believe that any form of brain capable of producing such scientific wonders could be housed in a body totally unlike that of man. The near-human appearance of the giants had seemed a definite confirmation that life on Mars had developed very much as on Earth. Since they were so mentally under-developed and obviously acted under instructions, it had been logical to assume that they received their orders from a race physically like themselves, but far superior in all other respects.

How greatly the captives had counted on that, and being able to ensure reasonable treatment by conveying their thoughts, they realized only now that they found themselves at the mercy of insects. The disappointment was so bitter that they felt faint and sick. Even their amazement was submerged in frantic half-formed speculations about the treatment they would receive from creatures so utterly unlike themselves; possessing intelligence far greater than their own, yet of a kind that might be utterly soulless.

In that awful moment they looked at one another, and each guessed that the others were thinking much the same thing; but none of them spoke. Before they had a chance to get their thoughts into any kind of order their attention became riveted by a new development. The whirring machine gave a loud click, then began to talk.

For a moment they grasped only that it was speaking in Spanish. New hope suddenly surged up in all of them. If the bee-beetles could understand human languages there was still a chance that things might not turn out so badly. They could be asked to provide for their captives some of the comforts that were enjoyed on Earth; better quarters, more water, and, if it were obtainable on Mars, food that would relieve the monotony of those dreary beans. Perhaps, too, when they had acquired all the information about Earth that their captives could give them, they might be persuaded to send them back.

Eagerly, they concentrated on what the machine was saying, but after a few moments disappointment showed in all their faces. It was not addressing them personally, and its theme appeared to be as irrelevant as had been the first film. It was an extract from a broadcast on knitting for young mothers. Only a few minutes of it were given, then the machine switched to a talk in French on Renaissance architecture.

Carmen cut in, her voice low but tense, "Did you . . . did I really see that creature set the machine going; or was it a trick of my imagination?"

To have asked the question at the time had not even occurred to her, because she was so positive of what she had seen. She asked it now only because it seemed so incredible, but without any real hope of reprieve from this new twist of the nightmare that they were actually living.

"If it was a trick, my imagination played me the same one," Escobar muttered glumly. Kem, too, confirmed her fears, but less directly, by whispering, "Anyhow, they don't seem hostile."

The French voice was cut short in the middle of a sentence and, after an interval of a few seconds, replaced by an English one reading poetry. There followed portions of broadcasts, apparently selected quite arbitrarily, in German, Italian, Dutch and several other languages, including one that Escobar said was Russian. As far as they were understandable by the captives, none of them had any bearing on the situation; but they continued to listen in the hope that, like the film series, they would later begin to make sense. In that they were disappointed. After the machine had been working for a little over half an hour it gave a louder click than usual and fell silent.

"Well; what do you make of that?" asked Kem.

"Nothing," replied Escobar, "except that these amazing insects wish to show us that they have means of recording human speech as well as filming human activities."

"I'm not sure you're right there. It may be only that they are in radio touch with Earth, and simply transmitted bits of the talks that are being given at the moment."

"I don't think so. To tune in to Earth would be pointless unless they were accustomed to do so. It seems more probable that those were recordings of broadcasts made some time back. In either case such a collection of extracts would only have been given in order to convey to us that they understand a number of Earth languages."

"I hope to God you're right. Anyhow, we'll soon put it to the test." Kem took a pace forward and addressed the two insects in English.

"Er . . . excuse me; we'd like to introduce ourselves. I'm Kempton Lincoln and my friends are Colonel and Madame Estévan Escobar. We fully realize that we are in your power; but all the same we feel that we are entitled to claim the honours of war. I mean, the furniture in this room shows that you can make the sort of things we are used to; so can't you provide us with beds and baths and a change of food from those awful beans?"

While he was speaking he was conscious of an urge to burst into hysterical laughter. The whole situation was so fantastically unreal. It could not happen outside a fairy story. Into his mind there flashed one of the illustrations from Kathleen Nesbit's delightful book, *Five Children and It*. He could see Cyril, Anthea and the others, in the gravel pit, grouped round the fat, furry, bewhiskered, antenna-eyed sand-fairy, just as the ill-tempered little beast was about to blow itself out and give them their daily wish—to "be beautiful as the day" or "have wings" or something like that.

The two bee-beetles remained perched on top of their machine and seemed to be ragarding him speculatively; but they made no sound or movement, much less did they blow themselves out and produce, like the Djin from *The Arabian Nights*, a seven-course dinner.

"It is no use expecting them to reply," said Escobar a little testily.

"The odds against their having developed human vocal cords as well as phenomenal brains puts that out of the question. If they do understand you the most likely way for them to show it is by making a drawing of some kind."

Carmen turned quickly towards him. "We have never seen them do that with the giants, and they must have some way of giving them their orders."

"It is possible that they have developed some form of thought transference," Escobar conceded.

At that moment Kem was conscious of an impulse to walk over to the long bench on which the scientific instruments were laid out. As he would not have known what to do with any of them, he dismissed it as one of those casual thoughts which are apt to cross the mind for no apparent reason; yet he had hardly done so when he saw Carmen take a step in that direction and Escobar turn to follow her.

"Stop!" he cried. "Stop!"

They halted and looked at him in surprise, as he added, "What were you going to do over there?"

"Er . . . I don't quite know," Carmen answered vaguely; but Escobar replied more definitely, "It suddenly occurred to me to examine some of the instruments they have made, to see how exactly they have succeeded in copying the detail."

Kem nodded. "I thought as much. I felt an impulse to go over there, too. It looks as if you were right about these creatures possessing telepathic powers; but we mustn't let them get a hold on us. I've often used a mild form of telepathy myself when doing conjuring tricks. All conjurers do, as a means of influencing people to take the card they wish; and it is well known that the more often persons allow themselves to be directed that way the easier it becomes to direct them. If we dig our toes in now we may remain immune; if we don't they may make us do all sorts of things in the future that we should hate having to do."

For some minutes there ensued a silent battle of wills; but forewarned is forearmed, and the captives now found little difficulty in resisting the insistent thoughts that impelled them towards the bench.

When they had shown quite clearly that they had no intention of moving, the two bee-beetles stopped staring at them and began to fuss a little and wave their claws as though consulting together. Then one of them lifted his right pincher, grasped another of the tiny levers and depressed it. Again the machine began to whirr, and through its transparent surface the complicated array of small parts could be seen working at frantic speed.

A sonorous snore from behind Kem caused him to glance over his shoulder. One of the giants was leaning back against the wall with his toothless mouth open, fast asleep; the other had his chin on his chest and was obviously dozing. Their state made it clearer than ever that they were not playing any part in the proceedings, or even possessed sufficient intelligence to take an interest in them.

The machine spoke again. It said clearly in Spanish, "Music while you work," then broke into a sultry rumba.

"So that's the idea," smiled Escobar. "They have brought us here because they want to be shown some of the scientific processes we employ on Earth."

"Then they are going to be unlucky," said Kem, "unless they are prepared to treat us decently. Now we have something to bargain with we may be able to get somewhere." He then proceeded to point first at the bench, then at his mouth.

One of the insects stopped the machine; the other flew across the room and buzzed once round the heads of the giants. They woke with a start and the monster nearer the archway wriggled out through it. Two minutes later he returned and, crawling across the floor, extended a huge hand to Kem, in the palm of which were a few beans.

Kem's fury was such that, regardless of possible consequences, he gave the great hand a swipe that sent the beans flying all over the floor. For a second he held his breath, fearing that the monster would seize and shake him; but the giant only looked surprised and set about collecting the spilled beans. When he had finished, as if he had received a silent order, he crawled out of the room again, evidently to return the precious beans to store.

Meanwhile, the bee-beetles who controlled the machine again pressed the lever; again the machine whirred and the words came, "Music while you work," followed by the rumba.

"Come on!" said Kem to Carmen; and, taking hold of her, he whirled her round in the first steps of the dance.

"Stop!" she protested. "Are you crazy?"

"No, just showing them what the music was really meant for, that's all."

"But to start dancing in such a situation is absolutely ludicrous. Besides, they may become angry if they think we are making a mock of them."

"Never mind. Let's risk it. We've got to stand up to the little devils. It's our only chance of forcing them to give us a decent deal."

The floor was so smooth that it was easy to dance on, and they executed a few figures with considerable grace; then the music was suddenly cut off.

After a short pause the bee-beetle clipped and depressed another lever. Still speaking in Spanish, the machine said, "Shoulder arms! Quick march!"

They looked at it and at one another, but did nothing. The sharp command was repeated three times; then, as they still remained motionless, the bee-beetle tried several other lines. In turn the machine said, "Run! I'll race you! Quick now! Get a move on! Get going!"

That, apparently, was the end of its repertoire, as the insect kept the last little lever pressed down and it reiterated over and over again, "Get going! Get going! Get going!"

Suddenly the second bee-beetle flew straight at them. They all ducked, fearing that it might have a powerful sting and meant to use it; but, having circled their heads, it streaked off to the laboratory bench, then back again, and so to and fro several times. It was soon clear that it had no intention of attacking them, but by its example was endeavouring to get them to follow it to the bench.

"It's no good!" Kem shouted, drowning the impersonal voice from the machine. "We're on strike! We're not going to lift a finger until you provide us with decent quarters and decent food."

Escobar shook his head. "It is useless to yell at them. I am sure they can't understand a word you are saying."

"All right," Kem retorted. "Let's sit down, then. That should show them we don't mean to give way. Suiting the action to the word, he sat down on the nearest chair, and the others followed his example.

After a few minutes the sit-down strike took due effect. The flying bee-beetle ceased to buzz angrily back and forth, and his companion shut off the machine. The two giants roused from their lethargy; one of them crawled out of the room and the other beckoned to the captives to follow. Evidently their first audience with the masters of Mars was over. Kem, who was last out, much elated to feel that his party had held their own, turned in the archway to give a derisive grin and make Churchill's sign of victory.

Having walked down the passages by which they had come in, they found that the entrance to the place was a hole about six feet from the ground in a low cliff-face. The giant who had preceded them lifted them down and on to the trolley, which was waiting there unattended; then the other took one of its control levers and set it in motion.

All trace of the sandstorm had disappeared, so as they moved off they could see the outside of the warren in which they had been. Although their hopes that the inventors of the Flying Saucers might live in marble palaces surrounded by gracious gardens had been shattered hours ago, it still seemed reasonable to expect that the exterior of their habitation would show some evidence of their achievements, perhaps in the form of carved windows and doorways, such as those that have for centuries delighted travellers to the rose-red rock-dwellers' city of Petra; but there was nothing of the kind.

On the contrary, the closest scrutiny of the long, twenty-foot-high cliff would not have revealed a single trace of the marvels within. The entrance used by the captives appeared to be no more than a jagged hole that might lead to a small cave. It was the only one of its size and had no doubt been made just large enough for the giants to enter when they were required to render their masters some service inside. All the other entrances, of which there were a number dotted inconspicuously about, were clefts or holes, in no case exceeding a few inches in width; but that they were entrances was shown by the fact that here and there some of the big insects were descending from the sky to land at them, or coming out to fly busily off at a high speed.

The cliff-face formed the only perpendicular side of a shallow depression in the desert, and they had been carried little more than a hundred yards up a gentle slope before it faded into the reddish-brown landscape behind them. As the trolley breasted the low crest they could see the bean-fields in the far distance across a great waste of sand, and, although they had been underground for several hours, the position of the sun in the heavens informed them that it could not be much past noon.

Carmen looked up at the sky and said, "We seem to have been in that place so long that I should not have been surprised to find it night on coming out."

"It seemed longer than it was because our minds had to grapple with so many startling new ideas," Escobar told her.

Kem grinned. "Anyhow, it's one up to us that those dictatorial little brutes should have thrown their hand in by mid-day. Look! There are the bean-fields. We are being taken back to barracks."

"That is a much more appropriate name for the giants' habitation than 'warren'," commented Escobar. "Although I am not sure that 'stable' would not be better still. It is clear now that they are not even a sub-race, as we at first supposed. In the Martian hierarchy they are definitely animals, and made use of only because they possess great strength coupled with a limited degree of intelligence and memory. They are probably regarded by the bee-beetles in very much the same way as man regards the trained elephants of India."

"That's about it," Kem agreed. "They are simply used for the heavy work. No doubt earlier generations of them were used to dig the canals, and they are still employed on mining and handling this foolproof form of transport, as well as in cultivating the beans."

"What about the Saucers, though?" Carmen enquired. "These great clumsy brutes could not possibly have made such wonderful pieces of mechanism, even under instruction. I know that elephants have been used to help build houses, but no amount of teaching would enable them to put together the parts of a motor-car engine."

"No, of course not. The bee-beetles must carry out all work of that kind themselves."

"How could four-inch-long insects possibly build flying-machines larger than anything we have on Earth?"

"Why not, when seventy-inch-tall men have succeeded in building great liners like the *Queen Mary*?"

"You are quite right there," Escobar put in. "And when one comes to think of it, they possess all the essentials that have given man his dominant position among the animals. Their heads are as large as ours in proportion to their bodies. Flight gives them a range of vision much greater than our own, with the ability to escape from their larger enemies; and having pincers on the ends of their horns enables them to grip things, just as we do with our fingers and thumbs."

As he finished speaking they entered the bean-fields. The sun blazed down mercilessly from a cloudless sky, but the families of giants were still working there. They now resembled groups of satyrs and bacchantes, as most of them were wearing wreaths of bean leaves to protect their bald heads; but they were still naked and Carmen commented that she wondered that they did not get badly sunburnt.

Escobar shrugged. "It can be as hot as this only for an hour or two in the middle of the day, and we know how tough their skins are. Elephants never get sunburnt, yet they are often made to work for long hours in much greater heats than this with no coverings except a head-cloth."

As they progressed through the bean-fields they noticed again the little black objects hovering over the giants' heads that in the morning they had taken for small birds; now they saw that they were really bee-beetles, and evidently playing the part of overseers keeping their gangs of big slaves hard at work. After remarking on this they fell silent, as they still found talking most laborious, and they did not speak again until they reached the barracks. There, the two giants took them to the room they had occupied the night before and left them to their own devices.

For a while they employed themselves in sorting out the things that had been brought back to them in the morning, and using such items as were suitable, together with some of the bean-fibre mats, to make up three beds. When they had done, Escobar, who had reset his watch approximately by the sun, said that it could not yet be much after two o'clock; so, unless they were sent for again, they had the whole afternoon as well as the night before them.

On the previous night they had naturally supposed themselves to be locked in their cell, but when the giants had come for them soon after dawn they had all noticed that the great door was not made of wood or any sort of metal and had a rough surface which made it look like a huge hurdle. Closer examination now disclosed that it consisted of several layers of coarse basketwork woven out of the thickest bean-stalks. Moreover, it had no lock and was secured only by a staple on its outer side. The staple could be seen through a two-inch gap, and by tapping it from underneath with the handle of Carmen's mirror Kem succeeded in knocking it out. A strong pull was then all that was needed to make the massive sheet of basket work swing inward on its creaking hinges.

Smiling over his shoulder at the others, he said, "Nothing venture, nothing win. Are you game to risk a spot of trouble by doing a little exploring?"

"Short of using physical violence they can't treat us much worse than we are being treated already," Carmen replied; and with Escobar behind her she followed Kem out into the lofty tunnel.

The light there was dim, but just sufficient for them to see by. Tiptoeing along to the next doorway, they peered through the crack down its side, and saw that it gave on to a room similar to the one they had left. In it two giants were sitting, quite motionless, with their backs against a wall.

When they had drawn back, Kem whispered, "I think they are our guards; but one can't be certain as there is so little to distinguish these great oafs from one another."

The next chamber into which they peeped was similar, but empty; and so it proved all along the row until they reached the entrance to the tunnel. As they emerged into the sunshine Escobar said:

"It looks as if you were right about the two we saw. They have probably been given the day off to look after us. Otherwise, it seems that the whole of this miserable race—men, women and children—are compelled to spend their days working in the bean-fields."

"They must have crèches for the little ones," Carmen objected.

Her husband shook his head. "To think of these people as even remotely human is to foster misleading ideas. What we learned this morning put an end to any lingering doubts about that. They are as far removed from the most advanced form of life on Mars as cattle are from men, and their resemblance to humans can be no more than accidental. If they were covered in fur, instead of having hide-like skins, and went about on all fours, we should have regarded them from the beginning as a species of huge ape; and baboons don't run crèches; wherever they go they take their young with them."

"I certainly saw some quite small ones crawling about among the bean-stalks," Kem said thoughtfully. "And, of course, their babies must be nearly as big as we are, which would give the impression that they are much older than they are in fact. But I think they are a good bit more intelligent than any of our apes."

"Than wild apes perhaps; but one could train a chimpanzee to do most of the things they do, and if a dog had hands its quicker mind would make it superior to them. As far as we know they are the only type of animal remaining on Mars, and it is by no means improbable that they owe their survival to having been chosen as the most suitable to domesticate. Given a race of great apes and hundreds of generations in which to train them, it should not have been difficult to teach them to perform all sorts of simple services in return for regular food and protection from their natural enemies. That, I am now convinced, accounts for both the activities and limitations of the giants. They are nothing more or less than highly trained animals."

While they had been talking they had walked a little way down the smoothly polished road, but the dreary sameness of the arid landscape on every side offered no temptation to proceed further; so they sat down on a sand-bank and, between intervals for rest necessitated by the effort of breathing, spent the next two hours or so discussing their extraordinary experiences of that morning.

When they had come out from the bee-beetles' hive the Saucer they had seen on their way there, or another like it, had still been visible in the sky, but low down on the western horizon. Since then it had climbed to the zenith and now, without the least deviation from a straight path, it was sinking at a slow, even pace towards the east. In the meantime another, smaller or more distant, Saucer had appeared above the eastern horizon and, at an even slower pace, was gradually mounting the sky.

As the afternoon advanced the temperature dropped with a swiftness they found surprising; but, as the only alternative to remaining where they were was a return to their cheerless cell, the increasing chill alone would not have driven them in before sunset. It was the sight of a distant duststorm that made them spring to their feet and run for cover in the tunnel. By the time they reached it the wind was already howling like ten thousand devils and the clouds of driven sand stinging their hands and faces. A few yards down the tunnel the air was still clear, so they were able to gasp it in; but running several hundred yards in that rarefied atmosphere had proved a frightful strain, and, having staggered back to their cell, they practically collapsed there.

It was the best part of an hour before they were fully recovered and soon afterwards the giants came in to give them their evening ration of water and beans. While they were doing so, Kem remarked:

"For future convenience we may as well christen these two. Unless anyone has a better idea, I suggest we call the chap with the birthmark Gog II and his pal Magog II."

As neither Carmen nor Escobar could think of any other famous giants, they agreed, and Carmen said, "That they really are animals makes it more awful, in a way, that those callous little insects should have left our original Gog and Magog to burn to death in the Saucer."

"I shouldn't think they had much option," Escobar shrugged, "if, as it is reasonable to suppose, they had decided that they dared not let the Saucer land from fear that it would form a centre of infection."

"They saved their own skins all right, though," Kem said quickly. "Of course, none of us realized what the Thinking Lights were then; but the bevy of them that appeared above the Saucer just after the fire in it started must have been its crew leaving the sinking ship."

"I expect they had themselves decontaminated by the same process as was used on us. But I don't see how they could have got Gog and Magog out of the Saucer without landing it, owing to their size."

"No; we agreed on that last night. It's queer, though, to think that for all those weeks a dozen or so of the bee-beetles must have been living within a few feet of us, and that we never even saw a sign of them."

"Yes, you did. Those shadows you saw moving about inside the lighted control tower, while the Saucer was still in the darkness of night on Earth, must have been cast by the heads of the bee-beetle crew as they busied themselves with the take-off."

"True; I'd forgotten that. I wonder what enables the little brutes to light themselves up at night. D'you think it is natural, or some invention that they carry about with them?"

"I should say the odds are greatly in favour of their possessing luminous organs similar to our fire-flies. They, too, are a species of beetle, and their luminosity comes from layers of cells mainly situated in the base of the abdomen."

"Maybe you're right; but, if so, the light these creatures give out must be far more powerful, because one can see them from quite a long way off."

"For a fire-fly's size its light is remarkably bright," Carmen put in. "At home the peasants often catch a few, then put them in a fine mesh wire cage and use it as a lantern, to save the expense of burning their oil-lamps."

"And," Escobar added, "these insects must be about a hundred times the size of a fire-fly."

Just then daylight in the lofty, cell-like chamber began to fade. With the same suddenness as dawn, twilight came and went; two minutes later darkness hid them from one another, until their eyes became accustomed to a light which seemed to have a much whiter quality than that which had lit the window high up in the wall all through the previous night.

Noticing it, Escobar remarked, "This evening, one or both of Mars' moons must be up."

"How queer it must seem to see two moons in the same sky," Carmen said. "Are they as big as ours?"

"Oh no, infinitely smaller. In fact, they are so small that their existence was not even suspected till 1877. But whereas our Moon is nearly a quarter of a million miles from Earth, Mars' moons are quite close to her, so they must look fairly large from her surface. One is called Phobos and the other Deimos."

"Those are the Latin words for Fear and Dread, aren't they?"

"Yes; they were named so as attendants on Mars—the God of War."

"And very suitably named, too," put in Kem. "But tell us about them. Do they go round and round together like Castor and Pollux?"

"No. Their behaviour is about as different as that of two moons could be. Phobos moves so quickly that she appears to break the universal law by rising in the west and setting in the east. That is because she goes round the planet faster than the planet turns upon herself. Her circuit takes her only seven hours and thirty-nine minutes, so she makes it a little over three times a day. Deimos, on the other hand, takes thirty hours and eighteen minutes to complete her circuit; so they can be seen at the same time at most only every other night, and then only for an hour or two when Phobos is near the western or eastern horizon, because she is less than 6,000 miles away, and therefore so near that she is eclipsed by Mars' shadow for the greater part of each night. Deimos is a bit over 14,000 miles off, so can be seen for longer; but both her distance and size would make her appear much smaller, as she has a diameter of only five miles."

"How big is Phobos?"

"Her diameter is ten miles. But the diameters of both are only guess-work, as from Earth they can be seen only as tiny points of light. They are, too, regarded as something of a mystery by our astronomers, because the complete absence of volcanoes on Mars would suggest that she is not the type of planet ever to have thrown out any moons at all, and neither of them shares her red tint; so they may be captured asteroids, but there are also strong arguments against that."

They now fell silent. The rough couches they had made up enabled them to settle down a little, if not much, more comfortably than had been possible the night before; and as, during the past twenty-four hours, they had been through more exhausting experiences than any they had ever met with in their lives, they soon dropped into dreamless sleep.

Dawn woke them, and shortly afterwards Gog II and Magog II appeared. They brought with them the usual ration of water, but to the captives' great surprise, no issue of beans. In spite of the fact that they intensely resented the deadly monotony of having nothing to eat but raw beans twice a day, they no longer complained on that account and had become accustomed to chew them with Spartan indifference. To be suddenly deprived of them now, either by design or oversight, seemed to justify the most violent protest. They made it, pointing at their open mouths, and shouting for beans with an insistence that, had they wit-nessed it in themselves a few weeks earlier, they would have taken for certain signs of madness. The fuss they created was in vain; either the giants could not or would not understand them. Angry and still break-fastless, they were put upon the trolley, which ran out of the tunnel and headed in the direction it had taken the previous day.

On reaching the canal zone, the now familiar sight of the giants picking beans caused them to realize that they were actually hungry; and had the trolley not been moving too fast they would have jumped off it with the idea of snatching a few beans before they could be recap-tured. But they were soon given something else to think about. They had left the fields barely a mile behind when they were caught in another duststorm. This time, however, it did not prove such a severe ordeal, as, before leaving their cell, they had taken precautions against such a possibility by bringing with them two silk scarves and a mantilla belonging to Carmen. Wrapping these round their heads, they huddled together and reached the cliff-face in which lay the bee-beetles' hive, breathless but still fully conscious.

With Gog crawling before them and Magog behind, they were taken to the room in which they had been shown the pictorial record of historical happenings on Earth. Two Thinking Lights had lit them down the inner passage, and now the captives knew what they were it was easy to recognize them at close quarters as large insects. The black blobs that Kem had taken for instrument boxes were their heads, and the things he had thought to be dangling wires were their legs. As on the previous day, they disappeared behind the screen and, after a few moments, a new series of short films was shown.

Kem and Carmen found them of little interest as they portrayed only factories and machines; but Escobar recognized some of them, and said that they were shots of atomic plants in various countries. All had been taken from the air and a few were close-ups of interiors photographed through roofs, as had been done in the case of his own laboratory. The series ended with the repeat of the shot showing the explosion of the Atom bomb on Bikini atoll.

The showing lasted for about an hour, then they were taken into the further room. It was evident that the bee-beetles needed only their own light, and that was, too, ample for the humans to see by; but here, seemingly to strengthen Escobar's impression that he was in his own room, the imitation electric lights flickered brilliantly, so the incandescence of the insects was no longer apparent. No change had been made there, but there were now a dozen or more bee-beetles in it. Two of them sat on the top of the talking machine; the rest were clustered on one of the side-tables, on which reposed a flat, square, plastic box that had not been there the day before. The talking machine whirred and the voice said, "Music while you work!" Then a jazz number began.

Kem glanced at Escobar. "You know what they're after, don't you?"

Escobar nodded. "Yes; the films we've just seen make that quite clear now. These clever insects have found out that we are developing atomic power on Earth; but they have not yet discovered how to make a fission bomb themselves, and they want me to make one for them."

"That's it; but it would be absolutely criminal to let them in on a secret like that."

As they made no move towards the bench the music was suddenly cut off. One of the bee-beetles on the small table touched the plastic box and its lid sprang open. In it there was a small heap of beans.

Stepping forward Kem stretched out his hand to take one. Before he could do so all except one of the bevy of insects rose and came buzzing at his head in an angry cloud. Fearing that they might sting him to death, he put up his hands to fend them off and swiftly drew back. At the same moment the bee-beetle who had remained on the table touched a hidden spring in the box, and its lid snapped shut.

Apparently satisfied at having driven him off, the other insects ceased to buzz round Kem's head and settled again on the table. The machine whirred again and its voice came sharply, "Get going! Get going! Get going!"

With a horrified glance at the others Kem exclaimed, "God help us! These little brutes have got us in a cleft stick. Either we'll have to do as they wish, or they mean to starve us to death."

CHAPTER XVII

THE DRONES

THERE could be little doubt that Kem was right. They were entirely at the mercy of their captors, so must do what was required of them, or starve.

Now they realized, too, that they had not been kidnapped at random, simply because the masters of Mars wanted to examine a few human beings at close quarters. They must have deliberately selected Escobar after having watched him at work in his laboratory. It was his bedroom, as well as Carmen's, to which they had come in the dead of night, and evidently they had chosen the time and place as offering the easiest prospects of capturing him. It seemed probable that the giants who had done the job were too stupid to take in detailed instructions, so had simply been ordered to carry off any humans they found in the room. In any case they would have expected Carmen to be with him, and planned to take her to prevent her giving an alarm before they could get him to the Saucer; that Kem had been roped in, too, must have been purely accidental.

But the fact remained. Escobar had been brought to Mars because its rulers wanted him to show them how to make an Atom bomb; and now that the captives were really beginning to feel hungry the beans in the fast-shut box seemed to them as desirable as Tournedo Rossini or a Lobster Cardinal. They looked at one another in consternation; then Carmen whispered:

"Estévan, you must not do it! But we can't starve. Pretend to do something."

"Careful!" warned Kem. "I had the same idea; but they may be able to understand what we say."

"That is most unlikely," Escobar declared. "If they had a real working knowledge of Earth languages they would have picked out the words they wanted from scores of broadcasts, then recorded them one by one in proper sequence, to make a record which, when played over to us, would have told us exactly what they wanted us to do."

"Perhaps; but they must have some knowledge of it; otherwise they wouldn't make their machine announce 'Music while you work', or shout ' Get going! Get going!' with the idea of inducing us to start on the job."

"I wouldn't mind betting that those, and a few more simple things like 'Stop!', 'Halt!', 'Fire!' and 'Go back', are about all it can say. Dead languages are almost impossible to decipher without some sort of key, and with brains so utterly different from ours they would find our speech a worse puzzle than we should that of prehistoric man."

"How do you account for their having got as far as they have, then?"

"By using the delicate instruments they have invented for simultaneous watching and listening. We know they can look into factories, and they have evidently studied troops at drill. Such orders as 'Quick march!' and 'Halt!' are always followed by action. That would give them the meaning of a few dozen words, but I should be greatly surprised if they know any more."

Kem smiled. "It's clever of you to have thought that one out; and I believe you're right. Anyhow, it seems that for you to start pottering around a bit is the only hope we have of getting any breakfast."

Evidently the bee-beetles thought they were arguing about whether they should or should not set to work, as they had switched off the machine and, while the two men were talking, remained quite still, watching them intently. Now, as Escobar walked towards the bench, they gave an excited buzz and flew up to vantage points from which they could watch what he was about to do.

Halting opposite the draughtsman's board, he glanced over his shoulder at Kem and said, "Instead of amusing them with any chemical experiments, I think I'll design a rocket for them with some unusual parts. They have ample sense to draw the inference that I shall want them made for me, and making the parts should keep them busy for quite a time."

As he spoke he picked up what appeared to be a pencil from the tray which, in all but colour, was an exact replica of the one in his own laboratory. But to his surprise and amusement he found that the pencil lacked a lead core. It was the right shape and carefully sharpened, but solid plastic, and so completely useless.

Having shown it to Kem and Carmen, he examined a pen. That, too, was solid plastic, and what passed for its nib had no split; but he thought he might make do with it, and opened the imitation cut-glass inkwell. Instead of blue, the fluid in it was dark green and slightly sticky. Dipping the pen he experimented on the edge of the paper and, finding that it would serve the purpose, drew a picture of a rocket.

When he had finished, he laid down the pen, then walked over to the small table on which reposed the box of beans and stood pointedly in front of it. The insects took the hint. Its guardian gave the box a flick with his claw, releasing a spring too small for the human eye to detect, and the box sprang open. Gathering round, the captives ate their belated breakfast, after which Escobar returned to his board and proceeded to draw on a larger scale some of the internal parts of the rocket.

There was nothing that Kem or Carmen could do to assist him; so they sat down in two of the chairs and would have been content to remain as spectators for a while; but the bee-beetles had other views about them. As on the day before, two of them kept circling their heads, then flying to the instrument bench, clearly endeavouring to induce them to go to it and set about some form of work. They could hardly ignore these importunities, so they kept shaking their heads and making gestures with their hands to indicate that they had no intention of complying.

After some time the two bee-beetles gave up their efforts and went into a huddle with their colleagues. The whole group settled on the desk and evidently took counsel together, as they waved their horns, clicked their pincers, and fluttered their wings. The result of this conference soon emerged, as Magog got to his knees and signed to Carmen and Kem that they should precede him through the archway.

Seeing that they hesitated, the giant simply picked Carmen up and pushed her out into the passage. As Kem made to follow her of his own free will, Escobar, who up to that moment had been absorbed in his drawing, swung round and exclaimed:

"What the devil are they up to? If they take you away I'm coming with you."

"No!" cried Kem quickly. "As our bread-winner it's up to you to stay here and keep them happy. I don't think you need worry about us. It is simply that they've tumbled to it that Carmen and I are drones, and the odds are they're sending us back to barracks."

Still most reluctant to be separated from them, Escobar attempted to follow Kem, but Gog barred his passage; so he had no option but to remain behind with the school of bee-beetles.

Kem knew well enough that in the insect world unpleasant things are liable to happen to drones; so he was far from sanguine that the reassuring prediction he had cried aloud—for Carmen's sake as well as Escobar's —would really be fulfilled. Concealing his apprehension as well as he could, he allowed Magog to put him on the trolley beside Carmen, then waited anxiously to see where the giant would take them. The trolley set off towards the barracks and by the time it had crossed the canal Kem was feeling a little more optimistic, but his fears were not fully allayed until they were back in their cell and Magog had stumped away, leaving them to their own devices.

They had been dismissed from the hive much earlier than on their first visit, and estimated it to be not yet ten o'clock; so they had the best part of the day before them and nothing to do in it. After Magog's heavy footfalls had ceased to echo in the tunnel, Kem at once set about prizing out the staple that secured the great wicker door, then he smiled at Carmen, and asked:

"Would you like to do some more exploring?"

"Yes, let's," she said. "I'll being my little torch," and having collected it she tiptoed after him out into the tunnel. This time they turned left, away from the distant entrance where daylight showed, and soon entered the great gloomy chamber to which they had been brought on their first arrival. They already knew that on its inner side, away from the cliff-face with its long row of cells and windows, there lay the catacomb-like lavatory; and they suspected that somewhere near it lay the cell in which they had been decontaminated.

In a few minutes they found the circular hole in the wall through which they had been pushed, or one like it; for soon afterwards they discovered that there was a row of six of them. The holes were much too high up to look into, but Kem found himself able to jump the distance with ease, and getting a grip on the edge of one of the holes he hoisted the forepart of his body over it. Beyond and below him lay pitch blackness, but as he switched on Carmen's torch and flashed it round, its beam showed him a bare, dank, circular chamber. Its floor unlike any others that he had seen in the warren, glistened with wet, and he came to the conclusion that these drum-like pits were used for a part of the year as cisterns in which to store a reserve of water.

When he had clambered down, they set out to explore a continuation of the tunnel that ran from the far end of the vault they had now examined. Two hundred and fifty yards down it they came to another chamber similar to the one they had just left. Crossing it, they walked on through a further section of the tunnel until they saw a faint glow lighting the murk ahead. At first they thought it was caused by daylight percolating from another entrance at the tunnel's extremity, but the curious quality of the light gave them a sudden hunch that it must emanate from some of the bee-beetles.

Advancing very cautiously now, they came to a great archway that gave on to a third chamber uniform with the other two. In it a score of the bee-beetles were milling round on a small section of the floor, while others were flitting up and down the inner wall.

Owing to a number of the cell doors on the tunnel's outer side having been left ajar no part of it was in total darkness, and a greyish suggestion of daylight penetrated even to the big windowless chambers. In consequence, in this semi-darkness the bee-beetles made but a poor show in their role of Thinking Lights. Instead of each one appearing to be a bright, dancing flame, it was easily identifiable as an insect. Their glow came from their underparts, just as Escobar had suggested that it might, and in the present circumstances was sufficient only to throw the un-luminous portions of their bodies into sharp relief.

Those in flight were alighting after each ascent on the edge of one of the circular holes by which the cisterns could be entered, pausing there a second, then flying down, clutching bundles almost as large as themselves between their legs. They added their burdens to several big piles on the floor, which the other bee-beetles appeared to be counting into smaller heaps. After a moment the watchers realized that the bundles and heaps were formed of beans, and that the insects were employed in issuing from store the giants' evening ration.

Fearing to draw unwelcome attention to themselves if they proceeded further, Kem and Carmen quietly drew back and began to retrace their steps. A quarter of an hour's walk brought them to the entrance of the tunnel, but instead of taking the road that led from it they clambered up the slope at its side on to the roof of the warren.

From there they could get a better view of the surrounding country than they had had so far, as even this slight eminence enabled them to see a great distance. A few miles away to their left they could make out the green belt of the bean-fields and a hundred yards in their rear a long ridge of boulders, at no point more than ten feet in height, broke the skyline. Otherwise, from horizon to horizon the parched red earth, marked only by its cracks and gaping crevasses, stretched away, desolate and menacing to anyone who should venture to journey across it.

The sun was now approaching its meridian; so, by mutual consent, they turned and walked towards the boulders with the idea of finding a little shade in which to sit down. All the boulders had been worn smooth from the friction of countless sandstorms beating upon them, but here and there they formed shallow caves, and selecting one of the larger they settled themselves in it.

For a time they sat in depressed silence. During the past two days their minds had been occupied by constant fears or physical discomforts; but now they had leisure to think, the hopelessness of their position came home to them with full force. As Kem silently contemplated the prospect that lay before them his mercurial temperament slumped to its lowest depths, and in a fit of bitter desperation he suddenly burst out:

"Oh, what are we to do? What are we to do? I just can't stand the thought of being condemned to this sort of thing for the rest of my life. I'll go crazy or commit suicide."

Carmen put a comforting arm round his shoulders. "It's ghastly, I know. But you must not talk like that. You've been awfully brave up to now in leading our explorations and defying the little brutes as far as you could. You've been more cheerful than any of us, too. You mustn't give way, darling. Your courage is the only thing I have to cling to."

It was the first time she had used an endearment to him since they had left Earth. He turned and looked at her. Their faces were very close together. Suddenly he seized her in his arms and greedily kissed her on the mouth.

For a moment she lay passive in his embrace, returning his kiss with a fervour equal to his own; then she broke away from him and cried, "No, Kem, no! You promised you wouldn't make love to me."

"And I've kept my promise," he said thickly. "But it was given six weeks ago, and things are different now."

"No, they're not."

"Oh, yes, they are! The night we arrived here Estévan buried the hatchet as far as you are concerned. He said that we must regard the past as though it had happened to other people and nothing in it should be counted as binding on us. That included your marriage to him. He gave us *carte blanche* to do what we liked."

"I am glad that he has forgiven me; but that does not alter things between you and me."

"It does, darling. He was generous enough to say that, seeing the ghastly plight we were in, we should take such comfort of each other as we could."

"Nothing he can say alters the fact that I am bound to him by the rites of my Church. And no one can give another person permission to sin."

"Oh, Carmen!"

"I'm sorry, Kem; but you must see how I feel about it."

"I think you are making a mountain out of a molehill. The canons of your Church were never meant to apply to men and women who had been carried off to Mars."

"Time and place can have no bearing on the unalterable laws of right and wrong."

"But, darling, I am desperate for you. All those weeks in the Saucer I was half-crazy with longing to hold you in my arms. Yet I fought it down and never attempted to lay a finger on you."

"I know, and I loved you all the more for the marvellous restraint you showed."

"That's all very well, but I can't go on like this. To be near you every moment of the day; to have to lie within a few feet of you night after night; it's positive torture."

Carmen took his hand and pressed it. "Poor darling. How I wish I had never let you make love to me in the first place. It wouldn't be so hard for you then. It is hard on me, too; but in time we'll get used to it."

"I'll never get used to it," Kem flared, and with a violent gesture he pulled her towards him. She jerked her head away, and his kiss fell on her neck. For a few moments they struggled wildly, but he was loath to exert all his strength from fear of hurting her, and by the use of all of hers she succeeded in defending herself. As her slim body writhed under his broad one, she gasped:

"Kem! Don't make me! Please! I won't give in! I won't give in! Stop! I swear by the Blessed Virgin that I won't let you!"

"Oh heil!" he muttered, and rolling off her flung himself face downward on the sand, his head buried in his arms, almost weeping with rage and frustration.

Their struggle had left them both panting for breath like two fishes out of water. Striving to draw the thin air down into their straining lungs they lay without moving for several minutes; then Carmen crawled over to Kem and put her arms about him.

She was crying now, and her warm tears fell on the back of his neck as she sobbed, "Oh, Kem, forgive me! I know you think I'm being hard and selfish; but it isn't that. It isn't that I still think we haven't paid for our sin, either. But no one ever stood in such need of the mercy of God as we do. In our obtaining it lies our only possible hope of protection and, perhaps, a chance to find happiness again in the future. We must be patient, brave and chaste. He knows how pitifully weak I really am and how terribly I want to give way to you. If you press me too far I may not be able to resist temptation. I beg you not to tempt me further, Kem, and so help me to keep my resolution."

Her appeal roused all the best instincts in him. Turning over, he took her in his arms, wiped away her tears and kissed her gently on the cheek. Then he murmured:

"All right. I'm sorry I was rough. It's not going to be easy but I'll do my best."

For a time they lay there quietly, all passion drained from them after their emotional outburst, until he said a little grimly, "You know, it is a very true old saying that God helps those who help themselves; and I'm damned if I'm going to give in without a struggle to leading this sort of life indefinitely."

"What do you mean?" she asked. "As far as we know there is no better part of Mars to which we might attempt to escape."

"No; from what Estévan says it is five-eighths desert and the canals run all over it. That makes it pretty certain that its civilization—if one can call it that—is the same all over. Of course, there must be scores of other barracks full of giants and hives full of bee-beetles scattered about near its fertile areas; but I am afraid the odds are enormous against there being other types of creatures who would treat us more decently."

"Well, there are no possible means by which we might get away from it."

"You're wrong there, my sweet. We came here in a Flying Saucer, so we might get back in one."

Carmen tucked a strand of dark hair under the headscarf she was wearing, and smiled. "It's a lovely dream, Kem, but I'm afraid it can never be more than that."

"Why? We might manage to steal one."

"If we could, we wouldn't have the faintest idea how to fly it."

"No; that's the real snag," he agreed reluctantly. "We might succeed in stowing away on board one, though."

"I'm afraid there are lots of snags to that, too. For one thing, we couldn't be certain that it was going to Earth."

"The odds are that it would be. According to Estévan all the other planets are uninhabitable."

"They may not be for the bee-beetles."

"Where they could survive there is a good chance that we could. Anyway, I'd willingly take that risk to get away from here."

"It might be making only a cross-country flight and land in another part of Mars."

"That would be disappointing; but we'd be no worse off."

Thinking it good for him to employ his mind on practical problems, she led him on with further objections. "But, Kem, say we did manage to stow away on a Saucer that was about to fly to Earth, awfully few of them land when they get there. I'm afraid we would only be tantalized by a few hours of looking down on our dear old planet, then find ourselves on the way back here."

He considered that for a moment. "Of course, even if they didn't find us during the voyage, we'd have to come out towards its end. But having got so far we might persuade them to land us."

"One can't do much persuading with beings to whom one cannot talk; and so far these creatures have proved anything but obliging."

"There are two kinds of persuasion. Ours might have to be with a big stick."

She shook her head. "I doubt if they would give way to threats."

"We might succeed in overpowering them."

"There would be more of them than there would of us and the sting of an insect their size might cause death."

"Bees sting, but beetles don't; so they may not have stings."

"All right; saying we did get the best of them, we should still be faced with the job of landing the Saucer ourselves."

"I know. That's the devil of it. Unless we can learn how to fly a Saucer first it's a hundred to one that we'd crash."

"There doesn't seem to be much chance of our learning anything about them as long as we are quartered here. We don't know yet where they are made or kept."

Kem glanced upwards. A Saucer which, from its apparent size and altitude, they judged to be the same as the first they had seen on the previous day, was now again nearly overhead. In the past two hours it had climbed at a steady pace from low on the western horizon, and seemed again to be pursuing a set course to the east. As Carmen followed his glance, he said:

"From the slow speed and undeviating path of that chap, he appears to be a patrol ship; but during the next few days it is a fair bet we shall see some more active ones coming and going about the place."

"Even if they were flying over us all the time, I don't see how that would help you to find out where their base is."

"Perhaps not; but I mean to try. Estévan should be able to help us there. After he has been pretending to work for our captors for a while they may show him one of their factories. They will have to if they want him to supervise the making of that phoney rocket he is designing. Given a little time we'll find out where they keep the Saucers. That should be comparatively easy. The really stiff fence we've got to get over is to think of some means by which we can induce them to show us how to fly one; or, failing that, if we have to go as stowaways, some sort of gun we can pull at the last minute which will compel them to land us on Earth."

As there seemed no more to be said on the subject for the time being, they talked for a while on other matters; then, the warmth of the early afternoon sun having made them drowsy, they fell asleep.

They were woken by wind-driven sand stinging their faces, and roused up to find themselves caught in another duststorm. Hastily, they pulled their scarves over their mouths and nostrils and huddled together until the worst of the storm was over. When the wind had ceased to howl they got to their feet and set off hand in hand through the yellow fog towards the tunnel entrance. They found it only after having twice missed their way, and were greatly relieved when they had got far enough along it to be clear of the stifling particles.

It was not until they were back in their cell that they were in any state to talk again. Then, as Carmen let down her dark hair and began to brush the grit from it, she said:

"What a curse these duststorms are! D'you think we shall have to suffer being half asphyxiated every day, or that they only occur like rain with us, or at certain seasons?"

"Estévan could give you a sounder opinion on that than I can," Kem replied, "but I'm afraid we shall have to put up with them as part of our daily routine. I'm pretty certain they are caused by the extremes of temperature between night and day here. Both yesterday and to-day storms have blown up about an hour after dawn and an hour before sunset. That looks as if, as soon as the sun has had time to warm up the earth, the cold air that has accumulated during the night is driven out towards the dark hemisphere of the planet; then when the earth begins to cool in the late afternoon it comes rushing back again."

He had hardly finished speaking when Escobar was brought in by

Gog, and, after expressing his relief at finding them safe and sound, he confirmed Kem's theory.

While they were being given their evening rations they exchanged accounts of their doings since they had separated. Escobar had little to tell, but he was depressed, angry and very tired indeed. The bee-beetles had kept him at his drawing-board for over eight hours without a break.

"Why didn't you go on strike?" Kem enquired.

The scientist shrugged. "I tried that, but each time I sat down in the armchair one of them started to open and shut the box that contained the beans. The little swine were saying as plainly as if they had spoken, 'Go on working or you get no supper!' So what the hell was I to do but get back on the job again?"

"Oh, Estévan, what soulless brutes they are!" exclaimed Carmen sympathetically.

He sighed. "To-morrow there will be no cinema show or arguments afterwards, so I suppose they will expect me to put in an eleven-hour day. I can't stand that sort of thing for long at my age. I shall crack up."

"No, you won't," said Kem with sudden firmness. "Not till we've got them where we want them, anyway. You've got to keep going somehow. On that hangs our only chance of getting back to Earth."

"Back to Earth!" repeated Escobar, staring at him wide-eyed. "How? There is nothing I can do which would give us the remotest chance of doing that."

"Oh, yes there is. I've been giving it a lot of thought this afternoon. At first it occurred to me that we might steal a Saucer, or stow away in one and get taken back to Earth like that. But neither idea is any good. There are too many snags to both of them. Since then I've had a much better idea. We were wrong this morning in deciding that you should only pretend to show them how to make an Atom bomb. You must make one. You must make half a dozen, while keeping some essential detail of their manufacture to yourself. Then we'll let one off. We'll blow a chunk twenty miles long out of one of their canals. And if that doesn't teach them we'll blow their hive sky-high. We'll scare the pants off the little bastards. We'll create such merry hell here that they'll come crawling to us on their knees, begging us to get into a Saucer and let them take us home."

"Oh, Kem!" Carmen exclaimed with shining eyes. "What a wonderful idea! How absolutely marvellous!"

Escobar gave a short, cynical laugh. "Yes; it's a good idea all right—but for one thing. As we shall never get back, there is no reason why I should not tell you now. That plant I ran in the Argentine had nothing to do with atomic energy. I have no more idea how to make a fission bomb than the man in the Moon."

CHAPTER XVIII

THE MENACE TO EARTH

FOR a moment Kem stared at Escobar in dismay, then he burst out laughing and cried, "Well, I'll be damned! After General Peron's public announcement that his atomic scientist had deceived him we got the idea that he might be bluffing, and really had something pretty terrific up his sleeve all the time."

"We thought the Great Powers might think that," Escobar smiled, "and, having told the truth, saw no reason to discourage them. In view of the state of the world to-day it is up to every nation to take any measures it can to make others think twice before attacking it. I suppose you were sent out to discover if we really had found a way to mass-produce Atom bombs, or had just allowed you to lead yourselves up the garden path?"

Kem nodded. "That's it. And now I've got the answer. The thing that does astonish me, though, is your disclosure that you know nothing about atomic energy. I never doubted for a moment that you were making Atom bombs; the only question was whether you had a new process by which you could make them much more swiftly and cheaply than anyone else."

"In view of the precautions we took to guard the place it is hardly surprising that you jumped to the conclusion that it was an atomic plant; but if you had given the matter serious consideration it should have occurred to you that we might be making some other type of weapon."

"I was told that you had been connected with nuclear research when you were working for the Nazis."

"Then you were misinformed. I am an astro-physicist and my speciality is stratospheric rockets. That is why I was stationed at Peenemünde. If you had read those papers in the brief-case you would have tumbled to that long ago."

"I have read them. I spent several hours going through them in the Saucer while you were asleep. But in science I got no further than elementary chemistry, so I could not make head or tail of the gibberish that most of them contained."

Escobar twirled up a point of his military moustache and smiled sardonically. "It does not say much for the people you were working for to have sent out someone totally ignorant of science on a job like that."

"If these cursed Martians hadn't come on the scene, and I'd got away with that brief-case, somebody else would have deciphered its contents quickly enough."

"You mean if you hadn't hung about to keep your assignation with Carmen."

"All this is getting us nowhere," Carmen intervened. "I think your plan for terrorizing the bee-beetles into sending us home was a fine one, Kem; and as I've never considered it my business to enquire into Estévan's work, I, too, thought he was producing Atom bombs. But since he wasn't, and has no idea how to make them, what can we do now?"

While she was speaking twilight began to fall and within a few minutes the cell was in semi-darkness; but they had already settled themselves on their hard couches for the night, so they went on talking in the starlight.

After some thought, Kem said, "It seems to me the best course would be for Estévan to continue to bluff the bee-beetles into thinking that he is making an Atom bomb for them."

"I can't go on doing that indefinitely," Escobar objected.

"No; but it will give us a little time to find out a bit more about them. Besides, the atom is not the only thing that can be used as an explosive. We might still pull off my plan if you could make some good old block-busters filled with T.N.T. Could you do that?"

"How can I say? Given the right ingredients and facilities I could; but the question is, can our new masters provide them? When I was first taken into the laboratory they have copied from my own, I naturally expected that everything in it would be usable. But look at that pencil I showed you. If all the other things turn out to be like it, I'd stand no more chance of making explosives there than I would here out of these bean-fibre mats."

"I hadn't forgotten about that dud pencil," Kem smiled. "I was rather glad to see it, in a way. It showed that these clever little devils aren't quite so omnipotent as we first thought them. They can copy the shape of anything from their stereoscopic photographs, but they've no means of finding out what things are made of, or if they have something else inside them."

It was getting really cold now, and Carmen poked her head up from under her blanket for a moment to say, "That would explain why the armchair in the laboratory has no springs. When I sat down in it the seat felt quite solid: I'm sure it was made all in one piece."

"It explains, too, their failure to learn how to make an Atom bomb by watching how it is done on Earth," Kem added, looking across at Estévan, "and since they decided to bring someone here to show them how to do it, I can't help seeing the funny side of their having picked on you."

"Because you were fooled yourself, eh?" Escobar replied grumpily.

"That's it. And, after all, they were better placed than I was to know what you were really doing: they could see into your plant."

"No doubt they were misled by seeing my new giant rocket. That is a further proof that in spite of their own achievements they are still very ignorant of science as it has developed with us. It is a great relief to know that, but it is also to our personal disadvantage. I shall be able neither to hold their interest by producing harmless wonders, nor make any kind of bomb that we might use ourselves, if all those instruments they have provided prove to be nothing but theatrical props."

"I should be surprised now if you found them of much use. One could see at a glance that the substances they were made of were different from those we use; and they have failed even to imitate the colour of ordinary ink."

"The colours of all the things in the room were wrong; but there is an explanation for that. Many animals and insects cannot see colour at all; so I think we may assume that these creatures see everything in black and white."

"I was rather surprised to see that none of their films was in 'glorious technicolor'," Carmen put in, "but that would account for it."

"Anyhow," said Kem, "whether those instruments are duds or not, Estévan, it is up to you to do three things. You must keep the flag flying so that they continue to feed us, find out all you can about the Saucers, and try to make some H.E. bombs for us to use. Even hand-grenades would be better than nothing."

"It is easy enough for you to lie there and talk; but how do you suggest that I should set about making such bricks if I find there is no straw?"

"You must persuade them to take you to one of their factories. They must have such places in order to make the Saucers and the films and talking machines. In them it is certain there will be raw materials and chemicals that you will recognize. By pointing out the ones you need, you could get them to hand over to you as much of each as you require. There is another angle to it, too. If you play your cards right they may let you examine one of the Saucers, and if you can find out how it works we might later steal one and get away in it."

Escobar grunted. "And how do you propose that I should convey such requests to them?"

"By making drawings. You could sketch little pictures of a crane lifting a rocket, of a blast furnace, of yourself with a hammer at an anvil, of yourself being led by the bee-beetles towards a Flying Saucer, and that sort of thing. After all, they are very far from being fools. When you have completed your designs for the rocket parts and they have had them made, they are bound to realize that you could still help enormously by showing them how the bits should be put together. And they could not possibly assemble a large rocket inside their hive. That's when your big chance will come to pull a fast one on them. In the meantime you must do your utmost to encourage them in the belief that, having brought you here, they've picked a winner. Unfortunately there is very little that Carmen and I can do that will help much, but you may be sure we shall do every possible thing we can to support you."

When Escobar had agreed that Kem's programme appeared the only prospect of sooner or later getting the better of their captors, they went to sleep; but on the following day it transpired that his companions were not to be given any chance to prompt or aid him. Soon after sunrise, and the issue of rations, Gog and Magog took all three of them out on a trolley. Still miserable from another night spent with only a few mats between them and the hard floor, and from the chill of early morning, they were taken to the bean-fields. There, the trolley halted; Gog lifted Kem and Carmen off, and Magog drove on with Escobar towards the hive.

As the trolley rolled swiftly away in a cloud of dust, Gog pushed his charges in among the ten-foot-high beanstalks, picked up one of the great floppy baskets that was lying there and proceeded to demonstrate that they should pick beans into it.

Kem's round face went red with rage and his black eyes flashed dangerously. "This . . . this is the end!" he choked. "The utter, outside limit!"

Carmen could not help laughing at the sight of his indignation. Picking a bean, she waved it under his nose and chaffed him, "Beans, Kem, beans! Surely you remember how eager we were to get hold of a few yesterday morning? Now we can eat as many as we like."

"But this is outrageous!" he spluttered. "I'm damned if I'll submit to being treated like a negro slave and made to labour eleven hours a day in a plantation."

"No, it's very far from funny really," she agreed with sudden seriousness. "But, after all, what else can we expect? If ever there was a perfect example of a Communist State, this is one. The bee-beetles are the Commissars and the giants the masses. The masses get the minimum possible to eat that they can be kept fit to work on, and it being a well-known precept that 'given an inch they ask for an ell', they are deprived of all comfort as a routine measure, in case they got spoilt and demanded better conditions. As we have bodies that are more like those of the giants than the bee-beetles, we have been classed with the giants. That must be why we have been given quarters in the barracks instead of in the hive. And now we have shown that we either can't or won't make ourselves useful to our masters in the way Estévan is doing, they have decided that we are fit only to labour with the masses."

"That's about it," Kem said angrily. "In a Communist State there are only bosses and slaves; and it would be quite illogical for the bosses to allow a couple of slaves to sit about all day doing nothing—even if we are very small ones."

Under Gog's supervision, and that of a bee-beetle who flew up to have a look at them and continued to hover nearby, they set about their uninteresting task; but they had picked only a few dozen beans when the morning sandstorm blew up. For over half an hour it put them out of action, then when it had abated they reluctantly started work again.

They had been picking for a further twenty minutes when a group of giants that was picking along the same row, and working much faster than they were, came up with them. Most of the giants in the group gave them a dull, stupid stare, then went on working. But one, about eight feet high, whom Kem judged to be not yet in his teens, stopped picking altogether and stood with his toothless mouth hanging open, gaping at Carmen.

Suddenly he rushed at her, seized her, threw her to the ground and sprawled on top of her. About the naked lout's intentions there could be no possible doubt. His clumsy hands, with their horny, broken nails, grabbed at Carmen's clothes, ripping them away from her shoulders and body in jagged strips.

As Carmen screamed Kem leapt upon the young monster's broad back, got his hands on his thick throat and endeavoured to dig his nails into it. But the skin was loose and tough, and with a sickening sense of helplessness he felt his grip was making little impression. Jerking back his bald head, the brute broke Kem's grip, then violently contracted the muscles of his great shoulders and threw him off.

In vain Kem shouted to Gog for help. The giant stood there contemplating the struggle with the brutish expectancy on his face that one might see on that of a village idiot watching a mongrel savaging a duck.

Rushing in again, Kem kicked the huge youth in the ribs with all his might. Then, as he winced sideways from the blow, endeavoured to land another kick in his most vulnerable parts; but he could not reach them. The second kick landed on the massive thigh and made no more impression on it than if it had been hit by a falling apple.

Frenzied with loathing and terror, Carmen clawed madly at her attacker's face. By chance rather than with intent her clutching fingers ripped away his eye protector. Evidently his eyes, unaccustomed to being exposed to the air, were stung by it. For a moment he ceased from his endeavours to strip her, and a low wail issued from his slobbering mouth. Blindly he began to strike at her with his hands; but Kem seized him by the lobe of the ear and wrenched him sideways, so that his flailing fists struck the earth instead of her.

Carmen's screams had brought the giants running from all directions. Scores of them of both sexes and all sizes now jostled one another among the bean rows, striving to get a glimpse of what was going on. But this herding together had also brought the bee-beetles on the scene. Like competent policemen dealing with a traffic jam, they split up the crowds of giants by diving at their faces, then harried them back to work. One whizzed round Gog's head like an angry hornet, evidently giving him an order; for he stooped, seized the cause of all the trouble round the waist, lifted him in the air and flung him a dozen yards to land with a screech upon the ground.

Kem knelt down by Carmen, raised her head on to his shoulder and took both her hands. Neither had breath enough left to speak for some minutes, then he panted:

"You poor sweet! I'm not standing for any more of this. Lie still till you can breathe quite freely."

She gave him a wan smile, and murmured, "What do you mean to do?"

"We'll make a bolt for it. We are lighter and faster than they are. I don't believe they'll be able to catch us."

"What . . . what about the bee-beetles?"

"They may sting us. Are you game to risk that?"

"Yes. I'd rather die than be raped by one of these loathsome animals. He was the first one who had really looked at me. And there are hundreds of them. Oh, Kem, that awful toothless mouth and those bristles sprouting from his nostrils. . . ."

"Steady! Lie quiet. Try not to think about it. Just let me know when you feel recovered enough to make an all-out effort."

They remained where they were for several more minutes, then she nodded to him. As they stood up they turned together towards a gap in the bean rows and began to run. The low gravity gave them a strength and speed three times as great as they would have had on Earth. With each bound they covered ten or twelve feet.

Gog's strides equalled that in length, and he came crashing after them. But they were more nimble and easily eluded him by dodging between the tall bean plants. Within two minutes they had left him well behind, but a bee-beetle came diving at them like a miniature aerial torpedo.

It pinged past Kem's ear, turned with incredible swiftness and zoomed up straight at Carmen's face. She ducked; it soared over her head, circled and dived again. Yet it did not strike or attempt to land on either of them. Time after time, as they ran on, zig-zagging from side to side, it came zizzing towards them; but each time they either ducked or it swerved aside of its own accord at the last second.

Although it would have been impossible for them to outdistance it, fear lent them additional speed. With their lungs threatening to burst their chests and their eyes starting from their heads, they raced on, finally to stagger clear of the bean rows and out across the open desert. It was only after they had covered several hundred yards of barren ground that the bee-beetle gave up its attempts to check their flight, and flew back to resume its normal duties.

Collapsing on the reddish earth, they gasped and panted with closed eyes until the intolerable pain in their lungs gradually eased. Then they smiled weakly at one another, knowing that their bid for freedom had succeeded. When they had fully recovered their breath they made their way slowly back to the barracks. On reaching their cell Carmen changed the rags to which her dress had been reduced for other clothes. Only then did reaction set in and she suddenly fainted.

Kem tucked her up in the coverings that she used at night to sleep under, bathed her face, and when she came to gave her two of the bromides. He sat by her, holding her hand till she went to sleep; and, fearing to disturb her, remained so through the long hours of the afternoon. She did not wake until Escobar's return, half an hour before sunset, roused her.

As soon as she was fully awake she declared that she now felt none the worse for the revolting experience of which she had been the victim, and while they chewed their ration she and Kem told Escobar of all that had happened that morning.

After he had expressed his sympathy and concern for her, he said that he had little to report. He had managed to improve his own terms of service to some extent by adopting the rule of a battalion on the march, and resting for ten minutes in every hour. At first the bee-beetles had fussed and worried him while he had sat resolutely in the hard armchair; but after two brief sit-down strikes of this kind they had accepted the practice, and had not even been unduly troublesome when he had taken half an hour's break in the middle of the day.

Nevertheless he was very tired and extremely depressed. He had examined all the copies of his scientific impedimenta and found that with the exception of a few items, such as slide-rules, test-tubes and graph paper, they were completely useless. So he had had to spend practically the whole day drawing further sections of his rocket, and now felt pessimistic about his chances of making any but the most primitive explosives, even if he succeeded in obtaining suitable materials.

As twilight fell Carmen looked up from her couch to say, "If the whole of Mars is inhabited only by bee-beetles and giants, I can't see why the insects are so anxious to find out how to make destructive weapons. They have the monsters under their thumb already and there is no one else for them to use them against."

Escobar gave a bitter laugh. "You don't need any higher mathematics to solve that problem. Surely you remember what I told you about Mars; and you have seen for yourself how desperately short of water they are here. What does a bedouin tribe do when their cattle have drunk all the water in the wells within reach of the encampment? They move on to the nearest place where there is more to be had. Nature is the same the world over—the universe over, I should have said. The masters of Mars know that if they remain here their race is doomed to become extinct in a few more generations through lack of water; so they are preparing to move on to the nearest place where water is to be had. That is Earth. They must conquer Earth or die. That is why they want to learn the secrets of our most destructive weapons. To use them against us and wipe us out."

Kem had already guessed that; and as they fell silent he thought of the ghastly fate that must overtake mankind if ever the bee-beetles succeeded in obtaining the secrets of the Atom bomb. They were far from desperate for water yet, so had no pressing need to hurry their preparations. There would be ample time for them to make a stock-pile large enough to blot out Earth's civilization in a few weeks; and when they did launch their attack it would come as a complete surprise. In their Flying Saucers they possessed vastly superior air power. That of Earth was infantile compared with it. London, Paris, New York would be reduced overnight to a few square miles of flaming ruins. All resistance would prove futile. Plague from the wrecked cities would sweep over the Earth, killing off the country-dwellers. Any remnant of mankind that survived would be hunted down by giants landed for that purpose, or enslaved and brutalized until it lost all memory of its former greatness.

It was a terrible picture; but he went to sleep on one comforting thought. The masters of Mars had slipped up in selecting Estévan Escobar from whom to learn the secret of the Atom bomb. Whatever pressure might be applied to him, his ignorance of it ensured that he would never disclose it to them.

Kem had not been asleep for long when he woke with a start. Some-one was shaking him by the shoulder. As he turned over, his half-conscious mind told him that it must be either Estévan or Carmen. But, to his amazement, he could see the dim forms of both of them still sound asleep a few feet from him. The touch on his shoulder had been too gentle for that of a giant. Wide awake now, he jerked his head round. The bright starlight showed him instantly that he had been woken by another human being. He was staring into the pale face of a fair-haired girl.

CHAPTER XIX

THE COMING OF ANNA

A TORRENT of excited thoughts surged through Kem's mind. Amaze-ment was succeeded by relief, joy and eager hopes. The sight of a human being in such circumstances conjured up all sorts of exciting possibilities. Evidently the bee-beetles controlled only a part of Mars. A species similar to mankind had, after all, developed there. As the planet was far more advanced in its life than Earth their state must have reached Utopian levels. They would be wise, gracious and beautiful through many generations of selective breeding. Their habitations would contain all the comforts that the mind could devise; and they would live frugally but well on all the choicest delicacies that long experience would have enabled them to produce with little effort.

Swift visions of escape from grim captivity to an earthly paradise were still tumbling helter-skelter across Kem's mental horizon when the girl spoke.

Her voice was low and pleasant but her words conveyed nothing whatever to him.

He shook his head and peered at her, trying, in the semi-darkness, to get a better impression of what she looked like. He had glimpsed her face only for a moment as she knelt above him, but on his starting up she had altered her position a little, so that she was now kneeling with her back towards the light.

She spoke again, and, half turning, pointed at the window. For a second her profile was outlined against it. He saw that her hair was straight and fell to her shoulders, framing a face that was round with plump cheeks, full lips, a determined little chin and a snub nose. From what he could make out, her outer garment appeared to be made of fur. In the vague hope that she might understand him, he asked in English:

"Where have you come from?"

She now shook her head; so he tried her again in French and Spanish; but it was clear that she no more understood him than he did her.

"Carmen! Estévan!" he called loudly. "Wake up! Wake up! Something terrific has happened."

His fellow-captives started from their sleep and poked their heads out from beneath their coverings. For a moment both of them stared speechlessly at the girl, thinking they must be dreaming. But Kem said with an excited laugh:

"You're not seeing things. She's real. She's warm flesh and blood like we are; but I can't understand her language."

"How . . . how on earth did she get here?" asked Carmen in amazement.

"Goodness knows! She woke me up a moment ago. She must come from another part of Mars where there are people like ourselves. Isn't it terrific! Just think of it! Where she comes from there must be warmth, comfort, and decent food instead of those accursed beans. Perhaps her people and the bee-beetles fought one another to a standstill ages ago, then agreed to divide Mars between them. She may have got over the frontier through some accident, and have been brought here as a prisoner. But if that's the way of it we'll all escape together and go back with her. Then heigh-ho for the fleshpots!"

With the volatile enthusiasm which was one of Kem's characteristics, he suddenly took the girl by the shoulders, drew her forward, and planted a hearty kiss on her cheek.

At that she laughed and kissed him back; then she spoke again in her own language.

Like a cold douche, Escobar's voice destroyed in a single sentence all Kem's joyous imaginings of Elysian fields only a few days' march away.

"She's not a Martian: she is speaking Russian."

For a moment they all remained completely silent, occupied with swift speculations on what that might portend. Then Carmen asked, "Do you speak enough of it to talk to her?"

"No, only a few words," Escobar replied, but sitting up on his pallet, he turned to the girl and said, "*Tovarishch.*"

Instantly her face brightened into a delighted smile, and lifting her clenched fist in the air, she cried, "*Tovarishch! Tovarishch!*"

"*Sprechen Sie Deutsch?*" he asked.

"*Ja,*" came the quick response. "*Genug um Sie zu verstehen.*"

"Thank God for that!" he muttered in Spanish; and that being the language he, Carmen and Kem had used habitually since their kidnapping, he went on in it quickly to them, "German is the only foreign language the Russians teach to any extent in these days, and then only in their higher schools. We're lucky that this young woman has had a decent education." Turning back to her, he asked:

"*Wie kommen Sie hierher?*"

She replied in a swift spate of heavily accented phrase-book German. Both Kem and Carmen had a smattering of that language, so by following her with strained interest were able to make out a little of what she said; but to get her full meaning they had to restrain their impatience until, from time to time, Escobar gave them a *précis* of it.

He told them that her story was very similar to their own. She had been kidnapped with two men companions at night by giants and brought to Mars in a Flying Saucer. They, too, had been parachuted out on arrival in sealed sacks, then decontaminated, and had come round to find themselves naked under a few fibre mats in a big bare cell. Next day they had been shown the film sequence of major historical events on Earth, then listened to extracts from broadcasts in various languages and been told to "Get going!" by the talking machine.

On Escobar asking her about herself, she replied, "My name is Anna Nitkin. I was born in Murmansk up in the Arctic Circle. My father is a high official in the department of Heavy Industry and as soon as I was old enough I was sent to the University of Leningrad. I took science, specializing in geology and radio-activity. I received a diploma in both, and after six months in the Ministry of Mines I was selected to be laboratory assistant to Doctor Kruger Harsbach."

As Escobar exclaimed at the name, she said, "You have heard of him, perhaps. He is one of the German scientists whom we brought to Russia after the war. He was already well known for his work on nuclear reactions and has since become one of our leading men in the atomic field."

"They, too, were brought here to make Atom bombs," Escobar said in a quick aside to Kem, as Anna went on:

"I was transferred from the Ministry in Moscow to his experimental station beyond the Urals. It was a lonely place, hundreds of miles from anywhere, in the depths of the pine forests. Except for a little group of scientists, all the comrades there were Asiatics, chosen because they could not read or write, so could understand nothing of what we were doing. Naturally I found life there rather dull after Moscow, with the excitement of the Party rallies, the political discussion circles, and the Young Communists' drives to increase production. But I was very proud to have been chosen for my work and became greatly interested in it. Sometimes Doctor Harsbach worked all through the night, and occasionally he permitted me to do a double shift so that I could help him. I had been stationed there just over ten weeks when we were captured. It happened at about three o'clock in the morning on a night that I had remained up working with Doctor Harsbach. Zadovitch had just come in——"

"Who is Zadovitch?" Escobar interrupted.

"Nickolai Zadovitch is the third member of our party. He is the M.V.D. man who was responsible for maintaining political purity in the camp. He had just come in, and was kicking up a fuss. He said that I should not work for such long hours and ought to be in bed. We were arguing with him that our work must come before all else, because on such work as ours depended the prevention of the enslavement of the free Soviet workers by the greedy American capitalists. Suddenly the windows were shattered and great hands came through them. Zadovitch drew his pistol, but he was knocked down before he could fire it. I tried to get through the door but I was pulled back by my hair. One pair of hands tore down the curtains, the other threw us upon them. Oddments of all kinds were then piled on us, the curtains were bunched up and we were carried off half dead in them to a Flying Saucer."

After having given Kem and Carmen the gist of her account so far, Escobar asked her, "When was this?"

"In mid-October. We arrived here towards the end of December. Our voyage occupied sixty-eight days."

"It took considerably longer than ours, then; but that might be accounted for by the two planets having been nearer their opposition when we were carried off. We have been here only three days, whereas it must be nearly five weeks since you landed. You must have found out quite a lot about Mars in that time. We should be most interested to hear all you can tell us."

"There is little to tell. As far as we know there are only three forms of life remaining on Mars: the insects, the giants, and the beans. We think that the insects must have liquidated every other species of animal, reptile and plant in order to economize water. The conservation of water is their greatest concern. They must know that in a measurable time there will no longer be enough to form the polar caps in winter and that soon afterwards their last reserves will evaporate. They are very clever about some things, and have probably already calculated to within a few years the date at which a universal drought on Mars will render life extinct. They brought us here to teach them how to make Atom bombs, and we have no doubts about why they are anxious to learn our secrets. If they could make a big enough stock-pile themselves they would use it to bombard Earth and crush all resistance; so that they could safely invade it and establish themselves there permanently."

Escobar nodded. "We reached the same conclusion. To learn atomic secrets was also the reason why they kidnapped us. They have threatened to starve us if we refuse to work for them. No doubt they did the same with you. What attitude did your party adopt?"

"They did; and Doctor Harsbach decided that we must play for time by pretending to humour them. He drew a number of blue-prints of extremely complicated mechanisms; but we are now becoming very worried. They have processes, as yet unknown to us, by which they can cast the parts shown in such designs far quicker than we could. For the past fortnight we have been taken each day to a plant they have some miles down the canal. There, we have been set to assemble the parts, and the work is nearly completed. What we are to do when it is finished, and we can no longer disguise the fact that we have constructed no more than an elaborate but quite useless shell, we cannot think."

"Before long, then, I shall find myself in the same awkward situation," Escobar told her. "But perhaps if Herr Doktor Harsbach and I get together we may be able to think of some way of fooling our captors for a bit longer. Whereabouts are your quarters; and how did you come to find us?"

"The three of us were given a cell near the far entrance to the tunnel. It is about half a mile away. I sleep very badly; so I often go for a walk alone in the middle of the night. The giants all sleep like logs, and no one has ever attempted to stop me. One could escape with the greatest ease; but there is nowhere to escape to. The insects must realize that, or they would guard us more carefully. Usually I walk for a while outside and look at the stars. The high albedo of Earth makes it easy to pick out. From here it is the brightest star in the sky, and I get some comfort from looking at it. But tonight I thought I would walk right through the tunnel and back, just to see if I had missed any feature of it when I first explored it soon after our arrival. It is very silent in the tunnel at night, and when I came opposite your door I heard some sounds that I could not understand. They were quite unlike the harsh, throaty cackle that the giants make when they talk; so I undid the staple and peeped in to see what it was. You can imagine my feelings when I realized that there were other human beings here. The sounds I had heard came from the man I woke: he was talking in his sleep."

When Escobar had again passed on to the others most of what Anna had said, they agreed that the sooner they met her companions, so that the two parties could hold a full-scale council of war, the better. On his suggesting that, she at once offered to fetch the Doctor and Zadovitch; and, promising to be back within half an hour, she left them.

As soon as she had gone, Kem began to bewail the fact that, instead of being a nymph of some superior Martian race, she had turned out to be, like themselves, just another prisoner brought from Earth. The others felt the same; but all agreed that considerable comfort was to be derived from the fact that they would now have other human beings with whom to share their anxieties, and that six heads would be better than three in plotting how to circumvent their captors.

Carmen was the least enthusiastic of the three about the possible benefits they might derive from this new development. "I think it is a bitter pill," she lamented, "that after finding that we have companions in misfortune they should turn out to be Russians. We shall find little in common with these atheists and enemies of freedom, and shall probably soon quarrel violently with them. How I wish that they had been Americans or British!"

"The Doctor is a German," Kem reminded her. "And as he was taken to Russia as a prisoner, he probably hates the Soviets as much as we do; so if we find we can't keep off politics we'll be four to two, anyway."

"You are wrong there," said Escobar seriously, "and it raises a point that I wanted to warn you about, Kem, before they get here. I knew Kruger Harsbach when I was at Peenemünde. He is a clever devil but a bit unbalanced—in fact some people might consider him insane on one particular subject. By origin he is not German, but South African Dutch, hence his Christian name of Kruger. He is about my age, so was a small boy at the time of the Boer War. When the British did their mopping up out there in 1902 they shot his father for sniping at them, then burnt down his farm. Kruger has never forgiven them for that. He and his mother migrated to Germany and he was educated there. By 1915 he was old enough to enter the Kaiser's war. On the Somme, I think it was, he was wounded when fighting against the British, and badly disfigured. Owing to that he was still not a very pleasant sight to look at when I last saw him. Not unnaturally, that added fuel to his hatred of your nation, and as a young professor in the 1920s he spent much of his time urging his students to prepare themselves for a war of revenge."

Escobar broke off for a moment, then went on, "As you can imagine, he was one of those who welcomed the emergence of Hitler, and he became one of the earliest members of the Nazi Party. When they came to power that enabled him to get the pick of the scientific appointments; and I must say he made the best of them. From early on he had been a great friend of Ribbentrop, and I have no doubt at all that he did a great deal to influence Ribbentrop in the belief that the Germans would come out on top if they had another war with England. While I was with him at Peenemünde his wife and only daughter were killed in one of the R.A.F. raids on Berlin. By that time he knew, as all those top Nazis did, that Germany had lost the war; but he swore that he would spend every hour left him till his dying day in working to revenge himself on the British."

Again Escobar paused, then added, "That young woman said that the Herr Doktor was sent to Russia as a prisoner. Don't you believe it. If I know anything about Harsbach he went there of his own free will. Like plenty of other people he could see that sooner or later the Soviets would have a showdown with the Western Democracies; so you can be certain that he has willingly given the Russians everything he has got. Probably the only reason he regrets having been brought to Mars is because he will never stand a chance now of seeing London in ruins. He is the most fanatical Britain-hater I have ever met; so as you are British, Kem, for goodness' sake keep off international politics and be careful of him."

CHAPTER XX

THE MAN WITH THE GUN

"ONE can't help feeling a bit sorry for him," Kem said thoughtfully. "To have lost his father, his property, his wife, his only daughter, and to have been disfigured into the bargain, is enough to make any man bitter. All the same it is unreasonable to blame the British as a race for his misfortunes."

"Is it?" asked Escobar, without any trace of aggressiveness. "I know you British regard yourselves as the benefactors of mankind, who have brought justice, hygiene and education to many of the more backward races; but other peoples have some cause to see you in a very different light. It can be argued that you robbed the Boers of their country because you wanted the gold that it contained; that you deliberately formed a coalition with France and Russia to smash the Kaiser's Germany because you saw in her a dangerous rival to your world-wide commercial interests; and that by robbing the Germans of all their colonies,

155

and every natura outlet for the expansion of their huge population, you brought the Hitler war upon yourselves. Anyhow, Harsbach probably looks at it that way and attributes the ill-fate that has dogged him to British unscrupulousness and greed."

Kem smiled. "I could make a very good case to show that our wars have been forced upon us through Germany having become the bully of Europe and the crazy determination of her rulers to achieve their ambitions at any cost. But that is not the point. As we are situated at the moment it is of the utmost importance that we should not allow these old race hatreds to divide us. Since anything British has the effect on this chap of showing a red rag to a bull, perhaps our best plan would be to keep it dark that I am an Englishman."

"I think that an excellent idea," Carmen agreed. "You have been talking nothing but Spanish now for the best part of three months; so no German or Russian could possibly guess that you are not an Argentinian, if we say you are, but you'll have to think of a suitable name for when we introduce ourselves."

"Yes, and it should be something as near as possible to my real one, in case either of you slip up and call me by that in front of them some time. Can you think of any Spanish name that sounds like Kem?"

"Sem is short for Sempa," she said after a moment.

"That will do splendidly. What about Lincoln?"

That proved a more difficult proposition, and after several suggestions they had to settle on Lináres as the nearest they could think of.

Some ten minutes later Anna rejoined them with her companions. Escobar greeted Harsbach as an old acquaintance, and they laughed together a little grimly about how utterly fantastic they would have thought it had they been told when they had last been together that they would next meet on Mars. Then general introductions took place.

The Herr Doktor was a tall, gaunt man in his late fifties. It was a part of his jaw that had been shot away in the first World War, and the taut skin of his left cheek pulled down the corner of one eye. But he was not as badly disfigured as Kem and Carmen had expected; or perhaps did not appear so because his face was redeemed by a good nose and forehead and remarkably fine eyes. He had his hair cut *en-brosse*, like a Prussian; his voice was pitched rather high, but all his utterances were quick and decisive.

Nickolai Zadovitch looked about forty. He was broad and powerful with a shock of yellowish hair, a beard of the same colour, and the flat high-cheekboned face of the typical Russian peasant. He was still wearing his uniform with the light blue facings and the black jackboots of the Political Police and, Kem was surprised to see, carrying a big pistol at his belt. He spoke nothing but Russian and favoured his new acquaintances with a suspicious look from his small, crafty eyes as he jerked his head abruptly in acknowledgment of Harsbach's introductions.

Harsbach could speak some Spanish, but Anna did not know a word of it; so as both of them and Escobar could speak German fluently, and Carmen and Kem understood a little, it was decided to carry on their conversation in that language.

The two scientists did nearly all the talking. Half an hour sped swiftly by as they swapped accounts of their kidnapping, their arrival on Mars, and what they had since learned about the planet. They were in full agreement on why they had been brought there, and in their determination to disclose no secrets which might assist the bee-beetles in getting control of Earth. They then went on to discuss the achievements of the insects and the economy they had imposed upon their planet.

"While they are far ahead of us in certain ways," Harsbach said, "they have no culture of any kind. That, I believe, is because they lack individuality. If one believed in souls at all, one would term them group-souled. There is much to be said for that term employed by the occultists, as it well describes the state of a number of physical bodies all animated by a common will. We see it in the migrations of our own animals, birds and insects at certain seasons, and with many of the last it is also demonstrated in their building communal nests."

Escobar stroked the black beard he had grown, and nodded, "I agree. And these bee-beetles have developed in a way which one would expect of insects. Their sole genius lies in constructional ability. We have embryonic examples of that in the hexagonal cells of our own bees and the beautiful symmetry of hanging wasps' nests."

"Like many of our insects, too," the German informed him, "they themselves process all the materials for their requirements. The development of ours appears to have been arrested after they learned that by selecting certain foods they could secrete substances suitable to their immediate needs. These have progressed a stage further: by including different chemicals in their diet, they can produce not one but a variety of substances; some transparent, others opaque; some with the elasticity of rubber, others which will harden nearly to the degree of steel."

"I take it you have found that out during your visits to their plant?" Escobar enquired.

"Yes. I have now been watching them at work for a fortnight. The thing that astonishes me is the simplicity of their operations. They use no furnaces; their own bodies are the crucibles in which they blend the ingredients for all their manufactures. The various types of excretions are stored in airtight vats, then run off into moulds as required. To construct large or complex objects several, sometimes many, parts are fashioned simultaneously in a number of moulds, then assembled before they are quite set. Thus the necessity for rivets is eliminated and, after polishing, the object presents a perfectly smooth and seamless surface."

"I suppose they lift the larger parts into position, and move the heavier things they make when they are completed with the aid of magnets?"

"Yes. The control of magnetic force appears to be their one great discovery. I imagine that, initially, they must have stumbled upon some magnetic law of which we are still in ignorance, and have since learned to apply it in a variety of ways."

"The basic principle of how to eliminate the force of gravity without effort, once known, would open up almost limitless possibilities. Do you know if they use magnetism for disruptive purposes, as well as for light and propulsion?"

"Not as far as I know. They do not appear to have any knowledge of explosives, or to possess weapons of any kind."

"How, then, do they keep a whip-hand over the giants?"

"Routine overseeing appears to be all that is necessary. With their superior intelligence it is reasonable to suppose that by the lure of easy food they succeeded in training the giants to passive obedience countless generations ago. The functions fulfilled by them have become almost automatic, so it is reasonable to regard them as little more than cattle."

"We thought of elephants as a better comparison," Escobar smiled. "In some cases, too, they function independently from the herd; witness those who kidnapped us and those who have since acted as our escorts. Their capability to carry out such orders infers that they possess a degree of intelligence considerably higher than that of most animals."

The German shook his bristly head. "Having watched them very carefully, I am inclined to think that in these special cases they have no idea what they are doing, and act only on orders that have been conveyed to them by a form of hypnotism. Of one thing I am certain: the insects can make their will felt by telepathy."

"Yes. We have experienced that; but found it comparatively easy to resist. However, I see your point: it would not occur to the monsters to offer any resistance, and even if they did they are not mentally equipped to resist to the same degree as ourselves."

"Have you tried the process in reverse? I mean, attempting to convey your wishes to the insects by concentrated thought?"

"No. Do you think that possible?"

"Yes. I have already met with a limited success. I practise every day, and am progressing slowly; although I regard it as most unlikely that I shall ever be able to carry on an intelligent conversation with them by such means."

"I take it that thought transference is their normal means of communicating with one another?"

"No," replied the Herr Doktor a shade hesitantly. "I don't think it is. That they are animated by common mental impulses, such as that which mysteriously impels all the flying ants in the nests of a whole district to take wing on the same day, I am certain. Ten days ago, at about two o'clock in the afternoon, they suddenly became subject to the sexual urge, and without a moment's warning abandoned everything they were doing to indulge it. But I think they have developed telepathy only as a means of conveying their orders to the monsters. Among themselves they use a language which seems to have been evolved in a similar manner to that used by our own bees."

Escobar looked his surprise. "I had no idea that our bees had a language. It has always been supposed that all such insects played their part in communal life owing to race instinct, and had no need, much less the means, to convey their thoughts to one another. Are you certain of what you say? If such a discovery has been made it implies a revolution in our biological knowledge which has never been surpassed."

"It is now regarded as proven by the greatest authorities on the subject." Harsbach shrugged. "Evidently you missed Herr Doktor Von Frisch's papers about his bee-keeping experiments in Austria. The first was published in 1946, and others followed in '48 and '49. As we all know, the bees' one preoccupation is the search for material with which to make honey. Von Frisch placed caches of sugar in various parts of his grounds on different days and at gradually increasing distances from his hives; then watched for results. Every apiarist knows that bees well laden with pollen often circle round the inside of the hive on their return, then do a little dance. That has always been put down to excitement; but Von Frisch proved conclusively that the bees behaving in such a manner were giving their brothers definite directions on how to find the lucky strike they had made themselves."

"You amaze me! How could they possibly do that?"

"Having made their circle, they cross it, making the bisecting line in what appears to be a drunken dance. But they are not in the least drunk. The angle of the line in relation to the position of the sun gives the watching bees the direction in which the cache lies; the drunken movements and wriggles of the stomach give the distance it is away. By timing the movements with a stop-watch Von Frisch worked out a scale of distances; and the final proof that the audience had received an intelligent message lay in their flying direct, and without pause, to the place a mile away where he had put the sugar."

"And you think that the bee-beetles here have a similar language?"

"I am certain of it. One must regard their horns and pincers as arms and hands. If you observe them closely you will see that they use the former as a type of semaphore, and the latter similarly to the motions by which deaf and dumb humans talk to one another."

"Does not the fact that they can talk invalidate your theory that they have no individuality?"

"I do not think so. Bees cannot be said to have individuality, or any other insects, whatever their achievements. They have no thought of self, but are dominated entirely by the urge to perpetuate their race. That postulates: firstly the procuring of sufficient food to feed it; secondly the creation of a suitable habitation to protect it from the elements and from its natural enemies, and to enable breeding to take place in the most favourable conditions; thirdly the instinct to migrate when it becomes apparent that the locality occupied no longer affords facilities adequate to support it."

After a moment's thought, Escobar said, "Your analysis of insect mentality explains many things that have puzzled us. Creatures entirely absorbed in the urges you mention would naturally give no thought to comfort, art or any form of self-indulgence; and would use such knowledge as they have gained only for labour-saving devices such as the trolleys, or to facilitate their migration to another world now this one threatens to become uninhabitable for them. That they are entirely ruthless in pursuit of their aims is shown by the way in which they have eliminated every species here with the exception of the giants and one form of vegetation."

"They must also have eliminated all forms of harmful bacteria. Since I have been here I have not seen a single instance of an insect or giant in ill-health. That they have performed this remarkable feat is made all the more certain from the fact that none of my party has fallen a victim to disease."

"What you say is a great relief to me. Having been decontaminated on our arrival would have prevented us giving them any of Earth's diseases, but it could not protect us from picking up other forms of disease which might exist on Mars. I have said nothing to my wife or Señor Lináres of my fears, but I have been expecting that at any time we should feel the first symptoms of some probably deadly complaint."

Harsbach smiled. "I think you may set your mind at rest. The metabolism of the giants must be very similar to our own; so if every disease to which their race was subject in the past has been stamped out, we, too, should be safe."

"To have achieved such a degree of hygiene is quite extraordinary, in view of the fact that many of the most dangerous types of bacteria are detectable only under our most powerful microscopes."

"For them to have waged a victorious war against disease would have been far easier than for us. At close range the eyes of most insects are far more powerful than our own; and, as you will have seen from their photography, their lenses are incomparably better than ours. There were other factors in their favour, too. By liquidating all animal and vegetable life other than the giants and the beans, they at the same time destroyed the majority of the breeding-grounds and carriers of pests. Again, Mars is now mainly arid desert in which even bacteria would find no means of subsistence, and all the remaining water being canalized it would not be beyond their powers to filter and disinfect it. That leaves only the bean-fields and the habitations, and a systematic cleansing of those over several generations would have completed the task."

After a moment, Harsbach added, "Another fact which convinces me that no harmful bacteria exists here is the use to which the excreta of the giants is put. Insect economy demands that nothing should be allowed to go to waste, so it is used to manure the bean-fields. Thus a form of perpetual motion is achieved, through the same chemicals of. which the beans consist being put back into the earth season after season and emerging again as a new crop. But that would not be practical if the excreta was not free of harmful germs."

Kem had become restless during this long conversation, and cut in to ask Escobar in Spanish if he and Harsbach had decided on a future policy; upon which Escobar said to the German:

"Señor Lináres still hopes that we may find a means of getting back to Earth. Do you think there are any prospects of our doing so?"

Harsbach pulled a wry face. "Naturally we have also given that much thought, but it is certain that the insects will do their utmost to prevent us, and it seems to me that without their co-operation any such attempt must prove hopeless."

"Have you seen any of the Flying Saucers since you landed? I mean, close to?"

"Yes. They make everything they require at the one plant. That is, in this part of Mars; there are doubtless other hives and other plants in other areas. Adjacent to the plant is a flying base and there are several Saucers stationed on it."

"Could we get hold of one?"

"I greatly doubt it. We have not yet discovered if the insects have stings; but if they have the sting of one their size would prove deadly. Besides, we have not the faintest idea how the Saucers are operated."

"Since you are already able to communicate with them to a certain extent, could you not induce them to show you over one on the excuse that you will have to fit the Atom bomb you are making to it? After a number of visits you might learn its secrets. If you could do that, and they are unguarded at night, we might succeed in stealing one and getting away in it."

With a shake of his head the Herr Doktor replied, "Even if I could manage to find out enough about them to get one off the ground, what of the problem of navigating it back to Earth on magnetic waves, about which I understand nothing. No; it is out of the question. I would rather take my chance in a rocket powered by atomic energy, with which we are familiar. You know much more about rockets than I do, and in making one you would have the co-operation of the insects. Such a plan seems to me to offer far better possibilities."

It was Escobar's turn to shake his head. "No; such a project is beyond me. I could, of course, make a giant rocket with their help, but its take-off is the problem that I see no way of solving. To reach Earth in one flight would necessitate an initial speed that, even allowing for the comparatively low gravity of Mars, would kill us."

"The use of nuclear energy instead of normal jet fuel would enormously reduce the mass-ratio required for such a rocket."

"True; but even so such an attempt would be a most hideous gamble, unless we had first carried out successful experiments in sending pilotless rockets to one of their moons, then to Earth. Perhaps, though, we might do that on the excuse of testing. To start with I could make a rocket and you could insert a fission bomb into its warhead; then we could launch it against Phobos or Deimos. Both are so small that if it hit the mark whichever it was aimed at would blow up. We would know then that we were working on the right lines, and——"

Harsbach cut him short with a harsh laugh. "If we did that they would never let us launch another. Have not you yet realized what Phobos and Deimos are?"

Escobar looked puzzled. "Some people argue that they are small burnt-out moons, others that they are captured asteroids. I know of no other theories concerning them."

"They are neither; but perhaps you have not been here long enough to notice the regularity of the movements of the two Saucers that are frequently to be seen above us. One appears to move from west to east and crosses the meridian three times in every twenty-four hours. The other rises in the east and crosses the meridian only once every thirty hours. It is those two Saucers that we have named Phobos and Deimos."

"Indeed! They are then the equivalent of the permanent aerial rafts that our own scientists are already planning to send up as second launching bases for despatching rockets to the Moon. In that case you are certainly right that it would be the end of us if we blew one up."

"We could send a trial rocket to Earth."

"No. It would be useless unless it contained a big enough explosive charge for us to observe the burst, and so make certain that it landed. We could not take the risk of its devastating some highly populated area."

"And without a trial you consider our chances of arrival would be too slender?"

"Yes. Even if we could make a large enough rocket to carry us without the bee-beetles suspecting our intentions, and take them by surprise in getting away in it, I think the attempt would be suicidal."

They were silent for a moment, then Escobar went on, "There is another possibility put forward by Señor Lináres; but in view of our fears that the bee-beetles have deadly stings, it would prove extremely hazardous. He suggested that I should manufacture some explosives and by their use terrorize the insects into taking us back to Earth themselves."

Harsbach's grey eyes suddenly lit up, and he exclaimed, "That had not occurred to me, but it is certainly an idea. Virtually it would amount to declaring war on them; so, as you say, it would mean gambling our lives in the attempt. But it would be less of a gamble than leaving Mars on our own in any form of space-ship that we did not know how to navigate. As insects are so dominated by routine it should be much easier to temporarily paralyse their activities by surprise than it would be with men. I believe Señor Lináres is right. If we laid our plans carefully, we might overawe them for long enough to make them place a Saucer and its crew at our disposal, and be glad to be rid of us."

"Have you yet come across any chemicals here from which we could make explosives?"

"Yes. They use nitric acid in some of their processes, and also mercury. But only in small quantities, and I doubt if I could get hold of enough to make the quantity of explosives we should require to really terrorize them."

"An Atom bomb would serve our purpose far better than anything else. You suggested just now using nuclear energy to power a rocket. Were you only theorizing, or could you stop pretending and actually produce it?"

"I could if I had the materials; but uranium is essential, and lead, for screens for our protection while we make it; and, as far as I know, they use neither."

Anna had been following the conversation, and she now put in, "There must be both on Mars. I took a diploma in geology, and if it could be arranged for me to go prospecting I am certain I could identify the type of ground in which they are to be found."

The Herr Doktor gave her a swift glance. "In that case I will try to make suitable arrangements. It may take me some days to convey to the insects that I cannot complete my work until you have found certain minerals for me, and that to find them may necessitate an expedition across the desert; but with patience I think I shall manage it."

Turning back to Escobar, he added, "This plan may be dangerous but I welcome it with relief. At worst it provides me with an excuse for failing to produce immediate results in a few days' time, when the insects have finished making the container for my bomb; at best it may lead to our regaining our freedom."

"I wonder what the best course would be for me to adopt in the meantime," Escobar said thoughtfully. "Do you think they would allow us to work together?"

"They might; and now that I am to make a real bomb I shall have much preparatory work to do while Anna is out prospecting; so I should welcome your help. But whether they will allow you to give it me is quite another matter. It is probable that their object in bringing two atomic scientists here from different countries is to have them make bombs independently of one another, then combine the best features of each."

Anna spoke again. "Why not make two bombs? The American

163

employment of atomic warfare against Japan was not decisive until a second bomb had been dropped. It may prove the same here.' '

"Why not?" Harsbach agreed, smiling at Escobar. "By the time Anna has found uranium and lead, and sufficient quantities have been mined for our purpose, you should easily have caught up with me in getting your casing and mechanism manufactured. Then we will have a race to see who can first complete the filling of the warhead. I am told that in the Argentine you have found a short cut to production. Well; we in the Soviet Union have found one, too. I challenge you to beat us."

Escobar gave him a rueful look. "You will recall, Herr Doktor, that at Peenemünde I was a rocket man. Whatever you may have since been led to suppose, I am a rocket man still. I know practically nothing about the production of nuclear energy. Enough perhaps to superintend the construction of a suitable bomb casing; but there can be no race between us. When it comes to the finer mechanism and the filling of my bomb, you will have either to give me your instructions or undertake the work yourself."

"So we are ahead of you, as well as of the Americans and those swinish British." Harsbach gave his short, harsh laugh again. "I challenged you in order to find out. That you should not even be able to compete is more satisfactory than if I had won by a good lead. However, Anna is right in her contention that with two bombs at our disposal we shall stand several times as much chance of emerging victorious as we should with one. I will, therefore, provide you with specifications for making your shell. By the time it is completed I should be able to transmit ideas to the insects fairly easily. I will convey to them that matters would proceed faster if you became my assistant, and we will carry out the finer work on both bombs, together."

Anna suddenly began to speak very fast in Russian. After a moment Zadovitch joined in. Harsbach turned and snapped at them both in the same language. A violent three-cornered argument ensued. Twice Zadovitch significantly tapped the holster of the gun that he was wearing on his belt. Then Harsbach silenced them both by a series of sharp staccato sentences which might have issued from the thin-lipped mouth of a typical Junker of the old German General Staff.

Turning back to Escobar's party the Herr Doktor waved an apologetic hand. "Please to excuse this little disagreement," he said smilingly, again using German. "My companion with the untidy yellow hair is a person of very low intelligence. At times he forgets that we are no longer in the Soviet Union, and that on Mars it is I, not he, who gives the orders. Be good enough to disregard the incident. It is closed."

It was now close on four o'clock in the morning; so both parties felt that they ought to get a little sleep before the long day ahead of them. Harsbach said that, as a first step, he would tackle the bee-beetles with a view to gaining their consent to the amalgamation of the two parties, so that they could communicate freely at all times in future; and that should he meet with opposition they would, in any case, get together each night in secret until such opposition could be overcome. Then good nights were said and the visitors departed.

As their footsteps died away Escobar began to tell Kem and Carmen all that had emerged from his conversation with the Herr Doktor, and of the decision they had taken. When he had done, Kem asked:

"What was the row about that they had towards the end? For a moment, from the way the M.V.D. man tapped his gun, I thought they were going to set about one another in earnest."

Escobar shrugged. "He is a stupid oaf, and has not yet fully realized that the orders he was given by his chiefs cannot possibly apply here. I admitted to Harsbach that I know very little about atomic energy, and he very sensibly agreed to share his knowledge with me, so that we could make two equally effective bombs. On the policeman learning that Harsbach intended to give away a Soviet State Secret, he threatened to shoot him. But the Herr Doktor told him that, in the present circumstances, nothing could matter compared with getting out of the clutches of the bee-beetles before they compelled us to show them how to blow every city on Earth to hell; and to stop being a fool. At least, that is the interpretation I put upon their quarrel."

"Then you were wrong," said Carmen quietly. "I've often told you how, when I was a young girl, I was threatened with deafness until I had that marvellous operation; and that during the time I found hearing difficult I was taught to lip-read. Of course, I could not understand what that Russian said, because I don't know Russian. But to lip-read one has to watch a person's expressions so intently that, quite apart from the movements of the mouth, one gets a sort of sixth sense about the thoughts they are expressing. I am certain that when that horrible man tapped his gun, what he was really saying was:

"'All right; if you consider that the help this Argentinian scientist can give you is essential to your plan, go ahead. But if you give away Soviet secrets to these people, I shall make it my business to see that none of them reaches Earth alive.'"

CHAPTER XXI

THE EXPLOSIVE PILL

In the morning Gog and Magog appeared as usual; but they brought with them only five beans, which Gog gave to Escobar. It seemed certain that this discrimination was aimed at penalizing Kem and Carmen for having abandoned work in the bean-fields the day before, and that assumption was promptly confirmed by the giant preventing the scientist from sharing the ration with his companions. Much concerned by this new piece of blackmail, the breakfastless couple anxiously waited to see what would happen next.

Their anxiety proved needless and the attempt at coercion ended in farce, as they were taken on a trolley with Estévan and dropped off at the bean-fields; upon which they proceeded to eat as many beans as they wished, then, eluding Magog, who had remained to keep watch on them, they ran away again.

Once more they were subjected to a few minutes' severe fright as two of the bee-beetle overseers pursued and endeavoured to drive them back; and, again, it was quite a time before they recovered from acute respiratory pains owing to the strain violent exertion put upon their lungs; but by eight o'clock they were fed, free and none the worse for their second act of defiance.

The long empty day hung heavily on their hands, as they had no way of spending it other than chatting and dozing among the boulders above the barracks. It would have gone quickly enough had they still actively been lovers, but all reference to their personal feelings for one another being barred by an unspoken mutual consent, their conversation soon became stilted. After having talked for a while of the staggering surprise, that the appearance of Anna had occasioned them on the previous night and discussed the members of the Russian party, they found little else to say; so they were not altogether sorry when the approach of the afternoon sandstorm drove them back to their cell.

As they sat there they were both conscious of a slight tension, which was broken only temporarily by Escobar returning, tired and grumpy; but the giants produced fifteen beans for the party's evening ration; so they took some comfort from this indication that the attempt to bully them into becoming plantation slaves was not to be maintained permanently.

Soon after sundown Harsbach came in to report that his first efforts with the bee-beetles had proved unsuccessful. So far he had failed to convey to them the idea of a prospecting expedition; and, although he had made rough drawings of the two parties—first separately descending from two Saucers, then together seated in one cell—they had either not understood what he was driving at or were opposed to the parties joining up, as he and his companions had been taken back to their cell and shut up in it as usual.

After some discussion it was decided to present their captors with a *fait accompli* by the Russians moving in with the Argentinians, and Harsbach went off to fetch Anna and Zadovitch. The one cell would easily have accommodated twenty human beings; so when the newcomers arrived with their mats and few belongings there was ample space for them. Both parties displayed the utmost courtesy towards the other; but as some members of each could express themselves in a general conversation only with difficulty, they soon gave up the attempt and settled down to sleep.

When morning came they were given a fresh example of the giants' indifference to any matter upon which they had not received definite orders. Gog and Magog arrived with rations for three, gave them clumsily to Carmen, Escobar and Kem, then sat down to wait patiently while they were consumed. They glanced at the Russians, exchanged a few clucking noises but, after a moment, took no further notice of them.

Harsbach then gave an interesting demonstration of his power to transmit thought, which in this case verged on hypnotism. His party also had two giants to look after them, whom they had derisively christened Uncle Sam and John Bull. Concentrating on Gog, the Herr Doktor willed him to go and find these two monsters. After a moment Gog stood up and left the cell; ten minutes later he returned with the Russians' keepers. They showed no anger at having been eluded, and had brought with them the party's rations. With expressionless faces they handed over the water flask and beans, then sat down beside Gog and Magog to watch their charges breakfast.

Meanwhile both parties had had their first opportunity to see the other by daylight, and Kem had been covertly observing his new companions with the keenest interest.

Zadovitch he dismissed at once at his face value. The yellow-haired Russian was obviously a very simple type, easily moved to anger or laughter, with the hearty appetites of an animal and, judging from his small, light eyes, imbued with an animal's cunning. He was typical of the lower ranks of the Soviet secret police, who were not expected to have any ideas of their own. Kem knew that such men were chosen for a dog-like fidelity to their masters, based on the fact that as long as they held their jobs they enjoyed an easy life with many privileges; whereas the loss of them meant a return to harsh physical labour as the only thing for which they were fitted other than routine spying.

The Herr Doktor presented an infinitely more complex personality. His disfigurement showed more plainly in daylight, but his eyes were such a dominant feature that it became almost unnoticeable to anyone at whom he looked direct. It could now be seen that they were grey, piercing, very large and widely spaced, and the latter characteristics lent support to what Escobar had said of his being a fanatic. Somehow he had managed to keep himself both clean-shaven and spick-and-span while on Mars, and this, together with his lean figure and decisive manner, gave him much more the appearance of a professional soldier than the bulky, hirsute Escobar; although the former had served in an army only in his youth, while the latter had become a colonel.

Kem soon decided that the German could display considerable charm when he wished and, as he was undoubtedly intelligent, would make a most pleasant companion provided his sore points were not touched upon. More, he was already convinced that Kruger Harsbach possessed resource and courage, so would prove a greater asset in any attempt to escape from Mars than any other member of the combined parties.

From such little chance as Kem had had to judge Anna, he estimated that, mentally, she stood about halfway between the two men with whom she had been kidnapped. Whatever the Communists might pretend for propaganda purposes about there being equality of conditions and opportunity for all in the Soviet Union, social classes very definitely existed there; so, as the daughter of a senior official, she must have enjoyed a far more spacious upbringing than Zadovitch. She was, too, a graduate of a university; yet she could not conceivably have had one-tenth of the Herr Doktor's experience of men and affairs, and she did not look in the least like an intellectual.

On the contrary, had Kem seen her in a dance-hall, or on the beach at some popular holiday resort, he would at once have put her down for what an old friend of his graphically described as "a smacked bot for uncle".

She was sturdily built, but several inches shorter than Carmen and possessing nothing of the South American's delicate beauty, grace or distinction. Her health and colouring were her best assets; for she looked as strong as a little mare and the silvery-blonde locks that framed her piquant face were set off by a pair of round, smiling china-blue eyes. She wore no trace of make-up and needed none, as her lips and cheeks were red from the warm blood pulsing under them and her skin was as free from blemish as a baby's.

As she had been captured up near the Arctic Circle she was well clad to face the bitter nights on Mars. Over a plain white sweater she was wearing a short musquash coat that buttoned across the front and had something of the appearance of a battledress blouse. Below it she had on a pair of thick, grey serge slacks, the bottoms of which were tucked into the tops of ugly, but practical, unpolished, square-toed boots that were lined with sheepskin. Suitable as the costume was to a young science graduate stationed in a cold climate, Kem could not help visualizing her well-rounded little person with nothing on but a *cache sexe* doing a high-kicking cabaret act at some night haunt in a Scandinavian city.

When they had finished eating and had paid a visit to the long dark gallery, they emerged from its archway into the big tunnel chamber to see that Uncle Sam and John Bull had manned a trolley and parked it behind that of Gog and Magog. The Russians were soon aboard it and Escobar aboard the other; but Gog prodded Kem and Carmen back to the cell and closed its door upon them. With mixed feelings they heard the two trolleys rumble away. Evidently no further attempt was to be made to enslave them, but, all the same, they felt rather as though they had been sent to Coventry, and the prospect of another long day with nowhere to go and nothing to do robbed them of any joy in their liberty.

They waited until the morning duststorm was over, then went for a long walk in the opposite direction to that in which lay the bean-fields; but the scene proved equally monotonous and they did not dare to stray far from the road from fear of getting lost in the desert. Once they saw a line of trolleys driven by giants and loaded with some earthy substance rolling along a road in the distance and, on breasting a slight rise which they had decided to make the limit of their expedition, they sighted a green belt a few miles further on, which showed that another canal lay there. In the pleasant warm hours of the middle day they slept for a while, then walked slowly back to the barracks, to await there with concealed impatience the return of the others.

During the week that followed no event of importance occurred and their plans for escape made no apparent progress. Harsbach got no further in his attempts to explain to the bee-beetles that certain minerals must be found and mined before he could complete his bomb; so all he could do for the time being was to modify its mechanism, in order that it should become operative when charged, and to furnish Escobar with specifications for designing the finer parts of his missile in a similar manner.

All of them looked forward to the evenings, as once they were well wrapped up in their bean-fibre mats they lay talking, often till midnight or later, on a great variety of subjects. With several hours' practice each night Kem and Carmen soon got back all the German they had ever learned and were constantly adding new words to their vocabularies. Zadovitch alone remained unable to participate in the general conversation, and had to content himself with scraps of Russian thrown to him from time to time by Harsbach or Anna.

Now and then the wars of the century and international politics brought them on to dangerous ground. Sometimes Kem had to exercise the greatest restraint to prevent himself from smacking Harsbach's face for the untrue and flagrantly unjust things he said about the British. At others the Argentinians were hard put to it to conceal their hatred of Communism in all its forms, and the Russian party to conceal their loathing of such dictatorships as those of Generals Franco and Peron. It soon became clear, too, that the mentalities of Carmen and Anna were such poles apart that, like oil and water, they would never mix; but recognizing the gulf that lay between them, the two girls rarely addressed one another direct.

Such tensions were, however, only occasional. For much the greater part of the time they thoroughly enjoyed these idle hours in the starlight or moonlight, during which they debated many matters, told stories and sometimes held sing-songs, in which Zadovitch, who had a fine baritone voice, was able to join. Kem, with his happy, tolerant nature, which took no account of creeds, prejudices or class distinctions, provided people were good-humoured and behaved decently to him, contributed more than any of the others to making their evenings a success; but he was far from happy in the daytime.

Had Fate decreed that he and Carmen should spend eleven hours a day alone together, in normal circumstances, anywhere on Earth, they would have found hundreds of things to talk about. The morning papers and radio bulletins would have daily provided a score of topics; he would have had financial problems and she household cares; leaving love out of the question, they could have confided their ambitions to one another with some prospect of achieving them. Food, clothes, entertainments, hobbies, games, books, pets, and even the weather, would have come up in due course for discussion. But here on Mars, with no foreseeable future, and no possible variation of regime, raiment, diet or conditions, there was positively no subject to discuss that had not already been worn threadbare. Had their walks been through countryside or jungle they would at least have had trees, flowers, beasts and birds to comment on, but the sandy wastes that they trod in their expeditions offered no conversational stimulus of any kind. As a final factor that prolonged the monotony of their day, almost unendurably, it held no breaks that they could look forward to, during which they could occupy themselves in preparing and eating lunch or tea; neither could they even offer one another a cigarette or a sweet to suck.

Carmen took this eventless existence much more philosophically than Kem; for, although she always appeared eager to talk on any subjects that did crop up, and produced her share of them, she invariably carried her rosary and, when they had been sitting silent for any length of time, employed herself by saying a number of *Ave Marias*.

Kem still thought her the most perfect living thing he had ever seen; but he was chary of looking at her too frequently, as it recalled memories of her face aglow with passion, and stirred in him fierce cravings that he had promised to subdue. Yet the very fact that he succeeded in banishing such thoughts from his mind had its repercussions. He became so bored that he could have screamed.

By the end of the week he was tempted to return to the bean-fields and start working there of his own free will, rather than continue to idle away interminable hours in semi-silence, while making pointless expeditions across almost featureless wastes, every boulder in which he already knew. He would have done so, but for the fact that he did not like to leave Carmen alone, and to take her with him was to risk that she might again be assaulted by one of the young monsters working in the fields.

At length he came to the conclusion that his only chance of escape from boredom lay in devising some way of forwarding their plans for attempting to leave Mars, and on the eighth night after the Russian party had joined them he put up a scheme to the Herr Doktor.

It was that Harsbach should steal some nitric acid and mercury and make a small quantity of explosive with them. Kem was then to produce the explosive and pretend that he had found its ingredients in one of his expeditions across the desert. By demonstrating an explosion to the bee-beetles he hoped that they would associate it with Harsbach's empty bomb-case, and thus be persuaded to agree to a prospecting expedition setting off to secure the minerals necessary to manufacture a larger quantity.

Escobar suggested that much trouble could be saved in demonstrating an explosion to the bee-beetles if Zadovitch simply fired off his pistol in front of them; but to that certain objections were raised.

Harsbach disclosed that he, too, had been carrying a pistol at the time of his capture, and added, "Since both Zadovitch and I were knocked out before we had a chance to use our weapons, when we came to in the Saucer we decided that we had better save them as a last card if our lives were threatened. Evidently the insects do not appreciate the use to which they can be put, or they would not have returned them to us after we were decontaminated; but as we have them still I feel most strongly that we should keep them up our sleeves against some great emergency."

"Besides," Kem pointed out, "the insects must have seen the bullets of your weapons when they examined your things a few hours after your arrival on Mars; therefore if they were shown one they would recognize it as something brought from Earth. The whole point of my plan is that the explosive should be some substance which we can make them believe that I found in one of their own deserts."

That clinched the matter, and Kem's plan having received general approval Harsbach promised to get to work on it next day. Two nights later the Herr Doktor handed him a little pill and said:

"This is as near an approach to fulmanite of mercury as I could get; but I feel pretty confident that it will do the trick. Be very careful of it, as fulmanite is extremely sensitive, and in spite of the small quantity it could make a nasty mess if it went off prematurely."

While they settled the details of how they would proceed with their demonstration, Kem wrapped the pill up in a piece of cotton wool from Carmen's dressing-case, and put it in the inner pocket of his colourful coat. Then they got under their coverings and joined the others in their usual evening's recreation.

After their first few trolley rides all of them had discovered that they did not need the giants to lift them on to a trolley's six-foot-high deck, as, owing to the low gravity, they could easily jump that height at a single bound. In consequence, they had now become accustomed to getting on the trolleys themselves; and, next morning, as soon as the

Russian party had got aboard theirs Kem and Carmen jumped up beside them.

Uncle Sam was squatting at the control lever and took no notice; but John Bull stared dully at his two new passengers for a moment, then made a movement to push them off. Zadovitch, in accordance with the instructions he had received, grasped the monster's great hand and, exerting all his strength, thrust it back, while Harsbach stood up and fixed his grey eyes on John Bull's saucer-like blue ones, willing him to take no further action. After a few seconds the giant relaxed, shook his head stupidly and turned away. As he did so, Uncle Sam pushed on his lever and the trolley ran forward, following out of the tunnel that upon which Escobar was being taken as usual to the hive.

When it reached the canal, instead of crossing the hump bridge towards the hive, it turned south along a road that ran parallel to the covered waterway. Kem and Carmen had never been so far in that direction before, so they now began to look about them with new interest; but, owing to the flatness of the landscape, they were carried another two miles before they could see anything other than the great half-pipe on their right and the interminable bean rows on their left. Then they saw ahead of them a second canal branching out at right angles from the first, and two minutes later the trolley sped over a bridge across it, bringing them into the oasis, where the plant was situated.

Harsbach had always referred to this place as the "Oasis" from association with the Earth-made maps of Mars, upon which all the big greenish-coloured spots where several canals crossed one another were so called; but it bore no resemblance whatever to the fertile patches in the African desert with their picturesque groups of palms. It resembled more a vast yard cut up into a number of square and triangular sections, the walls of which were formed by lengths of the semicircular coverings of the intersecting canals.

There were no tall chimneys, no great erections of steel girders, no dumps of coal, and no buildings of any kind resembling those usually seen at a factory. Neither were there any networks of railway lines. The floors of the yards were bare, spotlessly clean and, like the roads, of polished stone. Everything was moved about them on the magnetized trolleys, and to load them, or lift weighty objects as required, magnets on T pieces that appeared to be made of concrete were used. The only structures were cube-shaped storage tanks, from which ran pipes of varying dimensions, and a number of large concave discs on stands, that looked rather like the sound range-finders used by anti-aircraft batteries.

All work was carried out in the open, and the first yard was a scene of great activity. Hundreds of bee-beetles were busying themselves at a great number of troughs and moulds of all shapes and sizes, and scores of giants were acting under their orders. Some of the insects were adjusting the flow of liquids from pipes into the moulds, others were directing the knocking out of their contents after it had set, or superintending the despatch by trolley of finished articles to other yards.

As the trolley on which Kem sat rolled over the hump of another bridge he glimpsed the domed tops of three grounded Flying Saucers about a quarter of a mile away. Next second, beyond them, against the blue horizon he caught sight of the morning dust-devil.

Almost immediately afterwards there came a loud hooning sound and a violent wind tore at his hair and clothes, but not a particle of sand was carried on it. Harsbach leant over and said to him:

"Those things that look like sound-detectors are wind machines. All of them are oriented either upward or towards the circumference of the oasis. By turning them on whenever there is a duststorm the insects are able to keep their plant free of the particles of sand which would prove ruinous if they got into the more delicate parts of the things they are making."

A few moments later, and for some time afterwards, they witnessed a curious phenomenon. Immediately above the oasis there remained a large circular patch of bright blue sky, but on every side there had risen what appeared to be a solid yellow wall that shut them in. It was like being at the bottom of an enormous roofless gasometer.

Meanwhile the trolley had crossed two more bridges, and three yards in which a number of unfamiliar objects were being assembled. On the far side of the fourth yard it halted, and they all got down within a few feet of a torpedo-like structure that was obviously the Herr Doktor's bomb-case. A group of about twenty bee-beetles stood near it and, as he approached them, waved their horns in greeting.

Kem produced from his pocket three drawings he had prepared for the occasion. The first showed him picking up the explosive pill; the second showed three figures, distinguishable by their clothes as Carmen, Anna and himself, looking about for something on the ground; the third showed them again with several giants heaving clods of earth on to a trolley. Looking first at the group of bee-beetles, then at Harsbach, Kem asked:

"Have you any idea which are the top boys of this party?"

The Herr Doktor shook his head. "No; none whatever. The fact that there is no way of recognizing these creatures is one of the major obstacles to communicating with them. I can never be certain that I am endeavouring to convey my thoughts to the same ones for two days running. My recent lack of success may be due to my having tried to transmit ideas to a succession of different shifts, instead of having the advantage of being able to reiterate my wishes again and again to one group that would gradually become conscious of what was in my mind. But, of course, it may be that the idea of this expedition was too complex for them to grasp solely by telepathy and a certain amount of dumb show."

Kem laid his sketches down before the bee-beetles, then brought out the explosive pill and showed it to them. Harsbach, meanwhile, erected a simple apparatus he had made on the previous day, which consisted of a tripod carrying at its apex a receptacle to hold the pill, and a length of wire that when jerked would release a hammer. With the "nothing up my sleeve" sort of gesture that came so easily to Kem from his amateur conjuring, he placed the pill in its container and stepped back. Then Harsbach pulled the wire.

There came a blinding flash and a far louder report than Harsbach had expected. Instantly the whole plant was thrown into wild confusion. From the yard in which they stood, and those adjacent to it, thousands of bee-beetles flew up into the air, while the giants stampeded, cackling with fright, and flung themselves upon one another to huddle terrified in corners.

Carmen clapped her hands, Zadovitch and Anna waved their clenched fists in the air and shouted joyfully in Russian. They had suffered so many humiliations and discomforts at the hands of their captors that their delight at this first turning of the tables was understandable. They felt, too, that it was an earnest of more sweeping victories to come. But Kem and Harsbach exchanged a worried look. Both were wondering if, by this demonstration, they had not played their best card prematurely, and might, within the next few minutes, have to pay a very heavy price for it.

CHAPTER XXII

ZADOVITCH'S MISTRESS

STILL laughing and clapping, both the girls congratulated Kem and Harsbach on the result of their experiment. From fear of frightening them, the two men refrained from voicing their thoughts or showing their acute anxiety; but with secret concern they gazed skywards. Up there above them the bee-beetles now formed a solid black cloud that hovered ominously. Should it suddenly descend and attack, Harsbach and Zadovitch had their pistols, so might drive it off temporarily; but if the attack was persistent the hundreds of insects could smother them in a few seconds. In any case it would mean the opening of a war to the death, and that was the very last thing they wanted at the moment.

For a good five minutes, that seemed like fifty, the swarm remained almost stationary, then a score of insects broke away from its sides and began to circle slowly over the yard.

"We had better sit down," said Kem. "That may reassure them."

It was only then that the girls realized that there was any danger of their being attacked, and the whole party followed Kem's example.

This pacific move apparently had the desired effect, as the score of bee-beetles came lower and, after a further cautious circling, settled within about fifteen feet of the twisted tripod. For a further two minutes both the humans and the insects remained quite still; then, as though at a signal, the swarm above broke up and, coming down, its members began to chivy the still terrified giants back to their work.

Greatly relieved, Kem stood up, advanced towards the group on the far side of the tripod and again spread his sketches out on the ground in front of them. Cautiously they gathered round to examine the drawings. Then Harsbach joined him and kept pointing, first at the wrecked tripod, then at the empty warhead of his bomb.

Within a few minutes it was evident that the insects had got the idea, as some of them began to fly round Kem's head, then alight on the trolley, to which Uncle Sam and John Bull had now crept back on all fours. With a directness characteristic of them they obviously wanted Kem to start at once on his self-proposed mission; but he had no intention of doing so without adequate preparations.

Turning over one of his sketches he drew on the back of it two trolleys —as a precaution against one breaking down in the desert—four giants, a row of Pan-pipe water flasks and some beans: then on another a sketch of the sun rising and setting on Mars with twenty semicircles above it, indicating that they might be away about three weeks. Again the bee-beetles were quick in picking up his meaning. Three of them flew on to the trolley and by waving their pincers practically beckoned him to join them, while others ordered up another trolley with two more monsters.

Kem grinned at his companions. "Well! I will say this is service. I had no idea that we would get results so quickly; but since we have, there doesn't seem much excuse for us to delay our departure. As I started this excitement they will expect me to go, and Anna must do so, because she's the only one among us who knows in what sort of ground we are likely to find lead and uranium. Carmen, you'll come, won't you? The trip will provide a new interest for us."

Anna promptly walked towards the trolley, jumped, and landed lightly on it. Muttering something in Russian, Zadovitch followed her example; but Carmen made no move and said to Kem in Spanish:

"No, Sem. You must go; otherwise they might call off the expedition; but I prefer to stay behind. If I had to spend several days as well as nights with that little Russian we should end by tearing one another's eyes out. Besides, as you and I arrived here with Estévan, it would be unkind for both of us to leave him without even a word of warning."

"Oh, come!" Kem protested. "Estévan will have Harsbach to keep him company; and it is silly to get all het up just because Anna has been educated with completely different standards from yourself. Besides, I can't leave you to wander about day after day on your own."

Harsbach's smattering of Spanish had enabled him to understand the gist of this, and he said to Carmen, "Just now Zadovitch declared that wherever Anna goes he means to go, too; so that leaves me entirely without assistance. He was quite unskilled, but nevertheless in many ways I found him useful. Would you care to take his place and come here every day to help me?"

"Indeed I would, Herr Doktor," Carmen replied. "Nothing would please me better than to have a job to occupy my mind."

Kem gave her a rather unhappy look. Bored as he had been in her company for the past week, he was very loath to leave her; and now that he was about to set off into the unknown he felt a sudden impulse to seize her in his arms and hold her very tightly to him. But he repressed it and, a little awkwardly, held out his hand.

She took it and smiled into his eyes. "Please don't be offended, Sem; but I'd already made up my mind that if this expedition came off it would be a good thing for us to separate for a while; although I hadn't expected such a sudden parting. If I thought you were going into danger I should come, too; but there is no reason to think you will come to any harm, and when you get back we shall have lots of new things to talk about."

He grinned a trifle sheepishly at this disclosure that she had recently been as bored as himself, and gave her hand a squeeze. Then, as she wished him good luck, he turned, nodded to Harsbach and jumped up on to the trolley beside Anna and Zadovitch.

No sooner had he landed on its deck than Uncle Sam started it up and it rolled forward towards the nearest bridge. As Kem turned to wave to Carmen he noted that the second trolley was following them and remarked to Anna:

"Now we have another couple of monsters attached to us we must decide on names for them. How about Stalin and Molotov?"

His suggestion had been made as a leg-pull, and he had expected her to retort that she thought President Truman and Winston Churchill more suitable; but to his surprise he saw that her face had gone almost apoplectic with indignation. Her blue eyes popping and her cheeks bright red, she stuttered:

"How . . . how dare you liken those wonderful men to brutes?"

"Sorry," he apologized. "I didn't mean to offend you; but your national leaders are just statesmen like any others, and I don't see anything particularly wonderful about them."

"Of course they are wonderful," she protested hotly, "and quite different from those of other countries. The others are all greedy warmongers, whereas ours are idealists of great vision who work selflessly and tirelessly for the welfare of the workers of the whole world."

Kem saw that it would be pointless to contradict her. He suddenly realized, too, that the Russians had not christened their monsters Uncle Sam and John Bull from any sense of fun, but because they really thought those characters represented all that was hideous and brutal. Clearly, if he wished to remain on speaking terms with Anna he must remember that her sense of humour did not extend to matters concerning the Union of Socialist Soviet Republics. With a shrug he said, "Never mind: let's call them Mutt and Jeff."

With the three bee-beetles who had taken charge of the party buzzing above them, the trolleys crossed the other bridges out of the oasis and twenty minutes later reached the barracks. On the way through the tunnel the bee-beetles consulted with others of their kind who had charge of the store-rooms there. A whole basketful of beans, some fifty water flasks and a quantity of fibre mats were piled on to the second trolley, then the little cavalcade rolled on out into the sunshine again.

Turning to Anna, Kem said, "This is your party, as it is you who have to produce the goods. Which way do you wish to go?"

She had not spoken since her outburst but no longer showed any trace of ruffled feelings, and replied in a brisk, business-like voice, "As far as we know the deserts on Mars do not differ from one another, so we may as well go straight ahead. First I shall look for lead, as without it to protect him it would be dangerous for Comrade Harsbach to reduce uranium to its components. Lead, too, should be much easier to find; as there must be any amount of it on Mars. Our only difficulty will be to identify a high-content lead-bearing ore in a place where it is easily workable."

"What sort of ground must we keep a look-out for?" Kem enquired.

"The principal lead ores are galena and cerussite," she informed him; "the former being more common. It is usually found in veins in slaty clay, accompanied by copper and iron pyrites, but it also occurs in pockets in limestone; so our best prospect will be to examine any likely cliffs that we may come to."

Kem's German was progressing well, but, apart from the bit about cliffs, Anna's explanation proved too much for him; so he forbore from questioning her further on geological matters and left it to her to point out to Uncle Sam the directions in which she wished him to drive the trolley, or order a halt whenever she wished to get down to look at out-crops of rock.

By mid-day they reached the nearest canal to the north and found that, like the one with which they were already familiar, it had five-miles-deep belts of bean-fields on either side of it; but no giants were working in them. Crossing it, they entered another desert, which, again, was indistinguishable from the one they already knew. Every half-hour or so Anna pulled the trolley up to make an examination, but although she found indications of galena on two occasions she pronounced both sites much too unpromising for working.

Soon after they had suffered the evening sandstorm, sundown caught them about a mile off the road near a pile of big boulders; so they decided to camp there for the night. Apart from selecting the best protected places in which to arrange their coverings, there was no camp to make; but, once they had settled down, they found the change from the great gloomy cell to the open, under the starry heavens, a very pleasant one. For a while Zadovitch sang to them in his melodious baritone, then he wished them good-night in Russian and turned over to go to sleep.

But Anna was not sleepy, and now that Carmen was not present to resent it, Kem led her on to talk about life under the Soviets. She proved an even more fanatical Communist than he had supposed, and spoke with glowing enthusiasm of the time when the workers of the whole world would enjoy the fruits of their labours, instead of being ground down and robbed by the horde of parasites who battened on them in every country except Russia.

He did not attempt to argue with her, and knowing the miserable conditions under which the vast majority of the Russian masses still lived thought it rather pathetic that she should think them so much better off than the masses in the democratic countries. Yet it was obvious that she honestly believed her people to enjoy a freedom unknown elsewhere, and that it needed only a few more five-year-plans to make Russia a Utopia.

Next day they crossed two parallel canals about twenty miles distant from one another, and passed several parties of giants on trolleys, to whom their own monsters cackled greetings; then they entered another vast, desolate waste. Methodically, and apparently tirelessly, Anna examined every low cliff or group of boulders that they came to, but without any satisfactory result. Kem found the proceedings extremely monotonous, so he was very glad when sunset forced them to camp again, this time in a hollow by the roadside.

When they began to spread out their rough bedding, Zadovitch made one pile of Anna's and his own, then with a laugh pulled her down beside him. She playfully tweaked his yellow beard and pummelled his chest, but after a moment shook back her hair and nestled down in the crook of his arm. Kem tactfully moved his things some way away. He already knew that she was Zadovitch's mistress, as they had made no secret of the matter during the ten days they had been sleeping in the same cell as Kem's party. Their blatancy was one of the things that Carmen so intensely resented about them; but Kem had excused it in his own mind as not unnatural in two people coming from a country where two or three families often had to live together for years at a stretch in a single room.

On the following afternoon, as they were bumping over another seemingly interminable desert, quite casually, for something to say, Kem asked her, "How long have you been in love with Zadovitch?"

Her china-blue eyes went round with surprise, and she exclaimed, "In love with him! Why should you suppose that I am in love with him?"

"Well, you let him sleep with you, don't you?"

"Of course. He is an M.V.D. man."

Kem frowned. "What the devil has that got to do with it?"

"Everything," she replied promptly. "In Russia no girl would refuse to sleep with an M.V.D. man if he wished her to. It would be far too dangerous. I mean . . ." she corrected herself quickly, "they have considerable influence; so it would be foolish to quarrel with them. Besides, they are important servants of the State, so represent the People, and it is considered an honour."

Kem smiled to himself as he wondered how she reconciled such coercion with her vaunted ideas about freedom. It suddenly occurred to him that on the night she had been kidnapped, and Zadovitch had come into Harsbach's laboratory to protest about her working such long hours, he had not been inspired by concern for her health, but was simply impatient to have her in bed with him. The thought that the Russian had paid for his impatience by being seized by the giants and brought to Mars was amusing. After a moment Kem said:

"As you are no longer in Russia, there is no reason why you should go on sleeping with him if you don't want to."

"But I do," she admitted frankly. Then she gave Kem a little sideways smile, and added, "With him, or somebody. I enjoy it, and, after all, it is the only pleasure that is left to us here on Mars."

At that Kem let the conversation drop, but curiosity about her impelled him to ask her later in the day, "Was Zadovitch your first *affaire*?"

"Of course not," she laughed. "I am twenty-two, and I started at sixteen. That was not very pleasant, but two years later when I went to the University I greatly enjoyed myself with the young Comrades in my classes. But why do you ask? Do you wish to sleep with me?"

The directness of her question took Kem aback, but he swiftly raised a grin and hedged. "Not if it means a bullet in the back from your friend Nickolai Zadovitch."

At that moment they arrived at a lone rock standing about fifteen feet high. It made quite a landmark in the surrounding desolation, and Anna had directed Uncle Sam to it; so for the time being no more was said of the matter.

Night fell soon afterwards and they camped by another group of boulders. When the sun had set they had a sing-song, and afterwards, as Kem lay looking up at the stars before he drifted off to sleep, in spite of endeavouring to call up Carmen's image, he could not prevent the wicked little smile Anna had given him from keeping on recurring to his mind.

The fourth day passed no differently from the preceding ones, except that they made a wide semicircle and recrossed a canal that they had crossed the day before, in order that when they made a satisfactory strike, as Anna felt confident they would before long, it should not be too far from their base.

Just as they had decided on a place to camp for the night, Anna pointed at a low ridge about a mile away, and said, "It seems a pity not to have done that one before finishing for the day."

Kem looked across at it. The two giants had already stepped down to the ground while Zadovitch, eager to get his water ration, had jumped off with them and was walking towards the second trolley. The three bee-beetles who were acting as observers of the expedition had flown off as soon as the trolleys halted; as it was their custom to return to their hive every night and fly out to rejoin the expedition soon after dawn each morning.

On several occasions Kem had attempted to get the giants to let him try his hand at driving one of the trolleys, but they always pushed him away. This seemed an excellent opportunity; so he took a few paces along the deck, grasped the control lever and thrust it forward. As he did so the trolley ran on along the road. Having seen the giants work them so often he had felt certain that they must be almost fool-proof, and so it proved. He found that he could steer and regulate the pace without any difficulty.

At the sound of the trolley moving Zadovitch turned and shouted something after them, but Anna shouted back and pointed at the ridge she wanted to prospect; which apparently satisfied him. The giants, too, had turned and came running in pursuit, but the trolley was much too fast for them to catch, and they soon gave up the attempt.

Having run the trolley a quarter of a mile down the road, Kem cautiously manœuvred it across the sand between the gaping crevasses, until they reached the ridge. As he halted it the flaming sun went down below the horizon. Jumping to the ground, they covered the last fifty yards of broken ground on foot. By the time they had done so darkness had fallen and only starlight lit the desert scene.

Looking round, Anna said, "It's too dark now to do any prospecting; but that's no reason why we shouldn't stay here for a while. Let's find a comfortable place to sit down."

In silence they searched about until they came upon a little cave and, without exchanging a word, sat down inside it.

After a moment she said with a giggle, "I bet Nickolai is hopping with rage about our having run away from him. But we need not worry about that. He dare not try to follow us here now daylight has gone, from fear of falling down one of the crevasses and breaking his neck."

"That goes for us, too," replied Kem. "I'd never be able to manœuvre the trolley back safely in the dark. It looks as if we are marooned here for the night."

"Are you sorry?"

"No; it's a pleasant change to be free of him and of those four ugly brutes."

Anna pouted. "Is that all! I know you are in love with that awful anti-social Argentinian woman, but at least you might be polite."

He turned his head. It was very close to her round, piquant face, and he could see her eyes bright in the starlight. With a rueful smile he said, "Your guess is right; and since I can't tell you that I love you, what do you expect me to say?"

"You don't have to say anything," she smiled back. "There are better uses for a tongue and a pair of lips."

When she had said that she opened her mouth, put her little pink tongue out and waggled it at him.

It was three months since Kem had stepped off the liner on which he had met Carmen. Three months was a long time for a young man like Kem, at the height of his youth and vigour.

Grinning at Anna he now put out his tongue and leaned forward. Their tongues touched. Their mouths opened wide and closed on one another. Her arms went round his neck. Very slowly she leaned over backwards and drew him down on top of her.

They made love with violent, savage passion, hurting one another yet rejoicing in it. In everything but the sexual urge they were poles apart, but for the time being it dominated them both utterly. Straining their muscles they fought rather than caressed, and kissed and kissed until their lips were bruised and sore. Then, still clasping each other tightly, they lay gasping for breath while the stars above moved slowly on.

It was now very cold, but they did not notice it. The only thing that impinged upon their consciousness was the intense, utter silence of the desert.

Suddenly they heard a stone clink, then footfalls. Starting apart they sat up. At the same instant they caught sight of a figure against the sky-line. It was Zadovitch. He had risked the crevasses and found them. He was only about ten yards away, and as they moved he saw their white faces in the shadows. With a snarl of rage he took a pace forward and drew his gun. As Kem sprang to his feet he knew that his life was not worth the five beans he had missed for supper.

CHAPTER XXIII

ALL SET FOR A KILLING

THE instant Kem had seen Zadovitch he had realized that he could expect no mercy if the Russian believed he had made love to Anna. One imprudent glance from either of them, giving that away, and he would be finished. But he thought there was still a chance for him if they showed no sign of guilt. Zadovitch could have seen nothing. To all appearances a sudden impulse had caused his companions to go off to prospect a last pile of rocks before the light failed; sunset had caught them and they had become benighted there. Such was the fact, and Kem's intentions had been completely innocent. That he had succumbed to Anna's blandishments was neither here nor there. Everything hung on whether Zadovitch accepted their situation as the result of an accident, or believed that they had deliberately planned to evade and deceive him.

In that tense moment Kem had taken such comfort as he could from the thought that the Russian had no grounds whatever to suspect him of designs upon Anna, as he had never shown the least personal interest in her, nor she, as far as Zadovitch could know, in him. But the thought was cancelled while still half-born. The Russian's angry cry on catching sight of them, and his pulling his gun from its holster, demonstrated more plainly than any words could have done his conviction that their desertion of him had not been accidental. Now the whole attitude of his massive body, outlined against a background of innumerable stars, showed unconcealed menace.

Kem knew that in Soviet Russia life was held cheaper than among any race of savages. Tens of thousands of people were condemned, without trial, to death there every year, merely through being sent to endure the impossible hardships of the forced labour camps. And every M.V.D. man was an habitual killer. He could speak no Russian; so it was impossible for him to reason or plead with Zadovitch. Even could he have done so, he knew that it would have been useless. Zadovitch was a dangerous animal who believed that he had been robbed of his mate.

Kipling's famous line, "I have taken my fun where I found it, an' now I must pay for my fun", flashed with grim appropriateness into Kem's mind, to be followed instantly by the cynical rider that, in this instance, even if he hadn't taken his fun he would, all the same, be on the point of paying for having had the opportunity to take it.

About having done so he had no regrets, as it had been fun; if only on the same level as riding a fine horse at a breakneck gallop across a mile of firm sand, or making a perfect dive from a rock into the clear waters of the Mediterranean.

As Kem came to his feet and braced himself, these thoughts passed through his brain with the swiftness of the flickering of a morse lamp. Mingled with them were wild speculations on ways in which he might attempt to save his life.

Had he been in the open he would have turned and run, taking a chance on evading Zadovitch's bullets by ducking and dodging as he fled in the semi-darkness. But he was standing with Anna in a little bay of the ridge; behind them and on either side the rock was almost sheer, rising to a height of about twenty feet. Owing to his lightness on Mars, in three or four bounds he could have scrambled up it, but not before the Russian could put a bullet through his back.

For an instant he contemplated seizing Anna and swinging her in front of him as a shield; for it was highly improbable that Zadovitch would be such a fool as to cut off his nose to spite his face by shooting her. Yet such a display of fear would be equivalent to an admission of guilt, and it could only postpone the issue. There was still just a possibility that if he showed no concern, and could survive the next few moments, Anna would succeed in allaying Zadovitch's suspicions.

As the Russian took a pace forward, Kem decided that he would stand a slightly better chance if he relied on Anna using her wits than if he burnt his boats by endeavouring to shield himself with her body. In a low, urgent voice, he exclaimed:

"For God's sake speak to him! Tell him we couldn't help getting stuck here! Pretend to be pleased that he's found us!"

To his amazement no swift gabble of Russian followed his appeal. The only sound that broke the stillness was that of Zadovitch's boots crunching on the stones as he halved the distance between them.

Kem shot a quick glance at Anna. Her silence had suggested that she was too petrified by fear to speak; but no fear showed on her face. She was standing with her arms akimbo and her head thrown back. The starlight glinted on her pale gold hair. Her eyes were shining with excitement and her mouth hung a little open.

"Quick!" he gasped. "Say something! Ask him why he's got his gun out. Show amazement, and be indignant as hell if he accuses you of deceiving him."

Still Anna remained silent; apparently entirely absorbed in the same detached expectancy with which one witnesses the development of a crisis in a thrilling play. It was impossible to guess if her attitude was the outcome of Slav fatalism, of a conviction that it was useless to protest innocence because Zadovitch knew her too well to beleive her, or simply that she thought she would have less trouble with him later if she showed complete indifference to Kem's fate. In any case it was clear that she had no intention of making the least effort to save him.

Meanwhile, Zadovitch had halted about twelve feet from Kem. Raising his pistol he pointed it at Kem's chest, and said a few words in a harsh voice. At that moment Kem would have given ten years of his life to be able to speak Russian. Then he could have replied and, perhaps, with his far more subtle mind have argued Zadovitch into postponing his execution. As it was, he could do nothing but attempt to force a disarming smile, shrug his shoulders, spread out his hands and take a pace forward in the hope of getting near enough to grab the gun.

But Zadovitch was too old a bird to be caught by such a trick. He promptly took a pace back, thereby maintaining a distance which was too great for Kem to jump before getting a bullet through the head. Levelling his pistol again, he spat out a curse and squeezed the trigger.

As the Russian extended his arm Kem knew that his last moment had come. In spite of the cold, beads of perspiration had broken out on his forehead and the palms of his hands were damp. He hated the thought of death. Yet his principal emotion was not fear; it was surprise that he should actually have come to this. Somehow, even in the tightest corners in which he had ever been, he had never really believed that he would be killed while still quite young. Even now it seemed utterly preposterous that he, Kempton Lincoln, should be rendered as lifeless, stiff and un-savoury as a slaughtered horse lying in a knacker's yard, through a single bullet tearing a hole in the muscles of his heart. All the same, he had had more experience than most people of the sudden, grotesque and appalling change that even a small bullet could effect on penetrating a vital area of the human body.

It was now too late to seize Anna and drag her in front of him. There was no escape. Aghast, yet still half unbelieving, that at last death had really caught up with him, Kem stared down the gun barrel, expecting it to spurt flame and send crashing into his chest the little metal ball that would slay him as surely as if an Atom bomb had been dropped upon his head.

No flame leapt from the barrel; no violent impact of nickel-coated lead on bone sent him reeling back to spit blood and choke out his life. Nothing happened. There came only the sound of a faint click. Zado-vitch squeezed the trigger a second time. Again there came the click. Only then did Kem realize that something had gone wrong with the mechanism of the pistol. With a yell of triumph he flung himself at his would-be murderer.

Relief, even wild elation, at such an escape was justified; but any sense of triumph was premature. Even unarmed, Zadovitch was physically more than a match for Kem. He was a good two stone heavier, every bit as unscrupulous in a fight, equally courageous, and his muscles might have rivalled those of a strong man in a circus.

From their first clash neither gained any advantage. Kem's astonishment at finding himself still alive befogged his judgment. As he launched himself in a rugby tackle at the Russian's knees he miscalculated his distance and landed flat on the stones with his hands clutching empty air two inches short of their objective. Zadovitch wasted a precious minute in trying to find out what had gone wrong with his gun, so missed the chance to kick Kem's head in while he was still prostrate. On Kem lurching to his feet they struck half-blindly at one another, and his left caught the Russian's right wrist, knocking the useless pistol from his hand.

Zadovitch drew back for a second, then came sailing in with outstretched arms and clutching hands, hoping to seize Kem in a gorilla-like embrace. Kem, his wits now restored from the temporary paralysis that had affected them, realized the danger of coming to grips with his more powerful antagonist. He sidestepped and, as the Russian came charging past, landed a blow behind his ear. Zadovitch staggered sideways, but recovered and spun round with amazing swiftness for a man of his bulk. Again Kem dodged his charge, struck out and gave back; so that the movement brought him well out into the open, and he no longer had any reason to fear being pinned up against the steep side of the ridge.

Bellowing like a bull, the Russian came in again. Once more Kem sidestepped and struck out. Zadovitch, his eye cut by the blow, gasped and lurched away; but only to adopt a new tactic. Stooping, he picked up a boulder as large as a harvest-festival marrow and hurled it at Kem. Had they been on Earth he could never have thrown a rock of such a size, but here on Mars the lesser gravity enabled him to do so. That cut two ways. Although the great stone caught Kem on the shoulder, its weight was not sufficient to knock him down. Nevertheless it caused him to stagger backwards. His heel struck another large stone and he fell.

As he went over Zadovitch came pounding towards him. Only just in time, he rolled aside. Swerving, the Russian kicked at him, but missed. Panting, Kem got to his knees. While he was still on them a second kick landed in his ribs, driving most of the breath from his body. Gasping with pain, he heaved himself upright and struck out desperately at his enemy's face. The blow was a lucky one. It caught Zadovitch on the nose, causing tears to spring to his eyes that temporarily blinded him.

Kem was still too near winded to follow up his advantage. He knew that at all costs he must prevent those gorilla-like arms getting a grip on him, or he would be finished. He must get back his breath, then use the fact that Zadovitch knew nothing about boxing to land blow after blow on his head and body. Turning his back on his enemy, he covered thirty yards in a series of light leaps across the stones, until he reached a patch of open sand that would give him a surer footing.

Dashing the tears from his eyes, the Russian came bounding in pursuit only a few yards behind. As Kem's breathing eased a little he halted, turned and lashed out. His left landed squarely on Zadovitch's chin, his right took him in the midriff. But the two blows did not stop him: gravity again made them too comparatively light to do so. Instead, the impetus of his last leap carried him on, to fall right on to Kem and send him over backwards. The blow to the chin had knocked the Russian half-unconscious, but he managed to grab the collar of Kem's coat and hung on to it. Both of them struggled to their knees, then to their feet. Again and again Kem struck at his enemy, but Zadovitch used his left hand to protect his face while continuing to hang on like a bulldog with his right.

Gasping and panting they lurched across the sand, Kem striving to drag himself free, his antagonist striving to draw him closer to that he could get both arms round his body. All too well Kem knew that if once that happened it would be the end of him; yet he could now only jab at the Russian's head without enough power behind his blows to knock him out, and he was tiring rapidly.

Suddenly Zadovitch let out a terrified yell. His legs seemed to fold up under him and his head shot down to Kem's waistline. Unnoticed by either of them as they staggered this way and that, they had approached a deep crevasse. In swerving to avoid a blow from Kem, Zadovitch had trodden on its edge. The soft sand had given way beneath him.

For one frantic moment the Russian's feet scrabbled wildly at the ground as he strove to regain a foothold. Kem, seeing the yawning gulf into which his enemy was sliding, braced himself with all his might. But Zadovitch still had a firm grip on his coat. In vain he threw all his weight back on his heels; as the Russian dropped he dragged Kem down with him.

To save himself from going headlong after his enemy, Kem first fell to his knees, then jerked his legs out behind him. Stretched out at full length on his stomach he dug his toes into the sand; but his head protruded over the edge of the crevasse and Zadovitch was now clinging to him with both hands. Their faces were within a few inches of one another. Kem stared down into that of the Russian. The blood from his flattened nose had run all over his yellow beard, one of his eyes was closed, and his teeth were clenched in a hideous grimace from his effort to prevent himself hurtling to his death in the void.

Frantically Kem strove to thrust the Russian from him; but he could not break his hold. His enemy's whole weight now hung like a millstone from his neck, and inch by inch he could feel himself being dragged forward over the crumbling edge of the crevasse. With every movement he made the soft sand slithered from under him, so that within a few moments he was lying on a steep slope with his head a foot below the level of his legs. In vain he beat at Zadovitch's blood-smeared face with both fists. The Russian gasped and groaned at each blow but would not let go. More and more sand cascaded away from beneath Kem's chest, and he knew that in a matter of seconds now his legs would lose their grip; so that he must pitch forward into the black gulf with his enemy.

It was at that moment that he felt a hard object digging into his left collar-bone. It could only be a stone. Thrusting his right hand into the sand below his chest he drew it out, clenched it firmly and struck Zadovitch with it on the forehead. Still the Russian clung on. Again Kem struck. Zadovitch gave a last despairing groan, his grip relaxed and he plunged downward into the abyss.

Breathless, shaken and exhausted, Kem remained sprawled on the dangerous slope for a moment; then, with a cautious heave, he wriggled back to safety. As he did so Anna's voice, husky with excitement, came from behind him:

"What a fight! It was touch and go, wasn't it? But in spite of his greater strength I felt sure you would prove the better man; and I wanted you to beat him."

Still panting from his exertions, Kem turned over and stared up at her. "Then . . . then why the hell didn't you help me? . . . Since you . . . followed us here . . . you could have . . . hung on to me. . . . I might easily have . . . gone over with him."

She shook her head, then extended her hand. The starlight glinted on the open blade of a penknife that she was holding in it. "No," she smiled. "Had he dragged you any further I meant to lean over and jab this in his neck to make him leave go. But I did not wish to deprive you of the kudos of killing him unaided if you could."

"While you stood by and enjoyed the spectacle, eh?" he muttered angrily.

"Of course," she replied, obviously having failed to register the sarcasm in his tone. "It is a good saying that none but the brave deserve the fair; and it would have pleased any girl to see the way you fought your rival for me."

Her calm assumption that he had risked his life in order to keep her from Zadovitch annoyed him intensely; and, now he had got his breath back, he snapped, "It's no thanks to you that I had any chance to fight at all! As for wanting me to win—it's all very well to say that now, but what about when Zadovitch first came on us? You could have said a score of things to get him into an argument; but you didn't. You just stood there dumb as an owl and waited to see him shoot me."

At that she laughed. "No, no, Comrade: you are quite wrong there. I knew beforehand that his pistol would not go off."

"How could you?"

"Because I removed the bullets from it last night, and put stones in the magazine so that he should not notice the difference in the weight of the weapon."

"What led you to do that?"

She shrugged. "Had you not inferred earlier in the day that you would like to sleep with me? Once a man and woman start talking on that subject matters do not stand still. It was certain some such situation as that which occurred this evening must arise fairly soon. I was tired of Nickolai and preferred you to him; so naturally I took precautions to ensure that he should not shoot you immediately he realized that you meant to take me from him. I wanted you to have a fair chance to prove your mettle."

Apart from the fact that by her forethought she had saved his life, her words revealed to Kem a number of things. In spite of her university education she was, beneath the skin, just as primitive as Zadovitch had been. She did not expect men to woo her, but to take her. Love, according to Western standards, played no part in her life. Like a young heifer, she merely had preferences for males who by a combination of strength and cunning could overcome their rivals. Death meant to her no more than love, and with true Eastern ruthlessness she regarded it as quite natural that a man who proved incapable of defending himself should die by violence. Compassion was equally unknown to her. For many months now she must have enjoyed all the little kindnesses that Zadovitch had been capable of showing her, and on innumerable occasions have gone happily to sleep in his arms; yet, having tired of him, she would, without hesitation, have plunged her penknife into his jugular vein.

Most men would have found such a mentality unnatural and evil. Kem shuddered inwardly at its implications, but he was broadminded enough to make allowances. The cat that goes out on the tiles, to be mauled by the fiercest tom she can find, or even the female spider, who eats her lover's limbs while he clings to her in the sexual embrace, is not evil; both act only in accordance with their lights. Since he and Anna had been thrown together by circumstances, and would now have to spend at least several more days constantly in one another's company, he must regard her in that way. To take a high moral tone with her would be as futile as to attempt to teach one of the giants the Ten Commandments, and to quarrel with her might prove highly dangerous. Simple common sense demanded that he should look on her as neither more nor less than a young animal who, for the time being at all events, asked only to submit herself to him.

Getting to his feet, he said, "Well, what now? Shall we stay here for the night or attempt to get back to the trolleys?"

"I would rather stay here," she replied. "In the starlight it is easy to see the big crevasses; but not the little ridges where the duststorms have blown a layer of sand over the smaller ones. If one of us puts a foot wrong we might easily break a leg."

The temperature was now well below zero, and he shivered. "I know, that's the devil of it. But I'm so damnably cold. If you're willing, I'd prefer to take a chance on that, with the prospect of getting under our mats."

"I will do as you wish," she said submissively. "But I think it would be foolish to risk it. I am more used to a cold climate than you are, and I'm sure I could keep you warm. Come on; help me make a grave."

To Kem, who was still acutely conscious that deep down in the crevasse, only a few yards from them, Zadovitch was wedged and now slowly dying, her words had a horrifyingly sinister ring; but evidently she had already forgotten the Russian's existence. Kneeling down, she began to scoop a hollow in the loose sand with her cupped hands. Kem dropped to his knees and set about helping her. After ten minutes' hard work they had made a shallow ditch some six feet long and three wide. Shaking her hair away from her face she sat back on her heels and said:

"Now get your clothes off."

"What!" he exclaimed, aghast at the very idea.

"Go on," she laughed. "We'll need our clothes on top of us."

Reluctantly, but too played out now by the fierce ordeal he had been through to argue, Kem undressed. With chattering teeth and a good part of his body turned to goose-flesh, he lay down in the grave.

Meanwhile Anna had stripped herself. Although she was considerably shorter and plumper than Carmen she had a beautifully compact little figure; and, as she stood silhouetted against the night sky, notwithstanding the intense cold that bit into his exposed limbs, Kem found himself admiring it. For a second it drifted into his mind how utterly fantastic it was that he should be on Mars, lying naked in a ditch, where the temperature was below freezing-point, looking at a naked Russian girl who regarded Stalin as her god and was about to lie down on top of him.

"You will be warmer in a minute," she said as she knelt with her knees on either side of him. Then she hung her short fur coat across her shoulders, drew the rest of their garments up behind her in a pile, and leaned forward till her breasts came down on to his chest.

As he raised his arms to put them round her she shook her head. "No, no. Not yet. Use your hands to scrape all the sand up round us, so that it covers our loose clothes."

Silently he did as he was bid, while she shuffled with her feet until they lay nearly buried under sand and garments. Almost at once he was conscious of her gracious warmth. It seemed to radiate from her well-covered body with the strength of electricity, and the sand in which they lay submerged kept it in.

After they had been lying there for a few minutes she lifted up her face to kiss him once, murmured, "Comrade, I like you very much," then again laid her cheek against his shoulder. A few moments later he could tell from her gentle breathing that she had drifted off to sleep with the untroubled innocence of a little child. Utterly tired out, he took a last look at the myriad stars overhead, closed his eyes and sank into a heavy slumber.

The coming of dawn roused them. As Kem woke he became subtly aware that he was not only warm as toast, but feeling relaxed, more buoyant, and fitter in himself than at any time since he had set foot on Mars. That this should be so was morally all wrong he knew, but he had never made any pretence of being a moralist. Lifting his head he grinned into the piquant little face of the pleasant burden that still lay spread upon him, and which was undoubtedly the cause of his new sense of well-being.

Anna grinned back and stuck out her tongue invitingly. Had they been in bed he would certainly have made love to her; but, after giving her one long kiss, he shook his head and murmured, "No, no, not now. We've got other things to think about."

"What things?" she asked with a disappointed pout. "We have all day before us and nothing to do in it."

"Oh yes, we have," he contradicted her. "You've got to find lead, my pretty, then uranium; so that we can get away from this damned planet."

Reluctantly she levered herself off him; and, spurred on by the chill of the early morning, they quickly pulled their clothes on. Then they walked the few yards to the crevasse and peered over its edge. Zadovitch had stuck about twenty-five feet down. His head, with its crop of blood-stained yellow hair, lolled over backwards and his mouth gaped open. If his injuries had not killed him the icy cold had done so, for he was clearly as dead as a doornail.

Anna's only comment was, "It's a pity that we were not able to strip him of his clothes."

Kem gave an inward shudder at her callousness, then recalled that in Soviet Russia the standard of living was still so low that millions of people there would go to practically any lengths to secure a stout pair of boots or thick overcoat. Turning away towards the ridge, he replied:

"I've no use for his clothes, but I want to get hold of his gun, as that might prove a godsend in an emergency. I take it you've still got the load of bullets you removed from it?"

She nodded, and they walked quickly over to the bay among the rocks where Zadovitch had caught them. Kem had expected that it would be easy to spot so large an object as the pistol, but the ground was much more broken than he had realized in the semi-darkness, and to his great annoyance their search for the precious weapon was abruptly cut short.

They had been hunting about for no more than two minutes when they saw the four giants running towards them. There was nothing surprising in that, as they had expected their escort to be worried by their disappearance; but they were entirely unprepared for what fol-

190

lowed. John Bull seized Anna and Mutt Kem. Cackling like a couple of angry geese, the two monsters shook them both with such violence that they feared that their heads would be jerked from their bodies, then threw them, breathless, dazed and sick, on to the trolley on which they had made off.

This punishment for having played truant took so much out of them that they were barely conscious of anything except their strained limbs for the next half-hour. When they did recover a little they found that they were back on the road with Mutt standing guard over them while the other three were spread out in the distance, presumably still hunting for Zadovitch.

Soon afterwards the three inspecting bee-beetles arrived on the scene and evidently received a telepathic report from Mutt about what had occurred, as they flew off to join in the search for the missing Russian. Within a few moments they located his body and, summoning the giants, set them to fill in the crevasse with loose sand.

When they had been on the job for some twenty minutes, Anna expressed surprise that they should go to so much trouble; but Kem told her that, having stamped out all diseases on Mars, the bee-beetles would not consider any labour too great to prevent harmful bacteria breeding in an exposed corpse; and that as the body had fallen too far for them to get it out they would have to fill in the whole of the lower part of the crevasse before it could be safely buried. His assumption proved correct, and the best part of the morning had gone before the burial was completed.

Meanwhile, although they had recovered from their shaking, they had begun to suffer from hunger and thirst. They had missed both their supper and breakfast yet Mutt, evidently under instructions, maintained a firm refusal to all their pleas to be allowed to take their rations. When the rest of the party rejoined them they fared no better; and it became clear that the bee-beetles meant the severity of their punishment to be such that it would deter them from running away again.

Still hungry, and now suffering acutely from thirst, they were compelled to resume their search for lead, and the hours of the afternoon seemed interminable. At last sunset came, and with unutterable relief they gulped down the water that they were then given. Overcome by strain and fatigue they crawled under a pile of mats, and had barely muttered *"Schlafen Sie wohl"* to one another before they were asleep.

Next day, towards evening, Anna found some pockets of galena among a mound of rocks she was prospecting, and pronounced it to have a considerably higher lead content than any she had previously come upon; so they decided to start a mine there rather than continue their search for something better. When she had shown it to the bee-beetles and carried some of the lumps of ore to one of the trolleys, to indicate that she had found the material they needed, Kem drew a picture of a row of trolleys and a number of giants digging out lumps of rock to load on to them. Having examined it, the three insects waved their pincers to show that they understood and flew off in the direction of the barracks.

Camp was made and when darkness fell Kem and Anna resumed their love-making in a much more deliberate and leisurely manner than had characterized their fierce encounter forty-eight hours earlier. Then in the morning they set the four giants to work heaving aside the boulders in a search for further pockets of galena. That evening the reinforcements they had sent for arrived. These consisted of some eighty giants with rations, bedding and equipment on fifty-five trolleys and, flying above them, a dozen bee-beetle overseers.

The equipment they brought amounted only to a collection of hand implements, large scoops and stout bean-fibre baskets. The fact that it was so primitive seemed to indicate that open-cast mining had always proved sufficient to provide the bee-beetles with the various chemicals they used for their material-producing diets, but for present purposes it was perfectly adequate. Next day the company of monsters, whose labour was equivalent to that of several hundred humans, began operations under Anna's directions, and early in the afternoon the first convoy of trolleys loaded with galena was despatched back to the plant.

For four days the work continued from dawn to dusk, then Anna decided that they had secured an ample supply of ore for Harsbach's requirements, so on the fifth morning the camp was broken up, and she and Kem set out with the last load on their homeward journey. As, during their prospecting, they had covered the greater part of a circle, the run back occupied only a day and a half. They had been absent for twelve nights, and shortly after noon on the thirteenth day their trolley carried them over the bridges in the oasis to the yard in which they had left Harsbach and Carmen.

They were there now, and Escobar—who, it soon transpired, had completed the designs for his bomb ten days earlier—was with them. All three were engaged in assembling some of the newly-made parts for his projectile, but as soon as they saw Kem and Anna they stopped work and hurried over, shouting excited greetings.

As Kem waved back to Carmen the cheerful smile on his round face was very far from mirroring his state of mind. Intermittently for several days, and almost continuously for the past six hours, he had been worrying himself silly about the effect it might have on her when she learned that he had taken Anna as his mistress. He knew that it would distress her intensely; so he would have liked to spare her the knowledge, but could see no way of doing so.

It was not to be expected that Anna would make any attempt to conceal the matter out of deference to Carmen's feelings; and, although he had considered asking her to, he had decided against it. During the past six days she seemed to have developed a genuine affection for him; so on that account it was possible that she might have agreed to do her best to conceal, temporarily at least, their new relationship; but it was the very fact that she now showed such affection for him that had restrained him from asking her to keep their affair secret. He had felt that to do so was to offer her a gratuitous insult, and place her in the position of a housemaid whom the master of the house has seduced yet expects to hold her tongue out of respect for his wife.

And Carmen was not his wife. She was not even his mistress. She had been so only for a few nights three and a half months ago. Since then she had consistently denied herself to him, and had remained implacable in the face of his obvious distress and most urgent pleading. Reason told him that he owed her neither loyalty nor consideration. Yet the fact remained that it was her he loved, not Anna; and the second he set eyes on her again his mind was thrown into a fresh turmoil, in which delight at seeing her once more was mingled with guilty shame at having betrayed her.

A dozen swift questions and answers passed between the returned travellers and those who had stayed behind, then Harsbach asked:

"Where is Nickolai Zadovitch?"

Kem had naturally expected the question and replied calmly, "He's dead. He fell down a deep crevasse one night when we were out in the desert."

Anna turned and gave him a quick smile. "You are too modest. Why not admit that he threatened to shoot you, and that in spite of his superior strength you got the best of him?"

As they had never discussed what account they should give of the Russian's death Kem could not blame her for blurting out the truth. Obviously she had done so only because she held life cheap, and wished him to receive due credit for his bravery. He, on the other hand, felt that the circumstances in which he had quarrelled with and finally rid himself of Zadovitch might, in England, have been considered very near murder; so he had instinctively sought to conceal it. Since the cat was now out of the bag, he shrugged and said:

"It's true that we had a difference of opinion, and fought. But the fact that he missed his footing and fell down the crevasse, instead of myself, was a matter of pure chance. It just happened that his luck was out that night."

Carmen did not appear to be at all concerned at learning that he had been responsible for the death of the Russian. On the contrary, she smiled fondly at him and announced, "I'm simply dying to hear all about it; and how you found the lead, and everything. I can't even wait till this evening; so the Herr Doktor will have to give me an afternoon off."

Harsbach bowed gallantly from the waist. "Of course, Señora. Your time is your own to do what you will with." Then, with a slightly malicious smile, he added, "Your husband and I will be quite content to receive an account of the expedition from Anna."

Ignoring the innuendo, Carmen took Kem's arm and said, " For the past week our captors have been allowing us to drive the trolleys ourselves when we wish to, and they are quite easy to manage. Let's take one and drive up to our old haunt among the boulders above the barracks."

It was years since Kem had blushed; but he now felt the hot blood flush his cheeks to scarlet as he cast a swift, embarrassed glance at Anna.

She gave him a wicked little smile and, evidently fully convinced in her own mind that she had permanently hooked him, murmured meekly, "Don't think of remaining here on my account. I have no desire to monopolize your attention in the daytime." Then, like the little gamin she was at heart, she grinned and stuck her tongue out at him.

Her highly suggestive grimace was not lost on Harsbach. His harsh, abrupt laugh echoed round the yard, then he said to Kem, "Now we know why you killed Zadovitch and threw his body down a crevasse."

Kem swung upon him and retorted angrily, "You are wrong! I killed him to save my own life."

Carmen had already taken a few steps towards the nearest empty trolley; so her back was partially turned towards them. But she had heard every word they said and, out of the corner of her eye, had seen Anna stick her tongue out.

Without turning round, she said to Kem in a curiously muted voice, "Please don't start an argument, but come with me. I want to talk to you alone."

As he caught up with her he saw that her face had gone deathly white, and he felt as though he had broken some precious thing that could never be replaced.

CHAPTER XXIV

MURDER

CARMEN was first up on to the trolley. As soon as Kem had jumped up beside her she pushed over the lever and it ran forward. The scene that had just occurred made both of them tongue-tied from embarrassment. In an awkward silence they drove through the bean-fields—now empty of giants as the harvest in that area had been completed some days before —and on to the top of the great low mound under which lay the barracks. It was not until they had got down and settled themselves among the boulders that either of them spoke. Then Carmen simply said:

"Well?"

"Well what?" he retorted, with an edge on his voice; for during their silent ride the shame he felt had become sublimated into a growing anger and, having persuaded himself that she had no right to reproach him, he was now on the defensive.

"You know well enough," she said. "You have been making love to that little Russian slut."

"Yes. She has become my mistress," he replied with brutal frankness. "What about it?"

As Carmen turned to look at him he saw that her big eyes were incredibly sad, and she murmured, "Oh. Kem, how could you? She is a product of everything that is evil. I know it is not her fault that she has been brought up as an atheist and to be shamelessly immoral; but the fact remains that she and her kind are bent on destroying everything that is noble, honourable and decent in our world. What can you possibly have in common with such a woman?"

"A young and healthy body."

"Surely something more than that is needed by people like us before we can give ourselves in love?"

"This isn't love. I have no feelings whatever towards Anna but good, clean, honest lust."

Carmen sighed. "To admit that you have simply been behaving like an animal makes matters no better. I should have thought a man like you would have been ashamed to confess that you are incapable of controlling your baser instincts."

"You may be a saint, but I am not," he burst out angrily. "You know as well as I do how we are situated. We've found lead, but we have not yet found any traces of uranium, and we may have to search half the planet before we make a strike. Even when we do, it will be a long time before Harsbach can get his bombs finished. Then we shall still be faced with the problem of persuading or tricking these damned insects into letting us take the bombs up in one of their Flying Saucers. Given that we succeed in that, our attempt to terrorize them into taking us back to Earth may quite well fail. Whichever way you look at it, we shall be stuck here for months yet; perhaps years; maybe for good. You cannot possibly expect me to live like a monk for the rest of my life while constantly in the company of two pretty women; one of whom, at least, feels the same way as I do. It's utterly unreasonable. And, anyhow, I don't see that you have any right to complain about what I choose to do."

For a moment Carmen was silent, then she replied, "No: that is quite true. When I refused to sleep with you myself I gave up even the ethical right to question your actions. But that does not alter the fact that I love you; and it's only natural that your unfaithfulness should come as a shock to me, because I believed you loved me, too."

"I do love you," he said in a more gentle voice. "I've never ceased to do so. I swear that. The thought of having to hurt you like this has made me desperately unhappy for days past, and I only wish to God there was a way in which I could spare you further pain about my being physically unfaithful."

She laid a hand on his. "There is a way, Kem. Let's forget that you ever went on your expedition, and start all over again."

He swung round, his face beaming and exclaimed joyfully, "You mean you're ready to sacrifice your scruples and let me——"

"No, no!" she drew back quickly. "Not that! You know I can't. I meant that if you really loved me you would be willing to give up Anna; so that we could at least be again all we were to one another before you went away."

The sudden unexpected way in which she had unintentionally aroused his hopes made his disappointment all the greater; yet he gave a full minute to considering what she had said before replying, "If we were certain of getting away from Mars in a few weeks, or even a few months, I'd willingly give up Anna to retain your respect; but for all we know we may be stuck here for good. That being the case, it just isn't on; because I know myself too well to believe that I could keep it up indefinitely. Sooner or later the yen for her would get under my skin again, and you would feel even worse about it if you found out that I had started to deceive you with her behind your back. I know only too well how rotten it is going to be for you to see me being even civil to her now you are aware she is my mistress; but the remedy is in your own hands. You can't have it both ways. Either you must put up with that or stop playing the virtuous wife to a husband who doesn't give a damn for you. I don't have to tell you which course I would rather you chose."

She shook her head. "No, Kem. What I wouldn't give you for love I certainly will not give to prevent your making me miserable over another woman. Holy Mary be thanked, I have a little more character than that."

"I'm sorry," he apologized. "I shouldn't have put it that way. The very last thing I intended was to be brutal: it is only that I am looking at the future a little more realistically than you seem capable of doing. Naturally, loving you as I do, I shall do everything I possibly can to prevent Anna drawing attention to the fact that she is my mistress, in your presence. But, actually, after to-night, it's unlikely that she will even have a chance to do so for some time to come. The sooner we can find uranium the better; so I expect she will set off on another prospecting trip to-morrow. As things are between you and me, naturally I shall go with her."

Carmen smiled a little wanly. "As far as I am concerned perhaps that's just as well. Now, leaving Anna out of it as far as you can, tell me about your trip."

The air having been cleared between them, Kem became considerably more cheerful; and, glossing over Zadovitch's death, raked up the few amusing incidents from his twelve-day journey to recount them with gusto. Only the approach of the evening sandstorm drove them down into the tunnel, and while they waited for the others to return he took the opportunity to find an empty cell, into which he carried some bean-fibre mats; so that should Anna insist on vaunting her now proprietary interest in him, he could take her in there to sleep, and so minimize Carmen's distress at their relationship.

Actually the evening passed off better than he had expected, as most of it was devoted to a sing-song. Then, next morning, with fresh supplies, their four giant warder-retainers and three inspecting bee-beetles, he and Anna set out on their second prospecting expedition.

Before they had gone far Kem asked her what sort of minerals she would look for in seeking to detect the presence of uranium, and she replied:

"Both pitch-blende and carnotite contain uranium. The first is a glossy bluish-black substance found in igneous rocks; the second a canary-yellow mineral which occurs in sandstone deposits. In our world pitch-blende is the more common; but both are relatively scarce, and here we are much more likely to come upon carnotite. In fact I have already seen traces of it in some of the sandstone cliffs while we were prospecting for lead; but never in sufficient quantity to make a payload. From the distribution of the traces I found I think we should go north-east for two days, without wasting time in examining any rocky areas we pass, then start our prospecting on the third morning."

That night, and for many nights to come, the camps they made had few features to distinguish them from one another, or from those in which they had lain while on their first expedition. During the days they traversed endless deserts, intersected by occasional roads and bean-planted canal zones, both of which became separated by ever greater distances as they advanced into the vaster wastes to the north.

Had they been offered a wish, and chosen a honeymoon in which solitude should be the first consideration, their desire could not conceivably have been more completely gratified. The giants performed their duties in a manner so like automatons that, after a time, they seemed to become no more than detachable parts of the trolleys they operated. The inspecting bee-beetles came and went with the regularity of clock-work. Apart from these representatives of the two types of inhabitants of Mars, there was neither man nor beast, bird, reptile or insect, to disturb for one instant the even tenor of their days and nights.

On setting out Kem had been far from happy, as his talk with Carmen had shaken him badly. She had not lost one iota of her attraction for him, and he was more than ever convinced that she was the finest person he had ever known. While he resented the fact that her resolution had driven him into hurting her, he could not help but admire it, and was half inclined to wish that he had the strength of character to emulate it. But his Latin temperament was utterly averse to asceticism in any form, and he felt that he had been right in refusing to pretend otherwise. He felt, too, that it would be foolish to allow himself to drift into fits of contemplating how infinitely happier he would be had she been with him on the expedition instead of Anna; so he deliberately checked each thought of Carmen as soon as it came into his head, and by this means succeeded for the time being in getting her image out of his mind.

In that Anna unconsciously helped him; because to explore her personality was like endeavouring to understand an entirely new kind of book, that had no explanatory opening but a certain amount of interesting matter wedged in it between many pages of extremely dull nonsense.

Sexually he found her surprisingly immature. She was nice to cuddle, because she was fresh-skinned and sweet-breathed; but she knew nothing at all about love-making as a graceful art. It struck him that she was probably symptomatic of the Communist world from which she came. If one pressed the right button she worked, with vigour and precision, and no one who possessed a ration card with her number stamped upon it could have any reasonable grounds for complaint. Yet about her amorousness there was neither the enticement of gradual surrender nor the allure of tasting forbidden fruit, which added so much to most love affairs in the bad old capitalist world.

Her sense of humour was strictly limited. It consisted only of the custard-pie variety and occasional excursions into the realms of school-girl smut. Any forms of shaggy-dog story, play upon words, or satire, were entirely outside her comprehension. In mathematics, physics and various other practical subjects she appeared to have a sound education, and she could talk intelligently on the ballet; but art and literature were to her almost closed books. Her geography and scripture were extremely sketchy. She believed that Jesus Christ had lived in Constantinople and been made use of by the early Popes as a sort of soap-box orator, to persuade the masses to resign themselves to slavery on the promise of a future life on which he knew quite well they would never enter. Such history as she knew concerned either the development of Marxism or was an incredible tangle of perversions of the truth. She had never heard of the civilizations of Egypt, Greece or Rome, and believed that the past consisted of one long, black record of evil rulers driving their peoples into war, in order to enrich themselves, or holding them down by deliberately created famines and using a pampered soldiery to carry out mass shootings whenever outbreaks occurred. She was, too, fully convinced that the masses in every country outside the Soviet sphere still groaned under the feudal system, and that Churchill was the King of England.

Kem soon found that any attempt to educate her to the truth was hopeless. He was careful to preserve the fiction that he was of Spanish descent and an Argentinian; but he said that he knew London and Paris, as well as Buenos Aires, and endeavoured to give her some idea of the life led in those cities by ordinary people. She simply would not believe that most factory girls owned several frocks, could change their jobs whenever they liked, and worked only a forty-four hour week compared with the sixty-hour week usual in Russia; or that the cinemas had seats enough to accommodate everyone who wanted to go to them, that people incapable of work received the same rations as the most highly-qualified technicians, and that the vast majority of families enjoyed the privacy of a home of their own, which rarely consisted of less than four rooms. These, and many similar facts, were all stigmatized by her as capitalist lies invented to disrupt the solidarity of the Soviet workers; and, after a time, she began to show strong resentment that Kem should —as she thought—continue to treat her like a gullible child.

Sometimes she carried the war into the enemy's camp by dilating on how the 200 million inhabitants of Russia had eliminated the friction inseparable from the ties of blood relationship through converting themselves into one great big happy family, with the kindly, impartial State acting as parents to them all; by describing the wonders that the five-year plans would eventually produce; and by enthusing over the excitement everyone derived from rival factories competing to see which could get its workers to give up the greater number of leisure hours, in a drive to increase output as a gift for Comrade Stalin.

More for amusement than anything else, Kem usually retaliated by asking, with apparent seriousness, such questions as "Does the State employ officials to play bears with the children?" and "Does Comrade Stalin ever ask to dinner the workers who have given up their leisure for him?" But, after a time, the game grew wearisome, as it usually resulted in an argument that was terminated by Anna dragging in a lot of pompous, meaningless Marxist jargon, to which there was no sensible reply.

By their third week out they were running short of subjects on which they could talk without violent disagreement, and the monotony of the expedition was beginning to prey upon their nerves. By daytime the opaline tints of the desert scene were undeniably lovely, and by night the myriad stars made the ever-cloudless sky a thing of fairyland; yet that vast, lifeless emptiness had something inhuman and terrifying about it. The very silence seemed like the held breath of some intangible horror that was waiting to spring out on the unwary; and still more sinister were the false nights created by the duststorms, that often occurred several times a day, rendering them utterly defenceless and even for a while cutting them off from one another.

It was, therefore, a great relief to both of them when, on their twenty-fourth day out, Anna made her strike. Such samples of carnotite as she had found had proved disappointing, but this was a really promising deposit of pitch-blende, to which she had been led by coming upon traces of silica, calcium, iron and manganese in the same area. That she should have found pitch-blende pleased her particularly for, as she told Kem, both sulphur and saltpetre were among the chemicals used by the bee-beetles, and from them Harsbach could make sulphuric acid, with which uranium could be extracted from pitch-blende; whereas its extraction from carnotite would have proved considerably more difficult.

The site of their find was a more than usually rugged tangle of rocks that must once have formed an island, as it was surrounded by a depression which in some places was as much as forty feet below the general level of the desert. After showing the bee-beetles that they had discovered the material for which they had been searching, they made camp among the rocks, but owing to the distance they had covered it was eight days before squads of giants reached them to undertake the mining.

At first Kem had feared that it would prove impossible to secure any considerable quantity of the pitch-blende without sending back to Harsbach a request to make some more explosive pills for use in blasting; but the great strength of the giants, which was multiplied by the low gravity of Mars, enabled them to prise the rocks apart and break them up in a way that could have been equalled only by the fabled Titans. Within a week Anna declared herself satisfied, further work was called off, and the whole company set out on its return trip. The original expedition reached base forty-eight days after it had set out.

During the mining operations and the homeward journey Anna's spirits had remained buoyant from the consciousness that she had succeeded in a difficult task; but Kem, being nothing more than a supercargo, had had all his work cut out to conceal his true feelings. He was thoroughly sick of Anna, and suffering far more than she was from the cold. They had travelled to a point that was not far off Mars' arctic circle, and in the northern hemisphere of the planet autumn was now approaching. No trace of cloud obscured the blue sky, but even when they made their way southwards the mid-day heats were less and the nights much colder.

They arrived only a little before sundown, so were taken by their escort to the barracks and, soon afterwards, Carmen, Escobar and Harsbach joined them there. The first cargo of pitch-blende had come in five days earlier, and Harsbach congratulated Anna most heartily upon her discovery. Then, as the scientist now had the material necessary to manufacture atomic warheads for his bombs, they got down to discussing in more detail how they should make use of them.

One bomb would obviously have to be exploded in order to terrify the bee-beetles into submission, and if it were simply dropped in the desert they might regard that as only a satisfactory experiment; so some target which would shake their morale had to be selected.

"There are only three to choose from," Kem remarked; "the barracks, the hive and the oasis."

"I think it would be wrong to annihilate wantonly a number of either the giants or the insects," Carmen said. "Would not blowing up one of their canals serve our purpose?"

Harsbach shook his head. "No; our target is already dictated by circumstances. It must be the oasis. Firstly, because the Saucer carrying the bombs will ascend from there, and as we shall not know how to navigate it we could not fly it over any other target even if we wanted to. Secondly, it is at the oasis that all our work is being carried out. It is of the first importance that we should destroy all traces of it and the insects who have worked with us; otherwise they might succeed in making further fission bombs after we have left, and later bombard the Earth with them."

They saw at once that he was right, but Escobar gave a twirl to his black moustache and asked, "Having made our demonstration, what then?"

"We shall threaten the crew of the Saucer that unless they take us back to Earth we will use the second bomb to blow up the hive."

"Should they refuse, since we cannot fly the Saucer ourselves, how are we to get over it?"

That was a poser to which no one could provide an answer at the moment; but it was the general opinion that, even if the Saucer landed them with the second bomb unexploded, their possession of such a terrible weapon would enable them to force the insects into making terms with them.

After a moment Kem said, "Say we can force them to fly us back, where are we going to order them to land us?"

"In the Soviet Union," replied Anna, without a second's hesitation. "The bombs are ours and none of you stands any chance of getting away without them; so obviously the choice of destination lies with us."

"Not at all," Carmen disagreed sharply. "There are three of us and only two of you."

Harsbach shrugged. "I am sorry; but Anna is right. We shall have an unexploded bomb on board made from my formula, which is the property of the Soviet Government. I cannot possibly allow that to fall into the hands of any other government."

"You could explode the bomb after landing," Escobar suggested. But they all knew that there was much more at stake than the bomb, as the far more valuable secrets of the Saucer itself would become available to the country in which it was landed; and Harsbach promptly rejected the suggestion on the grounds that they would not have with them the necessary apparatus to explode it from a safe distance.

For a while they sat in silence, having, apparently, reached a deadlock; then Kem said, "What about Mexico? That is a neutral country with sympathetic leanings towards the Soviet. I would agree to that; but you can't expect Carmen, Estévan and me to go with you to Russia, with the possibility that we may be held there as prisoners for the rest of our lives."

"That seems a reasonable compromise," Harsbach commented thoughtfully, but Anna would not hear of it, and there ensued a sharp exchange between them in Russian. Apparently, however, she gave way, as the Herr Doktor turned from her to Kem and said:

"Mexico it shall be; but on the understanding that, having landed you there, you will not seek to prevent Anna and me making the insect crew fly us on to the Soviet Union."

Kem had very different views about the ultimate destination of the Flying Saucer, but as Harsbach held the key to the only possibility of their getting away at all, this was not the moment to give him any idea of them. So, after a brief consultation with Escobar and Carmen, he accepted Harsbach's terms on his party's behalf.

Next day they all went to the oasis. During the seven weeks that Kem and Anna had been absent both bombs had been completed, except for the filling of their warheads, and the Herr Doktor had finished making the lead screens to protect himself and Escobar from the radium rays given off by uranium. They were now engaged in manufacturing sulphuric acid for the reduction of the pitch-blende, and under their direction the other three helped with the work.

A few days later Harsbach succeeded in extracting a small quantity of nearly pure, whitish uranium from about a hundred-weight of the black, shiny pitch-blende, and declared that, if all continued to go well, the process he had invented should enable him to produce enough nuclear explosive to fill the two warheads in a little under a month. All of them were delighted to learn that there was a chance of their being able to make their attempt to get away from Mars so soon; but none of them more so than Kem, for since his return he had been plunged into the utmost depths of misery.

He and Anna had taken up their quarters in the empty cell they had occupied for one night on their return from their first journey, but his attitude to her, and hers to him, was utterly different now that they had been living together for nearly two months. Then, they had at least had the bond of mutual physical attraction and a considerable curiosity about each other. Now, there remained nothing whatever to hold them together, except the fact that they slept under one lot of mats from habit. They were quite incapable of understanding one another's points of view on practically every subject, and the more they learned about each other's mentality the less they liked it.

Not unnaturally, Kem had sought an early opportunity of unburdening himself to Carmen. He had frankly admitted how right she had been in asserting that he had nothing whatever in common with the little Russian, so therefore ought to have had more strength of mind than to allow himself to enter into a liaison with her. But Carmen had not displayed the pleasure at his repentance that he had expected. She had simply said that he had chosen Anna of his own free will and that she was not prepared to share him with her. She had added that during the seven weeks he had been away she had got to know the Herr Doktor well, and had found him extraordinarily knowledgeable; so she preferred to devote such leisure as she had to continuing her interesting talks with him, rather than to providing for Kem the companionship which Anna was incapable of giving him.

A further forty-eight hours had been sufficient for Kem to become the victim of violent jealousy. The sight of Carmen and Harsbach, each time they went off for a stroll together, turned the knife in the wound and he found the greatest difficulty in preventing himself from quarrelling openly with the German. Anna soon saw what was in the wind and maliciously began to twit him about it. Matters were brought to a head one night a week after their return by her casually announcing that she now knew for a fact that Carmen had become Harsbach's mistress.

Kem felt certain she was lying in order to torment him. He told her so, and that she was not fit to lick Carmen's shoes. Then he boxed her ears, and picking up his mats left her screaming insults at him. But his return to the fold got him no further with Carmen. She treated him politely, yet kept him at a distance, and continued to spend all her spare time in Harsbach's company.

Although Kem had not believed Anna, the thought she had put into his mind nagged at him so persistently that he felt he must try to get his peace of mind back by killing it once and for all. So when he was next able to get Carmen on her own for a few minutes he said to her:

"When I broke with Anna two nights ago it was because she said that you and Kruger Harsbach were living together. It's not true, is it?"

"Of course not!" she exclaimed scornfully. "You should know how I feel about that sort of thing better than to believe her."

"I didn't. I smacked her face and told her she was a liar. But you seem so keen on that damn' German, and never have a moment for me now. I couldn't help feeling that you might have fallen in love with him."

She smiled. "Poor Kem. I think I've punished you enough now for letting me down so badly."

His face lit up, and he exclaimed, "D'you mean you've just been using him to teach me a lesson?"

"More or less. I do enjoy talking to him, because he has done all sorts of interesting things, and he has been teaching me Russian. That helped a lot to keep my mind occupied while you were away, and I've got on quite well with it. But I'm not the least in love with him. I love you, darling, and I always shall."

At her words Kem found himself trembling with happiness. Taking her hand, he kissed it and said, "It is an age since we had a real talk together. Will you come up to the roof of the barracks for a while after sunset this evening?"

She hesitated. "It will be absolutely icy up there. Still, I suppose we could carry up some of our mats to cover us. All right: we'll go up immediately after we've had our rations."

A few hours later they were ensconced among the boulders. The cold was incredibly bitter, and as they arranged the mats she said, "We will have to cuddle up, or we'll freeze to death. You will behave, won't you, Kem?"

"Of course I will," he promised; and, as she laid her cheek against his, he took her in his arms.

In the frosty air the stars looked so near that by stretching out a hand one could have plucked them from the sky; but to leave their faces exposed for long was to risk frostbite, so they soon drew the mats right up over their heads. For an hour they talked in whispers, finding immense solace in once more being able to give free expression to their true feelings for one another after the two months during which Anna had come between them. Carmen admitted that during his absence the thought that had troubled her even more than his unfaithfulness had been suspicions that he had killed Zadovitch to get hold of his mistress; but he assured her that he had done so only to save his own life, and described what had happened in detail; upon which she agreed that he had had little choice.

As they talked on it was borne in upon him more strongly than ever before that Carmen represented everything that was best worth loving and striving for, and that he would never be really happy unless he could make her his wife, so he said:

"Listen, my sweet. In about three weeks now we shall be making our attempt to get away from this ghastly planet. Should we succeed in reaching Earth, how long do you think it would take you to secure an annulment of your marriage to Estévan?"

After a moment she sighed. "Oh, darling, I wish you hadn't brought that up. I've thought of it, of course; but it's out of the question."

"Why? Quite a lot of Roman Catholic couples who wish to marry again succeed in getting annulments."

"I know; but in my case there are no legitimate grounds."

"There must be ways in which that could be got over."

"It could if I were prepared to tell a lot of lies."

His voice hardened a little. "Surely you don't think such a minor crime too high a price to pay to enable us to get married. For my part there are jolly few things I'd stick at to make you mine for good."

She sighed again. "Dearest, if I could ensure that by hacking one of my hands off with a hatchet, I swear I would; and if these were ordinary lies I wouldn't think twice about it. But I'd have to swear them in front of a priest, so they would be perjury. If we do get away it will only be by God's mercy. How could I bring myself to mock the Holy Virgin and the Saints after they had hearkened to my prayers to intercede for us?"

Kem did not argue with her. He knew only too well how adamant she always became when her religion was in question. But the sadness of his tone wrung her heart as he said, "Then it seems we've no chance of permanent happiness till Estévan is dead."

She began to cry softly and one of her tears splashed, warm for a second, on his face as she whispered, "If we get away you must give me up, Kem. It would be all wrong for a man like you to devote his life to a woman in my position."

"No; I'll never do that," he muttered doggedly. "After all, we are years younger than Estévan, and one never knows what may happen." He did not add the thought that he could not help coming into his mind —that Escobar now appeared to be far from a good life. He had aged a great deal since their arrival on Mars and, whereas the younger people had gradually become accustomed to the rarefied atmosphere, his heart continued to give him trouble whenever he exerted himself.

For the moment Kem took such comfort as he could from the fact that Carmen had forgiven him. During the fifteen days that followed they resumed their old attachment as though it had never been interrupted and, in some ways, the link between them seemed stronger than it had ever been before. Harsbach grumbled a little about her giving him less of her time, but they were now all too occupied with the imminence of their bid to overcome their captors to think of much else; so when one night Escobar declared that he did not feel very well, no one showed great concern about him, except to express the hope that he would be better in the morning.

But he was not better. He said that he had not slept all night and complained of acute pains in his bones. There was little they could do for him, except give him some of Carmen's bromides, which had been hoarded for just such a purpose; and when the others went off to the plant she stayed behind to keep him company.

Kem was of the opinion that Escobar had simply caught a chill, and would soon recover if he spent a few days indoors beneath his mats; so he was somewhat surprised when, at mid-day, Harsbach declared his intention of going back to the barracks to see how his fellow scientist was. He was even more surprised when the German returned half an hour later to report that their friend was now delirious and very ill indeed.

It so happened that Kem had been put on a job that would have been ruined had he left it unfinished, so he worked on until nearly four o'clock; then, having completed his tricky task, he at once took a trolley and set off for the barracks to see if he could be of any help to Carmen.

As he entered the cell he saw at once that Escobar was dead. Carmen was kneeling in prayer beside the body. At the sound of Kem's footsteps she turned, and as her glance rested on him he saw her big eyes dilate with horror.

Suddenly, in a low, tense voice, she spoke. "Get out of here! Don't dare to play the hypocrite! I know you now for what you are. You killed Zadovitch to get Anna. Now you've killed Estévan in the hope of getting me. But you never shall. Never! And God will punish you for these vile murders."

CHAPTER XXV

THE LAST BEAN

KEM stared at Carmen in amazement. Escobar's illness had not even brought back to his mind the conversation he had had with her fifteen days earlier; now he recalled it in every detail. With an indignant gasp he cried:

"Carmen! You cannot possibly believe that I am responsible for this!"

Slowly she stood up. Her face was haggard, her voice rasping, as she said, "What else can I believe? You were only a boy when you went into the war. You were trained as a commando—educated as a killer. You have told me yourself of the tricks you used to lure German soldiers to their deaths, and of how you struck others down in the dark. You swear that you killed Zadovitch in self-defence; but it was because you took his woman from him first that he attacked you. A fortnight ago you said you would stick at nothing to get me for your wife, and——"

"I did not say that."

"You implied it. When you found that I was not willing to perjure myself in order to get an annulment, you made it plain that you did not mean to give me up. But poor Estévan stood between us. You said then, 'After all, one never knows what may happen to him'. What else *could* you have meant, but that he might die through a convenient accident? Knowing your record I should have guessed then what had come into your mind. I should have guessed, too, that you would not risk waiting to get back to Earth, where the law might find you out. Besides, it must have been so simple to bring about his death while he was engaged in such dangerous work."

"What the hell are you talking about?"

"About the way you killed him, of course. He died of radium burns, and it was——"

"How d'you know?"

"Kruger Harsbach told me. He recognized the symptoms when he came here soon after mid-day and found Estévan delirious. He told me, too, how you had removed that lead screen without warning yesterday from in front of Estévan. Neither of them had any idea at the time that so short an exposure would have such terrible results. And Kruger is much too decent to suspect anything. He thinks you mistook the signal and removed the screen prematurely by accident; but I know how ruthless you are at heart. I guessed at once——"

"Then you guessed wrong!" Kem cut her short, his eyes dark with anger. "As for that liar Harsbach, as soon as he turns up I'll wring his neck."

"You were talking of me," said a quiet voice in heavily accented Spanish.

Swivelling round, Kem saw that the Herr Doktor must have followed him from the plant, as he now stood just inside the doorway.

Taking a pace towards him, Kem cried, "I was! Can you give me any good reason why I shouldn't bash your face in for having poisoned Carmen's mind against me?"

"Yes!" came the German's prompt reply. "This!" and from his hip pocket he drew a small automatic.

Kem's scowl deepened. He was sorely tempted to turn a somersault and kick the gun from the German's hand. But there was always the risk that it would go off, and either of them, or Carmen, might get the bullet. Now that their attempt to escape from Mars was so near, it would be criminal to chance prejudicing it by one of them being *hors de combat*. He decided that, whatever the provocation, he must, for the time being, avoid violence.

With a cynical smile Harsbach went on, "You may have had good reasons for getting rid of Escobar, but I did not accuse you of it. I merely said that when we were packing up yesterday evening you removed the screen that protected him sooner than you should have done."

"I did so at your signal."

"Then you admit that you did move it?" Carmen put in.

"Of course I did," Kem snapped. "You were there at the time and must have seen me; but nothing was said about it then, and I was working under Harsbach's directions."

The Herr Doktor shrugged, and pocketed his pistol. "I have already said that I thought your act due to a misunderstanding of my order. To draw attention to it was pointless, as if damage had been done there was no remedy we could apply. I was hoping that Estévan had stepped aside in time, or at least been exposed for so brief a period that he would suffer no serious injury. Even this morning I could hardly believe that an exposure of a few seconds would prove fatal. A stronger man would have thrown off the effects by now, but Escobar was in poor health and that, no doubt, explains why he succumbed."

"Yes; his heart gave out," said Carmen, her accusing eyes still fixed on Kem. "But that was due to the pain he was suffering. Whether it was or was not an accident, it is you who are responsible for his death."

"Thanks for the implied doubt," replied Kem sarcastically.

"Oh, Kem!" she burst out. "Knowing how cheaply you hold life, and all the circumstances, how could I help suspecting you? But I would give anything to believe that it was an accident. Swear to me that it was and I will believe you."

"I'll do nothing of the kind," he retorted. "If you're not prepared to believe me innocent without that, you can believe what you damn' well like."

For a moment they stared at one another; Kem's round face distorted by furious anger, Carmen's showing misery and indecision. Then Harsbach said:

"Since you elect to leave us in doubt I think decency demands that you should relieve Carmen of your presence. I suggest that you should either take up your quarters again in Anna's cell or find somewhere else to sleep."

"Just as you wish." Kem stepped forward to collect his mats; but, to his surprise, Carmen checked him by a swift gesture.

"No!" she said in a sharp, high voice. "Before the end of another week we shall all either be dead or gone from here. These last few nights many things will have to be discussed. We agreed in the beginning that we must never allow personal differences to divide us in the face of our common enemy. That is more important than ever now."

Kem shrugged. "Very well. I'll stay if you like. You're certainly right about our sticking together, and that there will be all sorts of things we'll need to talk over. As a matter of fact, I think the time has come when we ought to ask Anna to rejoin us here; so that she can have her say, too."

The others agreed, and they sat down in awkward silence until, shortly before dark, Anna returned from the plant. She did not seem particularly surprised at finding Escobar dead, but soon sensed the tension between Kem and Carmen, and asked Harsbach in Russian why they should both appear so upset at an event which could be no matter for great grief to either of them.

Carmen, who could now understand enough Russian to get the gist of the question, told her sharply to mind her own business; but Harsbach said that as a member of the party she was entitled to know what had happened, and gave her a brief summary of the situation. Then he added:

"I've been waiting for you before doing anything about the body. It's far too cold for us to go out and dig a grave after sunset; but, to facilitate discussing our plans, we want you to move back in here, anyway. If you will do so at once we can then put the body in your cell for the night and bury it to-morrow."

Anna agreed to that, but the matter of the burial was taken out of their hands. Just as she was going off to fetch her mats, Uncle Sam and John Bull arrived with the evening's rations. They gave one startled glance at Escobar's still form and ran cackling from the cell.

A few minutes later they reappeared in the doorway and a bevy of bee-beetles flew in past them. The insects made a swift inspection of the corpse, then issued silent orders to the two monsters. With evident reluctance, they came in and picked Escobar up.

Carmen naturally wished to see her husband receive proper burial; so she made a futile attempt to prevent them, at the same time appealing to Harsbach to intervene.

During the past two months the German had made considerable progress in conveying his thoughts to the insects and receiving theirs, and he now endeavoured to influence them telepathically; but without success. As the giants carried the body from the cell, he said:

"I'm sorry, but they are determined to dispose of the corpse without a moment's delay, in order to prevent the least possibility of its germinating disease."

"It couldn't do that in this temperature," remarked Kem with a shiver.

"I know," Harsbach agreed. "But if I am interpreting their minds correctly they are so scared of the reintroduction of harmful bacteria through putrefaction that they don't even allow the giants to die naturally. They have some means of killing them off when they become decrepit, and so making certain of their being buried immediately they are dead. If I am right, that would explain the alarm these two displayed at the sight of a body that had been dead several hours."

When the giants and bee-beetles had gone, Carmen gave herself up to prayer and the others settled down for the night; but for Kem that did not mean to sleep. He was terribly upset that Carmen should have jumped to the conclusion that he had killed Escobar, yet he had to admit to himself that she had not done so without good reason. Considered dispassionately, his wartime exploits, the Zadovitch affair, opportunity, and a motive that stood out a mile, combined to form a damning case against him—that was when once it had been suggested that there was a case at all. In spite of their discussion about the annulment, and everything else, he did not believe that the faintest suspicion of him would ever have entered her mind had not Harsbach told her about the moving of the lead screen.

Their atomic workshop was naturally a very amateurish and make-shift affair, so certain of the screens had to be erected and dismantled daily. As Kem always attended to that, and no mention of the incident had been made at the time, he could not even recall it. There was a possibility that he had been careless, but, if so, it seemed strange that Escobar, as the person exposed to danger, had not noticed and remarked upon the fact.

Kem wondered if Harsbach had made the whole thing up. A motive for his having done so was not far to seek. During Kem's long absence, and even up to a fortnight ago, he had enjoyed a monopoly of Carmen's company. Being so much older than she was he had cleverly adopted the pose of the kindly, amusing uncle; but Kem had no doubt at all that he was in love with her. No doubt, too, the German had a very shrewd idea how matters stood between Carmen and himself. If so, what better means could he adopt of discrediting his rival than leading her to suppose that he had murdered her husband? There could have been more to it even than that. By the same stroke Harsbach might have got Kem banished from Carmen's presence, so that he would be left a free field for the ensuing nights alone with her in the cell. He had certainly attempted to bring that situation about; and it was, perhaps, only Carmen's realization that in such circumstances he might become troublesome which had led her to veto so promptly his proposal that Kem should leave.

All the same, it seemed unlikely that Harsbach had invented the whole story; otherwise what had caused Escobar's death? His complaint about acute pains in his bones certainly tied up with radium poisoning. Yet, once more, why had he said nothing about Kem having accidentally exposed him to the radium rays? Perhaps, though, it had not happened like that at all. Perhaps Harsbach had seized on an opportunity when they were alone together, and Escobar had his back turned for a few minutes, to expose him to a powerful concentration. But why should he? Surely that was going a bit far simply to discredit a rival? Could he have any other reason for murdering his colleague? Yes. They were hoping shortly to return to Earth. In working with Harsbach these three months past Escobar must have learnt many of the German's scientific secrets. His usefulness was finished. Harsbach could quite well put the final touches to the bombs unaided. Now was the time to get rid of Escobar quietly, and, without arousing Carmen's animosity, preserve for the Soviet Union any atomic data he had picked up while on Mars. To utilize the murder to detach Carmen from Kem had probably been only a secondary consideration, but nevertheless one highly gratifying to the diabolical mind that had conceived it.

The more Kem thought over these theories the more convinced he became that they were the only ones that satisfactorily explained Escobar's death; but they did little to relieve his unhappiness, as he knew that it would be practically impossible to prove them. And next day, when he managed to get hold of Carmen for a few moments, it was only with the greatest difficulty that he succeeded in persuading her to give him a hearing at all.

Having listened reluctantly to what he had to say, she said coldly, "Poor Estévan undoubtedly died from the effects of radium poisoning. He told me himself before he became delirious that he recognized the symptoms. That he had never, as far as he knew, been exposed to the rays, and could not understand why he should have been so seriously affected, even if he had been exposed for a short time accidentally, is neither here nor there. You always arranged the screens and removed them. Kruger Harsbach had nothing whatever to do with that; so I do not think you have the least justification for bringing an accusation against him. I would rather not discuss the matter any further."

During the four days that followed she did not discuss that or anything else with Kem; and, at nights, he found himself virtually sent to Coventry. Now that Carmen's Russian was fairly proficient, on the excuse of giving her further practice in it Harsbach always talked to her in that language; while Anna, who was now bitterly regretting that she had deprived herself of Zadovitch, and regarded Kem with additional hatred because he had proved such an unsatisfactory substitute for the Russian, seized on the chance to drop back to her native tongue whenever she wished to make any remark.

The only times they now used German were when they had to say something to Kem while working at the plant, or at night when they wished to have his opinion on some point connected with their plans for getting away. It was the fifth night after Escobar's death that such a point, and in this case one that looked like wrecking their attempt now, at the eleventh hour, before it had even started, was put to the whole of their small company by Harsbach.

For several weeks past they had all been labouring under the happy delusion that he had successfully sold to their captors the idea that, when all was ready, he and his companions should go up in a Saucer as its crew, and give a demonstration of atomic bombing in one of the Martian deserts. To this end a Saucer had been converted in accordance with Harsbach's requirements. Doors large enough for human beings to use had been cut in the sections of the control tower passing through both the upper and lower decks, and the machinery inside it had been rearranged in such a way that there would be space enough for them to clamber up or down from one deck to another.

That day the two bombs had been passed up through bomb ports in the underside of the Saucer and slung by specially constructed cradles from its lower deck. By evening the final adjustments had been completed; and, when the others had returned to barracks, Harsbach had remained behind to inform the bee-beetles who were supervising the work that he was ready to give the demonstration the following morning.

To his consternation they had conveyed to him that the services of himself and his companions would not be required. Had the insects had a sense of humour and been capable of expressing it they would have laughed in his face. As it was they had registered contempt, and given him plainly to understand that they had allowed the alterations to the Saucer to be made only in order that he should not suspect their real intentions and, perhaps, refuse to complete his work on the bombs. They meant to make certain minor adjustments which would enable them to launch the bombs themselves, provision the Saucer for a long voyage, and try out the effect of the bombs against two of the largest cities of Earth.

It was with mingled fury and horror the others learned that all their months of arduous work had brought them no nearer to escape; and worse—that the results of their labours were to be used in a trial attack against the people of their own world.

Harsbach could not be blamed. All of them had been equally misled by such concessions as having for a long time past been allowed to use the trolleys, and to work only such hours as they wished, into the belief that the insects had come to trust them. That they had never really done so was now infuriatingly clear; and it was equally clear that unless some entirely new and audacious plan could be thought out during the night, there was very little chance that Harsbach or any of his companions would be allowed on board the Saucer next day. It would set off for Earth, just as they had planned that, at their own orders, it should; but they would not be in it. They would be prisoners still, condemned to await its return and, if the trial proved successful, find themselves subjected to the choice of death by starvation or labouring at making Atom bombs for the Martians, while living on a diet of beans and water, for the remainder of their lives.

For a long time they gloomily discussed the bitterly disappointing impasse with which they had so unexpectedly been confronted, but none of them could suggest even a remotely possible way of getting out of it. At length Kem said:

"There is one thing that might be tried. It is based on a theory that I've toyed with ever since my first day here. The odds are that it is wrong. If so, to attempt it is suicidal. However, if there's no chance of my getting away from here, I, personally, have no wish to go on living. And since you all hate my guts none of you will miss me, so——"

"Oh, Sem! Don't say that!" The cry of protest was wrung from Carmen.

He ignored it, and went on, "I propose to go out on my own at dawn. All you have to do is to wait here and be ready to leave at a moment's notice. If I don't return within a couple of hours you'll know that I've had it. Then it will be up to you to do the best you can for yourselves."

The others all pressed him to at least give them an idea of what he meant to attempt; but he would not do so, and bade them a curt good night.

Just as dawn was breaking he woke to find Carmen kneeling beside him. She said in a whisper, "Kem, darling! Please don't go. Whatever you've done, I still love you. I can't help it. If anything happens to you I'll die, because I'll have nothing left to live for."

He sat up, put an arm round her waist, and said gently, "I must go. I'm pledged to it. Besides, as far as I can see it is the only chance left for us. But I'll go with a better heart from knowing that you still love me; and if you like I'll give you my oath, now, that I didn't kill Estévan."

"I don't need it," she murmured. "The fact that you are willing to do so is enough. I haven't slept all night, and my brain is so tired from turning things over and over these past four days that I can't think straight any more; but I suppose I ought to ask your forgiveness for having thought you capable of so horrible an act."

Drawing her to him, he smiled. "Don't bother; but you can kiss me now without having to reproach yourself. That will do instead."

Their lips met freely for the first time since they had left Earth; but almost at once they heard a stirring behind them and drew apart. Harsbach and Anna were waking, and a few minutes later the giants came in with the rations.

Kem drank his water and ate four of his beans; then he asked Carmen if he might take her work-bag. On her nodding, he emptied out its contents and tied it to his waist. Over it he pulled a long matting cloak that he had made for himself against the cold. As he reached the door he held aloft the fifth bean and, before popping it into his mouth, said with a laugh:

"Well, here goes the last bean I shall ever eat on Mars."

His gesture of bravado was made in an attempt to comfort and reassure Carmen; but his smile concealed a nervous twitching of the mouth, for he knew that the odds were on his being dead within the next half-hour.

CHAPTER XXVI

A GAMBLE WITH DEATH

THE success or failure of Kem's plan—or at least his life and the opportunity to attempt to carry the plan out—hung upon one thing. It was a question that had often exercised the minds of all six human beings who had arrived on Mars, and they had frequently discussed it; but none of them had ever been able to produce any evidence one way or the other. He was now about to settle that unsolved question, and it was the quite simple one—could or could not the bee-beetles sting?

If they could, it was a foregone conclusion that the contents of the poison sac of an insect a hundred times the bulk of an ordinary bee would bring instant death. It was this latent if unproven menace that, from the beginning, had restrained their captives from ever making the least gesture that the insects might construe as an intention to use physical violence against them; while, for their part, if they possessed such deadly striking power, they must have realized that their captives once killed would be useless to them; so, although they had many times been made angry, the fact that they had not used it proved nothing.

The complete lack of evidence on this all-important point arose from the extreme simplicity to which the bee-beetles had reduced life on Mars. They no longer had either enemies to fight or other species to kill for food; neither had they ever been seen to quarrel among themselves. The giants were the only other living creatures on the planet, and they were so completely dominated by the insects that they never showed the least sign of resisting an order. That might be from the knowledge that the insects had the power to sting them to death; but it might have another cause, and it was in that possibility that Kem's one hope lay.

He thought it certain that at one time the bee-beetles had had stings, as otherwise he did not see how they could have succeeded in dominating all other life on the planet, and eliminating every species on it except the giants; but there seemed good reason to suppose that their great battles for supremacy must have taken place thousands upon thousands of years ago.

It is common knowledge that in evolution Nature makes biological adjustments to all species according to the changes in their circumstances. Some creatures had rudimentary wings which have since been absorbed into their structure; others had gills that have shrunk and atrophied, because climatic changes in the localities they inhabited made it essential for them to hunt their food by different methods. Human noses are losing their keenness of smell because it is no longer necessary to use them for scenting danger, and with every generation human teeth are growing a little weaker because the age has passed in which they had to be strong enough to tear raw meat from freshly killed carcasses. It was, therefore, possible that if the bee-beetles had had no occasion to use their stings for several hundred generations their poison sacs had dried up, and that the giants, being creatures of very low mentality, continued their blind obedience only out of habit, and a race memory of the very real terror that had once been wielded over them.

With these mingled fears and hopes seething in his mind, Kem took a trolley and drove himself down to the bean-fields. As autumn had advanced the tall plants had gradually dried out, and for the past week large numbers of the giants had been employed in harvesting the stalks to make their baskets. Halting his trolley on the road near the largest group of giants in sight, Kem jumped off it and went towards them. They stopped work for a moment to stare at him with their usual vague curiosity. One of the overseer bee-beetles at once flew up with the evident intention of finding out why he had come there, and settled on a bean-stalk within a foot of him.

Nerving himself to take the plunge, he gave a loud shout to rivet the giants' attention, then stretched out his hand and grasped the insect.

He felt a sharp stab of pain in the cushion of his middle finger. For a second he went as white as a sheet, expecting a fiery poison to streak up through the veins in his arm; but the pain remained local. He realized then that the creature had only nipped him with one of its pincers. With a gasp of relief he held the struggling bee-beetle up for the giants to see, then proceeded to put his plan into execution.

The four-inch long insect was more bulky than a card, but no larger than many other objects with which in the past he had practised sleight of hand. Loudly declaiming the conjurer's old patter, he made several mystic passes and cried, "Hey presto!"

Before the eyes of the astonished giants the insect apparently vanished into thin air, while actually he had passed it swiftly through a slit in his bean-fibre cloak and dropped it into Carmen's work-bag, which he had taken and tied to his waist for that purpose.

He was still only just completing the operation when a second bee-beetle flew up. Sensing that its comrade had been attacked, it hurled itself straight in his face. Had he ducked or given back he would have failed in his object, which was to impress the giants with his power over the insects; so he took the blow of the light body squarely, then caught it as it fell, half stunned by the impact. Again, he went through his magical patter, and made the insect vanish.

Next moment he was face to face with the second terrifying ordeal that he must survive if his plan was to succeed. From afar a score of the bee-beetles had seen that something was wrong in that part of the field. They came zooming down upon him from all directions.

He knew now that they could not sting; but everything hung upon how many would attack him at one time. If they called up reserves they might overwhelm him by sheer weight of numbers. Planting his feet firmly apart he braced himself and gave battle.

His transparent duststorm visor protected his eyes; so he was able to use his left hand to guard his mouth, while with his right he seized one of the insects that came within easy clutch. Those he caught, he gave a swift squeeze, firm enough to frighten but not to kill, then tossed them as high as he could into the air. In half a minute he had dealt with a dozen in that way, and each of his victims, on finding itself free again, had flown off at high speed in evident terror.

But there were still a score of them buzzing furiously round his head and diving in at his face whenever they saw a chance to evade his darting hand. Both his ears were being fiercely nipped and his hands had been lacerated in half a dozen places; yet he knew that it was all or nothing. If he once faltered and ran the game would be up. In spite of the pain of his hurts and the terror inspired by the thought that they might yet succeed in tearing his face to ribbons, only by remaining there and fighting to a finish could he now hope to emerge victorious, or even save himself. Again and again he beat the insects off, or caught and flung them from him.

The end came quite unexpectedly. As though seized by mass panic, the remainder of the swarm suddenly abandoned the attack, rose high in the air and flew off towards the hive.

Two of their number were left, either dazed or slightly injured, on the ground. Stooping, Kem whipped them up, one in either hand, juggled with them for a moment as though they were a couple of black snooker balls, then caused them one after the other to vanish.

Meanwhile the giants were cackling like a flock of geese and jumping up and down in wild excitement. The original group had been joined by scores of others, who had come running from all parts of the field; so that there were now the best part of a hundred of the great bald, naked monsters gathered in a circle round the amazing human who had defied their age-long masters, and possessed the extraordinary power of causing them apparently to disintegrate at a touch.

Panting from his exertions though he was, Kem lost not a second in putting the next stage of his plan into execution, for to have done so would have been to risk the ebbing of the wave of hysteria that had seized upon the plantation slaves before he could use it for his purpose. Pulling a basket nearly as big as himself, that was half filled with lengths of bean-stalk, from a young female giant, he tipped its contents out on the ground and kicked it away from him. Next, knowing that the monsters were always desperately eager for their rations, he made the motions of drinking and, tearing off a piece of bean-stalk, began to chew it. Then, pointing towards the barracks, he jumped upon his trolley.

Waving and clucking, the giants ran to the trolleys they had been loading and flung their loads to the ground. Kem pushed over the lever of his trolley and, as it ran forward, yelled, "Up the Rebels!" The monsters could not understand his words, but it was abundantly clear that they grasped his meaning. Crowding on to a dozen trolleys, they came screeching along the road behind him, like groups of hideous demons just freed from hell. The mutiny, which he had scarcely dared to hope he would succeed in fermenting, had well and truly started.

On entering the tunnel through the barracks Kem kept his trolley well to its cliff-face side, so that when he reached the cell where the others were waiting he could pull up, leaving ample room for the trolleys behind him to pass. Jumping off he ran into the cell and cried:

"Our luck's in, so far! I took a chance on capturing one of the bee-beetles to see if they can sting, and then can't. Now that the giants have tumbled to that they're in revolt; so there's a packet of trouble brewing. But we haven't a moment to waste. The Saucer crew won't have had time to provision it yet, so we must take with us to the oasis enough water and beans to see us through the trip."

"You're hurt!" exclaimed Carmen, taking a quick step towards him. "Your face and hands are covered with blood."

"It's nothing," he waved her back; "only a few tears where the little devils managed to get at me with their pincers. You and Anna had better stay here for the moment. It may be dangerous along at the store-pits. Be getting your things together, and the mats, so that we'll have some bedding for the voyage. Come on, Harsbach!"

The two men ran out and hopped on the trolley, then Kem drove it to the big chamber where, three months before, he and Carmen had seen the bee-beetles busily counting out the day's ration of beans. It was now like a scene from one of the colder hells in Dante's inferno. The revolted giants had caught a company of the insects at an early stage in their daily task, and had promptly set upon them.

The massacre, for that was what it amounted to, had been in progress only a few minutes. The insects stood no chance except in flight; for in that confined space, owing to the great reach of the giants, it was extremely difficult for them to escape being caught, and they could not hide, as in such deep gloom their luminosity was sufficient to give away their positions. In frantic panic they darted this way and that, while the huge shadowy hands struck at them. Every few seconds one was seized and squeezed to death, or knocked down and trampled upon. Meanwhile many of the monsters were raiding the big store-pits and gorging handfuls of beans, or gulping down flask after flask of water.

It called for considerable courage on the part of two humans to mingle with the scores of monsters now engaged in an orgy of greed and slaughter, and they were still in the entrance of the chamber, endeavouring to nerve themselves for the ordeal, when they were temporarily reprieved from the necessity of facing it. The morning duststorm arose outside, and in a minute drained away the dim light that percolated to the chamber. For a few moments eight or ten surviving bee-beetles, now glowing in their full glory as Thinking Lights, flitted wildly about, casting an unearthly radiance on the grotesque faces of the monsters; then they were killed and the great hall of rock was plunged in total darkness.

Nearly half an hour elapsed before the blackness became grey, but soon afterwards Kem and Harsbach could again make out the forms of the mutineers. Just as the noise they made had gradually lessened, so had their activity. During the period of darkness they had continued to grope blindly for beans and water flasks, and now the majority of them lay or squatted round the chamber, gorged to repletion, their stomachs already swelling from their never previously experienced indulgence.

None of them made any hostile move as Kem drove the trolley cautiously in amongst them; neither did they interfere while he and Harsbach collected a quantity of empty baskets and filled them with supplies. When they had loaded the trolley with nearly as much as they thought it would carry, they picked up the two girls and their belongings from the cell and drove out of the tunnel.

As they emerged into the open, they saw to their consternation that a dozen or more Flying Saucers were circling in the sky over the oasis. If the Saucer into which they had fitted the bombs was one of them, it looked as if their hopes of getting away in it were already doomed; but as the others exclaimed in dismay Kem said:

"If ours is one of those, its having taken off is a pretty nasty setback. Still, we may make it yet. The insects on the ground must have means of signalling to their pals up in the air. If my plan comes off we'll make them bring it down for us."

Harsbach grunted, then said a trifle stiffly, "Anyhow, congratulations on this extraordinary situation you have succeeded in creating. This is the first chance I have had to discuss it with you. Please tell us your intentions."

Kem turned to grin at him. "That's simple. By exploiting the bee-beetles' panic I hope to persuade them tò let us form the crew of the Saucer."

"Persuade them!" echoed the German. "Surely it would be more correct to say 'coerce them' into giving us possession of it?"

"No, it wouldn't. The Saucer is no earthly use to us unless we can get it with bee-beetle pilots who are willing to fly it under our orders."

"That is true. But how, having led a revolt against the insects, can you hope to bring them to this complacent state of mind?"

"That will be up to you," Kem replied with a laugh. "And when I've given you the layout I hope you will agree that it should not prove beyond your powers. Under my cloak, in Carmen's work-bag, I still have the bee-beetles that I captured. They are certainly alive, as I can feel them moving about; and, as far as I know, they are uninjured. I intend to produce them with profound apologies. You must convey the idea that I intended them no harm and was only having a game. In fact, that the whole affair was entirely unpremeditated; so I was both astonished and distressed when the giants misconstrued my little act and began this mutiny."

Harsbach's quick mind had already grasped the logical outcome of this distortion of the facts. "I see," he said; "and we are to offer ourselves as the allies of the insects in suppressing the revolt?"

"Exactly. Nothing like this can have happened within bee-beetle memory. They will be at their wits' end. By this time the whole oasis will be in a ferment at the news of the mutiny, and the insects are probably on the point of taking refuge in their hive. But they must know that such a step can afford them only temporary safety. They are sunk for good unless they can find a new way of terrifying the giants into submission."

"And we have it in our bombs."

"That's the idea. The apparatus for releasing those bombs was made on the assumption that we should release them. It is far too cumbersome for them to operate. The giants could manage it, but are no longer available. We will volunteer to go up and drop an Atom bomb on the barracks. Once we are in the air we proceed in accordance with our original plan."

"Excellent," agreed Harsbach; "except for one point. If we leave Mars without provisions we shall be dead from the lack of them long before we could reach Earth. But to start loading all this stuff we have brought with us into the Saucer would at once give away our intention to escape."

"I realized that. We must drive a bargain with them. They must provide us with pilots to take us back to Earth in return for our promise to use the bombs to quell the revolt."

"If we can succeed in making such a bargain, I trust you do not suggest that we should really use the bombs in that way?"

Kem shook his head. "Certainly not! These insects brought us here against our will. They threatened to starve us to death unless we helped them to produce a terrible weapon for use against our own kind. They deliberately tricked us into completing the work by converting the Saucer to our requirements and promising that we should form its crew. We owe them nothing, and must give the people of our own Earth all the protection we can by any means succeed in affording them. If we can once get up in that Saucer it would be an unforgivable crime for us to fail to launch at least one bomb on the oasis, and so destroy every trace of the work you have carried out there."

The others agreed wholeheartedly with all he said. Then they fell silent, for by this time they were anxiously scanning the road ahead of them. There were no longer any giants to be seen in the bean-fields and not more than half the groups that had been working in that locality had gone back to the barracks; so it looked as if the remainder had taken the opposite direction and carried the revolt into the oasis. Five minutes later, as the trolley switchbacked over the first canal bridge, they saw that their surmise was correct.

All work had ceased in the first and second yards; the bee-beetles had disappeared from them and seventy or eighty giants were revenging themselves on the insects who had enslaved them for so long by indulging in much senseless destruction. Whether they possessed any sense of humour at all had always remained doubtful, but with a curiously high-pitched cackle, that was possibly their form of laughter, many of them were smashing the moulds, breaking open the great bins of chemicals and pulling down the pillars that supported the wind machines; while some of the younger males were chasing and throwing down females, who squeaked with mingled fear and animal pleasure.

In the third yard several flights of bee-beetles were still making futile efforts to protect their plant. Here they did not suffer the same disadvantage as had those who had been massacred in the vaulted tunnel chamber, as they could fly up out of reach; but they were clearly getting the worst of it. Again and again irregular formations of the insects launched themselves at the giants' faces, but the monsters were no longer frightened of them, beat them off with ease, and, now and then, caught and crushed one.

As the trolley rolled over the curve of the next bridge, all four of its passengers gave exclamations of relief. The Flying Saucer that had been brought into the fourth yard for conversion to carry the bombs was still there. Scores of bee-beetles were grouped about it and several of them were flying in and out of its entry port. As they had sent up the other Saucers, evidently to save them from being sabotaged, it seemed, at first sight, illogical that this one should still be grounded. But Kem was quick to see a possible explanation.

"I believe our luck's still in," he cried. "They must already have realized what a potent weapon they have in the bombs for suppressing the revolt; but they are not strong enough to operate the levers that discharge them, and are trying to work out a method of doing so before sending the Saucer up."

Whether he was right or wrong, it was instantly made clear that the insects did not regard them as potential allies. No sooner had the trolley appeared over the bridge than a swarm of them rose in the air and came hurtling straight at it.

Halting the trolley, Kem drew the bag containing his four captives from under his cloak, threw it to Harsbach, and shouted:

"Quick! We must use those boys as our ambassadors. Do your stuff on each one before you let it go. Send them back with my apologies and our offer of help. We'll keep off the swarm while you concentrate."

He had hardly finished speaking before the swarm was on them. The cloud of insects was ten times the number that had attacked Kem in the bean-field. The air seemed black with them. They beat on every part of the four humans, tearing with their sharp little claws at faces, hair and clothing. With flailing arms Kem and the two girls smashed at them, and with little cries of pain plucked them from their ears, chins and fingers.

Meanwhile Harsbach had thrown himself on his knees between two baskets of beans, and, crouching down with his head almost on the floor of the trolley, had drawn one of the bee-beetles out of the bag. Holding it between his hands he pressed them to his forehead, and strove to impart to it the simple telepathic message that they came as friends. To each of the four insects he gave a full minute; then, as he released the last of them, he stood up to join in the fight that was still raging. For a further two minutes it continued, then it ceased as suddenly as it had begun. The whole party were left breathless and reeling; their faces and hands were dripping with blood; the two girls were weeping unashamedly from the hurts they had received; but they knew that their message had been delivered, and that they would now at least be able to parley with their enemies.

Kem ran the trolley across the big yard and halted it beside the Saucer. Harsbach signed to the others to stay on it, got off, and proceeded to open negotiations. For some moments he remained standing with his eyes riveted on the black mass of insects that had now gathered there, occasionally making descriptive gestures, while they watched him intently but gave no apparent indication of their thoughts.

Nevertheless, when he did turn his head towards the trolley he declared himself quite certain about what was in their minds.

They had sent for help to all the hives in other parts of Mars, and when it came would overwhelm the local giants. But that would take time and every moment meant a further destruction of their property. If the humans would go up and stop the revolt at once by dropping the bombs they would have them flown back to Earth. But not yet. They must remain on Mars until they had made two more bombs. The insects were quite confident that they would manage to restore order without human aid, and were unshakable in their decision that, if the bombs were to be used, only by their replacement could the captives buy their freedom.

CHAPTER XXVII

TEMPTING PROVIDENCE

THE attitude of the bee-beetles was bitterly disappointing. Kem had felt confident that in their present desperate situation, once they understood that an alliance was being offered to them they would be only too eager to accept help at the price asked for it. He had forgotten the great advantage that the insects' immensely superior mobility would give them over the giants in a prolonged conflict. Within a few hours swift flight would probably bring hundreds of thousands of them from other oases; and the creatures had brains, whereas the giants were morons. They were at a temporary loss only because they had been faced by a totally unexpected situation; but they would soon get themselves organized and think of a way to subdue the few hundred stupid unwieldy slaves who could not hope for reinforcements.

Yet there was the Saucer all set to go up. A navigating crew must already be in it, ready to take off and save it from sabotage by the giants if they succeeded in breaking through to this yard. Kem felt that by hook or by crook he and his party must get aboard, as they might never get another chance like this to escape from Mars. It was natural that the insects should be most loath for the bombs to be used unless they could ensure that others should be made, so that they would still have prototypes from which to make hundreds more for their hellish designs against Earth; but there was still a chance that in their present extremity they would give way if they were treated with firmness. Jumping off the trolley, he cried:

"Tell them there's nothing doing!"

"Those are the best terms they will give us," Harsbach replied a little uncertainly.

"I bet they have no intention of keeping their word. Anyway, we couldn't possibly leave them with the secret of the Atom bomb."

"All the same, I feel we should accept. Once we are on board we may be able to think of some way to trick them."

"No amount of trickery will enable us to live through the journey to Earth without rations," put in the practical Anna.

The Herr Doktor gave her a worried look. "I know. I had not lost sight of that. I was thinking that we might adopt some modification of our original plan."

Carmen shook the drops of blood from her hands, and said, "You mean use one of the bombs and save the other to terrify them into doing as we wish? We could then make it part of our terms that they should put out a dump of rations for us to come down and collect."

"We'd never pull that off!" Kem's voice was abrupt and urgent. "The old plan might have worked if we'd been able to spring it on them as a surprise. But we've more or less shown our hand now, and when they've quelled the revolt they are far more likely to dig their toes in. Our one chance is to defy them while they are still up against it. If only we can get the rations aboard, we'll find a way to coerce the pilots when they have to take the Saucer up to save it from being sabotaged by the giants. Come on! It's now or never!"

Suiting the action to the word, he picked up a basket full of water flasks, sprang off the trolley with it, and leapt towards the Saucer.

In spite of the lacerating they had already received, both the girls gamely followed his example, while Harsbach made a great mental effort to dissuade the bee-beetles from intervening. His attempt was unsuccessful. As Kem bounded up the ramp to the entry port the great swarm of insects rose and again fell upon them.

To all of them the next ten minutes seemed a night-long nightmare. To lift and hold the big baskets they needed both hands, so only for brief intervals were they able to defend themselves. Had not the strong transparent shades protected their eyes, they would have been blinded and rendered *hors de combat* within the first few moments. The only factor in their favour was that their bodies and the loads they carried weighed only a third of what they would have done on Earth. That enabled them to transfer the provisions and their belongings from the trolley to the Saucer without great effort and comparatively swiftly. Yet as they worked all of them sobbed with agony from the tearing of their flesh by the pincers of the scores of insects endeavouring to stop them.

They had succeeded in getting little more than half their supplies aboard when there came a fresh development. At first it looked like proving helpful to them, but swiftly turned into a new menace.

As Kem had anticipated, the flights of bee-beetles that they had seen twenty minutes earlier, striving to check the depredations of the giants, could no longer hold the mutinous monsters in the third yard. Little groups of giants were now penetrating to the fourth yard, intent on further destruction. At their appearance, as though at a signal, the main swarm of insects ceased attacking the humans, and sped away to aid their comrades' attempts to repel this new incursion; while a dozen or so of them—presumably the crew of the Saucer—flew into it.

"Take a breather!" Kem cried, and only too gladly they all paused from their labours for a few moments to wipe the blood and sweat from their faces. Then, with renewed energy, they set to work again.

But they had hardly done so when they became aware that within a matter of minutes they would be faced with another crisis. Some of the giants had seen the beans that they were loading into the Saucer and, with a greedy cackling, were making most determined efforts to reach it. The clouds of insects beat upon and harried them; but, shaking their bald heads and flailing wildly with their hands, they continued to make swift progress across the yard.

While loading up, even the physical pain to which the four humans had been subjected had not entirely swamped in their minds the vital question upon which everything now hung—once they had got aboard the Saucer with their rations would they, or would they not, be able to induce its insect pilots to take it up?

Even as they laboured so desperately, they knew that all their efforts might be thrown away. It was quite certain that the pilots would not willingly take them back to Earth without having received definite instructions, and if they feared that there was any likelihood of their being coerced into doing so, they might refuse to go up at all.

Their fears that they had, perhaps, reached a dead-end were suddenly relieved by feeling the Saucer lift a few inches. Evidently the pilots had decided that it was preferable to take their machine up with the humans on board to allowing it to fall into the hands of the giants. Yet the time margin left for escape was of the narrowest.

Harsbach and Carmen were already aboard. Anna had brought the last load of mats from the trolley. The monsters reached it at the moment she tumbled through the port. Kem was still outside and about to scramble in after her. One of the giants flung himself forward and seized him by the ankle. The Saucer was now rocking a little from side to side, but had not yet fully taken off. For a moment it looked as if Kem would be dragged from it before it could get into the air. Desperately he clung on with both hands, his muscles strained almost to the limit of endurance as the monster tugged upon his leg.

Suddenly, beneath his left arm, he glimpsed a spurt of flame. A deafening report almost shattered his ear drum. Six feet away the giant's forehead dissolved into a mass of pulped bone that spurted blood. The grip on his ankle relaxed. With a gasp he tumbled inboard.

As he fell upon his back on its upper deck the port above him closed, and the ceiling of which it formed part began rapidly to revolve. At the same instant his glance took in the means of his salvation. Anna was standing over him, her small white teeth clenched, a pistol clutched in her hand, from the barrel of which a wisp of smoke still trailed upward.

"Thank you!" he muttered as he got to his feet; then pointing at the weapon, he added, "I didn't know that you had been carrying a gun on you all this time."

She turned and gave him a contemptuous look. "It is Zadovitch's. Surely you do not think that I am quite such a fool as to have left it where he dropped it; so that you could get hold of it? As to saving you, I did so because we shall yet be faced with many difficulties before we can get away, and we need you to help us overcome some of them."

Aware that certain of those difficulties would confront them almost immediately, Kem turned his back upon her without replying. Owing to the way in which they had had to get aboard the Saucer its upper deck presented a spectacle of wild disorder. Great piles of beans and water flasks littered the floor in all directions. Scattered among them were Carmen's bags, her original bedding, a score of fibre mats and numerous oddments that had reached Mars with the Russian party. All four survivors of the two kidnappings were now hardly recognizable, owing to the blood that oozed from scores of small wounds all over their faces. Anna, still clasping her pistol, but her nerve now gone, had collapsed in a flood of tears upon a heap of beans; Carmen lay moaning against one of the square tanks. The two men were in little better shape, but both knew that everything depended on their taking prompt and vigorous action within the next ten minutes. Harsbach had already pulled open the door to the control tower, and motioned Kem to precede him through it.

Their roles had long since been decided, when they had worked out their original plan and had expected to be allowed to go up as the crew of the Saucer instead of having to fight their way into it. Kem was to act as bomber, while Harsbach remained in the control tower, and used his utmost endeavours to dominate the insects there.

When the alterations to the Saucer were being carried out, Harsbach had persuaded those who were supervising the work to have the way through the tower made, on the excuse that it would be necessary for a human crew to pass from the upper deck to the lower in order to launch the bombs. Actually he could have easily worked out a way of releasing the bombs from the upper deck, and his secret reason for insisting on a means of getting from one deck to the other was to gain access to the control room. Only by stationing himself in it could he hope to prevent the pilot from flying the Saucer away from the oasis before they had gained sufficient height to release a bomb without danger to themselves. Moreover, by watching the insects while the Saucer was in the air there was at least a chance that he might grasp the principles upon which they flew it.

As Kem clambered down through the control tower he had little opportunity to take in anything but a general impression of its interior. He got a glimpse into one miniature cabin in which an insect was facing what appeared to be a complicated chart; into another that seemed to serve as the bridge, as there were three bee-beetles there, one of whom was looking into the lens of an instrument that resembled a camera, while the other two were perched on a thick rod with a number of small levers spaced out along it; and into a third, which contained five more of them who appeared to be off duty, as they were not occupied with anything. The remainder of the space was criss-crossed by a number of struts and wires, but there was none of the complicated machinery he had expected to see; so it seemed that the great magnet worked upon quite simple principles.

When he reached the lower deck he was faced with the tricky business of getting into position as, had he let go, the gravity of Mars would have caused him to drop on to the whirling lower surface of the Saucer. As a means of getting over this a number of hand-holds had been fixed to the underside of the deck and two strongly made box-like structures, each six feet in length and open at their ends, which were about four feet square. The two open-ended boxes were parallel to, and just above, the noses of the two bombs, and had been designed for the bomb-aimer to lie in.

Swinging from hand-hold to hand-hold Kem reached one of the boxes, stuck his legs into it, then wriggled inside. Turning over on his stomach, he lay there looking down the bomb-sights, past the nose of the bomb to the place where its port would open. Barely two hours had elapsed since he had gone to the bean-fields that morning, yet that now seemed days away, and he had been through so much that he felt almost at the end of his tether. His face, neck and hands ached intolerably; he would have given almost anything to be able to shut his eyes and relax his vigilance, but he dared not. The moment of crisis which would spell success or utter ruin was almost upon them. Racked by anxiety as well as pain, he waited, his nerves strung to fever pitch, for the signal.

Some fifteen feet above him Harsbach had already embarked on his delicate and difficult task. For the first few moments he had kept one eye on an altimeter of his own construction that was fixed to the wall of the control room, but his main attention was riveted on the bee-beetles. As the altimeter reached 1,500 feet one of them pushed forward a lever. The Saucer heeled over a little, and the Herr Doktor guessed that, as he and his companions had forced their way into it, the pilot had decided to accept their offer to drop a bomb on the giants' barracks. Instantly, he put out his hand and pulled the little lever back until the Saucer righted itself.

The insect waved its pincers in protest; but Harsbach put the tip of his finger on the needle of the altimeter, then raised it gradually, at the same time throwing out the thought that they must go very high to escape their own blast. Apparently satisfied, the creature quieted down. Soundlessly, but so swiftly that all the humans in it felt the pull of gravity strongly, the Saucer continued to gain height. In another two minutes the altimeter showed 25,000 feet.

Harsbach then stretched out his hand and began to fiddle with the row of little control levers. His job was to stop the Saucer spinning, so that a bomb could be dropped; but he did not know how, and could find out only by trial and error.

The first lever he touched enormously increased their speed; so he swiftly flipped it back. The second sent them heeling over sideways; again he withdrew it. The third apparently had no effect; but from the control room he could see neither the upper nor lower surface of the Saucer; so he shouted loudly to Kem:

"Watch out! This may be it."

Meanwhile, the two insects on the lever bridge were evidently much annoyed at his interference with their machine, and buzzed angrily up and down; but he ignored them and listened anxiously for Kem's reply. After a moment it came:

"O.K. She's slowing down."

From where Kem lay he could now see circular streaks in the under-surface as it revolved less rapidly; then, as it slowed still further, the streaks became identifiable as parts of the bomb ports that had been cut in it. Another ten seconds and it stopped; but not in the right position for the bombs to be launched. They had realized that all the chances were against its doing so, and the second it came to rest Kem jumped down on to it.

"She's stopped!" he yelled up to Harsbach, and bracing himself against one of the bombs he began to push with his feet against the surface, until it came round with the bomb ports under the noses of the bombs. Then, opening a section of the bomb's casing, he swiftly adjusted the mechanism controlling the plunger so that it should detonate the bomb when the altimeter inside it had fallen to 2,000 feet.

Harsbach was being kept busy with the bee-beetles. The one from the chart room had joined the other two, and the three of them were buzzing angrily up and down in front of his face. Keeping the lever pressed over with one finger, he waved them away with his free hand. He was hoping desperately that the Saucer was still over the oasis, as he had had no means of following their swift flight, and if they had risen at even a small angle from the perpendicular he feared he would find it difficult, if not impossible, to get it back over the oasis again. His voice sharp with anxiety, he shouted to Kem:

"Have you got a sight yet? Where are we?"

Kem was now back in his bomb-aimer's box. As he had been landed by night he had never had a bird's-eye view of the part of Mars in which they had lived for so many comfortless, unhappy months. Now that he was looking down upon it from a cloudless, sunlit sky, from his memory of the map Escobar had drawn he believed the great oasis to be one called Lucus Feronia. But this was no time to speculate on such a matter. Quickly he called back:

"We are not quite over it, but nearly. Perhaps a quarter of a mile from the south-east edge."

"Near enough!" Harsbach cried gleefully. "Nothing will be left but rubble within five miles of its explosion point. Let her go!"

Kem pulled over the firing lever. The thirty-feet-long bomb slid from under him like a huge silver fish. "Bomb's away!" he shouted, then followed its course as it floated downwards. Owing to the lightness of the material from which it was made it went down comparatively slowly. Gradually it diminished to vanishing point, but he continued to stare along the track it had taken.

Suddenly a small white puff appeared; it swelled unevenly, rapidly increased to a great cloud that displayed fantastic shades of orange, red, pink and purple; then seemed to rise up like a huge black monster that sought to tear them from the sky.

For a few minutes after Harsbach had stopped the Saucer spinning it had continued to rise; then it had seemed to hover; now it had begun to fall. In swift alarm Kem yelled:

"Switch on! For God's sake stop her falling!"

Harsbach had already felt their downward motion. At that very second he had turned over the little lever, and the surfaces of the Saucer again began to rotate, shutting off Kem's view of the sinister, radium-charged mushroom that seemed to be reaching up to engulf them.

Next moment there came a crack like thunder, and the air rush created by the explosion struck the Saucer's under-belly. It had had no time to gather upward speed from its own power, but was lifted like a frail bark upon a tidal wave. For a moment or two it rocked wildly, then settled down to pursue its upward course.

No sooner had it done so than Harsbach found himself hard put to it to deal with the situation in the control tower. It seemed probable that the lens through which one of the bee-beetles was looking was attached to some type of periscope that had enabled it to see the bomb burst over the edge of the oasis. In any case, the vibrations of the insects told him at once that they realized they had been tricked, and did not mean to take the destruction of their great plant lying down.

The nine he could see were joined by four more, who flew down from inside the stumpy mast that projected above the Saucer's roof. All thirteen of them swished wildly back and forth, showing signs of utmost fury. One dived back into the bridge cabin and hurled itself on a lever. Instantly the Saucer tilted sideways. Harsbach was thrown off his balance. By grabbing a girder he managed to save himself. Thrusting out his free hand, he pushed the lever back, but only just in time to prevent the Saucer turning over. The insect threw its weight against another lever. The Saucer stopped going up and shot forward; but Harsbach did not worry about that. He was now having all his work cut out to defend himself. Twelve out of the thirteen bee-beetles were violently attacking him. Once more he winced and swore as they tore at his exposed flesh with their pincers. Again the insect in the bridge cabin threw over a lever. Suddenly the Saucer went into a steep dive.

Realizing now that he could not overcome them single-handed, he shouted to Kem, "Come up here and help me! Quick!"

Kem, much perturbed by the alarming motions of the Saucer was already making his way by the hand-holds towards the control tower. Scrambling up, he squeezed himself into the narrow space beside Harsbach, and, while the Herr Doktor flicked the lever back, drove his attackers off him. As soon as the Saucer had come out of its dive and was soaring up again, Harsbach said:

"Keep them off me while I show them the diagrams we drew, and try to drive a bargain with them."

"Wouldn't it be best to give them a chance to settle down first?" Kem asked.

"I doubt if giving them time to think over what the destruction of their plant may mean to them would put them in any better humour. Besides, I don't think we dare risk it. The other Saucers may be chasing us by now, and they may have some means of cutting off our power. Unless we can persuade or coerce these little devils into carrying us off at full speed in the next couple of minutes, we may never get away at all."

As he was speaking Harsbach had taken from his pocket two sheets of Carmen's notepaper. On one there was a map showing the main features of the locality below them and drawings of the two bombs, one of which pointed to the oasis and the other to the hive. On the other sheet there was a diagram of the solar system with an arrow pointing from Mars to Earth. While Kem continued to keep the insects off him, Harsbach laid the two papers flat in the bridge cabin and sent out the telepathic message:

"Choose. Make up your minds. Which is it to be?"

For a moment all the bee-beetles ceased their attack to circle above the papers. Then they resumed their attack with increased fury. In vain the Herr Doktor strove to impose his will upon them. They conveyed as clearly as if they had been shouting their refusal to be intimidated by the threat to their hive.

Harsbach shot a worried glance at Kem, and muttered, "They are probably banking on our not being able to locate the hive now, owing to the huge dirt-cloud that the effect of the bomb must be spreading out below us. The only thing left is to try what terror nearer home may do."

As he spoke he caught one of the bee-beetles between his finger and thumb. Slowly he squeezed it, till the frantic waving of its legs and pincers ceased. Laying the crushed body on the map of Mars for the other insects to see, he jabbed his finger impatiently on the diagram with the arrow pointing to Earth.

To take such a drastic step was to tempt Providence; and its result was totally unexpected. The twelve remaining bee-beetles flew straight up into the hollow of the mast and disappeared.

Kem stared upwards after them. There were several small compartments in the upper part of the mast, which protruded above the Saucer's roof. It was possible that they had taken refuge in them; but somehow he did not think so. The memory of his arrival on Mars had brought to his mind a sudden awful thought:

"My God!" he gasped. "I believe they've abandoned ship!"

Harsbach's face went white. "If they have, we're finished. We'll never be able to get back to Earth without a pilot."

Before they even had time to consider the appalling situation in which they had landed themselves, they were faced with an infinitely worse one. A soundless flash of bright white light lit the lower part of the control tower. Next second a spurt of flame roared up towards them. Instantly, they realized that before abandoning ship the bee-beetles must have deliberately set it on fire.

CHAPTER XXVIII

WALKING LIKE AGAG—DELICATELY

THE Saucer was many thousands of feet up in the air. It carried no parachutes. There was no escape from it. Under extreme pressure the bee-beetles had had the last laugh. Their wings would enable them to glide back to *terra firma*, but one of them had set in operation the emergency destruction mechanism to ensure that no lucky fluke of navigation should enable their enemies to do so. Short of a miracle, within a few minutes the Saucer must become a white-hot furnace and everything within it be utterly consumed.

Miracles rarely happen without reason, and there are miracles of courage as well as miracles of faith. Had Kem been asked at the moment he saw the flame what he thought their chances of survival were, he would have answered, "Nil"; but that did not prevent his acting on the principle that "While there is life, there is hope."

Without a second's hesitation, he let himself drop to the level of the fountain of flame and flung himself at it. With arms outspread he fell upon the place between the struts, low down in the control tower, at which he had seen the bright, white light. An agonizing pain seared through his chest. Next moment his clothes and his hair caught fire. He heard himself scream; but he knew that he had found and was pressing upon the mouth of the small flask from which the fire-raising element was spurting. The pain in his chest became as though a hundred rats were gnawing a great hole in it. All about him flames were roaring, licking and flickering. He beat at them frantically with his bare hands. Then the eye protector, which he had worn on Mars for so many months that it had become almost a part of him, burst into flame. The confused scene of criss-crossed girders caught in a burning glow and casting sharp black shadows was wiped out by a sudden fierce glare; then darkness came, but the burning agony in all his limbs still went on.

It was not until Kem had actually smothered the incendiary machine with his body that Harsbach realized they had any hope at all of saving the Saucer and themselves. Swiftly, then, he flung open the door to the upper deck, yelled to the girls to bring water, and hurried to Kem's assistance. Between them, by sluicing the contents of some fifty flasks about the lower part of the control tower, they got the fire under.

In these terrible moments the Saucer had shown no eccentricity in its flight, but Harsbach was now fearful that at any second it might; so he was frantically anxious to get back to within reach of the little row of levers that controlled it.

Kem was still screaming. Blinded and helpless he hung with his body wedged among the girders, two-thirds of the way down the tower. Between them, Carmen and Anna got him out; but now that Harsbach was again halfway up the tower it was impossible to get Kem past him to the upper deck, and the lower was still rendered unusable through gravity pulling everything in it down to the Saucer's whirling under-surface.

For a moment the two girls supported the moaning, writhing man, wondering what to do with him, then, simultaneously, they though of the new closet. While having the Saucer converted, Harsbach had recalled the awkwardness of using the well-like tank-contained lavatory originally designed for a crew of giants, and had taken steps to arrange something better suited to humans. The control tower, acting as the hub of the great disc, did not revolve, and the soil pipe ran down through it. He had had the pipe cut off eighteen inches from its exit and had turned the bottom five feet of the tower into a small circular compartment which would give privacy and reasonable comfort.

The closet was just below them. Anna scrambled down into it and Carmen lowered Kem to her. As she did so tears streamed from her eyes at the sight of him. His clothes were falling in tatters from his scorched body; his face was blackened and burnt almost beyond recognition. His screams had ceased. His head had fallen forward and his limbs gone limp. After suffering a greater degree of torture than he had ever thought that he could bear, he had lapsed into merciful unconsciousness.

It was a long time before he became capable of any coherent thought. For what seemed an eternity his mind swam in a sea of pain, marked only by alternate ebbings and risings to new heights which even screaming could not alleviate. The ebbings were caused by Carmen drugging him with her remaining sedatives, and doing what she could to ease the devouring ache of his worst burns. During her three months on Mars, knowing that she would never be able to get any replacements, she had exercised the greatest economy in the use of her toilet preparations: now she had cause to bless the fact, as she still had skin oils and soothing creams which were invaluable; but their quantity was limited and to her heart-breaking distress there were times when she could do nothing at all to help him bear his agony.

The worst of his burns was in the middle of his chest; but it was his eyes which gave her the greatest concern, as she feared that lack of proper medical care might result in his becoming permanently blind, and in spite of his struggles to tear it off she kept a bandage always over them. He was often delirious, and it was only by the change in his tone that she recognized the fact when at last his mind cleared a little. She had been readjusting the bandage over his eyes, and he asked in a feeble voice:

"Who are you? Why are you preventing me from seeing?"

"Oh, darling!" she exclaimed. "This is Carmen. You have been terribly, terribly ill; but surely you remember me?"

"Carmen," he muttered. "Yes, but what's happened? Where are we?"

"In the Saucer. Don't you remember? We managed to get aboard it, but the bee-beetles abandoned ship and set it on fire. You saved us all by putting the fire out; but you received the most ghastly burns, and you must keep the bandage over your eyes for a little while yet."

He moaned and drifted off into unconsciousness; but a few hours later he had another lucid interval and asked her to give him an account of what had happened.

She told him how she and Anna had got him down to the closet, and later moved him into the bomb-aimer's open-ended box above the empty cradle of the bomb that had been dropped—as it made a wide, comfortable berth that was just large enough to hold them both—and that Anna brought rations down to them; so that she had never had to leave him for more than a few minutes. For an hour or so, while the Herr Doktor had striven to get the hang of the controls, they had all thought they would never live the day out. The Saucer had behaved like a bucking bronco and they had been flung about like dice in a box. Anna had been knocked unconscious for a while and Harsbach had sprained an ankle; but at last he had fathomed the functions of all the little levers, and set a course, at a moderate speed, so that they should not feel the effects of gravity too severely. Except that the Saucer was powered by its great magnet, they still had no idea of the principles on which it worked; so their situation was similar to that of children who had got into a motor-car with no knowledge of what lay under its bonnet, but by experimenting with its switches and pedals were managing to drive it.

"How long is it since we left Mars?" Kem asked.

"Five days," Carmen replied.

"I couldn't even have made a guess," he murmured; "except that we'd been long enough on our way to lose the pull of gravity. I feel light as a feather again."

"Yes; and I thank God for it. Your sufferings would be even worse but for the fact that after the first hour or so your weight went down to zero. You have no means of sensing it, but you are now lying with your back to the ceiling of the lower deck, although hardly touching it; and the lack of gravity has served better than a water-bed in keeping pressure off your burns."

After another sleep he woke with his chest still paining him acutely, but with a mind at last capable of fully grasping his situation. Close beside him in the box-like bunk he could hear Carmen gently breathing, and realizing that she was asleep he remained quite still, so as not to wake her. His thoughts at once centred on the state of his eyes. They felt gummed up, but were not quite closed. Cautiously he raised his hand to the bandage and lifted it a little. He knew that the Saucer would now be filled with perpetual daylight, but he could see nothing. For a long time he lay endeavouring to accept the awful fact that he was blind. Then came the consoling thought that they were on their way back to Earth. If they reached it safely a specialist might be able to operate and get him back his sight.

When he heard Carmen wake he stretched out a fumbling hand till he found her face, gently began to caress it, and said softly, "Thank you, my sweet, for looking after me so wonderfully."

She took his hand, pressed it and sighed, "I only wish I could do more for you, dearest. But, anyway, you're through the worst now, and will soon be about again."

"I've been thinking," he said. "The relative positions of Mars and Earth must have altered a lot since our outward journey. They may be much nearer or much further apart. Has Harsbach any idea how long it will take us to get back to Earth?"

For a second she hesitated, then attempted to brush aside his question. "Oh, I wouldn't bother your head about that now."

"But I want to know," he insisted.

"I . . . I hardly know myself. I haven't seen Kruger Harsbach since the fire. Anna shares the running of the Saucer with him, but she doesn't tell me much. Anyway, what does it matter?—we are bound to be stuck in this thing for two or three months."

His grip on her hand tightened. "It matters a lot to me. I doubt if my sight can be saved without an operation. You're hiding something, Carmen. Please don't lie to me. How long do they think it will take?"

She gave a sudden sob. "I meant to keep it from you; but perhaps it is best that you should know. They haven't found any instruments that they can use to determine our position, or any way of getting the Saucer on to a magnetic wave that would take it towards Earth. We have enough water to last us for about a hundred days. But we're out in space, and simply flying wild."

*   *   *   *   *   *

On learning that he had been unconscious for five days and that the Saucer was outside the gravitational pull of Mars, Kem had quite naturally assumed that Harsbach had found a means of setting it on a course for Earth. That he had not was extremely disturbing. It looked now as if, when the magnetism with which the machine was charged ran down, it would cease to be manœuvrable and become an asteroid circling round and round Mars—as that was still its nearest planet—for ever and ever.

The thought swiftly called up visions of a terrible finale for its crew. They would be like shipwrecked people adrift in an open boat many miles from land, with their water running out and death from thirst creeping nearer every day. Worse—on the most desolate ocean there was always the chance of an eleventh-hour rescue; but in space there was none.

Kem knew that if he had still had his sight and been perfectly fit there was nothing he could do that Harsbach could not; so he concentrated such little energy as his sadly weakened state enabled him to muster in trying to take Carmen's mind off the awful uncertainties that faced them.

On the morning following her disclosure, she told him that now there was no longer any fear of his injuring himself during a fit of delirium, she ought to leave him for a few hours each day until she could get the Saucer tidied up from the results of its terrifying loops and twists while Harsbach had been experimenting with its controls. Since the flight of the bee-beetles the highest priority had obviously had to be given to trying to find out how to navigate it; so Harsbach and Anna, with only short intervals for sleep, had devoted themselves entirely to that, and were relying on her to put things straight on the upper deck as soon as she possibly could.

When she got up there she found herself faced with a Herculean task. Not only had the thousands of beans and all the other things been thrown violently about, but many of them had drifted over the edge of the deck and now lay halfway between it and the lower deck, against the wall of wire formed by the outer surface of the great magnet.

She made a start by collecting the beans and water flasks that were still scattered about the deck, and storing them in the empty tanks; and that alone occupied her for the best part of four days. Next, she got from Harsbach two struts that he had removed from inside the control tower. To the end of one she tied an angle piece, obtained from the same source, and to the other a landing net made out of an expanding bag-top and the sleeve of an old blouse sewn up at the wrist. Then, with these two implements, she spent another five days fishing up the scores of items that had floated down between the two decks.

Meanwhile, Harsbach and Anna were systematically examining every feature of the control tower, and removing such parts as it seemed they could without danger, in order gradually to work a passage up into the hollow of its mast, as the Herr Doktor thought it possible that somewhere up there lay the mechanism by which it could be navigated.

Carmen completed her labours by removing her own belongings to the lower deck and, now that Kem no longer might require her instant attention, making up a bunk for herself in the bomb-aimer's box over the unexpended bomb.

Owing to the protection from the constant sunlight that these boxes gave, they made excellent sleeping places, but she still spent a good part of her time lying beside Kem in his, and doing everything she could to relieve the tedium of his gradual recovery. Yet, after she had finished her tidying-up, she continued several times each day to visit the upper deck for a while, in order to perform such small services as she could for the two workers, and learn how they were progressing.

It was on their eighteenth day after leaving Mars that she wriggled into Kem's bunk, and said a little breathlessly, "Darling, I have a present for you."

Into his outstretched hand she pressed a round, flat object. He held it up near his face and caught the sound of a rhythmical ticking. "Why!" he exclaimed. "This is Estévan's watch. It must be."

"It is. I meant to give it you on the morning you went out to incite the giants to mutiny; but I didn't have the chance, because after you got back everything happened so quickly. Now that you can't see, I'm afraid it won't be much use to you; but I wanted you to have it as a sort of symbol."

He groped for her hand, found it, and pressed it. "I understand. You mean the fact that it had belonged to him, and your decision to give it to me, signifies that you had made up your mind that I was innocent of his death. Poor old Estévan. I don't think we had enough in common ever to have become real friends; but he behaved damn' decently from the time we found ourselves kidnapped. I'm glad to have such a memento of him. And infinitely more so on account of the reason for your giving it to me. But why did you keep this sweet gesture till now, when I've been *compos mentis* for very nearly a fortnight?"

Her voice held a tremor of excitement as she replied, "As I had no chance to give it you when I intended, I thought I would keep it until some occasion arose which might call for a celebration. Perhaps I am being premature, but I believe we may have good reason to render special thanks to God today."

"Why?" he asked quickly.

"Because Kruger Harsbach has got up to the top of the mast, and found inside a little compartment there a disc like a gramophone record, set on a short pillar. It is under a small transparent dome that forms a crown to the mast, and has an attachment like a pair of sights fixed across its surface. He believes that by aligning them on any star the Saucer can be directed towards it."

Kem drew in his breath sharply. "Then there is . . . after all . . . a chance of our getting back to Earth?"

"He thinks so; but we'll have to wait for a bit until we can be certain."

The next few hours proved for all of them a period of even more nerve-racking anxiety than those after they had first left Mars. Then, the question had been whether they were to be wiped out by a painful yet sudden death; now, it was whether they were to escape the far worse fate of a lingering death from thirst, perhaps preceded by madness. During the eighteen days that Harsbach's efforts to keep the Saucer on a set course had failed, there had always been the hope that as he and Anna explored its machinery they might yet find a way to do so. They had reached the top of the mast. There was no other mechanism left to explore. If the thing that they had come upon there worked, all might yet be well. If not, their fate was finally sealed.

While flying wild the Saucer had, at times, kept moving steadily in one direction for several hours before, for no ascertainable reason, veering off in another; so they had to exercise all the patience they could muster until next day. Then, just before issuing the morning ration, Harsbach told the two girls that for the past twenty hours the Saucer had adhered steadily to the course he had set to Earth.

Carmen quickly carried the great news down to Kem, but she added soberly, "All the same, he warned us not to be too optimistic. You see, he has no instruments of any kind by which he can tell the speed at which we are moving, or the distance we are from Earth. There is always the possibility that our rations may give out before we get there, or that the Saucer's magnet is not sufficiently highly charged to carry us that far. If it isn't, and peters out, we should have no way of keeping on our course; and the Saucer would become like a piece of helpless driftwood floating in an illimitable ocean. Then, even if we succeed in getting to within a few hundred miles of Earth, there still remains the frightful problem of landing. We may find it impossible to reduce our speed sufficiently to get down without smashing ourselves to pieces."

Nevertheless, their chances of life seemed so immeasurably greater than they had twenty-four hours earlier, that all of them thrust these gloomy possibilities into the back of their minds, and in the weeks that followed showed no lack of confidence that they would now, somehow, survive their amazing journey.

A routine of games and exercises was started to while away the interminable hours, and at Kem's insistence Carmen joined the others in them on the upper deck. As his burns healed, he, too, began to take gentle exercise with Carmen's help; but he was now only a caricature of his former robust self. He had lost so much weight that both his face and body were thin to the point of emaciation; and although he was allowed as many beans as he could eat, they seemed to lack the properties necessary to build him up again. The terrible burn on his chest, too, had drawn up his flesh there so that he could no longer stand upright, and when he walked he was almost bent double.

Occasionally Harsbach came down to have a chat with him, but Anna never did so. She had long since ceased to want him for herself, yet she still resented Carmen having got him back from her; and, as she had since tried but failed to seduce Harsbach, her present enforced chastity increased her bitterness towards Kem to the point of hatred.

In consequence, for a great deal of the time the Saucer became a strange microcosm of Earth—on which Britons walk one way up and New Zealanders the other—as Harsbach and Anna sat on the so-called upper deck, while Kem and Carmen sat, theoretically, head downwards on the lower.

When the two lovers were together they often discussed what they would do if they got safely back to Earth. Carmen would not listen for one moment to Kem's objection that his blindness and crippled state now constituted a bar to their marriage; so, putting that aside, they built many lovely "Castles in Spain". Yet they knew that even if the Saucer landed safely all the odds would still be against the full realization of their dreams.

They had spoken of it only once, but both of them were fully agreed that there was now no prospect of Harsbach setting them down in Mexico. With Escobar's death they had lost even the advantage of numbers; the other two were armed, while they were not, and Kem was virtually helpless. Moreover, only Harsbach and Anna knew how to fly the Saucer. It was certain that they would not willingly bring it down

236

in any place where the risk would have to be faced that they might not be able to get it up again in order to fly on to Russia. Nothing bar force of circumstances could now prevent their flying it straight to the Soviet Union, and when Carmen had tackled the Herr Doktor on the matter, by an evasive reply he had admitted as much.

During the hours that Carmen was with the others Kem cudgelled his wits in vain for a means of persuading or tricking Harsbach into landing Carmen and himself outside Soviet territory; for, once they were in it, he would have bet his last penny that they would never be allowed out again. He would, too, have given everything he possessed to secure the Saucer and its secrets for his own country. But to pull off either coup seemed utterly beyond the bounds of possibility.

It was in the second week after Harsbach had got the Saucer on a course for Earth that a slight accident caused Kem's heart to bound in his warped chest with excitement. He had by then learned to feel his way about the deck without Carmen's aid, and sometimes got out of his bunk to stretch his legs when she was not there. On this occasion, as he crawled out he misjudged his distance, struck his head sharply on the empty bomb cradle, and jerked up his hand to the hurt place. In doing so he partially pushed aside the bandage over his eyes. Instantly the blackness before his face was broken by a patch of greyness, and he knew that his sight was coming back.

For a few days, by the exercise of the greatest will-power, he both refrained from telling Carmen—because he did not want to raise her hopes until he was quite certain—and forced himself to resist the temptation to make further trials. Then, with trembling fingers, he took the bandage right off. He could see brightness and shadows, and even make out the blurred outline of the great bomb on the far side of the deck. Quickly, he replaced the bandage, and lay with a fast-beating heart till Carmen joined him.

When he told her of his marvellous discovery, she burst into tears of joy and kissed his scarred face all over. Then she told him that she had never lost hope that if he kept the bandage on long enough his sight would come back, but had pinned her faith even more on her prayers that it should do so. Then, kneeling down beside him, she offered up her heartfelt thanks that those prayers had been answered.

It was half an hour later that she said to him, "Kem, dearest, you will continue to keep the bandage on for a long time yet, won't you?"

"Yes," he nodded. "It will be much safer not to rush things. To start with I shall take it off for only a few minutes each day."

"And you won't tell Harsbach that you are recovering your sight if he comes down on one of his periodical visits, will you? Or Anna?"

"Why shouldn't I?"

"Please don't. Keep it as a surprise for them until your sight is fully restored. Promise me you will."

237

He smiled. "I hardly think either of them is likely to turn a double somersault from joy on account of a surprise that means good fortune for me. Still, I'll keep it dark if you wish."

No more was said on the subject till the sixtieth day of their voyage. By that time Kem's sight was so nearly back to normal that he decided to abandon his bandage for good. Taking it off that morning, he said to Carmen:

"It's two months to-day since we escaped from Mars, and to mark this anniversary I mean to treat myself to an excursion. I'm going to pay my first visit to the upper deck."

The blood drained from her face, and she seized his arm. "Kem, you're to do nothing of the kind! And you've got to keep that bandage handy all the time, so that you can slip it on again whenever Harsbach comes down here."

"What on earth are you talking about?" he exclaimed in amazement.

"I could not bear to tell you till I had to," she gulped, then hurried on, "It's something I overheard weeks ago. When I am on my way up through the control tower I often catch snatches of their conversation before they know I am coming. They were talking about you; so I waited and listened. Anna was saying that you may have kept notes while you helped with the making and fitting of the atomic warheads of the bombs. Harsbach said he doubted if you had sufficient scientific knowledge to make notes of any value. She said that to take the least chance of his new formula falling into wrong hands would be treachery to the Soviet Union, and he agreed about that. Then she said that since you had become only a useless drain on the rations the sensible thing to do was to get rid of you as soon as possible. She wanted him to keep me out of the way for a while that evening, so that she could come down here with a free field and put a bullet through your head. He wouldn't let her; but only because of the difficulty of disposing of your body without stopping the Saucer. It makes me faint with horror to even think of it; but they agreed that they dared not leave it to putrefy, and Anna baulked at the job of having to cut it into pieces with the few small implements that are all we have with us. Harsbach closed the conversation by saying that as long as you remained blind you couldn't possibly play them any tricks, or escape from the M.V.D. police to betray any secrets you may have learned, after landing."

Carmen paused for a second, wrung her hands together, and cried, "So you see, darling, how terribly careful you've got to be. If they find out that you have recovered your sight, they'll never let you land. Rather than take any risks at all they'll come down here first and murder you."

*   *   *   *   *   *

Kem quieted her fears as well as he could with an immediate promise that from then onward he would act as though his blindness had become

238

permanent. He realized, too, that any slip-up on his part might now bring him into immediate danger. The disposal of a body without stopping the Saucer and risking its going off its course presented no real difficulty—only an unpleasant and fatiguing labour—so if the enemy were given the least reason to suppose that he had recovered sufficiently to make an attempt to get the better of them, they might quite well decide to insure themselves against trouble by shooting him out of hand.

The thought that he had made such notes as he could about Harsbach's new method for the swifter production of nuclear energy from uranium made him smile a little grimly to himself. He had devised a cunning method of concealing them; for he had made them in Spanish and apparently as additional paragraphs on a number of Escobar's papers about rockets. Carmen still had the red brief-case that contained them in her suitcase; but Kem knew that his chance of getting away with them could hardly have been more slender. It looked as if he was going to be extremely lucky even to get away with his life, and he knew that the only hope he had of doing so was from now on to walk like Agag—delicately.

After a moment he gave Carmen an anxious look, and said. "What about yourself, my sweet? If you have any reason to believe that their hellish designs include you, for God's sake don't conceal it from me."

She shook her head. "No; you need not worry about me. Even Anna hasn't the face to pretend that I am the sort of woman who is capable of ferreting out scientific secrets. Besides, Kruger Harsbach would not let her harm me. He is in love with me—if you can call it love. But he is much too clever to attempt to rush his fences. He has the patience that goes with middle age. He knows that I would never become his mistress willingly as things are; but I'm sure he is banking on my agreeing to accept that role, rather than be carried off to prison, when we land in Russia."

Kem gave a heavy sigh. "Heaven alone knows what will become of us when we do land. But the odds are that he will not take the risk of crashing into any buildings by trying to come down in their immediate vicinity; so will land in open country. If I can keep up my bluff about being blind, that may give us a chance to take them by surprise and get away before any villagers or police come on the scene. Anyhow, as he is not being difficult at the moment, I think your best line to ensure your protection would be to pretend to be a bit bored with me, now that I've become such a useless wreck. Encourage him to believe that you're ready to play on reaching Earth, but mean to stand out for marriage."

Carmen agreed to do as he suggested. Then, that same evening, she produced a curious object from her dressing-case and, handing it to Kem, said, "I have been wondering what this is, for a long time. Now you have the proper use of your eyes again, perhaps you can tell me."

It was a nine-inch length of thick lead piping, one end of which was sealed and the other open, showing that it was filled with some whitish substance.

"Where did you find it?" he asked.

"On the upper deck, when I was clearing up there."

Turning its open end away from her, he said, "I've never seen such a thing before, but I can give a pretty good guess who made it and why. That whitish stuff inside the pipe is a paste made of powdered uranium; so it must give off radium rays in whatever direction the open end is pointed. For lack of a better name one might call it a Radium Torch."

She nodded. "I had an idea that it was something of that kind; and, of course, it must belong to Harsbach."

"Yes. I've often wondered how he managed to expose poor old Estévan to radium rays while we were making those warheads—that is, for long enough to cause his death, and without Estévan or anyone else seeing what he was up to. The answer is that he didn't. This is the thing with which he killed Estévan. He must have trained it on him while we were all asleep, probably for several nights in succession."

They were silent for a moment, then Carmen asked, "Is it still dangerous?"

"I don't know enough about radium to say," he replied. "After all these weeks it may have lost its potency; on the other hand——"

"No, Kem!" she exclaimed, guessing from his eyes the thought that had come into his mind. "Whatever their intentions towards us, to use it on either of them would be to commit a horrible form of murder. I won't let you!"

He gave a cynical little smile, and handed the strange weapon back to her. "All right, then. Get rid of it down the lavatory chute. You had also better get rid at the same time of anything that it was lying near, and may have affected, in your dressing-case. But, anyway, it wouldn't enable us to get the better of those two devils on the upper deck. We could use it only on one of them at a time, and as that one began to show the symptoms of radium poisoning they would guess what we had been up to. The survivor would make short work of us. Besides, even if we could think of a way of getting rid of both of them, I should still be up against the fact that I haven't the faintest idea how to control the Saucer."

After further thought Kem realized that the latter fence might be got over far more easily than the former. If he could only get a free hand at the controls, there seemed no real reason why he should not find out how to manipulate them as successfully as Harsbach had done. It would mean another period of violent somersaults and swervings, and there was the risk that he might knock himself out while experimenting; but short of such a calamity, it was not unreasonable to believe that he would succeed in getting the hang of them before being faced with the tricky business of bringing the Saucer down to Earth.

The real problem lay in getting that free hand at the controls. To do so he must either kill, take prisoner or impose his will on both Harsbach and Anna. During the whole of the month that followed he tormented his brain endlessly with plots and plans, all of which he was forced to abandon in turn as either being based on wishful thinking or being so desperate as practically to amount to suicide. By the end of the month he was no nearer to devising a way to overcome his enemies than he had been at its beginning.

He was still a weak invalid, walking with a chronic stoop. They were fit, strong, agile and armed with automatics. The opportunities for surprising and overcoming them in sleep were nil, as they took turns at keeping an eye on the controls, and never since leaving Mars had they been known to abandon their routine of keeping watch and watch about. Carmen, Kem knew, would brave any risk to aid him in an attempt to overcome them, but it was unthinkable to expose her unless he could conceive a plan that had a reasonable prospect of success; and, cudgel his wits as he would, in that all-important matter they remained utterly barren.

Nevertheless, from habit and conviction he acted as if he had no cause to despair of their situation. While they were on Mars Harsbach had never given him the chance to examine either of the great bombs closely, but now he had ample opportunity to study the one that remained. It was about thirty feet in length and three feet in diameter at its broadest part. The material of which it was made was similar to that used in the manufacture of the Saucers, so both were very light in weight and very strong. The central section of the bomb was hollow, to allow for the ten-foot fall of a plunger during its drop that, by a calculated adjustment, had the effect of exploding it at the desired height above its target. Sections of its sides could be opened on the same principles as those of a motor-car bonnet, but automatically clamped back into place much more tightly, thus rendering it airtight. For many days in succession Kem opened up these sections one by one, unscrewed various parts of the mechanism until he became fully conversant with the principles on which they worked, and, on the last sheets of Carmen's notepaper, made careful drawings of them.

It was on the ninety-first day since their leaving Mars that, on going to the lavatory and looking down its pipe, he realized that the crisis would soon be upon them. There was old Mother Earth, framed in the circle made by the bottom of the chute, now appearing as large as a cricket ball.

Next morning the globe overlapped the circle. It looked very different from Mars seen under the same conditions. It was much whiter. The sun, shining on its great areas of cloud, made them look like vast snowfields, and it was difficult to determine where they merged into the real snow-fields of its much larger Polar caps.

Carmen came down the control tower with their rations while he was still staring through the pipe. In a swift whisper she warned him to put on his eye bandage and get back to his bunk, as Harsbach might at any moment be coming down to take a look at the planet. From that time on Kem had to adopt his role of blind man in earnest, and sit about with his hands folded in his lap, apparently incapable of doing anything; for either Harsbach or Anna were constantly in the vicinity of the lower deck, watching the Saucer's swift approach to Earth.

That evening they began to feel the pull of gravity, and Harsbach cautiously altered the Saucer's direction in order to enter on the first of the breaking ellipses, which he hoped would reduce its tremendous speed. Twelve hours later they entered the cone of shadow thrown by the Earth as their approach caused its bulk to hide the sun from them. For the first time in three months they went to sleep in true night.

When they woke the Saucer was completing the second of its breaking ellipses. A few hours afterwards they entered the outer fringe of Earth's atmosphere and were rapidly gaining weight. When Kem next stole a quick look down the pipe it was mid-day. He was able to identify the great sweep of Hudson Bay, so knew that they were over northern Canada. They were still travelling fast, many miles up and heading eastward with the world spin.

During an afternoon greatly foreshortened by the fact that they were rushing away from the sinking sun, they crossed the tip of Greenland; then twilight fell. All day Harsbach had been paying periodic visits to the closet to observe the Saucer's progress, and after one made about ten o'clock he informed Carmen that the groups of lights below them were those of villages in Iceland.

For a time the darkness remained blank; then the Moon came up and Carmen told Kem that ahead of them she could see it glinting on a great chain of mountains. He said they must be the coast of Norway, and Anna, coming down shortly afterwards, confirmed that they were. At about one o'clock in the morning Kem decided to snatch another look himself. By then he expected the Saucer to be passing over either Sweden or the northern Baltic. To his amazement he found that without his noticing it they had changed direction. He was peering down at the unmistakable outline of northern Scotland, and the Saucer was travelling south.

Hastily adjusting his bandage over his eyes, he hurried back to Carmen and said, "I can't make out what Harsbach is up to. We should be approaching Soviet territory by now, but during the past hour he has altered the Saucer's course. He has brought us hundreds of miles south of the line we were travelling on and at the moment we are heading for Edinburgh. Please go up: tell him you've been looking down the chute, and see if you can find out his intentions."

Carmen was away for about five minutes. When she rejoined him her eyes were staring and her lips trembling.

"Kem!" she gasped. "This is terrible! Unbelievable! But he has gone mad. He must have, or he would never have told me about the frightful thing he means to do. He was frothing at the mouth, gibbering with unholy glee. Before flying on to Russia, he is going to drop the Atom bomb on London.

*　　*　　*　　*　　*　　*

Kem drew in a sharp breath. "I think I guessed it while you were up there. It is his insane hatred of the British. He means to revenge himself for his ruined life; for his disfigurement; for the deaths of his father, wife and daughter; and for the way we smashed Hitler—all by this one diabolical stroke."

"We can't let it happen," she whispered, aghast.

"We'll have to work fast," he muttered. "I wonder how long we've got."

"Anna told me a little time ago that we had slowed down to about four hundred miles an hour."

"Then we have an hour, or perhaps a little over."

"What are you going to do? Sabotage the bomb?"

"That's no good. One of them will come down presently to adjust the plunger mechanism for detonation height. They may not look at the warhead, but if they do they would discover what we had done, shoot us, and put it right." He paused, swallowed hard, then went on quickly, "I'm afraid this means curtains for us, darling; but the only certain way of fooling them is to use the bomb to blow the Saucer up."

She smiled at him. "Go ahead, Kem. What do the two of us matter compared with all those helpless millions?"

"Bless you, my sweet. Go over and sit in the bottom of the control tower while I get to work. Cough if you hear either of them coming down."

Kem's task was by no means an easy one, as lack of gravity no longer enabled him to move about freely. Moreover the light was far from good, although the bright moonlight outside penetrated the Saucer's surface just enough for him to see by it.

By using the hand-holds in the ceiling of the deck, he swung himself from his bunk to the other bomb-aimer's box, in which Carmen kept her things. From her dressing-case he took a piece of string, her manicure-set and the few other small implements he had used when examining the interior of the warhead; then he lowered himself cautiously on to the bomb, and crawled along it until he reached its nose. Opening the bonnet that covered it, he began to work with sure, swift fingers. Had he not made a prolonged study of the bomb's mechanism it would have been quite impossible for him to carry out his intent; but knowing every

243

part of it intimately enabled him to convert the warhead into a booby trap. The nuclear charge itself was no larger than a cricket ball, and by adjusting the leads to it he ensured that anyone opening the bonnet would set it off.

The job took him nearly half an hour, but he suffered no interruption and when he had finished he told Carmen what he had done. Then he added, "Of course, Anna may not open the bonnet. If she doesn't, we shall have to set the bomb off ourselves."

Swinging himself over to Carmen, he stood looking at her for a moment, then he said, "What an appalling thought it is that this maniac should make necessary the obliteration of anything so indescribably lovely as you."

She smiled at him. "Dearest Kem. It is sweet to hear you say that, but what is beauty anyway? The scars on your face are disappearing now, but I loved you just as much while your eyes were made hideous by them. It is what is in our hearts that counts."

He took her in his arms and their mouths met in a long, sweet kiss. Then, as they drew apart, they heard the sounds of scrambling feet above them. Carmen remained where she was, but Kem swiftly adjusted his bandage, and swung himself back to his bunk.

A moment later Anna appeared beside Carmen. Her smooth silvery gold hair and fresh complexion made her look as much like an empty-headed good-time girl as ever; but her china-blue eyes were hard as agates, and in her hand she held Zadovitch's automatic. Pointing it at Carmen, she said:

"I shall be acting as bomb-aimer. Go over and move your things from the bomb-aimer's box to Sem's bunk."

Carmen did as she was told. Then Anna spoke again. "Now get into Sems' bunk with him. And don't move. If either of you lifts a finger I shall shoot."

With Kem and the cases in such a confined space it was a tight fit, but Carmen managed to squeeze herself in. Anna then stuck her pistol inside her short fur coat, and swung herself along the ceiling until she could get down on to the rear end of the bomb. Opening the casing there she began to adjust the plunger mechanism.

After a moment Kem asked her, "At what height are you going to set it?"

"For impact," she replied.

"Really!" he exclaimed in surprise. "But won't that lessen its effect?"

"No. The Herr Doktor intends it to explode in water. The atomized particles will then spread far and wide in great radium-charged clouds, and kill an infinitely greater number of the accursed British capitalists."

"What about the wretched workers?"

"They deserve no consideration as long as they continue to serve their bourgeois imperialist masters. Only when they become politico-party-conscious will they have earned the right to the protection of their comrade-workers in the free Socialist Soviet World State."

"You couldn't possibly hope to hit a river, as narrow as the Thames is near London, from a safe height." Kem said after a second.

"Oh, yes, we shall!" she retorted. "Now the Herr Doktor knows how to control the Saucer he has worked it all out. The bomb is so light that its dropping speed will be comparatively slow, whereas the Saucer can be shot up at a terrific rate. We can afford to come right down to 2,000 feet, and there will still be time for us to rise to 10,000 before it hits the water. The Herr Doktor has described to me the Tower of London. At 2,000 feet I should be able to land the bomb in the river below Tower Bridge without the least difficulty."

As she finished speaking she closed down the casing, then she cautiously began to crawl forward along the bomb. Kem and Carmen lay tightly locked in one another's arms. They believed that she now intended to open the bonnet over the nose, to make certain that everything was as it should be inside the warhead. They could feel one another's hearts pounding. Both were convinced that their last moments had come. The second Anna lifted the bonnet there would be a blinding flash—then eternity.

But when she reached the middle of the bomb she stood up, gripped the hand-holds above her and began to swing herself towards the opening to the control tower.

Carmen was trembling with excitement. She could not have said if she was pleased or not to be given this short reprieve. It meant that she would have a few more precious minutes with Kem; but there was the ghastly thought that they would now have to explode the bomb themselves.

Kem had arranged his bandage so that he could watch Anna. Suddenly, as she reached the entrance of the control tower, he spoke:

"How I wish I had my sight back, so that I could look down the chute and see what happens when the bomb explodes."

Anna turned and glanced towards him. "Well, you can't, so you will have to imagine it."

"Carmen could," he replied quickly. "And she could describe it to me. Have you any objection to our getting out of this bunk now and occupying the closet? We shouldn't be in your way there, or be able to interfere with you when you come down to launch the bomb."

She shrugged. "No. You can do that if you like. But keep the door shut. "I don't mean to take any chances of your throwing something at me at the last moment."

"All right," he agreed. "How long will it be before we are over London?"

"About twenty minutes."

As Anna turned away and disappeared up the tower, he gripped

245

Carmen fiercely and whispered, "Darling! What she said just now means we've still got a chance. It's only one in a million, but pray for us now, my sweet, as you have never prayed before."

Pulling the bandage from his eyes he got out Estévan's watch and said, "We shall need this and your suitcase. Quick, help me to empty it."

*   *   *   *   *   *

When Anna came down to the lower deck twenty minutes later it was empty. The silent Saucer stopped revolving. Running lightly across its under-surface she got a grip on the bomb and kicked until the bomb port came under its nose. Then she climbed up into the bomb-aimer's box and lay down there. Below her now she could see the lights of London and the silver ribbon of the Thames lit by the moon. With a smile of hatred she adjusted the bomb-sights until they were directed on the Pool below Tower Bridge. She pressed the trigger. The bomb port opened. The great missile slid smoothly forward.

Faintly her yell to Harsbach reached Kem and Carmen, "Bomb's away!"

*   *   *   *   *   *

TOP SECRET

Personal from Director-General M.I.-X. to Prime Minister.

Sir,

Further to my telephone call early this morning, reporting that a large cylinder had been retrieved from the Thames below Tower Bridge some hours after the unexplained aerial explosion a few miles short of the Belgian coast. The cylinder is made from an extremely strong but light, almost feather-weight, substance. That, no doubt, is the reason for its not having either broken in pieces on hitting the water, or embedding itself in the mud of the Thames bottom. On being opened up it was found to contain the bodies of a man and a woman.

The man has now been identified as Kempton Lincoln, one of my agents, of whom we have lost all trace since his disappearance while on a mission in the Argentine eight months ago. From a Sacred Heart locket worn by the woman, she is believed to be Señora Carmen Escobar, the wife of Colonel Estévan Escobar; both of whom disappeared at the same time as Lincoln.

With the bodies in the cylinder a number of papers have been found. They are contained in a red brief-case, formerly the property of Colonel Escobar, who is said to have been General Peron's chief atomic expert. At first sight our own experts have expressed the opinion that these papers appear to contain information of exceptional value. They consist of:

(a) A series of sketches of the mechanism of a type of fission bomb so far unknown to us.

246

(*b*) *A number of documents in Spanish, giving particulars of an improved type of long-range rocket.*

(*c*) *Pencil notes made in Lincoln's hand, on the blank spaces in the above, from which it may prove possible to secure the clue to a new and faster method of producing nuclear energy from crude uranium.*

Our present theory is that Lincoln was a prisoner in some form of aerial craft, the crew of which intended to test a new type of fission bomb by dropping it on London; but that he and Madame Escobar succeeded in removing the atomic nucleus from the bomb's warhead and attaching it to some form of time fuse; so that it later blew up the aircraft, after they had concealed themselves in the hollow shell of the bomb and allowed themselves to be launched into space.

Both Lincoln and Madame Escobar are suffering from bad bruising and severe shock; but the doctors report that they should be in a fit state to answer a few questions this evening, and fully recovered in a few days' time.

I have the honour to be, Sir,

J.J.J.

THE END